LAURIE BRETON

DIE BEFORE I WAKE

MIRA®

MIRA

ISBN-13: 978-0-7783-2590-1
ISBN-10:   0-7783-2590-3

DIE BEFORE I WAKE

www.MIRABooks.com

Printed in U.S.A.

For Grace,
who's more than a boss,
but also a friend,
and who puts up with me
as graciously as her name implies
whenever I'm on deadline!

Thanks to my amazing editor, Valerie Gray, for the past six years. They've been great! Thanks also to the members of the MIRA art department, who always give me awesome covers. And, of course, to everyone else at MIRA Books who's involved in the process of turning words typed on a page into a living, breathing book.

One

I've always been a white-knuckle flier.

Normally the most rational of people, I have trouble trusting any law of physics that expects me to believe that a fifty-ton aircraft loaded with two hundred people is going to stay in the air because of something having to do with lift and thrust and air currents. In my narrow world view, gravity wins out every time. Every ounce of common sense tells me that the only possible outcome to such a scenario is for the plane to plummet from the sky, carrying me, and 199 other passengers and crew members, to a fiery death.

The flight from L.A. to Boston had taken about eight hours, and somewhere around Pittsburgh, we'd hit turbulence in the form of a hurricane that was battering the Northeast. I'd been forced to close my eyes to keep from seeing lightning tap dance all around the 747's wing tips. Eventually, the thunder and lightning gave way to rain, and I relaxed a little. But it was more than the storm, more than my customary terror of falling from the sky in a ball of fire, that had my fingertips pressing permanent prints into the armrest of my first-class seat; it was the fear of what waited for us on the ground.

The plane began its descent into Boston. Beside me, Tom sat calmly leafing through an in-flight magazine as though he did this kind of thing every day. Thomas Larkin, OB/GYN, small-town New England doctor, widower, father of two and all-around heartthrob, was my new husband. And I still couldn't believe it.

Julie Larkin. Julie Hanrahan Larkin. I kept mentally trying out the name, just to see how it sounded inside my head. What it sounded like most was disbelief. We'd met on a cruise ship, off the coast of Barbados. The trip had been a birthday present from Carlos and the girls at Phoenix, the L.A. boutique I managed. Because thirty was a significant birthday, and because the last couple years of my life had been a complete train wreck, my bighearted co-workers had thrown me a birthday bash, complete with black balloons, a male stripper and a ticket for a Caribbean cruise. They'd joked with me about finding Prince Charming somewhere on that floating palace. He would look like Johnny Depp—minus the eyeliner and the sword—and have more money than Donald Trump.

I'd gone along with the joke, even though I wasn't in the market for a man. After the unimaginable losses of the last two years, I'd made it my mission to fill the empty void inside me with work. I had no room—or desire—for romance. After my divorce from Jeffrey, I'd expected to take a lengthy hiatus from the dating scene. Like maybe the rest of my life.

But, as John Lennon so famously said, life is what happens while you're making other plans. Eighteen hours into the cruise, I found myself seated next to Dr. Thomas Larkin at dinner. Tom fit all the romantic stereotypes: He was tall, dark and handsome. Smart and witty and charming, with vivid blue eyes and a smile that drove like an arrow directly into my heart. Best of all, he made me laugh, when I hadn't laughed in a very long time.

There were other things I also hadn't done in a very long time. Following the guiding principle that what happens on the Princess line stays on the Princess line, I threw myself wholeheartedly into a shallow, scorching, unabashedly shameless shipboard romance. Ten days, I reasoned, and I'd be back in L.A., selling rhinestone bracelets to anorexic young blondes who played tennis and spent half their lives at the beach. In the interim, a little sun, sand and sex were just what the doctor ordered.

Except that, somewhere along the way, what was supposed to be no more than a shipboard fling turned into something else. And on the morning when Tom, his hair as rumpled as my bed sheets, pulled out a blue velvet box that held a single diamond solitaire, I realized he was offering me more than just marriage. He was offering me a second chance. A fresh start. And the opportunity to leave L.A., and all its sorrows, behind.

There was nothing left for me in L.A. Dad was gone. Jeffrey had moved on to bigger and better things. And Angel, the baby I'd lost, was nothing more than a sweet, painful memory. For a while, I'd been thinking about quitting my job, climbing into my beloved yellow Miata, and driving off alone into the sunset.

But Tom offered me so much more than that.

Anybody who knows me will tell you that I'm a born cynic. After all, I'm Dave Hanrahan's daughter. He taught me pretty much everything I know, and if there was one thing Dad didn't believe in, it was romance. Right now, he was probably spinning in his grave over the knowledge that his only daughter, high on moonlight and hormones and God only knew what else, had stood on a white-sand Bahamian beach at midnight, a month after her thirtieth birthday, and married a man she'd known for five days.

I was still having trouble believing it myself.

Beside me, Tom turned a page. "How can you do that?" I said.

Without looking up, he said, "Easy. I just lift the corner with my finger, and—"

"Ha, ha. Very funny. Aren't you nervous?"

"Why should I be?" He flipped another page. "Seems as though you're nervous enough for both of us."

"With good reason. I'm serious, Tom. It's not every

day your firstborn son comes home from a Caribbean cruise with a brand-new wife in tow. What if your mother hates me?"

He closed the magazine and looked at me. He smiled, and the corners of his eyes crinkled, and my heart did this funny little thing it'd been doing since the first time he smiled at me. "She's not going to hate you," he said. "Even if she did, it wouldn't matter. I'm thirty-eight years old. A little too old for my mother to be running my life. Besides, she'll love you."

"Why should she love me?"

He leaned and placed a kiss on the tip of my nose. "Because I love you. Stop worrying."

Easy for him to say. He wasn't the one who was uprooting his entire life, leaving behind friends, coworkers, career and home, to move to some tiny town in Maine, all in the name of love.

He must have seen the expression on my face. "Having second thoughts?" he asked.

God knows, I should have been. What I'd done was so out of character, I still couldn't believe I'd really done it. In spite of being Dave's daughter— or maybe because of it—I'd never done anything this crazy. This was risk-taking behavior, something I'd spent the last decade avoiding. This was stepping off the edge of a cliff into free fall, without a parachute or a safety net to slow my plunge. This was insanity at its terrifying, spine-tingling, exhilarating best.

The days we'd spent aboard ship had been heaven, days of sparkling turquoise water and ice-cold margaritas, days we'd spent lying on matching chaises, fingers loosely clasped in the space between his chair and mine as we soaked up the sun's rays, nearly purring with mindless contentment.

And then, there were the nights.

In light of my legendary cynicism, it seemed far-fetched that the word *besotted* kept coming to mind. It sounds so undignified. So junior high school. And I'm a woman who has walked a hard road to maturity. But none of that seemed to matter, because at that particular moment, as we touched down smoothly on the runway at Logan International Airport on an early September afternoon, it was the only word that came close to describing how I felt about my new husband.

Tom was still looking at me, still waiting for an answer, his blue eyes pensive, as though he wasn't quite certain what my response might be. Was I having second thoughts?

Was he out of his mind?

I grinned and said, "In your dreams."

Nobody was at the airport to meet us.

"I don't get it," Tom said. We stood with our baggage, lone islands in a sea of arriving passengers who flowed around us like salmon swimming upstream. "I told Mom what time we'd be landing. Which gate we'd be coming through. Where to meet us." He flipped his cell phone closed. "There's no answer at the house."

"Maybe she's running late because of the

weather. She could've hit traffic. Does she have a cell phone?"

A vertical wrinkle appeared between his eyebrows. "In spite of my constant nagging, she's too stubborn to buy one."

Until now, I'd never seen him frown. I hoped it wasn't an omen. I couldn't help wondering if his mother's failure to arrive on time was a deliberate snub aimed at me, her new daughter-in-law. Tom had described his mother as formidable. Intimidating. Difficult. All of which went a long way toward explaining the unease I'd been feeling ever since we took off from Los Angeles. I'd already built up a picture of her in my mind, one that involved horns, a tail, and sharp teeth.

But I was determined to win her over. After all, Jeannette Larkin was the woman whose DNA would be passed on to my children. "I'm sure she'll be along shortly," I said.

"Maybe." But he didn't look convinced, which did absolutely nothing to alleviate my apprehension. "You have to understand my mother," he said. "She's a bit set in her ways. This wouldn't be the first time she's done something off-the-wall just to prove a point."

In other words, maybe my theory was right. Great. "Okay," I said, trying to focus on the primary problem at hand. "If she doesn't show up, how do we get home?" We still had at least a hundred miles to go.

Scanning the crowd, he said, "We'll have to rent

a car. Damn it, I knew I should've driven down by myself and left my car in long-term parking. But you can't imagine how much I hate to do that. You never know what you'll find when you get back. Scratches, dents, slashed tires, graffiti—"

I patted his arm in a gesture of comfort. "She could be wandering around the airport, lost. Maybe you should try having her paged."

Some of the frustration left his eyes. "Right," he said. "Good idea, Jules."

Nobody in my entire thirty years had ever gotten away with calling me Jules. Until now. A lot of firsts going on here.

"You stay with the bags," he said, and began moving in the direction of the American Airlines ticket counter. He'd taken just a couple of steps when a male voice separated itself from the babble and hum of the crowd.

"Tommy! Yo, Tommy-boy!"

We both swung around. The face that belonged to the voice wasn't hard to pick out, since most of the crowd was moving in the opposite direction. Even with the aviator glasses covering his eyes, the family resemblance was unmistakable. He was a slightly younger, slightly watered-down version of my husband. Not quite as tall. Not quite as dark. Not quite as smooth.

Just plain not quite as.

"What the hell are you doing here?" There was an edge to Tom's voice, one he smoothed over so quickly I would have missed it if it hadn't been so uncharacteristic of the man I'd married. He shot me a brief glance before continuing. "I thought you were in Presque Isle."

"Finished the job early. Heard you needed a ride, so—voilà! Here I am."

Tom's eyes narrowed, and something passed between them, some kind of animosity that they weren't quite verbalizing. They rubbed each other the wrong way. Even I, a virtual stranger, could see it. "Lucky us," he said.

Instead of rising to the bait, the guy laughed. He turned his attention to me, all trace of hostility gone. His smile was genuine, warm and welcoming. "And this must be Julie." He pulled off the glasses and held out his hand. "I'm Riley. Tom's black-sheep brother."

Tom hadn't mentioned that he had a brother. Judging by the sour expression on my husband's face, he must have had good reason for that omission.

I shook Riley's outstretched hand. "Nice to meet you."

"Where's Mom?" Tom asked.

"She didn't come."

The two brothers exchanged a look that was layered with meaning. I tried to decipher one or two of those layers, but it was impossible.

In an attempt to inject some levity into the atmosphere, I said, "Maybe we could just settle here instead of going all the way to Maine. I hear Boston's nice in the fall."

Tom's frigid demeanor instantly thawed. "Christ,

Jules," he said, "I'm sorry. Don't worry about it, honey. Mom's just being Mom. She'll come around."

"Tommy's right," Riley said. "It's nothing personal. It's just that—" he slid the aviator glasses back on his face "—nobody's ever been quite good enough for our boy here."

The look Tom gave him could easily have frozen water. "Just cool it," Tom said. "Okay?"

"Whatever you say," Riley said easily, bending and picking up my suitcases. "After all, you're the boss. I'm just a lowly chauffeur."

In the rear seat of the Ford pickup, Tom rode in silence. I sat up front with Riley, who spent most of the two-hour drive regaling me with family stories and childhood memories. I half listened to him, made appropriate responses at the appropriate times, but for the most part, as we drove steadily northward through a drizzling rain, I simply stared out the window at the passing foliage. Was northern New England made up of nothing but trees? This had to be the most godforsaken, isolated place on the planet. What the hell was I thinking? Was it too late for me to change my mind, hop back on a plane and fly home to California?

Not that I would have left Tom behind, not for an instant. But I had myself halfway convinced that we'd gotten it backwards, that I wasn't supposed to uproot myself and move to the end of the earth. That instead, it was Tom who was supposed to be moving his medical practice to some thriving metropolis nestled snugly in the heart of the sunbelt.

Then, finally, we left the highway. And all my doubts vanished in an instant. Because Newmarket, Maine was enchanting.

I grew up in Los Angeles. But not in the glamorous part of town where the movie stars hang out. We lived in one of the seedier neighborhoods, the kind of place where hookers plied their trade on the sidewalk two stories below my bedroom window. A zillion years ago, my dad used to be Somebody. But when the mighty Dave Hanrahan tumbled with the momentum of a California landslide, nobody even noticed. My dad's life was one cliché after another. *The bigger they come, the harder they fall.* When he fell, it wasn't pretty. Not that it was his fault. Life just goes that way sometimes. It's that old story about the windshield and the bug. When you get up each morning, you never know which one you're going to be that day. Here's another cliché. *Nothing lasts forever.* Take that one apart and analyze it. Does losing it all hurt worse than never having possessed it in the first place?

I don't know the answer to that question. I just know that, growing up the way I did, I used to dream about getting out of there, about leaving it behind for something better. Just like Audrey in that movie, *Little Shop of Horrors,* I wanted to leave skid row and move someplace that was green. Newmarket, Maine, was that green place I'd spent my childhood fantasizing about.

It was like a postcard from Currier & Ives, or a painting by Thomas Kinkade, Painter of Light. The village green, shaded by elms and flanked by white-steepled churches. The picturesque little downtown shops with their mullioned windows and wooden signs. The old-style faux-gas lampposts that lined the brick sidewalks. All of it softened by raindrops on the windshield and the blurred reflections of brake lights on wet pavement.

"This place is lovely," I said.

"It's home," Tom said, the first words he'd uttered in a half hour.

I turned around. Behind me, Tom met my gaze and shot me a wink. I relaxed. Whatever it was that had sent him into a snit, he was over it now. Obviously, there was some kind of long-standing sibling rivalry going on between my husband and his brother, but over the course of the drive, Tom's customary good nature had been restored.

We left the downtown area and drove down a side street of manicured lawns and dignified Victorian homes. Just as Riley turned the car into the circular drive of a massive white house, the sky opened up, and the drizzle became a pounding downpour. There were several cars parked in the drive, including a silver Land Rover and a powder-blue Caddy of indeterminate vintage. Riley pulled up behind the Land Rover and parked opposite the front steps.

A movement at a second-story window caught my eye. The curtain was drawn aside and for just an instant, a face peered out, pale and chalky against the storm's dark backdrop. Then the curtain dropped back into place, leaving me to wonder if I'd imagined it.

"This is it," Tom said. "Home, sweet home."

The house was exquisite. Even through the driving rain, I could appreciate its beauty. I'd taken a course at UCLA in the history of art and architecture, so I recognized the spindles, the balconies, the stained glass and the graceful turret as classic Queen Anne–style architecture. Set back from the street behind a wide swath of green lawn and embraced by a broad veranda, the house was flanked by ancient elms and one enormous pine tree. Hung at precise intervals from the ceiling of the veranda, baskets of pink and purple fuchsias danced madly in the wind kicked up by the storm.

"Damn crazy weather," Riley muttered. "When I left a few hours ago, there wasn't a cloud in the sky."

"You know what they say about Maine." Tom fumbled on the floor by his feet and came up with a black umbrella. "If you don't like the weather, wait a minute."

He opened his door, popped open the umbrella, and stepped out of the car. The wind immediately caught the flimsy nylon and aluminum device and did battle with it. Tom danced and ducked like a champion fencer, the umbrella twisting this way and that, before he won the battle. He opened my door and reached in a hand. "Hurry," he said, rain streaming off his shoulders. "This can't last long. We'll get the luggage after it stops."

Together, we sprinted around the nose of the

pickup, skirting the broken pine branches that littered the driveway, and pounded up the steps to the veranda with Riley close behind us. As the rain hammered down on the roof above our heads, Tom closed what was left of the umbrella while I took quick inventory. My feet were drenched, my simple canvas flats probably not salvageable, but the rest of me was relatively unscathed. Except for my hair, which was famous for behaving perfectly fine until the first sign of humidity, at which point I could have been mistaken for Don King's slightly paler twin sister. I'd hoped to meet my new mother-in-law under more favorable conditions, but there was little I could do at this point.

Besides, it could have been worse. I could've looked like Riley. In the twenty-five feet between the car and the porch, Tom's brother had taken on more water than Lake Michigan during spring runoff. His hair was plastered to his head. Rivulets of water trickled down his cheeks and his neck. He swiped at his wet face with a coat sleeve that only made it worse. Then he shrugged, pulled off the aviator glasses, and shook himself dry like a golden retriever who'd just returned from a dip in the duck pond.

Behind us, the front door creaked open. "Better get inside," said the woman who stood there, "before the wind blows you away."

Either I'd misunderstood, or Tom had greatly exaggerated his mother's imperfections. It wasn't possible that the graying, matronly woman who greeted us could be the dragon lady he'd described. Nothing about her—from the tightly permed salt-and-pepper hair to the pink pantsuit adorned with rhinestone kittens—fit with the image of the she-devil that I'd been carrying around inside my head. This was Tom's mother, the terror of the town? The woman who was so hardheaded and difficult? The one who'd blown me off by sending Riley to meet us in her place?

No way.

Over her shoulder, I shot Tom an inquiring glance. He just shrugged. Jeannette Larkin stepped back to study me, and I tried to imagine what she saw when she looked at me: a young woman nearly a decade younger than her son, a little too tall, a little too thin, with dark, frizzy hair and bony knuckles. There wasn't a doubt in my mind that I fell far short of Jeannette's expectations of a daughter-in-law. Still, I boldly returned her assessment, hoping she'd find me acceptable. For Tom's sake, if nothing else.

"How was your flight?" she asked.

Relief coursed through me. I'd apparently passed the initial inspection. "Rough," I admitted. "Very rough."

"Jules doesn't like to fly," Tom said, moving smoothly to my side, "and this storm didn't help her nerves any. Here, honey, let me take your coat."

"I'm a bona fide phobic," I clarified, shrugging off the jacket and surrendering it. "Flying's at the top of my phobia list, followed closely by anything that slithers."

Footsteps sounded overhead, and two little girls in matching white sundresses thundered down the stairs. Amid cries of "Daddy! Daddy!" they flung themselves at Tom.

He scooped up the youngest and tossed her over his shoulder. She squealed in protest. The older girl buried her face against his side and clung to him with both arms, as though fearful he'd disappear if she loosened her grip.

Tom lowered the little one to a more comfortable position against his hip and said, "Did you really miss me that much?"

"You were gone forever, Daddy. Did you bring us any presents?"

The older girl pulled her face away from her father's side just far enough to peer up hopefully at him.

"Presents?" he said, wrinkling his brow as if in puzzlement. "Well, gee, I don't know. We'll have to check my luggage. Maybe somebody dropped something in there while I wasn't looking."

The younger girl giggled, but the elder daughter narrowed solemn eyes and said, "Oh, Daddy, stop being silly."

"Guess I can't put anything over on you two, can I?" He adjusted the little girl against his hip, placed an affectionate hand atop the older girl's head, and turned to me with a grin. "Jules," he said, "I'd like you to meet my daughters, Taylor and Sadie. Girls, this is Julie."

I'd thought meeting Tom's mother was nerve-racking, but this was ten times worse. So much was riding on it. I'd already heard a great deal about his daughters. Like any proud father, Tom had talked nonstop about his girls. Whenever he mentioned their names, his eyes lit up and his voice softened. A blind and deaf person could have seen that these two little girls were his life. If we were going to have any kind of successful marriage, Taylor and Sadie needed to accept me.

"Hi, girls," I said. "I'm so glad to finally meet you."

Taylor just stared at me, clear challenge in her eyes. Seven years old, she was the spitting image of her father. She had Tom's dark hair, his narrow face, and his blue eyes, which right now were studying me with a wariness I understood better than most people would. It was the same wariness I'd shown toward the various women my father had brought home over the years. Not quite welcoming, not quite trusting. The word *stepmother* had such negative connotations, and Taylor was no fool. She'd adopted a "wait-and-see" attitude that I found totally understandable.

Four-year-old Sadie, on the other hand, was as guileless and open as a six-week-old pup. There was no trepidation in her eyes, just avid curiosity and a willingness to accept me for what I was, her dad's new wife. The two girls couldn't have been more different if they'd come from different parents. Not just in attitude, but in looks. Although I searched Sadie's face for any trace of resemblance to Tom, I didn't find it. Taylor might have inherited her father's dark good looks, but Sadie, with her peaches-and-cream complexion and her blond curls, must have taken after Tom's late wife.

She smiled shyly and buried her face against her father's shoulder. "Hi," she said.

Life hadn't been easy for these little girls. They'd been so young when they lost their mother. According to Tom, Elizabeth's death had hit both girls extremely hard. Even now, two years after their mother's death, Sadie still had nightmares, and Taylor had trouble trusting new people. It hadn't been easy on Tom, either, playing both mother and father while trying to maintain his medical practice and his sanity. He'd freely admitted to me that without his mother's help, he wouldn't have made it through.

That was one of the things that had drawn me to Tom. After the initial attraction, of course, when I first saw him sitting in the next chair at the dinner table and felt the jolt all the way to the marrow in my bones. But it was the subsequent conversation, the hours we spent together, that cemented my feelings. They say every woman seeks out a man like her father to marry. On the surface, Tom Larkin and Dave Hanrahan were as far apart as the poles, but there were a few things they did have in common. I'd lost my own mother at a young age, and I'd spent my childhood watching Dad struggle to raise me alone. I believe it takes a special kind of man to do that. So I knew where Tom was coming from. And I respected him for it.

Because I'd been through it myself, I knew I

needed to tread carefully with Tom's girls. I couldn't expect to just jump in and take over where their mother had left off. Sadie might let me get away with it, but Taylor would never allow such a thing. She was old enough to remember, old enough to resent anyone who tried to take Elizabeth's place. If I hoped to win Taylor over, if I hoped to mold us into a family, I'd have to practice patience.

But I didn't have to rush. There was plenty of time for that. After all, we had the rest of our lives.

Wind battered the house in a relentless siege. Pine cones and debris rapped at the windows. Somewhere at the rear of the house, a loose shutter banged. But the place held fast. It had been built during an era when homes were designed to withstand a little wind, a little rain. That was a good thing, because we already had three inches of rain, and it was showing no signs of letting up. With wind gusts up to seventy-five miles per hour, the ancient pine that towered over the house creaked and moaned like an arthritic old man. I hoped to God it stayed upright; according to the radio Jeannette kept running in the kitchen, trees had been uprooted all over the county, and if it fell, that pine tree would go straight through the roof. Power lines were down everywhere. Twelve thousand people in the state were already without electricity, and that number was expected to rise.

But indoors, we were cozy and warm. Although we hadn't lost power, Tom had brought out the candles, the matches, the flashlights, and he'd lined them up on the kitchen counter, just in case. Dinner was roast pork, with steamed asparagus and tiny red potatoes swimming in butter. After an initial hesitation, I forgot manners and just chowed down with my customary enthusiasm. I have what people euphemistically refer to as a healthy appetite. The first time Tom witnessed it, at the buffet table aboard the *Island Princess,* he'd been floored by the amount of food I was able to ingest without gaining an ounce. He actually found it charming that I have the appetite of a stevedore. I find it annoying that no matter how much I eat, I still look like Olive Oyl, Popeye's seriously anorexic girlfriend.

Conversation around the dinner table was light and innocuous; Tom and I were asked about the cruise, about how we'd met, about our moonlight wedding and how we'd known so quickly that we were meant for each other. I was just reaching for my third potato when his mother dropped the bomb.

"You haven't told us anything about your family, Julie," she said with a smarmy smile. "I'd love to hear about them."

I hesitated, my fork hovering over the serving dish, and met Tom's eyes. My husband knew it all. I'd told him everything, the good, the bad and the ugly, and I wondered whether I should regale his mother with the whole sordid truth or a slightly sanitized version thereof.

Beneath the table, Tom slid his foot over to touch mine. His reassuring smile gave me strength. I glanced around the table at all the expectant faces, all these people waiting with bated breath for the life story of the anonymous woman who'd quite literally blown into their lives on the winds of a hurricane.

I speared the potato and put it on my plate. "Well," I said as I sliced it in two and slathered it with butter, "I'm pretty much alone in the world. Or I was, until I met Tom." I gave him a shaky smile, and he returned it full force. "I was divorced about a year ago. Before I married Jeffrey, there was just my dad and me. My mother, in her infinite wisdom, left us when I was five years old. Dad died six months ago. Liver cancer."

I didn't bother to elaborate. I didn't tell them that Dad had died of a broken heart and too much boozing. Let them read between the lines if they wanted to. I'm all for honesty, but some skeletons are better left in the closet.

I ate a bite of potato. "My father was…" I trailed off, wondering how on earth to describe Dad in words that normal people would understand. People who'd never had the privilege of knowing him, with all his quirks and oddities. "Very independent. A freethinker. A little to the left of center."

The girls watched me with wide eyes. Jeannette's brows were drawn together into a small frown. Probably wondering if there were some family history of severe mental illness that was about to infect her future grandchildren. Directly across the table, Riley seemed curious, waiting. "He was a musician," I said.

"Ah," Riley said, as though that explained it all.

"A musician?" Jeannette said. "How interesting."

Having grown up as Dave Hanrahan's daughter, I understood only too well that *interesting* was a euphemism for *horrifying*. I speared another piece of potato. When I saw the affection and approval in Tom's eyes, I decided to go for broke. Dabbing my mouth with my napkin, I said, "He was pretty well known at one time, until his career went south and my mother left him. When his career tanked and his band broke up, my mother ran off with the drummer. At that point, his life sort of fell apart."

That was a polite way of putting it. The truth was that after my mother left, Dad drank himself to death. It took him twenty-seven years, but Dave Hanrahan was nothing if not persistent. The day she walked out the door, he decided that life was no longer worth living, and he spent the rest of his days proving the validity of that theory.

"Good Lord," Jeannette said, looking as though she'd swallowed a persimmon.

I knew that my life—or, to be more accurate, my father's life—sounded like a train wreck. It wasn't as bad as it sounded, but I could understand Jeannette's horrified expression.

Beneath the table, Tom's ankle looped around mine. Riley appeared intrigued, so I directed my next words at him. "All the money disappeared. We barely survived. But he was a great dad. The best."

"Are you going to tell us?" Riley asked. "Or are you keeping his identity a secret?"

"No secret," I said. "His name was Dave Hanrahan."

Riley's face changed, the way it often does when people first hear my father's name. "Get out of here! *The* Dave Hanrahan? The front man for Satan's Revenge?"

"That would be my dad."

"The guy who wrote 'Black Curtain'? Oh, man. Tommy, remember how we used to play that record over and over and over? That guy was the epitome of cool. We all wanted to be him." Riley braced his elbows against the table and leaned forward eagerly, his eyes focused on me, everything and everybody else forgotten. "You must've had an amazing childhood," he said. "Hanging around with all those musicians. Listening to their music. Their stories."

I opened my mouth to answer him, but I never got the chance. The lights blinked and, from outside, there arose a massive splintering sound, a roar so deafening that it sounded like a freight train passing through. The ground actually shook, and if I hadn't known better, I would have sworn that the earth itself had opened up and revealed the gateway to Hell.

Then the window behind me imploded.

Two

"It's not that big a deal," I said. "Really."

"You're lucky to be alive." With intense concentration and quick, efficient hands, Tom dabbed antiseptic on the gash on my cheek while I tried not to wince. "Another six inches, and—" He closed his eyes and muttered something indecipherable. Darkly, he added, "I knew I should've cut down that damn tree last spring."

He capped the bottle of antiseptic, picked up a Band-Aid, and held my chin in his hand to size up the injury. "It's too old," he said, turning my head to the left, then to the right. "Too brittle. Too dangerous."

"It was just a limb." *A big one.*

"Next time, it's apt to be the whole tree. Damn thing took ten years off my life."

"I'm fine. Honest."

"You talk too much. Hold still." He tore open the Band-Aid, peeled off the paper backing, and gently applied it to my cheek. Sitting back to admire his handiwork, he said, "There. You'll probably live to talk a little longer."

I gave him a radiant smile and said, "My hero."

He grimaced. Crumpling the Band-Aid wrapper, he said, "Some welcome you got. If I were you, I'd run as fast as I could back to Los Angeles."

"What? And miss all the excitement around here? Surely you jest."

Humorlessly, he said, "It's usually a lot more boring than this."

"Oh, I don't know," I said. "I think I'll stick around for a while and see for myself."

He shoved the bottle of antiseptic back into his first-aid kit. "Tomorrow, I'm calling the tree service and having that pine cut down."

"It seems a shame. It's probably been standing there for a hundred years."

"And I'd like to make sure that you're standing for another hundred." He closed the lid on the kit and zipped the cover. "The tree goes. Don't even bother to argue."

"I suppose you're saying that because you believe a good wife always obeys her husband."

Some of the somberness left his face. The corners of his eyes crinkled as he said, "Do you have any idea how tempted I am to say yes?"

I smiled. "But you're refraining."

"For now, anyway. We may have to revisit the issue at a later date."

"Nice save."

"I thought so."

The sound of rattling glassware and cutlery drifted in from the kitchen. "Now that I'm all better," I said, "I should be helping your mother clean up the mess." We'd left the dining room littered with pine needles, broken branches, and rain water. Shattered glass was everywhere. On the floor. On the dining table. Tiny slivers of it embedded in what was left of our dinner.

"You're excused from kitchen duty tonight. Doctor's orders."

I raised an eyebrow. "Tom? You do realize that you're an obstetrician?"

"You have a complaint, file it with the AMA."

Outside, the chain saw had finally stopped its high-pitched whine. Now we could hear a rhythmic hammering as Riley boarded up the broken window. In the moments after the tree limb had made its unceremonious and unexpected foray into the dining room, chaos had reigned. The girls had been semi-hysterical. Jeannette had tried to calm them while simultaneously herding them away from the broken glass. Riley had thrown on a pair of snowmobile boots and a yellow slicker and rushed outside, flashlight in hand, to assess the damage. Meantime, Tom hovered over me like a mother hen, frantically cataloguing and documenting every scratch and bruise. For a man who spent half his life in the delivery room, he'd gone surprisingly pale at the sight of blood. Or maybe it was just the sight of my blood that frightened him.

Once Sadie and Taylor were convinced that nobody was seriously injured and the house wasn't in imminent danger of collapsing around them, Tom's mother had bribed them by promising that if they went upstairs and got ready for bed without argument, they could forego their baths for tonight. That was all it took. We hadn't heard another sound from them.

Until now. They came padding into the living room wearing flannel pajamas and matching Miss Piggy slippers. Taylor had a book in her hand and a sly expression on her face. "We're ready for our bedtime story," she said.

"Say good-night, then, and run along to bed," Tom said. "I'll be right up."

"No." She held the book in both hands and teetered back and forth from one foot to the other. "We want Julie to read it to us."

Tom and I exchanged glances. "Do you mind, Jules?" he said.

Did I mind? This was an opportunity for bonding, and I wasn't about to pass it up. "I'd be honored," I said, standing and taking Sadie by the hand. "Come on, girls. Let's see what you're reading."

The book was *Where the Wild Things Are,* one of my own childhood favorites. Upstairs in their bedroom, Sadie slipped beneath the covers and I settled beside her to read, while Taylor perched on the edge of her own bed a few feet away. Both girls were engrossed in the story, but after a few minutes, I could see that Sadie was having trouble keeping her eyes open.

"Enough for tonight," I said. "Time for bed."

"We're supposed to say our prayers now," Taylor informed me. "Before you tuck us in."

"Oh," I said. "Right. Of course." Nothing would have made me admit to them that I wasn't familiar with this particular bedtime ritual. Dave Hanrahan had nursed a lifelong contempt for anything that smacked of religion, a result of his uptight Catholic upbringing. Dad had attended Our Lady of All Saints School until eighth grade, and the nuns had traumatized him for life. So there'd been no praying in our house. But I'm an obliging soul, and I've learned to fake it if I have to. When in Rome, and all that jazz. I could handle a little praying. It might even do me some good.

Taking a cue from the girls, I knelt beside Sadie's bed, my stepdaughters beside me in their flannel jammies, their oversized Piggy feet stuck out behind them. Hands folded, I closed my eyes and tried to look pious. In unison, they spoke the words of the prayer:

"Now I lay me down to sleep
I pray the Lord my soul to keep
If I should die before I wake
I pray the Lord my soul to take."

"Amen," Taylor said.

"Amen," Sadie echoed. Her eyes popped open and she exclaimed, "Oops! I forgot!" Bowing her head again, she added, "God bless Daddy, and

Grandma, and Uncle Riley, and Mommy up in heaven. And—" She opened her eyes, glanced at me, and smiled. "And Julie," she finished. "Amen."

A tiny crack appeared in my heart. Maybe winning over Tom's daughters wouldn't be so hard after all. They were such precious little girls, and so very needy. And they seemed to genuinely like me.

I pulled back the covers. Sadie scrambled beneath them, and I tucked them up tight under her chin. She lay there beneath the blankets, a dreamy smile on her face, and said, "Are you my mommy now?"

Time stood still. While my heart beat in the silence, I glanced across the empty space between beds to Taylor, who seemed to be holding her breath, awaiting my response.

I lay a hand atop Sadie's head, felt the cool, soft tickle of baby-fine hair between my fingertips. "Your mom," I said, "will always be your mom."

Sadie yawned. "Even though she's not here any more?"

"Even though. I would never try to take her place. How about for now, we'll just say we're friends, and leave it at that? Okay?"

She gave me a sleepy nod and rolled over, burying her face in her pillow. I stood and crossed the room to Taylor, who lay beneath her own covers. Tucking the snow-white bedspread tightly around her, I said, "All set?"

She nodded. I reached out to touch her cheek, then hesitated. I didn't want to rush things with her. Instead, I simply said, "Good night."

As I turned to go, she said, "Don't get too used to being here."

I paused, not sure I'd heard her correctly. Turning, I said, "Excuse me?"

Her eyes, so like Tom's, held none of his warmth. Instead, they were glacial. "I said you shouldn't get too used to being here. Grandma says you won't last any longer than any of the others."

I told myself she was just a little girl. Only seven years old. There was no real malice in her words; she was just repeating what she'd heard. But when I thought about the hostility on her face, I wasn't so sure. Children were capable of cruelty, and Taylor was an intelligent child. She knew she'd upset me. That had been her intention. I'd seen the satisfaction in her eyes before she reached out and turned off the bedside lamp, leaving me to find my way in complete darkness.

I could almost forgive her for her animosity. After all, she was just a child, and she'd suffered an irreparable loss. I could still remember how I'd felt when my mother left us. The fear, the guilt, the knife-edged sense of betrayal. The years spent wondering if it was something I'd done that had driven her away. It had taken me a very long time to get over it—as much as anyone gets over that kind of loss— and I'd sworn that no matter what happened in my life, I'd never, ever do that to a child.

Taylor's mother hadn't run away like mine had, but Tom's daughter had to be feeling some of the same emotions that I'd felt. Death was the ultimate betrayal. And for a girl to lose her mother at such a young age—a mother whose absence would be keenly felt at all life's most poignant and significant junctures—the loss was immeasurable.

We all grieve in different ways. I'd walked in Taylor's shoes, and I couldn't fault her for how she'd chosen to grieve her terrible loss.

But Tom was right. This was some welcome I'd gotten. Wondering just who were these "others" that Taylor had referred to, I headed downstairs to find my husband and demand some answers.

I heard them arguing as soon as I reached the ground floor. They weren't exactly trying to be quiet. "She can't stay," Jeannette said. "You know that as well as I do."

"I don't know anything of the kind." My husband sounded agitated. Furious.

"You don't know anything about her. For all you know, she could be a gold digger. I cringed when I heard that pathetic story she told about her impoverished childhood. What if she married you for your money?"

Heat raced up my face. Normally, I was adamantly opposed to eavesdropping. But, damn it, this was *me* they were talking about. Wild horses couldn't have dragged me away. I crept a little closer to the kitchen door and pressed myself against the dark paneling of the hallway.

"That's ridiculous," Tom said.

"You're a doctor, Tom. She probably took one look at you and decided you were her meal ticket."

Wearily, my husband said, "I make a decent living, Mother, but I'm hardly in a league with the neurosurgeons of the world. I'm a small-town baby doctor."

"The perception's still there that doctor equals money. I just can't imagine what you were thinking. What happens when she finds out—"

"Finds out what? That I've been eaten up by loneliness ever since Elizabeth died? I can't believe you'd begrudge me a little happiness. Julie's amazing, Mom, and you'd see that if you gave her half a chance."

"What about your girls? They need you, Tom. How can you justify stealing what little free time you have away from them to give it to some stranger?"

"They need a mother!"

Sounding hurt, she said, "What do you think I've been doing for the past two years?"

Tom's voice softened. "I know what you've been doing," he said, "and I truly appreciate all you've done for us. But it's not the same thing. The girls need stability, an intact family."

"It's not going to work. You know it as well as I do. It's not too late to have this marriage annulled. I'm begging you to end it before it gets messy. Send her back where she came from and move on with your life."

Indignation had me holding my breath. *Send her back where she came from.* What did this woman think I was, a FedEx package?

Tom's voice again: "She has a name, Mom. It's Julie."

"Fine. Send *Julie* back where she came from,

back to L.A., to her hippy-dippy life and her fond memories of her wastrel of a father."

In a deadly quiet voice, Tom said, "I'm only going to say this once, Mother, so you'd better listen. I don't give a damn whether or not you like her, but Julie is my wife and, by God, you'll treat her with respect. If I hear one more negative word about her—"

A sound behind me tore my attention away from the sparring in the kitchen. Riley stood at the foot of the stairs, water dripping off his yellow slicker. I'd been so caught up in the drama being played out in the next room that I hadn't even heard him come in the front door. I had no idea how long he'd been standing there, or how much he'd overheard. Our eyes met, but neither of us said a word.

"Forget it," Tom said in disgust. "This discussion is over."

"Where are you going?" his mother demanded.

"Out. I need to cool off before I say something I'll regret."

"For God's sake, Tom, don't be an idiot. There's a hurricane going on out there."

"And it's a welcome reprieve from what's going on in here!"

A door slammed, and a moment later, I heard a car engine start up. My gaze still locked with Riley's, I saw something there that I didn't want to see, something that looked remarkably like pity. Without saying a word, I stalked past him to the staircase and fled upstairs.

* * *

I closed the bedroom door and slumped against it, my chest heaving with suppressed fury. The luggage standing neatly by the foot of the bed seemed to mock me, and I wondered if I should even bother to unpack. To his credit, Tom—who'd vowed to cherish me until death—had stood up to his mother for me. How long would he be able to stand up to her before she wore him down? I was crazy about my new husband, but if this was the direction my marriage was headed, how long would it be before I decided I'd made a colossal mistake?

I lifted my overnight bag to the bed, unzipped it, and pulled out my pajamas. Stomping into the bathroom, I tossed the pj's on the toilet seat, started up the shower, and began to strip.

I came to an abrupt halt when I caught sight of my reflection in the eight-foot-long bathroom mirror. I looked like the Wild Woman of Borneo, my cheeks flushed with fury, my eyes wide and wild. Even my hair seemed to be in on the act, standing electrified, as though I'd stuck my finger into a light socket.

How dare she call me a gold digger? The woman didn't even know me. And she'd already tried to turn Tom's daughters against me. What kind of monster would poison a child's mind like that?

I had half a mind to march back downstairs and tell the woman exactly what was what. I'd never been one to mince words or to retreat from a fight. If there was one thing I'd learned firsthand from my dad, it was that quitters never win. Dave Hanrahan had been the poster child for how not to live your life. He'd allowed a run of bad luck, a few lousy decisions, and the hazy comfort of alcohol to destroy his future. Because I'd been witness to his slow and painful deterioration, I'd vowed that I would never let life defeat me the way Dad had. No matter what, I stood up for myself and for what I believed in. And I never, ever backed down.

But, damn it, the woman was Tom's mother.

And I was the woman who wore Tom's wedding ring.

Scooping my hair back from my face with both hands, I let out a ragged breath. None of this was his fault. I couldn't blame Tom because his mother was a monster. He already knew that. He'd been living with the woman for nearly forty years. That was punishment enough for a lifetime. How could I justify giving him the added burden of lunatic behavior?

So I didn't go back downstairs. For tonight, I'd let it go. Today had been stressful for everyone. Maybe tomorrow, in the clear light of day, things would look different. Maybe tomorrow, after things settled down, Jeannette would see the error of her ways.

But as I stood in the shower, steaming hot water pounding down on my shoulders, I wasn't at all sure it would happen. Tom's mother seemed so unyielding that I wondered if there was more going on here than I was privy to. Was there some deep, dark secret that Tom hadn't bothered to tell me? Was it possible that Jeannette's train had simply run off the tracks? There'd been something in that look Tom and his brother exchanged at the airport, something about their mother that remained unspoken but understood by both of them. I couldn't help wondering if a woman so determined to deprive her son of happiness might be a little unbalanced. Would a sane, rational woman attempt to poison the minds of her grandchildren because she didn't want their father remarrying? No matter how I looked at it, there was no rational explanation for her behavior.

One thing I did know as I stepped from the shower and toweled my hair dry: I'd never felt so alone in my life. Not even after my baby died and the world became a barren, empty place. This was far worse. The world after Angel's death had been indifferent to my pain; I'd experienced none of the malevolence, none of the deliberate and focused hatred, that I felt here in this house.

I was wrapped in my fluffy white chenille robe, yanking a brush through my wet hair, when Tom came back. He closed the bedroom door quietly behind him. Brush in hand, I paused between strokes. Our eyes met: his uncertain, mine accusing. "Hi," he said.

"I heard you," I said bluntly. "In the kitchen. Arguing."

He grimaced. "How much did you hear?"

"Enough."

"Jules," he said, "I'm so sorry."

"That makes two of us. I don't understand, Tom. Make me understand."

"I don't know what to say. My mother's overprotective. She's always been that way."

Overprotective? Was that what he called it? If so, we might as well be speaking different languages. "I can think of a few other adjectives that fit even better," I said. "How about mean? Spiteful? Vicious? Just for starters."

"I don't have a response for you, Jules, because you're right." He raked slender, pale fingers through his dark hair. "I knew things would be a little awkward. I knew she wouldn't be happy about our marriage. But I never thought she'd be insulting to you."

"She called me a gold digger! And my father a wastrel!"

"And if you were paying attention, you know that I stood up for you."

"Yes. You did. And I'm grateful. But if this is the way she's going to treat me, I'm not sure how long I can refrain from giving her a large piece of my mind."

"Aw, honey." He took a step toward me. "She'll adjust. Just give her a little time."

"That's not everything, Tom. There's more." I told him what Taylor had said to me, the terrible things his mother had taught her, and he winced as if in pain.

"Christ, Mom," he muttered, rubbing his face with his hands. "What the hell are you thinking?"

I hated to see him this way. Hated even worse knowing I was the one who'd put that look on his face. "I'm sorry," I said. "I didn't want to tell you, but I thought you should know."

"I swear to God, Jules, I had no idea I was bringing you into this kind of nightmare. I wouldn't blame you if you walked away. It would kill me, but I wouldn't blame you."

"I'm not going anywhere. I take my marriage vows seriously. For better or for worse, remember? I'll do whatever it takes to win her over. If that doesn't work, then I'll just have to learn to live with her. Somehow." The picture that painted in my mind was bleak enough that I had to shove it aside.

"I'm not sure it could get much worse. This isn't fair to you. It's unacceptable. If Mom keeps this up, she'll have to live somewhere else."

Aghast, I said, "You can't throw her out, Tom. She's your mother."

"And you're my wife! There's another vow you should remember: forsaking all others. Yes, she's my mother. But you're my family now. You and the girls. If she's determined to come between us—" he scowled "—or between you and my daughters, I won't allow it."

I wasn't sure if I felt better or worse. It was a comfort to know that Tom was solidly in my corner. On the other hand, I didn't want to be responsible for the dissolution of his family. Wishing I could avoid asking, but knowing I couldn't, I said, "Tom? What did your mother mean when she told Taylor I wouldn't last any longer than any of the others?"

My husband rolled his eyes. "All those others," he said. "All the screaming, swooning hordes of women I've dated since Elizabeth died."

This was one thing we hadn't talked about, not in detail. His sexual history. Mine. We'd been too busy falling for each other to get around to the topic of our collective romantic past. At first, we hadn't thought much about it. Once we were married, it didn't seem to matter.

But now, suddenly, it did. "Have there been screaming, swooning hordes?" I asked.

"Come on, Jules. Do I look like Jon Bon Jovi to you?"

In my book, he looked far better than Jon. Which was saying a lot. But he was deliberately missing the point. "I'm serious, Tom. How many were there?"

He crossed the room to me and took my hand. "Elizabeth's been dead for two years." He tucked a strand of wet hair behind my ear. "I haven't lived like a monk. I've dated a few women. None of them stuck around. None of them stuck around because I wasn't serious about any of them. I swear, Jules, you're the only one who ever screamed or swooned."

Coyly, I said, "I don't seem to recall any swooning."

He leaned over me and buried his nose in my hair. "You smell so good. What's that scent you're wearing?"

"Strawberry. It's my shampoo."

"Don't ever stop using it." His chin brushed my temple, his five o'clock shadow grazing my skin. His breath warm on my ear, he crooned softly: "Julie, Julie, Julie, do you love me?"

"Stop," I said weakly. It was a private joke between

us, that hokey old Bobby Sherman song. "Please stop."

"You know you love it. So tell me, Jules, is the honeymoon over yet?"

I toyed with a strand of his hair and said, "Not quite yet."

"Then why are we wasting time? Hand over your weapon."

I gaped at him stupidly until he pried the hairbrush I'd been brandishing from my fingers. "You could do a lot of harm with that thing," he said, "depending on where you're aiming it."

"Ouch."

"Exactly. So what do you say, Mrs. Larkin? Time to end the foreplay and cut right to the main event?"

I flashed him a huge grin and said, "I thought you'd never ask."

It was hours later and inky dark when his cell phone rang. Peeling his naked body away from mine, Tom fumbled on the nightstand until he located the offending object. He cleared his throat and said, "Dr. Larkin." Listened a moment, then said, "Yes, of course. Not a problem."

I raised my head and looked at the clock, then hooked an arm around him and pressed my cheek against his sleek, broad back. Leaning into me, he said, "How far apart are the pains?" A pause. Then, "All right. I'll meet you at the hospital."

He hung up the phone and turned to me. "Sorry, Jules. Gotta go."

Sleepily, I said, "It's two-thirty in the morning."

"Might as well get used to it. Life would be a lot easier if babies were courteous enough to plan their arrivals between 9:00 a.m. and 5:00 p.m. Unfortunately, it doesn't work that way." He kissed the tip of my nose and left the bed. I listened as he dressed in the darkness, then walked to the window and peered through the blind. Quietly, he said, "Looks like the storm's over."

"Be careful anyway."

"Always. Go back to sleep, Jules."

When I woke again, the blinds were open, the sun was pouring in, and the clock read 8:37. I rolled over and spied the note propped against Tom's pillow. *Didn't want to wake you,* it read, *you looked so beautiful asleep. Make yourself at home. Mi casa es su casa. Literally. Oh—if you want to go anywhere, the Land Rover's all yours. Keys are hanging in the kitchen. Can't wait to see you tonight. Love, T.*

Smiling, I lay back against the pillow. I must've been dead to the world, because I'd never heard him return, never heard him leave a second time. It must have been the fresh Maine air or something. I got up, showered and dressed, then headed downstairs, anticipating a run-in with the dragon lady. But the house was deserted, silent, the morning sun flooding the kitchen with warmth. My new mother-in-law must be a cog in the wheel of the American work-force. Or else she'd fled the house because she didn't want to deal with me any more than I wanted to deal with her. Wasn't that the way with most passive-aggressive types? They tended to avoid conflict. And being nice to my face, then talking trash behind my back, was classic passive-aggressive behavior.

Or maybe she was just a two-faced bitch.

With some satisfaction, I pondered that possibility before telling myself to let it go or it would spoil my day. And what a day it was! Abundant sunshine and cloudless cerulean skies. Not a hint of the storm that had raged a few hours earlier. Except, of course, the damage it had left behind. With a bowl of Cheerios in hand, I flung open the French doors that led to the patio and stepped outside. The lawn was littered with branches, leaves and assorted debris. A small tree had been uprooted, and it lay forlorn, felled by the storm's fury. I found a wooden chair that wasn't too wet and sat down to eat my breakfast. A pair of bright yellow birds flew past, darting and swooping and twittering before they disappeared in the branches of a massive elm tree. I thought they might be goldfinches, but I wasn't sure. On the ground beneath the bird feeder, a cluster of sparrows pecked at spilled seed.

Around the corner of the house, a chain saw started up, its obnoxious whine tearing a jagged hole in the smooth fabric of the morning. Startled by the noise, the sparrows scattered. I finished my Cheerios and went back inside to put the bowl and spoon in the dishwasher. Then I went in search of the chain saw.

It wasn't hard to find. The noise level was appalling. In Riley's capable hands, the lime-green monster sang its own peculiar aria, the whine working its way up and down the scale. Dressed in a Hard Rock T-shirt, jeans, and safety glasses, Tom's brother finessed the saw with smooth, efficient motions. The branch that had fallen was as big around as my waist, and the chain saw protested loudly as he sliced it into neat, foot-long segments. I stood watching him until he became aware of my scrutiny. Then he took a step back, turned off the chain saw, and removed his safety glasses.

Birdsong filled the sudden silence, and for an instant I felt awkward, remembering what he'd witnessed last night and wishing he hadn't. "Sleep well?" he said.

"As well as can be expected." I raised a hand to shade my eyes from the bright sun. I knew we were both thinking about our last meeting. I might as well bring it into the open instead of dancing around it. "Your mother," I said, "doesn't seem to like me."

Fiddling with the pull cord to the chain saw, he said, "You did seem to bring out the worst in her."

"It's a talent," I said.

He balanced the butt of the saw against his booted foot. "I wouldn't let her get to me if I were you."

"I don't intend to. I'm indomitable."

He studied me with blue eyes very much like Tom's. And the corner of his mouth twitched. "Yeah," he said. "I can see that."

"So where, exactly, is she this morning? Your sainted mother?"

"She's at work. Tessie's Bark and Bath."

I raised an eyebrow. "Tessie's Bark and Bath?"

He grinned. "Mom's a dog groomer."

"And I'll bet she frightens the poor things into submission." Changing the subject, I pointed to the pile of wood he'd cut. "This pine branch is enormous. What'll you do with all this wood?"

"Split it. Stack it. Come winter, it'll keep the house warm."

"Winter," I said. "That seems like such a foreign concept. I'm a Southern California girl. I'm used to sunshine. The beach. I've never done winter. Does it really get as cold as I've heard?"

"Take whatever you're expecting and multiply it by ten. February may be the shortest month, but it's also the coldest. And the darkest. You'll want to buy an extra-warm coat. Fur-lined boots. Thick gloves. And a wool scarf. That is, assuming you're still here come February."

I shoved my hands into the pockets of my jeans. "Are you saying there's some reason I might not be here?"

"I didn't say that."

"She's not going to drive me away, Riley."

"I didn't say that, either. It's just—"

"What?"

His blue eyes studied me, but I couldn't decipher what was going on behind them. "Nothing," he said. "I have to get back to work. This tree won't get cut up by itself."

I stepped away as Riley fired up the chain saw. He adjusted his safety goggles, nodded to me, and went back to cutting.

I suspected I'd been snubbed, although I wasn't wholly certain. But I was definitely starting to feel as if I'd stepped through the looking glass and into some otherworldly dimension where everything was a little off center.

But I didn't allow myself to wallow in it; I had no sympathy for people who sat around bemoaning their fates. Pity parties aren't my style. I had far too much to do. Since I'd decided against making a run for it, I needed to unpack and try to find space for all my things in Tom's bedroom. *Our* bedroom, I reminded myself.

I headed back to the house, rummaged through my purse for a notebook and pen, and sat at the kitchen table to make a list of what needed doing. I'm a compulsive list-maker. I simply can't seem to stop. Jeffrey used to make fun of me because of it, but list-making helps me keep my life organized and running on track. If I didn't make lists, I'd never re-member anything. I use them in both my private and business life, and my friends and coworkers always point out how utterly organized I am. I just smile enigmatically and accept the compliment, while mentally thumbing my nose at my ex-husband. What can I say? Sometimes even a mature woman has to let her inner child out once in a while.

First on the list: *Go to bank*. I'd already closed my bank account and had the balance transferred elec-tronically to Tom's account, but I still had to drop by the bank and fill out paperwork to make it official. I'd managed to put away a small amount of money in savings, and the sale of my Miata had added a couple thousand to that. I'd hated selling my car, and I'd nearly cried when the used car salesman drove it away. But Tom had said that come winter, the sports car would be useless in the snow, and he'd promised to replace it with a brand-new four-wheel-drive SUV of my choice. So I'd caved. My life in California was over. Big changes were taking place. If I intended to live year-round in Maine, I needed to start acting like a Mainer. I would drive the SUV, even if my heart did secretly ache for a two-seater sports coupe.

Items two, three and four on the list were more housekeeping stuff: *Get a Maine driver's license, Apply for a new social security card,* and *Notify credit card company of new name and address.* Item five was more generic: *Contact old friends I've lost touch with.* People I talked to once or twice a year, exchanged Christmas cards with. Old school chums, friends of my dad, people Jeffrey and I used to socialize with. A couple of great-aunts. People I had little in common with, but that I didn't want to lose complete contact with.

I paused at number six. Chewing absently at the cap of my Bic pen, I pondered. At some point, Tom and I needed to figure out where to store my household belongings, which were in a moving van headed east on an Interstate highway somewhere between California and Maine. My entire life, packed into a green-and-yellow box truck. The ETA was next Sunday; I expected it would take me some time to go through everything and decide what to use, what to keep in storage, and what to discard. But we hadn't yet discussed where the boxes and furniture would go in the interim. Number six: *Talk to Tom about storage!* I underlined it, then circled it several times in heavy black ink just in case there was any chance I might miss it next time I looked.

I thought about putting *Find a job* on the list. I'd been working since I was fifteen. No slacker, I'd worked my way through college, then bounced around the L.A. job scene for a couple of years before I landed at Phoenix. There, I worked my way up the ladder to store manager. I'd always been a high-energy person, and it seemed odd to have no place I needed to be every morning at eight, hi-test cup of java in hand.

But looking for a job now would be pointless. Tom and I had talked it over, and in January, I was going back to school to get my master's degree. I'd been thinking about it for some time now. Although I'd loved my job at Phoenix, I didn't aspire to a career in retail. Actually, to my surprise, I'd realized that what I most wanted to do was teach. My degree in business management hadn't prepared me for that particular career choice, so it was time to hit the books again. Tom had been extremely supportive, reassuring me that he was fully capable of supporting me financially while I trained for a new career.

When my list was as complete as I could make it, I went back upstairs to unpack. The master bedroom suite had been designed with his-and-hers walk-in closets. I opened the door of the left-hand closet and found Tom's clothes, his suits and shirts and pants, arranged by color and hung with care, evenly spaced a half-inch apart. His shoes were lined up neatly on two shelves. Some fancy contraption built into the wall held his neckties, hung with a meticulousness that prevented any one tie from touching any other. Good God. I hoped he didn't expect me to share his neatness fetish. I generally took off my clothes and flung them. If I managed to hit the chair instead of the floor, I figured I was doing exceptionally well.

Because snooping in my husband's closet seemed like an invasion of his privacy, I closed the door and moved to the other closet. Not so much as a dust bunny inhabited its vacant space. Ditto for the bureau drawers. Tom kept his underwear and socks— stacked with razor-sharp precision—in the upright dresser. The bureau must have been Elizabeth's territory. I was a little surprised to find no evidence that she had ever lived here. No clothes, no knickknacks, no wedding photos, no froufrou female stuff. At some point after her death, Tom had removed all her belongings. Now that I thought about it, I'd seen no evidence of her presence anywhere in this house. Downstairs, photos of the girls were displayed here and there: school photos as well as candids of them with Tom, and with their grandmother and their uncle Riley. But not a single likeness of Elizabeth graced the house.

I wondered why this made me uneasy. It seemed odd that a man who'd loved his wife, a man who'd spent years with her and made babies with her, would keep no physical reminders of her after she was gone. No little personal objects, no mementos of any kind. It was as if the moment Elizabeth was gone, Tom had tried to pretend she'd never existed.

Had their marriage been unhappy? Tom hadn't mentioned any problems with his first marriage, so I'd simply assumed theirs had been a satisfactory union. On the other hand, I hadn't bothered to ask. For all I knew, they could have been on the verge of divorce when Elizabeth died. If there were problems, that might explain why all trace of her was gone from the house.

Trying to rationalize away my unease, I told myself I was probably just identifying too closely with Tom's late wife. More than likely, my subconscious was wondering what would happen if I died. Whether I, too, would be erased from this house as though I'd never set foot inside it.

Because that thought bothered me more than I cared to admit, I distracted myself with unpacking. It didn't take long; I'd traveled light. Most of my clothes were packed away on that moving van. Until they arrived, I'd manage quite nicely with the jeans and casual shirts I'd brought with me. I'd packed only one "serious" dress, and I doubted I'd be needing it here; I couldn't imagine that, as the wife of a small-town Maine doctor, I'd have many formal social engagements.

I managed to fill one bureau drawer, and I hung the rest of my clothes in the closet. They looked pathetic hanging in all that empty space, as did my toiletries, lined up on one end of the massive white marble bathroom counter. I sneaked a peek in one of the medicine cabinets. Empty. I opened the other and found Tom's toiletries—razor, toothbrush, deodorant, aftershave—all shelved neatly, again carefully spaced so that no two objects touched. I closed the cabinet, looked at my cluster of mismatched items cluttering up the counter, and decided to move them to the empty medicine cabinet, where my neatnik husband wouldn't be forced to look at them every time he walked into the room.

It was an improvement. I closed the mirrored door on my hair care products and perfumes, returning the powder room to its formerly immaculate state. Because I had no excuse to kill any more time up here, I headed back down to the kitchen. I still had the whole house all to myself. Except for Riley, but he was still outside, wielding the chain saw with its ferocious growl.

I took the keys to the Land Rover from the hook in the kitchen, let myself out the screen door, and marched over to where my brother-in-law was working. He shut down the saw and watched me approach. "Can you give me directions? I need to go to Tom's bank, the DMV, and the social security office."

He swiped at his brow with a shirtsleeve, picked up a bottle of water, and took a long swig. "The bank's downtown," he said, wiping his mouth with the back of his hand. "First National Bank on Main Street. You can't miss it. Social security office is in the federal building across the street from the bank.

Second floor, above the post office. The nearest DMV office is in Portland."

I thanked him and headed across the lawn to the driveway. It wasn't until I got into the Land Rover that I discovered it was a stick shift. *Crap on a cracker.* My Miata had been an automatic. Yes, I know what you're thinking. Bright yellow, automatic, four-cylinder convertible. You're thinking, *chick car.* I plead guilty as charged. But I liked driving an automatic, and I was a disaster with a stick. Jeffrey had tried once to teach me how to drive his five-speed Corolla, but the lesson had been a catastrophe I didn't want to repeat. The shifting part I got down without much trouble. It was the clutch, the dreaded clutch, that was my downfall.

In theory, I understood how it worked. The clutch goes to the floor, the car starts, the clutch comes up slowly as the gas pedal goes down. When it catches, you give it more gas and ease the clutch the rest of the way up. It sounds so simple, but a crucial piece of the puzzle, the kinetic understanding of when to ease up on the clutch and when to press down on the gas, had thus far eluded me. I could probably manage to drive the damn thing, but it would be a herky-jerky, humiliating experience.

My options ran the gamut from A to B. A, I could stay home, tell Tom that I couldn't drive a standard shift, and see what happened. Or, B, I could teach myself to drive the car, no matter how humiliating it might be.

I thought about my determination not to let life

defeat me. Thought about my dad, who had. Thought about how I'd survived the death of my newborn, and the subsequent death of my marriage. I was a strong woman. An intelligent woman. A determined woman. I'd survived the loss of everyone I loved, then moved on and started life over with Tom. I'd moved three thousand miles away from home to be with him. If I could do all that, I could drive this damn car.

I took a breath, pressed the clutch to the floor, and turned the key. The engine roared to life. So far, so good. I locked the seat belt into place, made sure the shifter was in first gear, then slowly, smoothly, eased up on the clutch with my left foot while stepping on the accelerator with the right.

The car lurched forward and came to a rocking, shuddering halt.

A trickle of sweat ran down my spine. I started the engine again. Concentrating hard, again I eased up on the clutch. This time, I gave it a little more gas than I had the first time. When I felt the car begin to roll, I stepped down hard on the gas pedal and let up on the clutch. The engine roared, and I actually managed to move forward a couple of feet before coming to a stop so abrupt that if I hadn't been wearing my seat belt, the windshield and I would have experienced a close personal encounter.

I was not having fun. I wiped sweat from my eyes and bit down on my lower lip. *Concentrate,* I told myself silently. *Just concentrate. You can DO this.* I let up on the clutch and pressed the gas, and the car jerked and shuddered so hard my teeth clacked together.

"Fuck," I said, thumping the palms of my hands against the steering wheel. "Fuck, fuck, fuck."

"Having a little trouble?"

I flushed crimson when I saw Riley standing there. "Go away," I said. "I really don't need a witness to my mortification."

"You're thinking too hard. You don't drive a car by thinking. You drive by feel."

Slumped over the steering wheel like a beach ball with a puncture wound, I said, "Then I believe my feeling apparatus is faulty."

"No, it isn't. Slide over."

"I thought you had work to do."

"It'll still be there when I get back. Go ahead. Scoot over."

I climbed awkwardly over the gearshift and plunked down hard on the passenger seat. Riley slid in behind the wheel, started the car, and together we listened to the purr of the engine.

"You can't think your way through it," he said. "You have to turn off your brain and tune into the vehicle. Become one with the car. Feel what it's feeling."

"How new age-y. Will we be hearing Yanni playing in the background anytime soon?"

"It has nothing to do with any new age bullshit. Close your eyes."

"Excuse me?"

"Don't worry, I'm not a serial killer. Just do it."

"You know, your family might be a little unusual… but you certainly aren't boring people." I closed my eyes and waited for what would happen next.

"Instead of thinking," he said, "I want you to use your other senses. Hear the sound of the engine. Feel the vibrations. Let the car tell you what it wants."

"Whatever you say, Yoda."

"Stop being a wiseass and pay attention. We're going to take a little spin around the block, and you're going to feel how I drive the car. Without filtering it through your left brain thinking mechanism. No talking. Just feel."

Eyes squeezed tightly shut, I gamely settled back against the passenger seat. This little experiment was doomed to failure, but I was a good sport, and it wasn't as though I had anything to do that wouldn't wait.

But a funny thing happened on the way to failure. As we cruised the suburban streets of Newmarket, Maine, population 8,931, I began to get a sense of what he'd been trying to tell me. Experiencing the motions of the car, listening to the up-and-down hum of the rpm's, I thought I understood. Just a little.

Until he pulled over. "Your turn," he said.

He left the shifter in neutral and the parking brake on, and we swapped places. "Remember what I said," he told me. "Don't think. Just feel."

"Do I get to keep my eyes closed while I drive?"

He reached around behind him, found the seat belt, locked and tightened it. "No."

"I sort of figured you'd say that."

I made a couple of false starts. "When you feel it start to catch," he instructed, "synchronize your left and right foot. Don't think about it. Feel it catch, feel the car start to move, feel how much gas it needs, and follow through."

Right. Like that was going to happen. But this time, I actually got the car moving. No shuddering, no jerking. Just a smooth ride down the street. I shifted at the proper time, with a minimum of disturbance, and Riley nodded.

"You're a good student," he said.

"I do all right once I'm moving. It's the stopping and starting that bother me the most. Where to?"

"Keep going straight." Apparently without fear of imminent death, he slumped comfortably on his tailbone and stretched out his legs. "I'll tell you when to turn."

"All righty then." I upshifted until I reached cruising speed, then sneaked a glance at him from the corner of my eye. "So," I said. "What's the story with you and Tom?"

I could feel his eyes on me, but I kept mine on the road. "What story?" he said.

"Don't be oblique. It's obvious to anybody who isn't deaf, dumb and blind that there's some kind of bad blood between the two of you."

"Maybe you should be asking Tom."

"Tom's not here," I said brightly. "So I'm asking you."

Riley casually pressed the button for the car

window. A little too casually, I thought. The window lowered with a soft hiss and he turned his face to the fresh air. "There's no bad blood," he said, scrutinizing the passing scenery. "We just don't always see eye to eye. Maybe you've noticed that we don't have a lot in common."

Looking at him, with his torn T-shirt, wrinkled jeans and shaggy hair, I thought of my husband. Thought of his buttoned-down neatness, his trim haircut, his meticulously clean fingernails with the cuticles pushed back to reveal the white half-moons. Thought of his closet, the clothes hung with such precision that he could have measured the distance between them with a ruler. "Yes," I agreed, "I think it's safe to say that your styles don't quite mesh."

"That's one way of putting it."

"What's another way?"

He thrust his arm out the window and held it there, his palm open to deflect the wind as we drove. "Tom," he said, waggling his fingers, "was always the golden boy. Star quarterback, class president, head of the debate club. National Honor Society. Prom king. Everybody loved him. Everybody knew he'd go far. He played basketball. Soccer. Golf, for Christ's sake."

"Golf?" I said skeptically.

"Stupidest game ever invented."

"And what did you play?"

"The Doors and Kurt Cobain, for the most part."

It explained a lot. "So you were one of those anti-establishment types."

Riley drew his arm back into the car. "I was a loser. That was my assigned role in the family. While Tom was out running touchdowns and winning awards and getting laid by every blue-eyed blond cheerleader in sight, I was sitting in my room with the curtains closed, smoking weed, contemplating my teenage angst, and plucking minor chords on my Gibson."

"It must've been hard," I said, "growing up in his shadow."

"It was torture. Everyone thought he was God. That he could do no wrong. I was always being compared to him, and always falling short. I wasn't perfect like he was. I was actually capable of making mistakes. I wasn't interested in the same things Tom was. Athletics bored me to tears. I was into music. I wasn't a clone of my brother, and it made people uncomfortable. They didn't understand me. Because I wasn't like Tom, I must be defective in some way." His voice held no bitterness; he was simply stating facts. "It never occurred to anybody that there was nothing wrong with me, that I just needed to be me."

"So you rebelled."

"I smoked and drank and raised hell. I totaled a couple of cars, got into fights, got kicked out of school two or three times. I didn't go looking for trouble, it just seemed to follow me around. Which, of course, made my faultless older brother look even better. If they'd only known." When he smiled, his eyes crinkled the way Tom's did. "Tommy wasn't anywhere near as perfect as Mom wanted to believe."

"Oh?"

"Don't get me wrong. He wasn't a bad kid. Just a normal one. He did his share of wild and crazy things, only he was smarter than me. He never got caught. But everybody—the entire town—had him on a pedestal. It wasn't any easier on Tommy, growing up here, than it was on me. That's the big drawback to living in a small town. Everybody knows you, or at least they think they do. You get a certain reputation, a label, and it sticks. *The perfect kid. The troublemaker.* In a small town like Newmarket, those labels are the kiss of death, because people wear blinders. They see exactly what they expect to see, and nothing more. Most of them wouldn't know the truth if it hit 'em upside the head."

"I'm sorry."

"Why should you be? You had nothing to do with it. It all happened a long time ago."

"Maybe so. But a lousy childhood sucks, no matter who or where you are. How did Tom deal with it?"

"He played the game, the same as I did. Except that it was a different game he played. After Dad died, as far as Mom was concerned, it was Tommy who'd be our savior. He was the good son, the one who always did exactly what was expected of him. It was actually easier on me, because I was the invisible one. Everybody's attention was so focused on Tom that most of the time, they forgot I was even there. I did pretty much whatever I wanted. Tom was the one who toed the line. He graduated with honors, went to college on a full athletic scholarship. Continued on to medical school. Married Elizabeth, started his own practice, and started raising a family. He's almost forty years old, and he's still doing what Mom wants him to do."

"Not necessarily," I pointed out. "He did marry me."

"His one act of rebellion. I have to admit I was impressed when I heard what he'd done. It was so out of character. Turn left at the next intersection."

Following his directions, I lost speed during the turn. The car shuddered and nearly stalled, but I feathered the accelerator and pulled out of it. Riley nodded approvingly.

"And you," I said, once I'd upshifted again, "it looks as though you're still playing your assigned role, too. Bad boy. Prodigal son."

"We humans are most comfortable with the roles we find most familiar."

"There's another little ditty I've heard: *Familiarity breeds contempt.*"

"I manage to sleep quite nicely at night, thank you, in spite of being the black sheep of the family."

"Good for you," I said, not sure I really meant it. Riley was the classic underachiever, and I identified with him more closely than I wanted to admit. It wasn't necessarily an admirable trait. "Can I ask you something else?"

"I doubt I could stop you if I wanted to."

"Tell me about Elizabeth."

Silence. It stretched out for an endless five seconds

before he said, "Why?" There was something in his voice, something that hadn't been there before, but I couldn't identify it. "Shouldn't that be Tom's job?"

It was too embarrassing to admit that my husband had told me virtually nothing about his first wife. Instead, I left Tom out of the equation. "I want to hear what *you* have to say about her. For starters, why aren't there any pictures of her in the house?"

"I'm the wrong person to ask. I don't even live there anymore. I have my own apartment, upstairs over the carriage house."

"It just seems odd. If only for the sake of the girls, there should be something. But it's as though she never lived there."

"The Lord and my family both move in mysterious ways. I gave up years ago trying to figure either of them out."

"Then tell me about her. What was she like?"

"She was the ideal life partner for my brother, so much like him it was nauseating."

"In what ways?"

"She was perfect. Maybe a little too perfect. Smart, pretty. Not in a glamorous way. More a Katie Couric than a Sharon Stone. Elizabeth was the quintessential freckle-faced girl-next-door. She was a cheerleader in high school, one of those girls you love to hate, except that in her case, it was impossible. Nobody could hate Beth. She was sweet, in a genuine way that softened the heart of even the hardest cynic."

"So you liked her."

"Everybody liked her. Just like Tom, she was universally loved, and placed on a pedestal by the good citizens of our fair city."

Wondering how I could possibly measure up to this paragon of virtue, I took a deep breath and tightened my fingers on the steering wheel. "Did she and Tom have a good marriage?"

I could feel his eyes on me again. "Julie," he said, "you're barking up the wrong tree here. I can't answer that question. Nobody knows what goes on inside somebody else's marriage."

"Of course not. But you must have an opinion, based on what you witnessed. Did they seem happy together?"

Riley shifted position and stared out the window. "I'm probably not the person most qualified to judge."

"Oh? Why is that?"

"I guess you could call it a conflict of interest." He turned away from the window, and when his eyes met mine, I saw something in them that looked an awful lot like resentment. "You see, before my brother stole her away, Beth was engaged to me."

Three

The accounts manager at the First National Bank of Newmarket was friendly and efficient. Millicent Waterhouse had gone to school with Tom, and she had nothing but good things to say about Newmarket's dashing young obstetrician. "You're a lucky woman," she told me as I filled out paperwork. "As far as I'm concerned, Tom Larkin is the best thing that ever happened to this town. I was thrilled when he came back here to start his practice. He could've made more money just about anywhere else, but he chose to come home instead, and nobody around here has forgotten that."

I glanced up from my clipboard and gave her a bland smile. "Is that so?"

"You'd better believe it. When Tom came back, old Doc Thompson was getting ready to retire. Nobody was sorry to see him go. He was a cranky old curmudgeon, and he usually smelled like a stinky old cigar butt that's been sitting in a dirty ashtray for three days." Millie's eyes twinkled. "But Tom's nothing like Doc Thompson. He's patient and kind, he always smells nice, and he just puts you at ease. He delivered both of my youngest kids, and when my sister started going through early menopause, he explained everything to her and helped her decide whether or not to take hormone replacement therapy."

This was the Tom I knew, the charming, kindhearted patron saint of mothers-to-be, menopausal sisters, and bent-but-not-broken thirty-year-old women in need of rescuing. Not the Tom that Riley had described, the man who'd come back from college, medical degree in hand, and proceeded to steal his brother's fiancée. There had to be more to it than that. Tom was a good man, a man with strong ethics. I couldn't imagine him crossing that fraternal boundary.

Finally managing to escape from the loquacious Millicent, I crossed the street to the federal building and took care of my business at the social security office. The DMV, thirty miles away in Portland, would have to wait for another day. Maybe, if Tom could get a few hours free, we could combine that with car shopping, as I suspected the selection would be greater in a larger city. Wandering up and down Newmarket's block-long main street, I inspected the window displays and played tourist. A teenage girl feeding coins into a parking meter smiled at me. An elderly man with a buff-colored Pomeranian on a leash sat on a bench outside the barber shop. I passed an old-fashioned apothecary shop with a soda fountain. Two doors down, showcased in the window of The Bridal Emporium, was an elegant ivory satin-and-lace vintage wedding dress that shot a pang of longing straight through me.

Of their own volition, my feet slowed and then stopped. I stood before that plate-glass window, admiring the dress, for a long time. This was my one regret. I'd been married twice, yet I'd never had a wedding gown. Like most adolescent girls, I'd spent endless hours imagining what my wedding would be like when I finally met my prince. Whenever I'd pictured it, I was wearing a dress like this one. But fate had other plans in mind for me. Jeffrey, ever the romantic, had dragged me off to city hall to get married on our lunch hour. I should have known right then and there that the marriage was doomed. On the other hand, my wedding to Tom, on that beach in the Bahamas, had contained nearly all the elements of my teenage dream: the breathless bride, the handsome groom, the heartfelt and intensely personal vows. It was exotic, romantic, almost perfect. The only thing missing was the dress.

When I'd looked my fill, I moved on, to Lannaman's bakery. If I'd previously doubted the existence of God, the smells emanating through the screen door were enough to make me reconsider. I went inside and bought a half-dozen assorted doughnuts and two chocolate éclairs. The doughnuts were for the girls, a blatant attempt at bribery. The éclairs were for Tom. They were his favorite dessert, and I intended to save them for later, during a private moment together, as I had a few dessert ideas of my own.

Carrying a cardboard bakery box tied with string, I was about to cross the street to my car when I noticed the bead boutique. I'd missed it on the first go-round, although I wasn't sure how I had overlooked the mouthwatering window display of Chinese turquoise. I'd never been able to resist turquoise. The shop entrance was around the corner, tucked into an alcove. When I opened the door, a bell tinkled overhead. The woman behind the counter was unpacking boxes of merchandise. She glanced up, said, "Good morning," and returned to her work.

As a bead shop pro, I didn't need a road map to find my way around. The shop was organized by material and by color. I went directly to the turquoise gemstones that were hung on nylon strings along a side wall. I lifted a string of round beads, weighed its heft in my hand, rubbed my fingers against the cool, polished stone. No two natural stones are ever identical, and there are often subtle variations in color, shape and smoothness. Sometimes consistency is important in a piece. At other times, a little diversity makes life more interesting.

"They're on sale right now," the proprietor said, without looking up from her work. "Thirty percent off all gemstones."

I checked the tag. The price was reasonable for a small shop in an equally small town. I was mentally calculating the thirty-percent discount when a voice from beside me said, "I like the turquoise, but with your coloring, have you considered the leopard jasper? I think it would be smashing."

I glanced up. The woman who'd spoken had a narrow face, with green eyes and dark auburn hair tied back in a ponytail. "I'm partial to jasper," she explained, then held out her hand. "Claudia Lavoie."

"Julie Larkin."

Her handshake was firm. "Yes," she said. "I know who you are. I saw you get out of the car and I followed you in here. I recognized the Land Rover. You're Tom's new wife."

A little nonplussed, I said, "That would be me."

"Nice to meet you. I hear you had a little excitement over there last night."

"Excitement? Oh, the tree. Wow. News travels quickly around here."

"The chain saw was a pretty big clue. Riley filled in the rest for me. I'm your next-door neighbor. I live in terror that one of these days, that entire tree will fall—in my direction."

"Your worrying days are over, then, because Tom told me last night he's having it cut down."

"That's a relief. If it went through my greenhouse and murdered my babies, I'd have to kill him." She smiled to show me she was just kidding. "You should stop in sometime. I'm always home. Except when I'm not."

"I'll think about it."

"I'm serious, you know. People always say these things to be polite. I'm happy to report that I've never been polite. Or, for that matter, politically correct. If I didn't mean it, I wouldn't make the offer. Please come. Dylan—my four-year-old—has spent the last few days with his dad. I'm used to having him home with me, and my afternoons have been long and boring. Besides, I make a mean margarita."

"In that case," I said, "I'll be sure to stop by."

"Drop in anytime. If the car's in the driveway and I don't answer the door, come around the back. I'm probably in the greenhouse."

I watched her leave, the bell over the door jangling cheerfully as she exited the store. I'd have to ask Tom about her. Unless he told me she was some kind of psycho, I'd probably take her up on her offer. She seemed a nice enough person, and I had a sneaking suspicion that Team Julie would need a cheerleader or two in order to balance things out.

Back on task, I selected two strings of turquoise that I really liked. And then, just because I could, I chose another string—of the leopard jasper.

When I got back to the house, Jeannette's Caddy was parked in the driveway, and the chain saw was silent. Grabbing up the bakery box, I took a deep breath and girded my loins for the inevitable confrontation.

My mother-in-law was at the kitchen counter, mixing a meat loaf. The girls sat at the table, hunched over coloring books, scribbling away purposefully. I held the bakery box aloft and said brightly, "I come bearing gifts."

All action stopped. Taylor dropped her purple crayon and examined the box with interest. "What's in it?"

"Doughnuts."

Sadie scratched the tip of her nose and said solemnly, "I like doughnuts."

I felt not even the merest twinge of guilt at my blatant attempt at bribery. I was willing to pay whatever price it took to unlock the doors to their little hearts. I set the box on the table and lifted the cover to reveal an assortment of doughnuts. The coloring books were instantly forgotten. Their faces painted with identical expressions of delight, both girls craned their necks to see what was in the box.

Behind me, my mother-in-law cleared her throat. "Tom doesn't allow the girls to eat sugar." Her tone implied that I, as Tom's wife, should already know this salient fact. "Besides, it's only a couple hours to supper. You'll spoil their appetites."

I stiffened. It was at least three hours until supper. God forbid I should spoil their appetites. God forbid a single grain of sugar should pass their lips. The girls looked crestfallen, and suddenly that guilt, heretofore absent, reared its ugly head.

"I'm sorry," I said. "I had no idea."

Jeannette covered the meat loaf pan with foil and put it in the refrigerator. Untying her apron and pulling it off over her head, she said, "As long as you're here, I need you to run to the grocery store and pick up a few things. You'll have to take the girls with you, because the babysitter's sick. I'd do it myself, but I have to go back to work. I have a shampoo and clipping at four-fifteen. Late in the day, but not much I can do about it." She folded the apron with precise motions, tucked it into a drawer, and reached up to smooth her hair. "If I'm not back by five, you might as well go ahead and put the meat loaf in the oven. Potatoes are already peeled and in the fridge. They just need to be put on to boil." Her eyes, peering at me over the rim of her glasses, were skeptical. "You do know how to cook?"

What idiot couldn't boil a potato? Did she really think I was that incompetent? "Of course," I said, an ingratiating smile glued firmly in place. "I'm much more than just a pretty face. What do you need at the store?"

"I'll give you a list. Girls, pick up your crayons and coloring books and take them upstairs. And put them away. I don't want to come home and find them strewn around your room."

"It's not fair," Taylor said. "I want a doughnut!"

"Yeah," Sadie said, taking a cue from her older sister. Tiny fists planted on her hips, she echoed, "It's not fair!"

"Life isn't fair," my mother-in-law snapped, "and you shouldn't expect it to be. The sooner you learn that, the better off you'll be."

Yikes. Glad I wasn't on the receiving end of her cutting comment, I carefully arranged my face in the most neutral expression I could manage. The girls made a few more token protests, but it was obvious that in this house, Grandma ruled. So while

Jeannette wrote out a list for me, the girls put away their toys.

Afterward, I got them settled in the backseat of the Land Rover and, as I drove away from the house, I marveled at my amazing transformation from big-city career woman to small-town mom, complete with husband, two kids, and an SUV. I felt a little like Barbie, after she and Ken had built their Dream House somewhere in American suburbia. The only thing needed to complete the picture was a large, hairy dog.

I slowed for a red light. It turned green before I reached it. I stepped on the gas, and forgot to shift gears. The car stalled halfway through the intersection. Muttering under my breath, I pumped the accelerator, popped the clutch, and took off, tires squealing on the pavement.

From the backseat, Taylor said, in a tone that was far too accusatory for a seven-year-old, "Why are you having so much trouble driving?"

I glanced in the rearview mirror. Her eyes were narrowed with suspicion. Whatever happened to children being seen but not heard? "I'm not having trouble," I said through gritted teeth. "I'm just a little rusty."

"My mom never had trouble driving it."

I checked the mirror again. This time, my stepdaughter looked smug, and far older than her seven years. Why was it that she always made me feel as though she were the adult and I the child? I took a breath and forced myself to be civil. "This was your mom's car?"

A smile flitted over her face. The little wretch had hit a nerve, and she knew it. "Yes," she said. "And Mom was a good driver. Sadie never got carsick when she rode with Mom."

Mild panic assailed me as I imagined myself cleaning vomit from the backseat of a very expensive Land Rover. "Sadie?" I said in alarm. "Are you carsick?"

"I'm not sick," Sadie piped up. "I love to ride."

In the mirror, Taylor was grinning. *Gotcha!* her face seemed to say.

I reminded myself again that I was the adult, and far too mature for the kind of retaliation I was contemplating. I had other, more important things to focus on. Like the fact that the car I was driving belonged to a dead woman. A dead woman who happened to be my predecessor. *Thanks, Tom.* It would've been really nice if he'd bothered to drop a hint.

I wasn't sure why it gave me the willies. Did I think Beth's spirit was still hovering around, clucking in disapproval as I stole her husband, laid claim to her children, and burned out her clutch? It wasn't as though she'd died in the vehicle and was therefore doomed to haunt it for all of eternity. Although, come to think of it, I was sure Tom had told me his wife died in an accident. If that was true, and if this vehicle really had belonged to her, then what had she been driving?

Maybe she hadn't been driving at all. Maybe she'd been a passenger in somebody else's car. Tom hadn't gone into any detail about her death. I could tell it bothered him to talk about it; the wound was still a little too fresh to start picking at the scab, so I hadn't pried. But I had to admit I was curious.

I glanced in the mirror again. Sadie was staring out the window, humming under her breath, some tuneless little ditty that kept repeating itself, over and over. Or maybe that was just Sadie's interpretation of how the song went. Taylor had tired of toying with me and was now focused on her Game Boy. The self-satisfied look on her face confirmed what I already knew: She was going to be a challenge. But one way or another, I'd win the war. After all, I'd once been a seven-year-old know-it-all. To paraphrase an old country song, I'd forgotten more than she would ever know about being a brat. The kid didn't stand a chance against me.

I eventually found the grocery store—the town was too small for it to stay hidden for long—and I pulled into a parking space. Just to satisfy my curiosity, I opened the glove compartment and rummaged around until I found the auto registration. I told myself I wasn't snooping. After all, the vehicle belonged to Tom and, as his wife, that meant it was half mine. Besides, if I got pulled over for some infraction, I'd need to know where the registration was. I had a right to snoop.

I could rationalize until the cows came home, but in the end, it didn't matter. The registration didn't answer any of my questions, because the car was registered to Tom. It might have been Beth's vehicle, as Taylor had said, or my stepdaughter might have been needling me. It was impossible to tell. The only way I'd know would be to ask Tom.

I shoved the registration back into the glove compartment and slammed it shut. "Okay, girls," I said briskly. "Let's do this!"

For a weekday afternoon, the store was busy. Lots of harried housewives and elderly people pushing their shopping carts up and down the aisles. Zippy muzak, designed to move shoppers along at the optimum pace for picking and choosing, blared out of overhead speakers. I checked Jeannette's list. It was extensive, but not detailed. Standing in front of the milk case, I pondered all the choices, wondering what brand my mother-in-law usually bought. Did I dare to ask Taylor? If I did ask, could I trust her answer? Would she tell me the truth, or try to sabotage my already shaky relationship with Tom's mother by pointing me in the wrong direction?

I wouldn't put it past her. The kid was sly, and I'd once walked in her shoes. I could remember a time or two when I'd done just about anything I could to get rid of my father's latest girlfriend. I hadn't cared how obnoxious I was, hadn't cared how childish some of my stunts were or how much trouble I might get into afterward. All that mattered was the end result: one more irritating woman out of our lives. One more opportunity for our nuclear family—that would be Dave and me—to remain intact. I'd been a real piece of work. And Taylor was so much like me it was scary.

From her perch high in the cart, Sadie kicked her legs and said, "Can I have orange juice?"

Orange juice hadn't been on Jeannette's list. I weighed the relative merits of garnering brownie points with Sadie against the pain of being reprimanded by my mother-in-law for the second time today, and decided to make the ultimate sacrifice. After all, I'm one tough *chica*. Just ask my friend Carmen. She's told me that so often, I've started to believe her. I knew I could stand up to Jeannette Larkin and whatever she dished out. This was a simple matter of survival. "You tell me what kind of milk Grandma buys," I told Sadie, "and I'll let you have orange juice."

Without hesitation, she pointed. "That one."

My bribery skills were being honed to a fine edge. I opened the cooler door and took out the milk, grabbed two miniature bottles of OJ, and consulted my list. Next item: cat food. As descriptions go, it was beyond vague. There were eight trillion brands of cat food on the shelves, enough to take up one entire side of the pet food aisle. Was I supposed to guess? Did she want dry food or canned? Enough for one cat, or several? Were we talking kitten chow, or something specially designed for geriatric felines? I was clueless, especially considering that in the twenty-four hours since I arrived at Casa Larkin, I hadn't seen any evidence that a cat actually lived there.

I was about to ask Sadie for clarification when I looked around and realized Taylor was nowhere to be seen. "Sadie?" I said, mildly alarmed. "Where's your sister?"

She shrugged with childlike unconcern. "I don't know."

Great. This was all I needed. Tom's mother already hated me. I couldn't wait to hear what she'd say if I lost her grandchild.

With my heart thudding and visions of an Amber Alert dancing through my brain, I wheeled the cart around the corner of the next aisle. There, at the far end, was my missing stepdaughter, deep in conversation with some blonde who looked more like Julia Roberts than Julia Roberts.

I mentally cancelled the Amber Alert. Taylor and I were going to sit down later this afternoon and have a long talk about sticking together in public places. Pedophiles and serial killers lurked around every corner, even in small towns like this one. "Who's that lady your sister's talking to?" I asked Sadie.

Her head swiveled around. "Auntie Mel!" she shrieked so loudly they probably heard her in the next county. I struggled to regain my hearing, relieved to know that Taylor hadn't been about to waltz out of the store hand in hand with some fabulous-looking stranger. Before I could stop her, Sadie had scrambled out of the cart and down to the floor. I stood glued to the spot as she ran the length of the aisle and wrapped herself ecstatically around the woman's legs.

"Hey, yourself," almost-Julia said, sticking a roll of price tags into the pocket of her teal-colored smock with the red-and-white Shop City logo stitched just above the breast. She gave me a long, assessing glance, then turned her attention back to Sadie and said, "How are you, baby doll?"

"I'm wonderful! When are you coming to visit?"

"I don't know, hon. I'm pretty busy. But I'll call your Gram one of these days soon and we'll make plans."

I maneuvered my cart to a stop. "Hi," I said. "I'm Julie Larkin."

The look she gave me was glacial. Crouching down, she hugged both girls and said, "Why don't you girls run over to the bakery and see what Yvette has for you? I'm pretty sure she just baked a new batch of chocolate-chip cookies. Tell her I sent you."

The girls hugged her and disappeared, their homing instinct infallible when it came to cookies. I propped a foot on the undercarriage of my shopping cart and said, "Tom doesn't allow the girls to eat sugar."

Almost-Julia stood up to her full five-foot-zero. "Yes," she said, her expression challenging me to do something about it. "I know."

Ah. A fellow subversive. We had something in common. "And who are you?" I asked, since she'd failed to provide me with a name, rank, or serial number.

"Melanie Ambrose. My sister used to be married to your husband. Before he killed her."

"Come again?"

"You heard me. Tom Larkin murdered my sister."

She was obviously deranged. While I gaped at

her, an elderly man who smelled of sweat and pipe tobacco took an inordinate amount of time picking out a box of breakfast cereal. When he'd finally moved on, I said, "I don't understand what you mean. Beth died in an accident."

Melanie cocked her head to one side and looked at me with a sad, knowing smile. "Really? So that's what he told you?"

"Well, I, uh—" I struggled to remember whether he'd used those exact words or whether I'd simply inferred them. For the first time, I wasn't sure. "I think."

"That lying sack of shit. Beth didn't die in any accident. That's just his guilt talking. He doesn't have the *cojones* to speak the truth."

My fingers tightened on the handle of the shopping cart. "Oh? And just what is the truth?"

"You want to know the truth? I'll tell you." Her pretty face twisted into a skeletal grimace of a smile. "Congratulations on your marriage. I hope you survive it."

Four

I slid the meat loaf into the oven and set the timer. The girls, still on a sugar high, were in the living room watching SpongeBob SquarePants. I turned on the burner under the potatoes, opened the bakery box, and took out a jelly doughnut. If I kept this up, pretty soon the box would be empty. Nibbling, I mentally wandered back to what Melanie Ambrose had told me. Two years ago, on a lovely moonlit summer night, Beth Larkin had driven her Land Rover—the same Land Rover I was now driving—up onto the Swift River Bridge, where she'd proceeded to remove her shoes and her glasses, leaving them on the front seat to weigh down the suicide note she'd written before she left the house. Then she'd climbed barefoot and half-blind onto the bridge railing, leaned forward, and taken a header off the side.

Jesus Christ. How was I supposed to respond to that?

Like a mother grizzly with her cub, I'd stead-fastly defended my husband. In part because he's the love of my life, and in part because I firmly believe that each of us is responsible for our own happiness, or lack thereof, and have no right to blame our failings on other people. Anybody who chooses to deal with their problems by jumping off a bridge surely has mental health issues that are not the result of anything another person may have done—or not done—to them. After mounting a defense of Tom so brilliant it would have made F. Lee Bailey proud, I grilled Melanie for more details. Of course, she couldn't pinpoint a single concrete reason that would have led Beth's unhappiness back to Tom. No, she admitted, he wasn't an alcoholic or a drug addict. No, he didn't beat his wife. Nor, as far as Mel knew, did he run around behind her sister's back. All she really had to go on—and it was pretty damn flimsy evidence—was that her sister had been deliriously happy for the first few years of her marriage to Tom. Then, as time wore on, Beth's demeanor changed. She became withdrawn and distant. She started keeping secrets. She stopped participating in life, became more of an observer, wearing her unhappiness around her like a heavy, black cloak.

And, of course, somehow this was Tom's fault.

This sounded to me like classic symptoms of clinical depression, but there was no point in suggesting to Mel that her sister suffered from mental illness. It would only exacerbate her already considerable pain, and she wouldn't believe me anyway. Her sister was dead, and she needed somebody to blame it on. As Beth's husband, Tom was the nearest and most likely target. And as Tom's new wife, I was firmly rooted in the enemy camp.

So I let it go. But it gnawed at me, this newly gained knowledge that not only had Tom's first wife chosen to take her own life, but that he'd lied to me about it. Or, at the very least, if he hadn't lied, he hadn't been fully forthcoming. It bothered me. It bothered me a lot. I'm a very open person. I say what I think and I think what I say. My candor is legendary among my friends and acquaintances. I don't hide things from the people I care about; my life is the proverbial open book. Tom's, it seemed, wasn't. As much as I hate seeing people toss around psycho-babble buzzwords like so much confetti, I had to admit that I was seeing a significant amount of dysfunction in this family. And if there was one thing I was familiar with, it was family dysfunction.

Tom and his mother arrived home at the same time, with Riley, who might not sleep here but appeared to eat all his meals here, straggling in a couple of minutes later. I already had the dining room table set, the girls washed up and their hair combed, and was just finishing dinner preparations when the rest of the family came in. Jeannette checked to make sure I had everything under control, then disappeared upstairs, presumably to remove the odor of wet doggie from her person. Riley headed to the sink to wash his hands. Tom came directly to where I stood at the stove, checking the potatoes for done-ness.

He planted a kiss on the back of my neck and murmured in my ear, too low for anybody else to hear, "I missed you today."

Turning around, I wrapped my arms around him. He pressed me back against the oven door and kissed me the way a woman wants to be kissed by the man she loves. I drew in the warm scent of him, leaned into his body and kissed him back.

"Christ on a crutch," Riley said from across the kitchen. "Why don't you two just get a room?"

Tom drew back and gave me a wink. "We already have one upstairs."

"Then go up there if you have to play kissy-face. Although you two might be wildly enthusiastic about your sex life, the rest of us have appetites we don't want ruined."

"Jealousy," Tom told his brother. "It so doesn't become you."

Rolling his eyes, Riley wandered off to somewhere, leaving us alone in the kitchen. "Tom," I said, "we have to talk."

The now-familiar furrow between his eyebrows— the one I'd never seen until we arrived in Newmarket—put in an appearance. "If it's a problem with my mother—"

"It's not about your mother. It's something else. But it can wait until after we eat."

"Should I be worried?"

"As in am I about to pack my bags and run back to L.A.?"

"As in precisely that."

I rested a hand against his abdomen, felt it rise and fall with his breathing. "Stop worrying," I said. "There's not a snowball's chance in hell of me leaving you."

"Hold that thought," he said as the girls bounced into the kitchen. "We'll discuss it in more detail later."

Supper was over, the table cleared, the dishes washed, the girls read to and tucked into their beds. Tom and I were finally alone. Perched cross-legged on our bed, my hands clasped around my ankles, I watched my husband's mirrored reflection through the open bathroom door as he peeled off his dress shirt and dropped it into the hamper. His body was lean and sinewy, with nice shoulders, well-defined muscles and a narrow line of dark hair that ran from breastbone to navel. My breath quickened at the sight of all that male pulchritude. He opened the medicine cabinet, took out toothbrush and toothpaste. "What's in the bakery box?" he said.

"Éclairs. I bought them to soften you up."

He uncapped the toothpaste and turned on the faucet. "I thought you liked me better hard."

"Ha, ha. Very funny."

"If you think that's funny, you should see my summer stand-up act in the Adirondacks."

"I'm sure it's a scream and a half."

I waited until he was done brushing his teeth, watched him as he leaned over the sink and splashed cold water all over his face. New as it was, this kind of familiarity still felt odd. Awkward. A little too intimate. I turned my face away from his reflection and said, "Tom?"

He put away his toothbrush and toothpaste, wiped down the marble counter, and tossed the washcloth into the hamper. Still shirtless, he leaned against the door frame, towel in hand. "What?"

I took a deep breath. Might as well jump right in with both feet. "Why didn't you tell me the truth about Beth?"

I'd caught him by surprise. I could see it in his eyes. He finished drying his hands and returned the towel to its hook in the bathroom. "What truth?" he said.

"Oh, for the love of God. You know what truth. She killed herself."

His gaze was cool. "Yes," he said. "She did."

"It would have been nice if you'd bothered to tell me. It was a little disconcerting, hearing it from someone else."

He shoved both hands into the pockets of his pants. "Who told you?"

"Her sister, Melanie."

"And I bet she told you exactly what she thinks of me. That I'm just as responsible for Beth's death as if I'd shoved her off that bridge railing myself."

"That might have come up somewhere in the conversation. She's clearly not one of your biggest fans. Damn it, Tom, why didn't you tell me?"

His expression remained emotionless, as if I were a stranger. "The time just never seemed right."

"She was so smug about the fact that you'd lied

to me. As though it corroborated her ridiculous accusations. I felt like a fool."

"I didn't lie to you. I just didn't tell you everything."

"In the end, what's the difference? I still ended up looking like a fool. Damn it, Tom, she blindsided me."

"What the hell do you want me to say, Jules? Maybe I should've turned to you that first night and said, *Hi, I'm Tom. My wife was so miserable living with me that she killed herself. Say, can I buy you a drink?* That would've gone over really well."

"I'm not saying you should have dumped it in my lap during the first five minutes of our acquaintance. But somewhere between dinner that night and our wedding, you might've found the time to tell me."

"I might have. I chose not to. You know, Jules, the world doesn't revolve around you. Other people have feelings, too. Talk about being blindsided! Instead of confiding in me, my wife—the woman I loved, the mother of my children—decided to jump off a bridge. How the hell do you think that made me feel?"

The guilt was instantaneous. If I thought this was difficult for me, I could only imagine how hard it must be for Tom. He had to live with it every day for the rest of his life, the knowledge that Beth didn't love him or their children enough to keep trying.

"I'm just a man, Jules," he said. "I'm not perfect. Sometimes you scare me. Your expectations are so high. I can't possibly live up to the image you have of me."

I slid off the edge of the bed and crossed the room to him. The hurt in his eyes tore at my insides. I rested a hand against his chest, felt the strong, steady beat of his heart. "I'm sorry," I said, embarrassed by the tears I was fighting back. "It must have been awful for you. I'm so very, very sorry."

"Aw, Jules." He wrapped his arms around me and rested his chin on top of my head. "That's the real reason I didn't tell you. It was just too damn hard to talk about it. And the last thing I wanted was your pity."

"Pity is not something I feel for you. Trust me."

"I have my pride. Maybe that's wrong, but I can't help it. I'm a man. I don't like to show weakness, and I don't like to complain. No matter what life throws at me, I deal with it." His arms tightened around me. "And of course, I know that for the most part, I've been lucky."

It was true. Tom had been blessed with a fine mind, a handsome face, a healthy body and an education that not everybody could afford. Two beautiful daughters, an extended family who loved him, in spite of their differences. A lucrative and satisfying career, a lovely house and a new wife who would walk over hot coals for him.

The only fly I could find in that particular ointment was the first wife who'd killed herself.

But that was then. This was now. A new beginning, a new life. Tossing aside logic and operating strictly from emotion, I stretched up on my toes and wrapped my arms around his neck. Tonight, Tom needed comforting. Regardless of our differences, we were husband and wife. I'd agreed to stand by him, in good times and bad. And the kind of comfort he needed tonight, only I could offer.

He raised his head, looked into my eyes, and smiled.

And I took his hand and led him to the bed.

They say that make-up sex is the best kind.

It must be true, because that night there was a poignancy to our lovemaking that hadn't been there before. We'd weathered a storm together and, perhaps because it reminded us of the fragility of life and the uncertainty of relationships, it had brought us closer. Left us more attuned to each other.

Our marriage was solid. I had no doubts about marrying Tom; this was a forever thing. We'd had a little spat, but that was an inevitable result of couplehood. It might be the first, but it wouldn't be the last. Marriage isn't a static thing; it's a fluid entity, one that involves continual adjustments and constant negotiations.

Tonight, we'd foregone all that in the name of something more primal. It wasn't until later, after the éclairs were gone and Tom was sleeping silently beside me, that I realized we'd never gotten around to discussing Riley's accusations. We hadn't gotten around to discussing much of anything. The aforementioned make-up sex had taken precedence over everything verbal. We'd let our bodies do the talking for us.

Which wasn't a bad thing, but I didn't want it to become a habit. Although our coupling was delicious, sex can't solve every problem, and trying to use it as a problem-solving mechanism only leads to bigger problems down the road. Some issues need to be talked out or they fester and grow. Sometimes, guidelines need to be drawn. Not every problem can be resolved with a quick—or not-so-quick—roll between the sheets.

But it was too late tonight for talking. Tom lay snoring quietly beside me, and I had no intention of waking him to ask further probing questions that would just upset him. There was nothing I needed to say that was so important it couldn't wait. Satisfied that all was right with my world, I plumped my pillow, snuggled down next to my husband, adjusted the bedding until I was comfortable, and promptly fell asleep.

The first bloodcurdling shriek ripped through the fabric of my consciousness, tore me from sleep and sent me bolt upright in bed. "What the—"

It came again, a piercing scream that subsided to shuddering sobs. Beside me, Tom sat up and yanked on a pair of jeans. "Sadie," he said curtly. Heart thudding, I threw on my robe and raced down the hall behind him. In the light cast by the Dora the Explorer night light, I could see Sadie flailing about her bed, sheets tangled around her slender limbs and eerie, unearthly noises coming from her throat.

In the other bed, Taylor lay motionless in slumber.

I marveled at her ability to sleep through all that noise. Was she the kind of kid who would sleep through the crashing of an asteroid through the roof, or was this behavior from her younger sister so common that it no longer registered with her?

Tom sat on the edge of the bed. "Sadie," he said firmly, "wake up." He shook his daughter's shoulder, but the sobbing continued. "Sadie, honey. You have to wake up. You're having a nightmare."

Sadie awoke with a jolt, her breath coming in short, labored gasps. She gazed wide-eyed at her father and then at me, as though she'd never seen either of us before. And then she began to sob in earnest. "It was Mommy," she said. "I saw her. She was alive. And there was a bad man there—"

"Shh." Looking tortured, Tom gathered her onto his lap and rocked her. "It's all right, sweetheart. It was just a bad dream."

"But I saw her. She was alive. And then—"

Still rocking, he said gently, "It was a nightmare, Sadie."

"No, it wasn't!" Sadie shook her head vehemently. "She was really there. She's not dead. She's not! She's alive!"

Tom glanced at me briefly, then his gaze came to rest on something beyond my shoulder. I turned and saw his mother standing in the doorway, her face pale, her hair down and a ratty flannel robe wrapped around her. "Let me talk to her," she said.

"No-o-o-o!" Sadie wailed. She turned her tear-streaked face to me. "I want Julie! Just Julie!"

Jeannette's mouth thinned, but it was pain, rather than anger, that I saw in her eyes. I gave my mother-in-law an apologetic look, then quickly moved to the bed and sat down beside Tom. He relinquished his daughter to me, and she buried her face against my chest. "How about some hot chocolate?" he said softly, and Sadie nodded.

They left us alone. I glanced down at the child held tightly in my arms, her tears soaking the front of my robe, and breathed in the sweet, baby-powder scent of her hair. She wrapped a single hand around my upper arm, and I studied it in wonderment. The tiny fingernails, the delicate bone structure, the dimpled, baby-soft skin.

I think that was the moment I fell in love, the kind of gut-wrenching, visceral, inexplicable mommy-love that changes your life forever. This tiny person, who'd placed her trust in me—only me—had torn a hole in my heart and wormed her way inside it in a way no other human being, except for Angel, had ever done. The emotion was so overwhelming that I felt weak. Humbled. Unworthy of something so pure and good.

Swiping a tear from my cheek, I said with false bravado, "Want to talk about it, Lady Sadie?"

She shook her head and burrowed more closely against my breast.

"You just want to cuddle?"

Sadie nodded and stuck her thumb into her mouth. While she sucked it, I ran my fingers through her hair, so fine and damp and delicate. Instinctively,

I rocked her back and forth, humming some lullaby I didn't realize I knew. *Hush, little baby, don't you cry.* It had lain buried somewhere in my memory, a remnant of my own childhood, when my mother used to rock me to sleep and sing it to me in a sweet, clear voice. Another memory that had stayed buried until this moment. As the tears trickled down my face, I wasn't sure if I was crying for Sadie and her lost mother, or Julie and hers. Somehow, they were all jumbled together. Somehow, I'd tapped into Sadie's emotions, and they were mine.

Tom returned with the cocoa. "I sent Mom back to bed," he said. "There's no sense in her losing sleep. We can handle this ourselves."

Remembering the longing I'd seen in his mother's face, I thought he was wrong. Sadie might not need her grandmother at this moment of crisis, but Jeannette needed her. My mother-in-law's need to be needed was clearly written on her face. But I couldn't tell him that. It wasn't my place. I'd already caused enough trouble between them.

Latching onto the cup of cocoa, Sadie drank it down. With a shuddering sigh, she handed the cup to Tom, lay back against me, and closed her eyes.

At that moment, I couldn't have loved that little girl more if I'd been the one who carried her inside my womb for nine months. Her purity, her innocence, her pain, all struck a place deep inside me. Tom and I sat together on the bed until she'd gone to sleep again. He pulled back the covers and I gently laid Sadie on the bed. Together, we pulled the blankets back up to her chin. Our sleeping angel. I pressed a tender kiss to her forehead while Tom checked on Taylor, who was still sound asleep. And we tiptoed out.

In the kitchen, Tom leaned over the sink, his shoulders slumped in despair.

"How long has she been having these nightmares?" I said.

"They started shortly after Beth died. It happens once or twice a month. I keep hoping she'll grow out of them, but—" He shrugged. "It hasn't happened yet."

Standing behind him, I began to massage his shoulders. "Tom," I said gently, "I think your daughter needs counseling."

"No."

His answer was so immediate, so vehement, that it shocked me. I paused, fingertips still pressed deep into hard, uncompromising muscle. "Tom, the girl is in denial. She can't even accept that her mother's dead. How can you refuse to do something that might help her?"

"I already tried," he said. "It was a disaster."

"You need to relax. Your muscles are all bound up." I resumed the massage. "In what way was it a disaster?"

"It made things worse instead of better. The nightmares started coming with greater frequency. Dr. Weinrich said it was healthy, that this meant we were starting to see progress. But there was no way I could consider torturing my child as progress. I couldn't take it. She couldn't take it. She's too young to be put through that. So we stopped the therapy sessions."

I moved down to his shoulder blades and began to knead them like bread dough. "I'm not sure I agree. The longer she stays in denial, the harder it will be for her to accept that Beth isn't coming back."

The tautness wasn't leaving his muscles. "Jules, with all due respect, you've never raised a child, much less one who's recently lost her mother. I know you're trying to help, but you're not an expert."

I took a breath. "No. I'm no expert on child rearing. But I was a little girl once. And I lost my mother. So I think I have a pretty good idea of what I'm talking about."

He expelled a breath. I continued kneading. Emboldened by his silence, I said, "Nobody around here ever mentions Beth's name. There aren't any pictures of her in the house—"

"My girls have lost so much. I'm trying to help them forget."

"But maybe—" I moved my hands farther south, wrapped them around his rib cage, heard his soft groan of pleasure as I squeezed and manipulated stiff, tense muscles. "Has it occurred to you that forgetting might not be the healthiest thing for them?"

"No. It hasn't occurred to me."

"How can you expect them to heal when their mother's death—and her life—are shrouded in secrecy? Instead of giving legitimacy to their feelings of loss, you're invalidating them. Making it seem as though they shouldn't be grieving, because their mother was never here in the first place. If I were a little girl, I think that would confuse the hell out of me."

"It's a great theory, Jules, but that's all it is. You don't have a degree in psychology, and even if you did, that doesn't mean you'd be right and I'd be wrong. Let's just agree to disagree, and go back to bed."

"Fine," I said, giving up on the massage. "I'll agree to disagree. Are you happy now?"

He turned and planted a kiss on my mouth. "Yes. An obedient wife is a good wife."

"Good thing I know you're kidding."

"Oh?" He played with a strand of my hair. "Just for future reference, what would happen if I wasn't kidding?"

"My aged granny had a philosophy that covered this particular contingency. She passed it on to all the female cousins. Sort of a rite of passage."

"Aged granny, eh?"

"You betcha. *Walk softly and carry a big frying pan.*"

"Ouch. Does that really work?"

I grinned. "It did on Grampa."

Five

At 10:00 a.m. on Sunday, right on schedule, the moving van chugged up the street and stopped in front of the house. When Tom and I had packed up my apartment, a few days after our wedding, I'd marked the boxes carefully, so it was easy to let the movers know where everything should go. The furniture went to the carriage house, to be sorted out when Tom had the time to help me. Most of it would probably end up at Goodwill, but there were a few pieces I wanted to keep. My clothes and my CD collection went to our bedroom. Everything else was carried up to the attic by a pair of burly guys who wore T-shirts and jeans, a couple days' worth of blue-black facial hair, and perpetual scowls. Frick and Frack. In the absence of shirts with their names embroidered on the front, it was impossible to tell them apart. Because they reminded me of the deliverymen in the old Dire Straits music video—*money for nothing, chicks for free*—I had trouble keeping a straight face.

The liberal tip Tom gave them wiped away the scowls, and they left us with smiles and best wishes on our marriage. When they were gone, Tom headed out for his regular Sunday afternoon tee time with the guys, and I spent what was left of the afternoon unpacking. With the eager and oh-so-helpful assistance of two curious little girls, I unpacked clothes and shoes and handbags and jewelry and arranged them in the bedroom closet. Working in the boutique, I'd gotten an employee discount, and I'd taken full advantage. Tom was about to find out how much of a clothes junkie his new bride was. Hopefully, he wouldn't immediately send me to a twelve-step program.

Sebastian, the fat gray Maine coon cat who'd spent my first few days in the house hiding from me, lay purring contentedly in the middle of our bed while in the background, Paula Cole asked the musical question, *Where have all the cowboys gone?* Sadie, posing in front of the mirror, asked, "Can I try on this lipstick?"

Already world-weary at seven, her sister told her, "You're too young for lipstick."

"Poppycock!" I said.

They both stared at me. "What's poppycock?" Taylor said.

"It's a more polite way of saying bull—uh, baloney." I finished hanging up the emerald silk blouse that brought out the green specks in my eyes and snapped off the overhead light in the closet. "Sit on the foot of the bed," I told Sadie, and she scrambled up onto the mattress, setting it to bouncing. As a small child, there'd been little that I enjoyed more than playing dress-up and pretending to be a grown-up lady. "Purse your lips," I said, "like this." She complied, and I neatly applied the color to her lips, careful not to damage the lipstick I'd paid fourteen dollars for. The color was called Broadway, and was wildly inappropriate for a little girl. Which was what made it so much fun. I yanked a tissue from the box on the bureau. "Blot," I said, and Sadie obediently smooshed her lips against the tissue.

I stood back to study my handiwork. The bright lipstick was garish against her pale skin. "Stay there," I said, and rummaged through my makeup case until I found a complementary shade of blusher. I applied it to Sadie's cheeks, blended it until it looked natural, and then I held up a hand mirror so she could see the result.

The little girl squealed in delight. "Your turn now," I told her sister, who'd stood by watching the entire process, on her face a look of intense scrutiny, as if she weren't quite sure whether or not she approved of this frivolity. But when her turn came, she was as eager to be beautified as her sister. For Taylor, I chose a darker shade of lipstick and its accompanying blusher. I was pretty good at this. If my marriage didn't work out, I could always aim for a career in cosmetology.

Deciding to go for broke, I found a couple of brightly-colored shirts, a pair of silk scarves, and a cluster of dangly bracelets to complete their ensembles. By the time I was done, the girls looked sweet and silly and theatrical. A miniature version of the Gish sisters. They were so adorable that I ran for my digital camera to take a couple of pictures.

"Tell you what," I said, once I was satisfied that I'd properly documented the moment. "Have you ever been to a tea party?"

The girls exchanged glances. "No," Taylor said solemnly.

"There's no time like the present. What do you say, Sadie?"

"I say yes!"

I made a pot of Earl Gray and, because there were no cookies or sweets in the house, we drank it with saltine crackers glued together with strawberry jam. I showed the girls how to lift their teacups with their pinkies curled, and we giggled at the silliness of it all. "When you were a little girl," Taylor said, "did you have tea parties?"

"Sure," I said. "My mom and I used to have them all the time." It was something I hadn't thought of in years. When Dave was away on tour, we used to paint our nails and curl our hair, dress in our jammies, and have tea parties with my Barbies. Before she disappeared from my life forever.

"Where is your mom?" Sadie wanted to know.

"Y'know…I have no idea."

They gaped at me, Taylor through narrowed eyes, reluctant to give up her innate suspicion. "How can you not know?" she demanded.

"She and my dad split up and she left us a long time ago. When I was a little girl. I haven't seen her in twenty-five years."

"So you mean," Sadie said, "she could be dead, and you wouldn't know?"

"I suppose that's possible."

"And she never called you?" Taylor said. "Or wrote you a letter?"

I knew they were curious because they'd lost their own mother. They needed to process this information, compare it to their own experience of loss. It was a part of the healing process. I knew that intellectually. But emotionally, it wasn't that simple. The pain I thought I'd buried long ago shifted position and poked, needle-sharp, at my insides. "No," I said. "She never did."

"That's sad," Sadie said matter-of-factly.

"Why don't you have any kids?" Taylor wanted to know.

Oh, boy. I hadn't counted on this turning into a full-fledged therapy session, with me as the patient. I wondered whether they were old enough to hear the truth, decided they were. "I had a little girl." I could see that I'd caught the attention of both girls. "Something went wrong when I was giving birth, and she died. We named her Angel."

"Because she lives in heaven with the angels?" Sadie wanted to know.

I smiled at her, hoping she wouldn't see the tears that hovered just beneath my eyelids. "Exactly," I said.

"If Daddy had been your doctor," Taylor said, "I bet Angel would still be alive."

Tom Larkin as superhero. If only life were that simple. But they were young. It was far too soon to disillusion them. "I bet you're right," I said.

"But it's okay," Sadie said, "because you have us now. And our mom is up there in heaven, watching over Angel."

In her eyes, it was an equitable trade, Beth as caretaker for my daughter, me as caretaker for both of hers. Sometimes it takes a child to dig through the layers of complexity and reduce an issue to its core. "Yes," I said, grateful that I'd been given this second chance. "I have you. And you have me. We're very lucky, aren't we?"

Sadie flashed me a shy smile, then ducked her head and took a sip of tea. "Julie?" she said. "You won't leave us, will you?"

I was afraid to breathe. Across the table, Taylor met my eyes. Beneath her suspicion, I thought I saw a glimmer of something else. Hope, maybe? I thought about my mother, walking out the door one rainy Sunday night and never returning. Thought about Beth Larkin, climbing up on that bridge railing and taking the easy way out, with no thought for the destruction she was leaving behind. Damn them. Damn them both for tearing out the hearts of little girls whose only crime was loving them.

"No," I vowed. "I will never, ever leave you."

By Wednesday afternoon, I'd had enough of hanging out in the attic, sorting through the stuff that Dad and I had accumulated over the course of the last thirty years. My knees hurt, my allergies were acting up, and every box I opened was starting to look identical to the dozen boxes that had preceded it. It was definitely time for a break, so I dusted myself off, brushed my hair, spritzed myself with a wisp of my favorite body spray in the hopes of making myself presentable, and headed next door.

Tom had given me the lowdown on Claudia. She'd grown up next door, and had inherited the house from her grandmother, along with a big enough pile of money to afford her a comfortable lifestyle. She played at raising flowers. According to Tom, she sold some of them to local florists, but she didn't really need the money. Her gardening was more a hobby than a source of income. Her ex was some kind of pharmaceutical salesman who spent half the year on the road. Their divorce had been bitter, but they shared custody of their son, who was the same age as Sadie. Whenever his dad was home for a few days, Dylan stayed with him.

Claudia's house was smaller than Tom's, and had an eclectic New England–cottage feel. There were lots of multipaned windows, a wooden front door with a rounded top, and a trellis thick with some kind of wild and wooly climbing greenery. I rang the bell and waited. When there was no answer, I remembered that she'd told me to come around the back. So I followed a slate walkway that led me, like the yellow brick road, directly to the emerald city.

Or so it seemed. The greenhouse dominated the

backyard, but even this late in the season, flowers bloomed everywhere in the garden. Seemingly random splashes of color, which upon closer inspection had obviously been carefully planned, stretched from the patio to the brook that marked the rear property line. The grass, what there was of it, was green and level and recently mowed. The scents were enticing, and the entire place possessed an immensely appealing earthiness.

As predicted, I found Claudia in the greenhouse, repotting a geranium. Her work station was a silvered wooden plank set atop a pair of sawhorses. A shelving unit, nailed together from pieces of the same plank, held gardening tools, bags of potting soil and mulch, a stack of empty terra-cotta pots, containers of various fertilizers and insecticides, and God only knew what else. The rest of the greenhouse, every inch of it, was filled with plants. I'd never seen so much green—or such a profusion of color—in one place in my life.

With her hands buried up to the knuckles in rich, black soil, she sang off-key with Michael Bolton: "When a ma-an loves a woman—"

I cleared my throat. Her head whipped around and she saw me. "Oh, good," she said, apparently without embarrassment at being caught. "I was just thinking about you."

"Hello, yourself. This place is impressive."

"Welcome to my world," she said. "My obsession. Gardening keeps me relaxed, helps me work out my aggressions, and prevents me from tumbling over the edge of reason into insanity."

"You certainly seem to be good at it."

"It's the only thing in this world that I can call mine alone. I don't have to share it with anyone else. Even my son I have to share with his father. Whether I want to or not." While she talked, she tamped down the soil around the roots of the transplanted geranium. "When I get mad at my ex," she confided, picking up a small watering can and dousing the soil, "weeding the garden is my favorite activity. As I lop off their little heads with my hoe, I imagine it's him I'm decapitating." She grinned. "It's so freeing."

"Remind me not to get on your bad side."

"Oh, you're safe." She picked up a towel and wiped the dirt from her hands. "I only take out my aggressions on stubborn weeds and ex-husbands. But, Julie—I'm so glad you came! I'm dying of thirst. Let's make a pitcher of strawberry daiquiris, sit on the patio, and get shitfaced."

Her enthusiasm was contagious and, although shitfaced probably wasn't in my future, we sat in lounge chairs on the patio with a pitcher of daiquiris on the table between us. Her face turned up to the sun, Claudia said, "So how's it going so far? Is the transition difficult?"

"Oh, it's going just great." I took a sip of my daiquiri. "My mother-in-law hates my guts, I've been threatened by a seven-year-old, and a total stranger accused me of marrying a homicidal maniac."

"Let me guess," she said over the rim of her glass. "Melanie Ambrose."

"The lady gets it in one."

"Ignore Melanie," she said. "Everyone in town knows she's a few sandwiches short of a picnic. And that mother-in-law of yours? Woo-hoo, she's a piece of work. But I'll admit I'm intrigued by the threat from a seven-year-old. I assume we're talking about Taylor?"

"We are. And it's not as though I don't understand where she's coming from. I'm a stranger to her, and she's reluctant to take me at face value. I believe that's a sign of good judgment."

"But?"

"But—" I realized that the alcohol had loosened my tongue, and I wondered if I were saying too much. But Tom had known Claudia Lavoie all his life, and after five minutes in her company, I felt as though I had, too. "It isn't so much what she said. The poor kid was just repeating what she'd heard. I guess what bothers me so much is that she was parroting something Jeannette had said to her. Something toxic and hurtful that should never have been said in front of her."

"What did she say?"

"She told me I shouldn't get used to being here, that I wouldn't last any longer than any of the others."

Claudia raised a single, elegant eyebrow. "Yikes."

"Exactly. When I told Tom, he was—"

"You told Tom what she said?"

"He's my husband. He's supposed to support me in times of need. And since I didn't find it appropriate subject matter for Jeannette to be discussing with his daughter, I thought he needed to know."

"You do like to live dangerously, don't you?" She leaned forward eagerly, her stemmed glass of bloodred liquid dangling between two elegant fingers. "So what'd he say?"

"He threatened to throw her out. His mother, that is. Not Taylor."

"That might be a little hard, chickie. Since the house belongs to her."

It was my turn to raise my eyebrows. "*Jeannette* owns the house?"

"Unless she sold it to Tom. And if she'd sold it to Tom, I would have heard. Nothing stays a secret for long in this town."

"I just automatically assumed the house was his."

"You assumed wrong. Tom grew up in that house. I should know. I grew up in this one. Your husband gave me my first kiss when I was six years old. I'm thirty-seven now, and still comparing every man I meet to my first crush."

"But why? Why would he tell me he had the power to remove his mother from the household if it wasn't true?"

Claudia leaned back, adjusted her gold watch strap. "He's trying to save face, sweetie. He wants you—his blushing bride—to be impressed with him. What would you think if you knew he was still living with his mama? Instead of the other way around."

"But Tom isn't like that," I insisted. "He's very forthcoming with me."

Yet, even as I said the words, I remembered that he hadn't bothered to tell me the truth about Elizabeth's death. Instead, he'd allowed me to assume something that was untrue. How forthcoming was that?

Seeing the crestfallen look on my face, Claudia squeezed my arm. "Don't feel so bad, hon. Tom's an all right guy. He may not be perfect, but compared to my ex-husband, he's a saint. He always was, as far back as I can remember."

"Not according to Riley, he wasn't. He says Tom was a normal kid who pulled normal juvenile shenanigans; he was just too smart to get caught."

She dismissed that idea with a wave of her hand. "Forget Riley. He's just jealous. Always has been, always will be. Tom was always the Crown Prince of Newmarket, and Riley just a humble footman. It drove him crazy. Whatever Tom had, Riley wanted. Up to and including the lovely Lady Elizabeth. Remember the Bible verse that says you shouldn't covet your neighbor's wife? I guess they forgot to put in the part about brothers."

"But Riley said—"

She raised her sunglasses and studied me beneath them. "He said what?"

"He said that he and Elizabeth were a couple before she started dating Tom."

"Well, I suppose that's true enough." Claudia dropped her sunglasses on the table, next to the pitcher of daiquiris. "They dated for a couple of years, while Tom was away at college. But they broke up before he came back, primarily, I believe, because

Riley didn't seem to have any ambition. Beth wanted more than to spend the rest of her life married to a self-employed carpenter. Tom was a doctor. With him, she and her future children would live the kind of lifestyle she craved. She knew exactly what she was doing when she married Tom Larkin."

"Riley implied that Tom stole Beth right out from under him."

Claudia laughed, a sweet, musical sound. "Trust me," she said. "Beth was not the passive type. Nobody stole her out from under anybody. She was a strong woman, with strong convictions. She knew what she wanted, and she went after it."

"Then what happened to her? If she was such a together person, why did she commit suicide?"

Something in Claudia shut down, right before my eyes. Some of the lightness, the vivacity, left her. "That's a question," she said, "that I've asked myself every day for the last two years. We were close, you know. I thought I knew her so well. But she changed. The last year of her life, she wasn't the same person. Something was wrong, something I couldn't fix. And then—" She studied me through narrowed eyes. "Promise you won't repeat this? Scout's honor?"

"I promise."

She continued to study me, as though gauging my sincerity. Then, with the briefest of nods, she said, "I never believed Beth killed herself."

The daiquiris had slowed my reflexes. It took me a minute to follow her line of reasoning to its chilling and far-fetched conclusion. "Are you saying that—"

"Yes. I'm saying exactly that. I don't believe Beth killed herself. I think somebody helped her over the side of that bridge."

Six

Following that afternoon with Claudia, I became mildly obsessed with Elizabeth Larkin. Was it morbid curiosity that fueled my fascination? Some kind of survivor guilt, because she was dead and now I was sleeping with her husband? Or was it an empathic reaction that arose from identifying too closely with her motherless daughters? I had no idea. I only knew that I'd been furious with her for deliberately deserting her girls, and now, in a 180-degree turn, I'd circled back to viewing her as a victim. Except that this time, the fabled Beth who lived inside my head wasn't a victim of random fate. Instead, she'd fallen prey to some dark and sinister evil. Somebody with means and motive had intentionally chosen to end Elizabeth Larkin's life.

Maybe. Or maybe not. Had she really been pushed over that railing, or was Claudia's homicide theory simply a figment of her daiquiri-fueled imagination?

Either way, an injustice had been done. Whether victim or perpetrator of that injustice, Beth Larkin haunted me. I even started dreaming about her, this faceless woman whose life I seemed to have inherited. In the morning, I could never remember the dreams, only that Beth had played the starring role. The knowledge left me with a vague unease. Why was I dreaming about Tom's first wife? Was I looking for justice? Retribution for the death of a woman I hadn't even met? I'd never before been consumed with righting a wrong; I'm no crusader, no espouser of causes. I live my life my way, and I expect others around me to do the same. I'm not the kind of woman to pursue a killer.

If, indeed, there even was a killer.

Tom finally got a Saturday off. I'd already discovered that a doctor's wife pretty much lives alone, especially the wife of an obstetrician. Sleeping solo comes with the territory, and though I'd hoped to have more time with him, I understood the demands of his career. So when Tom was working, I found other things to keep me busy. I'd begun making jewelry again, and catching up on my reading. But on that particular Saturday, with no gynecological emergencies and no babies whose arrival appeared to be imminent, I had my husband all to myself. Or as much to myself as I could manage with two pint-sized chaperones. That morning, beneath a brilliant blue sky, we packed the girls into Beth's Land Rover and drove to Portland, where we traded it for a shiny new burgundy-colored Toyota Highlander. Automatic, of course. I liked the look of the small SUV, there was plenty of room for the girls, and Tom said the four-wheel-drive would get me through the worst winter storms. I still missed my Miata, but I was grateful I'd married a man who made my welfare a priority. That was something Jeffrey had never done.

Afterward, we took the girls apple picking. I sat cross-legged on a blanket and watched the three of them: Tom, standing high on a ladder selecting apples and handing them down to the girls to be bagged; Sadie, whose ponytail had come undone, her hair askew and tangled with twigs; and Taylor, whose ruddy cheeks played a nice counterpoint to the grass stains on the knees of her formerly white pants. Tom glanced over at me and grinned, and like the Grinch, my heart grew three sizes that day. It was one of those golden moments, the kind of moment that you can pull from your memory in ten or twenty or fifty years, and it'll still be there, frozen in time with every detail intact. In that moment, I realized I had it all. The little tableau in front of me was everything I'd ever needed, everything I'd ever wanted. Tom and the girls. A package deal. My family.

That night, after the girls went to bed, we ordered pizza, took it up to our room, and had our own private candlelight dinner. No kids, no mothers, just the two of us. While we ate pepperoni and mushrooms, we talked, bouncing around from topic to topic: the events of the week; Taylor's math grades; the article Tom had recently read about a promising new cure for cancer. Tom was a talker, and so was I. We never ran out of things to say. We'd spent more than one night on board ship sitting up into the wee hours, talking. Communication came easily to us; we seemed to have a palpable connection, an unbreachable bond.

But we were equally good at other methods of communicating. That night, when we were done talking, we made love on crisp, clean sheets, a cool breeze drifting through the open window and a single candle flickering on the dresser. Afterward, as I lay cradled in his arms, I said sleepily, "You're pretty good at that."

"I pride myself," he said, "on my skills in the boudoir."

"You know—" I lay my cheek against his chest, absorbing his heat, and listened to the steady thud of his heart. "Considering your choice of career, I'd think you'd be so tired of looking at women's hoo-ha's all day long that when you come home at night, sex would be the last thing on your mind. Seen one hoo-ha, seen them all."

"Ah," he said, "but that, my darling, is business. This is pleasure." He ran a finger down my arm, sending a tiny *frisson* of delight through my nerve endings. "There's a line I'm not allowed to cross. Diagnosing endometriosis and making love to my wife are very different activities. Besides, if I may be so bold as to say so, I find your hoo-ha infinitely more attractive than any of the ones I meet on a daily basis."

Groggily, I said, "You are so full of it."

"You say that like it's a bad thing. Jules?"

Half-asleep, I said, "What?"

"Let's make a baby."

That woke me up fast. In the soft flicker of candle-light, his face was all light and shadow, lines and angles. Dramatic, mysterious. "Isn't this a little soon?" I said. "We haven't even been married a month."

"Why wait? When you know it's right, why wait? It would be nice to have a baby while the girls are still young. It's easier for kids when they're closer in age. They have a built-in peer group."

I searched his eyes, saw nothing there but sincerity. "You're serious," I said. "You've actually given this some thought."

"I have. I've watched you with the girls, Jules. If ever any woman was meant to be a mother, it's you."

The pain caught me by surprise. It always did, like a tiger crouching behind the door, waiting to pounce. "In case you forgot," I said, "I tried it once. It didn't go so well."

"What happened with Angel wasn't your fault. It was a fluke. There's no reason to believe it will ever happen again."

I rolled away from him and balled up my pillow, holding it tight against my stomach. "Don't start spouting statistics at me," I said. "I don't want to know the percentage of infants who die at birth. Those numbers are meaningless. Angel wasn't some statistic, she was my child. And we don't know why it happened. That scares me." I took a breath to calm myself. "It scares me a lot."

He dragged me back into his arms. I kept the pillow between us, maintaining my distance, not ready to give in. "I'm an obstetrician," he pointed out. "Of course I'd turn your care over to a colleague, but I'd still want to be closely involved in the pregnancy. And being aware of your previous problem, if I thought you or the baby were in any danger, I'd send you to a specialist I know in Boston. He deals with high-risk pregnancies, and he has a very good track record."

It seemed to me that he was reducing this, a life-altering decision of the heart, to simple biology. *Just the facts, ma'am.* Okay, so he was a doctor, and that's what doctors deal with. Biological facts. I'd give him that much. But I wasn't a doctor and, for me, there was more to this than percentages and risk factors. This wasn't a medical decision, but an emotional one.

I sat up in bed and wrapped my arms around my knees. "I'm not sure I'm ready, Tom. I think I'm afraid to try again. What if I fail a second time?"

"Then we'll know better than to go for a third try. But what if you don't fail? What if you're capable of producing a beautiful, healthy child? If you don't try, you'll never know. And that would be a damn shame. A major loss to us both."

I thought about it. Thought about my unfulfilled longing for a child. Weighed the possible benefits against the very real pain I'd felt when I lost Angel. "I want a baby," I said. "Very much. I just thought—"

"What?"

I bit my lip and hunched my shoulders closer together. "I guess I thought we'd spend a little more time getting to know each other first."

His eyes crinkled at the corners, and I struggled to maintain my equilibrium against the wattage of his smile. "What's to know?" he said. "I already know you're the most beautiful, amazing, exciting woman on the planet. I know I want to see you grow and blossom with my child inside you. And I know you love the girls, but, damn it, I want something more with you. I want the bond only two people can generate when they create a child together."

His sentiments were heartfelt, his logic well thought out, and I found myself weakening. "If I do this," I said, "and I truly mean *if,* do you promise you'll be there with me every step of the way? Because this is not something I can do alone."

Tom sat up beside me and took my hand. "Every step of the way," he promised. "What do you say, Jules? Do we lose the condoms and see what happens?"

Scraping the hair back from my face, I closed my eyes and took a breath. He was right. I knew he was right. It was like falling off a horse; you had to get back in the saddle as quickly as possible or the fear would paralyze you forever. *Here I go again,* I thought, *jumping off into the unknown without a safety net.* I opened my eyes. "Yes," I said.

If I live to be a hundred, I'll never forget the way he smiled at me. As if I'd just offered him the moon. "You're sure?" he said. "You're absolutely certain you're committed to this? Because once it happens, there's no going back."

"No kidding. I might not have an M.D., but I'm aware of the basic biology involved. Of course I'm sure." I'd made the commitment; now all I had to do was stick with it. See it through to whatever conclusion nature chose to bestow on us.

"Darling, Jules," he said, "I love you so much."

And I loved him, more than I'd ever imagined loving any man. I just hoped to God I was doing the right thing because, as he'd pointed out, there was no turning back. Once sperm introduces itself to egg, it's all over but the shouting. It's either abort— something I could never bring myself to do—or endure nine months of pregnancy and the pain and screaming that come at the end. There's no middle ground. No get-out-of-jail free card. Once that baby's in there, one way or another, it's coming out.

"I love you, too," I said.

He leaned forward and kissed me. Sweetly, with a tenderness that hadn't been there before. Sitting, I tilted too far forward, swayed, and he caught and steadied me. We rolled back onto the bed and lay pressed together in the shadowy light from that single candle. His eyes gazing into mine, his warm hand on my breast, sent a shaft of longing through me. I reached up and touched his face. "Tom," I whispered.

He caught my fingertips in his mouth and nibbled them. "What?" he said.

"Just Tom."

Our bodies were so attuned, so in sync with each other, that I was already primed. When he entered me that first time with nothing between us—just heated flesh against heated flesh—I let out a long sigh of bliss. Here, with Tom, with our bodies joined intimately and plans made for the future, I'd reached the pinnacle of happiness. I knew, without a doubt, that life couldn't get any better than this.

He smiled. And then he made me forget everything but him.

Jessica Kenner lived out in the middle of nowhere. She was Taylor's best friend, and my stepdaughter had been invited to her house for a sleepover. The customarily quiet Taylor was brimming with excitement as we drove the winding country roads. Maine, I'd quickly learned, became rural about a half mile outside any given town. From the edge of civilization, you could drive for miles in any direction before you hit a settlement larger than a four-way stop with a Grange hall, a church, and a convenience store that sold Budweiser and lottery tickets. All the essentials. This part of the state was mainly farmland, and as I headed west on the Old County Road, we passed farmhouse after farmhouse, most of them dilapidated, their ancient, unpainted barns collapsing from age and neglect.

There were still a few working farms. Dairy farms, mostly, their pastures dotted with black-and-white Holsteins, a big sign displayed in each front yard proudly announcing to the world that they sold their milk to Hood, or Oakhurst, or some other big-city dairy. A few had farm stands that sold potatoes and honey, zucchini and home-made apple pies. There was a quiet dignity to the landscape, a sincerity and simplicity that I found appealing. These honest, hard-working people struggled for every bite of food they put in their mouths. Nothing had been handed to them, and I admired their rugged independence.

The Kenners lived in a blue-and-white trailer parked on a small lot between a cow pasture and a big cornfield. The trailer had seen better days; rust streaks marred the siding, and last year's Christmas lights—those ubiquitous "icicle" strands that looked as though they'd been crocheted—dangled from the eaves. But the yard was tidy, the grass neatly cut, a well-tended flower bed of purple and gold chrysanthemums circling a concrete birdbath that held clean water.

The trailer was as neat inside as out. Jessie and Taylor greeted each other with so much excitement that if I hadn't already known they'd parted ways two hours ago at the end of the school day, I might have mistaken them for old war comrades reuniting after fifty years. Amid the excited babbling of two seven-year-old girls and the equally excited barking of a small white dog who was so happy to see me that he insisted on running between my legs and trying to trip me up, I introduced myself to the vivacious, apple-cheeked Mrs. Kenner. Once I'd determined that she probably wasn't a serial killer and it was safe to leave Taylor in her care, I made a swift and grateful escape.

Finding my way back home wasn't as easy as I'd expected. Taylor had navigated for me on the trip out here, but we'd taken so many turns that after a while all these back-country crossroads, with their faded red Stop signs and their fields awash in milkweed and goldenrod, looked the same. A couple miles back in the direction we'd come from, I took what I thought was the correct turn. But once I left the main road, nothing looked even remotely familiar. A little nervous, I checked my fuel gauge. I still had half a tank of gas. As long as I didn't spend the next three hours driving around in circles, I shouldn't have to worry about running out.

But I was hopelessly lost. I took another turn, trying to chart my course using the afternoon sun. I knew I'd driven west out of town. Now the sun sat low on the horizon behind me, a fat orange ball that nearly took my breath away. I must be headed east. Back toward home. But the next road sign I saw— the first one I'd seen in ages—told me I was headed north on Route 37. If I didn't figure out where I was pretty soon, I'd end up in Canada.

Vowing to buy a road map at my earliest opportunity, I continued on in a vaguely northeasterly direction. At my next right, I turned, figuring this would put me back on track. I might end up overshooting downtown Newmarket by a mile or two, but eventually there'd be something to point me in the right direction.

I was so focused on continuing east that I almost missed the sign. *Swift River Road.* I checked the mirror, hit the brakes, and sat studying the sign, my heart beating a little too fast. This was it. The place Claudia had told me about. Somewhere down this road, spanning the river, lay the Swift River Bridge. The place where Elizabeth Larkin had died.

It wasn't even a conscious decision that made me take the turn. Once I'd seen the sign, there was no question about what I'd do. I simply followed the path that providence had laid out for me. I *had* to go there. *Had* to see where Tom's first wife had spent her final moments. Had to breathe in the surroundings and try to put myself in her place, try to imagine what would have led her to such a tragic end.

I'd left the farmland behind. Here, headed toward the Swift River, the woods grew thick, with heavy branches meeting overhead in a leafy red-and-gold canopy. I thought of the Robert Frost poem, something about the woods being lovely, dark and deep, and I shivered. Dark and deep for sure, but maybe not so lovely. I was a city girl, and these woods, with their dense autumn foliage and the road tunneling through, felt too much like a tomb. I'd never experienced claustrophobia until now, but the eerie sensation that the trees were closing in on me was so strong I almost turned back.

I rounded a curve, and suddenly there it was, springing up before me so abruptly I gasped. An old, rusted green bridge with a sign that read Heavy Loads Limited.

I parked on the shoulder and got out of the car. There were no sounds of traffic; the quiet here was filled with the sounds of nature. Rustling leaves mingled with birdsong and the gurgling flow of the river. A hawk circled slowly overhead, wings spread as he glided effortlessly on the air. I walked up onto the bridge, my footsteps sounding loud in the silence. It was one of those old-fashioned bridges designed with wire grating instead of a solid roadbed, and the river, rushing beneath me, made me a little dizzy at first. On one side, the cement curbing had started to crumble, revealing the rusted rebar inside. Forcing myself not to look down, I walked the length of the old dinosaur, grateful when I was again on solid ground.

From the opposite shore, I turned and looked back. The bridge seemed so ordinary, so harmless. Not a weapon of death, merely an old river crossing in need of replacement. I heard the sound of an automobile approaching. It came around the bend, an old Chevy pickup, and crossed the bridge, tires singing on the grating. The driver waved to me. I waved back, and he continued on his way. I stood listening until the sound of his engine had faded. Then I walked back onto the bridge.

Partway across, I stopped, walked to the railing and, resting my hands on it, looked over the side. The river moved rapidly, carving its way around boulders and gravel sandbars. Near either shore, it was shallow, but the center looked deep and thick and murky. I imagined climbing up onto the rail, going into freefall, knifing through that smooth, wet surface and sinking into the muddy depths below. I imagined the struggle, the white-hot agony of burning lungs as I fought for breath. For life. Imagined the final, inevitable release as nature, and the river, won.

I was so deep into my imaginary scenario that when a hand touched my arm, I screamed and spun about in terror. The man who stood behind me was as ancient as the bridge, and in about the same condition. His shock of unruly gray hair encircled his head like a lion's mane, and a week's worth of scraggly whiskers did their best to cover his chin. His eyes were blue and watery, his clothes tattered. And he smelled god-awful, as if he'd spent the last month sleeping at the town dump. "I didn't mean to frighten you," he said in a reedy, high-pitched voice. "I just wanted to make sure you were all right."

I took a deep breath, hoping to slow my racing heart. "Yes," I said. "Yes, I'm fine. I just—you startled me, and—who are you?"

He gave me a small, courtly bow that belied his tattered appearance. "Roger Levasseur," he said. "I live just around the bend."

My heartbeat had slowed almost to normal. "Thank you, Roger. I was just looking at the river."

I hoped he'd take the hint and leave. The guy was creeping me out, and I couldn't find a discreet way to move upwind of him.

He studied me through red-rimmed, rheumy eyes. "Be careful. Bad things have happened on this bridge. I wouldn't want anything happening to a pretty lady like you."

Was he a protector or a threat? Because I didn't know the answer to that question, I stayed silent. The wind grabbed at a strand of my hair and blew it across my face. I reached up and shoved it back behind my ear. "Well," he said at last. "Have a nice day."

"You, too."

Agitation warring with relief, I watched him walk out of sight. When he was gone, I ran for my car. I'd had enough of this place. I checked the backseat for intruders, got into the Toyota, and locked all the doors. For a few minutes, I sat there with the driver's window rolled partway down, trying to dispel the *eau de* Roger that still assaulted my olfactory nerves. Good God, when was the last time the man had bathed? Or changed his clothes? Did he lack running water? Soap? Had he been filthy for so long, he could no longer smell himself?

Dusk had begun to settle over the river. It was time to get out of here. I had no idea which direction would lead me home, but at this point I didn't care. I just wanted to get away from the bridge, away from Roger, away from this dark place where the sun barely broke through. I couldn't wait to get home and take a shower. A long, hot one.

I put the key in the ignition and turned it. The engine cranked, and then…nothing.

I turned the key a second time. Again, the Toyota failed to start. I thumped the steering wheel in frustration. I couldn't believe this. My beautiful new car, the car I'd bought less than a week ago, the car Tom had picked because it would be safe and reliable, was dead. For all it was worth, it might as well have been a plastic toy. I didn't know what had gone wrong, but one thing was obvious: the Toyota wasn't going to start.

And I wasn't going anywhere.

I called Tom at his office, but he'd just left for the hospital. Hoping to catch him en route, I tried his cell phone, but it bounced directly to voice mail. I'd be getting no help from that quarter. It looked as though, for the third time this week, he'd be spending the evening in the delivery room. There was a mini baby boom going on, his expectant mommies popping all at once. I checked my watch. It was nearly six o'clock. I really, really hated having to do this. Jeannette wouldn't take too kindly to my interrupting whatever earth-shattering plans she had for the evening. As a matter of fact, she'd probably tell me to call a cab and then hang up on me. But I didn't know what else to do. If worse came to worst, she could at least provide me with the number of the local cab company.

So I called the house. To my relief, Jeannette wasn't home yet. Monica, our part-time after-school babysitter, answered the phone instead. "I'm in a bind," I told her. "My car broke down and I need a ride. Is there anyone around who can pick me up?"

"Jeez, Mrs. Larkin, that really bites. I'd come get you myself if I had my license."

Monica was fifteen, and her mother had promised that as long as she stayed out of trouble—she hadn't specified to me what kind of trouble her mother was referring to—once she turned sixteen, she could take driver ed. In the meantime, Monica hoofed it.

"That's all right," I said. "Is Jeannette around?"

"Not yet, but she's due any minute. She's running a little late today. Maybe she had an uncooperative client. Sometimes, they bite, you know. The dogs, not the owners."

"I don't suppose you've seen Riley around?"

"Actually, I think he just got home a few minutes ago. Want me to check the carriage house and see if he's there?"

I felt a little foolish; he'd already bailed me out with the driving thing, and I hated to ask for another favor so soon. But this was an emergency. Right now, I had no other choice. "Go check," I said.

Three or four minutes later, minutes that seemed more like hours, I heard a rustling sound and then Riley's voice, strong and male and reassuring, said, "Julie? What's wrong?"

"My car won't start, I'm somewhere in the boonies, and it's getting dark. I don't suppose you could come rescue me?"

"Where are you?"

I took a breath. "Swift River Road," I said. "Parked in a turnout just before the bridge."

There was a moment of silence at the other end of the phone before he said, "I'll be there in twenty minutes."

I wasn't sure whether to feel relief or guilt. He hadn't asked the expected question: *What in bloody hell are you doing out there?* It wouldn't have been an unreasonable question for him to ask; it's just that in retrospect, the truth seemed silly and childish, and I wasn't sure I wanted to admit to my newly minted hunger for the details of my predecessor's demise.

In the deepening twilight, I huddled in the Toyota, not even daring to run the radio for fear of draining the battery. Who knew what was wrong with the damn thing? I didn't want to make it worse. This dark place, already at the bottom of my list of favorite locations, got even creepier once the sun went down. It was not the kind of spot where a girl would choose to break down, if she were lucky enough to choose. I nibbled at my thumbnail as headlights came around the bend and approached my car. They pulled up behind me and went dark, and I recognized the shadowy hulk of Riley's Ford pickup. Embarrassed by the depth of my relief, I got out of the Toyota and greeted him.

"What seems to be the problem?" he said.

"I stopped to look at the river—" he shot me a long, hard glance, as if he knew I was lying, and in the semidarkness I felt my cheeks go hot "—and I turned the car off. When I came back, it wouldn't start."

While I stuffed my hands in the pockets of my jacket for warmth, Riley lifted the hood. With a penlight, he looked around, fiddled with whatever it is men fiddle with under the hood of a car. I suspected that as the owner of a Y chromosome, he had some idea of what he was looking at, but it was all Greek to me. "I'm not a mechanic," he said. "But it seems to me that this belt—or what used to be a belt—just might be your problem."

I moved closer, leaned over the engine, my gaze following the beam of his flashlight. A piece of thick, black rubber hung at an awkward angle, unattached to anything. "Golly gee," I said. "Look at that."

"You just bought this thing. If I were you, I'd call up the dealer and give him what-for. You have roadside assistance?"

"I, um—maybe. I don't know. Tom did all the talking."

I sounded like an idiot. What kind of woman didn't keep track of important details like that? Had marriage turned my brain to mush? It was obvious that Riley was thinking the same thing. The words *ditzy female* were undoubtedly flashing through his brain like neon lights. "Get your owner's manual," he said. "Leave the keys. It'll have to be towed back to the dealership. I doubt anybody around here will have the part."

Back in the pickup, he called the towing service, told them where to locate the dead vehicle, and then he pulled a hard U-turn and headed back in the direction he'd come from. We drove in silence, a silence that grew heavier with each mile we traveled. "I drove Taylor to her friend Jessie's house," I explained. "Somewhere in West Newmarket. I got lost coming back, took a wrong turn somewhere, and ended up at the bridge. I just thought I'd get out and take a look at the river, and—"

"You know." The words were hard and flat, not spoken as an accusation, but as simple truth.

"Know what?"

"You know that's where Beth died."

Oh, hell. At my sides, my hands balled into fists. I considered lying, but what was the point in continuing the charade? He already knew the truth. "Yes," I said.

When he didn't respond, I continued, "But I really did take a wrong turn. And once I saw the sign for Swift River Road, I couldn't seem to stop myself. I had to see where Beth died."

I was digging my own grave, going deeper with every word. Riley gave me another of his long, hard looks, and said, "Why?"

"Because it doesn't feel right to me. Beth's suicide. I realize I didn't know her, but from what I do know about her, she seems like the last person on earth who'd kill herself. I just—" I studied his silent profile, his callused hands gripping the steering wheel. "It bothers me," I said.

He said nothing. In the silence, I fidgeted. "Could we not tell Tom?" I asked. "Please?"

"Stay out of it," he said. "Let it be. Stop trying to turn over rocks to see what's underneath. You could end up hurt. I don't want to see that."

"I don't understand. Why would I get hurt?"

He squared his jaw and said, "What's it to you,

anyway? You should be glad she's dead. You got Tom out of the deal. Be grateful for small favors."

It was like being kicked in the diaphragm. For an instant, all the oxygen left my lungs. And then the anger rushed in to take its place. "That's a terrible thing to say!"

"You're right. It is."

I waited for him to apologize. It didn't look as though he intended to. In the fading light, I studied his profile. "What is it you know?" I said.

"I don't have a clue what you're talking about."

"Oh, come on, Riley. You obviously know something I don't. What is it you're afraid I'll find out? Tell the truth. Don't you think you can trust me?"

He laughed, a short, cynical bark. "You want to know what I think? I think you've watched one too many episodes of *Murder, She Wrote.* Take my advice. Be a good little wife, stay home, and bake cookies."

It was an interesting response. Especially considering I hadn't said anything about murder. "That's pretty sexist," I said.

"I'm a sexist pig. So sue me. If baking cookies doesn't float your boat, get a job. Something to keep you occupied, so you'll forget about playing amateur sleuth. Stop poking into other people's business. You'll only stir up things that are better left untouched."

Aghast, I stared at him. I'd been fishing, casting my net into the unknown, throwing paint at the wall, just in case something stuck. I hadn't expected a bite. But damned if it didn't look as though my new brother-in-law actually knew something he wasn't telling me.

For the first time, I realized the man sitting beside me was a stranger. What did I really know about Riley Larkin? I knew he was handy with a chain saw and comfortable handling a stick shift. I knew he was something of a loner who'd grown up in his brother's shadow, playing antihero to Tom's golden-boy persona. I knew he was attractive, but it wasn't the same kind of stop-dead-in-your-tracks-to-take-a-second-look handsomeness that Tom possessed. Riley's looks were quieter, the kind that grew on you gradually. You had to know him for a while before you noticed how good-looking he was.

But that was the extent of what I knew about my brother-in-law. He could be an axe murderer for all I knew. The idea wasn't comforting, especially considering that we were alone in a car together in the middle of nowhere.

"Julie? Are you listening to me?"

I dragged my attention away from my vision of Riley as serial killer. "Yes," I said. "I hear you."

"Just drop the whole thing, okay? It's better for everyone involved."

He was probably right. I still didn't understand why I found it so important to know the truth, except that I felt a kinship with Beth Larkin. In some inexplicable way, we were sisters. But I wasn't about to admit that to Riley. "Truce?" I said.

He glanced at me from the corner of his eye. Then sighed. "Truce."

If he thought that meant I was going to stop searching for the truth, I'd allow him to continue thinking it. After all, what Riley didn't know wouldn't hurt him. I wasn't quite so sure it wouldn't hurt me.

Seven

I could hear Claudia grumbling as she approached the door. She swung it open midrant. "—God's sake, give me a minute to—" She saw me and stopped abruptly. "Oh," she said. "It's you. You were pounding so hard I thought you were the cops, come to confiscate the lone cannabis plant that's growing so magnificently in my kitchen window."

"Did they consider homicide?" I said, blowing past her, moving down the corridor and into the bright, sunny kitchen. It was decorated in Southwestern colors, brick-red and sage-green with highlights here and there of bright yellow and teal. And in the window, basking merrily in the sunlight, sat the aforementioned cannabis plant. "Nice kitchen."

"Homicide? Over one little plant? Isn't that what you'd call overkill? No pun intended."

"Not the plant," I said impatiently. "*Beth.* Did the police rule out homicide? Did they even consider it?

Or did they automatically focus the investigation on the obvious?"

"Oh," she said.

"I haven't been able to stop thinking about what you said. I went out and looked at the bridge, and—"

"Why in God's name did you do that?"

"I was in the neighborhood. I saw the road sign. It seemed like a good idea at the time."

Calmly, she said, "Tea?"

"Yes, thank you. My car died on me—my new car—so Riley came to pick me up, and I swear to God, Claudia, that man knows something. There's something really shady about Beth's so-called suicide, and Riley knows it. Which is why—" I let out a rush of accumulated breath. "Which is why I want to know if the police looked into the possibility of homicide."

Claudia moved smoothly to the sink and filled the teakettle, set it on the stove, and turned on the burner. "Amazingly enough, they didn't share the details of their investigation with me. Imagine that. But the newspaper report said they found no evidence of foul play." She cocked her head to one side, looking for all the world like a pixie come out to play. "Don't take too seriously anything I say when I've been drinking. A couple of daiquiris and my imagination goes into overdrive."

"Don't you dare recant your story now! This was your idea." If I caught Claudia backpedaling away from her original position, I'd be livid.

"And I'd been drinking since noon."

"I can't believe this. First Riley, and now you. What is *wrong* with you people?"

"All I'm saying, hon, is that I don't really know what happened. Nobody does, except Beth, and she's not about to tell us."

"Beth, and whoever killed her."

Claudia shrugged. "*If* she was killed. So far, we have no evidence that she was."

"Damn it, Riley's hiding something."

The kettle whistled, and Claudia removed it from the burner. "So what are you saying? That you think Riley killed Beth?"

I'd given the idea a great deal of thought. As a matter of fact, since yesterday afternoon, I'd hardly thought of anything else. But no matter how I looked at it, it didn't wash. The idea seemed ludicrous. "No," I admitted. "I can't imagine it. But there's something strange about all this. Something that's off-kilter. There are no pictures of Beth in the house. Nobody ever speaks her name. It's as though she's been erased from the family archives. And that bothers me. It bothers me a lot."

Claudia calmly arranged tea bags in two delicate cups painted with pink rosebuds and filled them with hot water. "And what does Tom have to say about that?"

"He gave me some song and dance about trying to help the girls heal by removing all the reminders of what they'd lost."

"That sounds reasonable to me."

"It's not reasonable, damn it! It's creepy."

She set the kettle back on the stove and held out a cup of tea. "Sit down. Drink your tea. It'll help calm your nerves."

"My nerves are fine." But I sat. And drank. "Riley knows something," I said. "I'm not crazy, I'm not overreacting, I'm not imagining it. He told me to stay out of it because he didn't want to see anything happen to me. Come to think of it—" I paused, eyes narrowed, trying to remember the exact wording the strange old man had used. "That's pretty much the same thing Roger said."

"Roger who?"

"He's this hideous old man who talked to me on the bridge yesterday. Gray hair, missing teeth, and a stench worse than a three-day-old mackerel."

"Oh," she said. "That Roger."

"You know him?"

"Everybody knows him. Roger Levasseur. Used to be a physicist. He taught at MIT. They say he's brilliant, or at least he was until he lost his marbles. Now he lives alone in a little trailer out by the river. He smells bad, but he's harmless. They say he built some sort of fishing shack under the bridge, out of old plywood and roofing nails. Sometimes he sleeps out there. The property's not his, but nobody seems to care. He doesn't bother anybody."

"That awful man was a physics professor at MIT? Impossible."

"Not really. Some academics from those prestigious institutions have IQs so high they have trouble functioning outside of academe. I had a great-aunt who taught at Harvard for twenty years. One day she just snapped. Stripped off all her clothes and ran buck-naked up and down the Widener Library stacks. As you can imagine, Harvard's austere administration wasn't impressed. She had tenure, so they couldn't fire her. Instead, she went on an extended leave of absence, and spent the rest of her life in a sanitarium, eating pablum and staying away from sharp objects." Claudia paused to gaze at me fondly. "Julie," she said, "what is it you want?"

"I don't understand what you mean."

"You just came here. This is a small town. We're quirky. Give us a little time before you start rocking boats. I guarantee you'll sleep better at night."

Had she and Riley gotten together last night and compared notes? Or had I accidentally wandered into Stepford? Who was this stranger, and what had she done with the Claudia I'd met a few days ago? I drained my tea and slipped down from my wooden stool. "Sure, Claudia. Whatever you say."

"Oh, now you're mad. Don't be that way."

I lifted my chin and said, "I'm not mad."

A dimple appeared in her left cheek. "Right. And I'm the Queen of France."

I glared at her. I'd thought she was my friend. How could I have been so stupid? I barely knew the woman. Jeffrey had always told me I was too trusting. "I have to go," I said. "Have a nice life."

"Julie! Oh, for Christ's sake." She got up from her stool and chased me to the door. "Look, I'm just trying to protect you."

I turned on her. "I don't need protecting! Do I really look like that much of a babe in the woods? Do I wear a sign on my back that says Dunce?"

"It's not that."

"Then what is it? What quality do I possess that makes everyone I meet think I need to be protected from the big, bad world?"

"Everybody doesn't think that."

"Roger does. Riley does. You do."

"Okay," she admitted, "maybe I think you do, just a little. Look at your behavior. What else am I supposed to think? You make wild accusations and then go off half-cocked when I don't rush to agree with you. How many other people have you said this to? Has it even occurred to you that if you're right, if Beth was murdered, you might be placing yourself in jeopardy by showing too much interest? No," she continued, seeing the expression on my face, "I can see you hadn't even thought about that until I reminded you. That's dangerous behavior. That, my dear, is why we all think you need protection. Not so much from the world as from yourself."

I stood silent, stunned by her accusation, even more stunned by its truth. "Besides," she said, looking pained, "it's not about you. Not really."

My recovery from mortification was amazingly rapid. "Now you're contradicting yourself," I said. "Which is it? You can't have it both ways."

"Fine. If you must know, it's my own ass I'm protecting. If anything happened to you because of me,

Tom would have my head on a platter. And that's the truth."

All the starch went out of me. It wasn't what I'd expected to hear, but her face told me it was the truth. "I think," I said, "you'd better tell me what you're talking about."

"Come back in the kitchen. We'll talk."

"We can talk here."

"Fine." Claudia crossed her arms and leaned against the wall. "Tom and I go way back," she said. "We rode our tricycles together, up and down my driveway because he was a year older and my grandmother wouldn't let me out of the yard. When I was six, he gave me my first kiss. We climbed trees and caught frogs together. We went out together on Halloween and egged people's houses."

I couldn't help myself. The words just popped out of me. "My Tom did that?"

"He did. We were about as close as two kids could be. Then Beth came along, and we became a threesome. The Three Musketeers. Through adolescence and into adulthood, it was all for one and one for all."

"Does this story have a point?"

"The point is that Beth and I became like sisters. We told each other everything. Or I thought we did. So when she died, Tom blamed it on me."

"Why the hell would he do that?"

"He felt that as Beth's best friend, I should have seen how depressed she was. I should have realized she was suicidal. Plus, his wife was dead and he needed somebody to blame. He chose me."

"I don't get it. Why was it your responsibility? He was her husband. Surely that trumps a best friend in the closeness category. If there was any blame to be handed out, he should have stepped up and taken his share."

"Beth put on a good act. She kept her depression hidden. She managed to fool me, and not too many people can pull that off."

"So you didn't know she was depressed?"

"I didn't. I knew something wasn't right with her. The last few months of her life, she changed. But, like most people, I was too wrapped up in my own life to pay attention to hers. If anything, I suppose I imagined she and Tom were having marital problems. He works long hours, and Beth was home alone with the girls. I thought she was ticked off because he didn't pay enough attention to her. Attention was one of Beth's big priorities. To tell you the truth, the possibility of depression never even crossed my mind."

"Tom claims she was clinically depressed and had been for some time."

"Yes, well, he's a doctor. If anyone should recognize the symptoms, he should."

"Yet according to what you're telling me, he didn't."

"Not until it was too late."

"Anyone can be a Monday-morning quarterback," I said. "You don't need a medical degree for that. And I still don't understand what any of this has to do with me."

"It's quite simple. The truth is, I don't want to lose Tom. He's my dearest friend in the world. My parents are gone. So is my Gram, and Beth, my closest girlfriend. Even my worthless ex-husband has moved on to greener pastures. Except for Dylan, Tom is the only family I have left. He's like the older brother I never had. If he thought I let you walk into trouble without doing my best to save you, he'd never speak to me again. I'm not willing to risk that. I don't know why you're so obsessed with Beth, but I don't think it's healthy for you or your marriage. And it's certainly not healthy for me. So I beg of you, give it a rest. You have a good man there, one I suspect would lay down his life for you. If you love him, don't force him to make that choice. Back off and focus on what really matters. Tom and those two beautiful little girls."

I didn't know what to say. "Answer one question for me," I said, "and then I'll leave you alone."

"Fine."

"Do you think Beth killed herself? Gut feeling, not the polite thing to say, or what you think I want to hear. What do you, Claudia, really believe?"

"Oh, boy." She moved to the hall mirror and stood there, looking at her own reflection. "Some days," she said, "I don't believe it at all. I look at everything Beth had going for her. Tom, the girls, a lovely home. She was so headstrong, so determined, and I can't imagine that she would throw that all away."

"But?"

"But." Claudia squared her shoulders. "But then,

on the days in between, the days when I'm feeling more rational and less emotional, I tell myself I'm looking for something that simply doesn't exist. Looking for unicorns, when horses will clearly do. The whole sordid affair is pretty straightforward, after all. Beth parked her car on the damn bridge, penned a suicide note, and jumped off the railing. End of story."

Maybe she was right. Maybe it really was the end of the story. She was certainly right about the obsession. I'd become fixated on Beth Larkin. Claudia's words had hit a nerve: *Back off and focus on what really matters. Tom and those two beautiful little girls.* She was right. They were my future. Tom, the girls, the baby we were trying to conceive. Beth was the past. A fleeting shadow, too insubstantial to be real. Dead and gone, and nothing I could do would change that. Uncovering the truth might pacify me, but it wouldn't do a thing for poor Beth. The best I could do for her, the most respectful act I could commit, would be raising her daughters to be decent, caring human beings. Beth would want that. It's what I'd have wanted, in her place.

So I made the decision to take Claudia's advice. To stop looking for answers. To give up the witch hunt. Starting tomorrow, I'd climb those attic stairs and get back to unpacking. There were books to be shelved, knickknacks to display or discard, Dad's belongings to sort through. Maybe, while I was up there, I might even organize some of the clutter that had been accumulating for what looked like decades.

If I took my time and did it right, I could find enough work up there to keep me busy for a month.

Besides, I told myself, up there I surely couldn't get into any trouble.

"It was cut."

"Cut," Tom repeated, his rising inflection turned the single syllable into a question.

"Ayuh." The mechanic was about forty-five, with a mullet that was two decades past its expiration date, Elvis-style sideburns, and a gray-and-white pin-striped shirt. The patch over his breastbone said *Randy* in a lively, flowing red script. "This belt's rugged," Randy said. "These babies don't just up and quit on you. Especially not on a new car like this one. See where it let go?" He held out the belt and we both leaned closer so we could see what he was talking about. "There's just one little tear, right here." With a greasy index finger, he pointed to a ragged spot on one side of the belt. "The rest of her's cut off clean as a whistle."

Tom looked frazzled. He'd cancelled a half-dozen afternoon appointments to make this trip to Portland to pick up the repaired Toyota. "Are you telling me," he said, "that somebody cut this belt deliberately?"

"You can see it with your own eyes. They didn't slice it all the way through. Left just enough attached so it wouldn't let go right away. But once it was left hanging by a thread, so to speak, the result was a foregone conclusion. Car won't run without it. The intention, as far as I can make out, was for you folks to get out on the road somewhere before it broke the rest of the way through and left you stranded."

Tom uttered a foul word. It was the first time I'd ever heard him use that particular word, and my eyes widened in appreciation of his creative usage. "Why?" he said. "Why would anybody do such a thing?"

Randy shrugged. Not his problem. His was a simple existence. He dealt with broken belts, not with vandals.

"It was probably kids," I said. "You know how teenagers are. They think this kind of thing is funny."

Tom's face, a juxtaposition of sharp lines and angles, appeared thunderous. "Well, I don't," he said. "This is so not funny that I can't even find words for it. I don't like this. I'm filing a police report."

"Come on, Tom, do you really think that's necessary?"

"Are you serious? Somebody—and I don't give a damn whether that somebody is twelve years old or a hundred and twelve—came onto my property, apparently while I was sleeping, and deliberately vandalized my wife's car. Damaged it so she'd end up stranded somewhere. They didn't care whether she ended up there alone, or with one or both of my girls, as long as the car broke down while she was behind the wheel. You're damn right I think it's necessary. What if you didn't have a cell phone? What if somebody had done you harm? What if nobody'd been there to pick you up when you called?"

"Then I would have called the police. Or a taxi."

But Tom wasn't to be dissuaded; I'd never seen him so agitated. "That's not the point," he said, while Randy, fueled by the wisdom culled from his vast experience, nodded sagely in agreement. "What if the belt let go just as you were pulling out onto a busy street? Into heavy traffic, with only a tiny window of time to make a safe turn? You could've been killed. You, or one of the girls. Or maybe our unborn child. So yes, I'm reporting this. I'm calling Dwight Pettingill as soon as we get home, and I'm filing a police report. And if they catch the little shit who did this, I'll push like hell for jail time."

Still nodding, Randy said, "You can't let people get away with hurting your family. You're doing the right thing, Doc. Make the bastards pay."

I rolled my eyes. *Men.* No matter how long I lived, I would never understand them. It looked like we had our own little vigilante group started. I wondered if they had a twelve-step program for that kind of thing. *Hi, my name is Randy, and I'm a revenge junkie.* Damn it, Tom was too smart to overreact like this. It was obviously kids. Kids who didn't have the brains to realize the possible consequences of their actions. But there was nothing I could do to change his mind; my husband was on a tear, already prepared to wreak vengeance for the imagined death of a baby we hadn't yet conceived. It was a little over the top, but at the same time, there was something endearing about it. I tried to imagine my ex getting this fired up over anything, but that was a station I just couldn't tune in. Oh, for sure, if anything had happened to me during our marriage, he would have grieved. Jeffrey wasn't a complete ogre. He'd cared about me. But Jeff was too passive to don a suit of armor, mount a white stallion, and ride to my rescue. Not without major prodding. Tom, on the other hand, was determined to be my white knight, whether I wanted one or not.

We drove home in separate vehicles, Tom riding my bumper so close I was tempted to slam on the brakes just to teach him a lesson. *Thou shalt not tailgate.* It had come as something of a shock, the sudden appearance of my balanced, rational husband's inner Neanderthal, and I was torn between justified horror and a faintly mortifying thrill at the realization that even the vaguest of threats against my person had sent Tom on a zealous mission to preserve my delicate well-being. I'd always been an independent woman, and I knew my card-carrying feminist sisters would drum me right out of the club if they knew about the side of me that was secretly delighted to be fussed over by a man.

Tom must have made the phone call from the road, because when we pulled into the driveway, a Newmarket police cruiser was already waiting. A uniformed officer leaned against the fender, in his beefy hands a half-eaten Big Mac. When he saw us, his ruddy cheeks turned even redder. "It's this low-fat diet Dolores has me on," he explained. "A man can only eat so much tofu. If I didn't sneak in a real meal once in a while, I'd starve to death. Damn woman even has me limited to two beers a day." He grimaced in disgust. "Lite beer."

Tom clapped him on the shoulder in sympathy. "She's just looking out for your health," he said. "Dolores loves you."

"Yeah. That's what she keeps telling me. I don't know, but I'm pretty sure I'd be happier if she showed her undying affection by frying me up a big, thick steak. Hell, it doesn't even have to be fried. Grilled would be close enough." Dwight swiped at his mouth with a paper napkin and hid a discreet belch behind his hand. Crumpling up the remains of his sandwich, he stuffed it into his empty McDonald's bag. Suddenly all business, he straightened and said, "I hear you had an incident of vandalism."

Tom showed him the ruined belt, explained what had happened and what Randy had told us. "Hell-raising is one thing," he said. "I wasn't a perfect kid. I egged a few houses in my time, toilet-papered a few trees. But I never did anything to endanger anyone. We were lucky. My wife was stranded, but nobody was hurt. It could've been a lot worse. If this belt had given out on I-95 on a busy Saturday during leaf-peeping season, we could be looking at something a lot more serious than vandalism."

Dwight rubbed the back of his neck. "You realize there's not a lot we can do," he said, "not unless you have some idea who might've done it." He looked mildly hopeful until Tom shook his head and crushed his hopes. Dwight sighed and pulled a notebook and pen from his shirt pocket. He flipped open the notebook and clicked the pen. "I guess that means we ask the obvious questions. Do either of you have any known enemies?"

Talk about overkill. I opened my mouth to protest the ridiculous turn this conversation had taken, but Tom beat me to it. "My wife just moved here," he said. "She doesn't even know anybody yet. How could she have enemies?"

It wasn't quite what I would have said, but at least it was a protest. Dwight nodded at Tom, turned his attention to me. Every inch the cop, pen poised over his notebook, he waited.

I cleared my throat. "Nobody I can think of," I said.

"No previous boyfriends or husbands? Somebody who might have an axe to grind?"

"No. I mean, I have an ex-husband, but we parted amicably." Dwight said nothing, and his steady gaze made me squirm, even though I'd done nothing wrong. "No," I said with finality. "There's nobody."

With a sigh, he returned to Tom. "What about you? Any disgruntled lady friends? Pissed-off patients? Husbands who think the baby looks more like the doctor than the daddy?"

"For Christ's sake, Dwight."

"Look, I have to ask. You wanted me to investigate. That's what I'm doing. Investigating."

"No," Tom said firmly. "There are no disgruntled lady friends or vengeful husbands hiding in my private woodpile."

"No pending litigation? No accusations of malpractice? No new mother who's ticked off because her episiotomy scar's crooked?"

"My patients are all satisfied with the care they've received from me."

Dwight adjusted his sunglasses. "That's what I've heard. How about somebody you've had words with? I hear there's no love lost between you and Melanie Ambrose."

Tom's eyebrows went sky-high. "Isn't that what they call leading the witness?"

The corner of Dwight's mouth quivered, but he held a straight face. "It would be, if we were in court. Since we're not, I figure I have a right to ask."

"Melanie's made no secret of the fact that she doesn't like me," Tom said. "But she wouldn't do something like this."

"You'd be surprised what people will do when the pressure's on."

"Come on, Dwight, we've both known Mel since we were kids. Can you see her sneaking out here in the dark of night with a switchblade, crawling under my wife's new car, and hacking her way through the serpentine belt?"

This time, Dwight grinned. "That would be a picture worth a thousand words."

"I still think it's teenagers," I broke in. "And I think you guys are taking this way too seriously."

"Can't ever take something like this too seriously," Dwight said. "Not when it impacts your personal safety." He closed his notebook and shoved it back into his pocket. "But you're probably right.

Most likely it was teenagers. Mind if I take a look around?"

"Please," Tom said. "Whatever you have to do."

"I'll file a report," Dwight said, "but you need to know you shouldn't expect much to come of it. We can check the belt for prints, but if your mechanic's had his hands all over it, he's probably destroyed any evidence there might've been."

"I know you'll do your best."

"If either of you think of anything important, don't be afraid to call."

"Trust me," Tom said. "I have your number on speed dial."

I'd kept Sadie home from preschool this morning because she wanted to help me in the attic. I knew just how much help I could expect from a four-year-old, but I wasn't in any real hurry to finish; besides, I was eager for any bonding opportunity that presented itself. After a Tom-approved breakfast of oatmeal and fresh fruit, we trooped up the back stairs to the attic. It was a shadowy, foreboding place, long and narrow, with low eaves and corners that never saw daylight. There were a pair of windows at one end, but today they weren't letting in much light because of the steady gray drizzle that fell outside. Bare lightbulbs, strategically placed every ten feet along the center of the ceiling, provided pools of weak illumination separated by areas of inky darkness, and I'd brought a couple of flashlights with me to make up for the dearth of light.

Like so many attics in houses of a certain age that had been inhabited by the same family for any length of time, this one was packed with the minutiae that accompanied years of living. A couple of old trunks, a wire mesh dress model, an old black Singer treadle sewing machine. Boxes of Christmas decorations, outgrown children's clothes, a tennis racket and somebody's long-forgotten roller skates.

The movers had left my belongings near the stairs. When Tom and I packed up my apartment, I'd labeled the boxes clearly so I'd know what was in each one. Most of them held books, so many books I wasn't sure how to deal with them. The few wobbly bookcases I owned were far too shabby for this elegant house. All my furniture had been either inherited from my dad—cheap discount store stuff he'd been using since before my mother left us—or acquired during my brief marriage to Jeffrey. None of it was notable in any way, except by its sheer lack of notability.

While Sadie held one of the flashlights aloft, I grabbed the first box off the top of the pile, wrestled it into compliance, and dragged it through the dust to a clear spot out of the main traffic route. "What's in that box?" Sadie said.

"Books." I dusted off my hands and went back for a second. "We're going to stack them by the back wall."

"Why? Don't you want them?"

"I need new bookcases. I don't have any place to display them."

"Uncle Riley could build them for you. He's a carpenter."

"An idea worth considering," I said.

The flashlight beam wobbled. "Can I look at them?"

So much for being my right-hand woman. I reminded myself that time wasn't a consideration here and that keeping Sadie happy was at least as important as organizing my stuff. "You probably won't find it very interesting. There aren't any picture books. But you can look at them. Just treat them with care."

While I lifted and stacked boxes, Sadie knelt and pulled open the flaps to a box of paperbacks. She rummaged around inside, pulled out a book. Studying the cover with a frown of concentration, she said, "*J-A-N-E.* That spells Jane. What does *A-U-S-T-E-N* spell?"

The boxes were heavy, and by now, I'd started to sweat. I paused, swiped my sticky hair back from my face with a grimy hand, and said in surprise, "You know how to read?"

"A little. My best friend at preschool is named Jane."

"But you're four years old."

She looked at me, unblinking, as though puzzled by what her age could possibly have to do with her reading ability.

I hurried to explain. "It's just that most four-year-olds I've met didn't know how to read. I'm impressed."

Solemnly, she told me, "Daddy says I'm precocious."

"Apparently so."

While Sadie lovingly paged through *Pride and Prejudice,* I went back to the heavy boxes of books. I heaved the last of them on top of the pile and returned to where the rest of my belongings waited. Sitting on the dusty floor, I dragged over a box labeled Dad. I cut the seal with a steak knife I'd brought up from the kitchen and peeled back the top.

It was Dad's record albums. A lump formed in my throat as I thumbed through his well-loved collection. Ella Fitzgerald. T-Bone Walker. Robert Johnson. Dave Hanrahan might have been a rock musician, but his heart, his poor, shattered heart, belonged to the blues. And his daughter had grown up listening to these old recordings. I knew them all by heart, had even entertained the idea, during a brief bout of adolescent madness, of becoming a blues singer myself. Common sense, aided by an utterly mediocre singing voice, had prevailed. But I still loved the old music Dad and I had listened to on those long-ago Saturday nights. I'd been too young at the time to understand that he was mourning my mother. By the time I was old enough to understand, I'd become too self-absorbed to care, one of those snotty adolescents for whom life's biggest tragedy is to be uncool, and the epitome of uncoolness was staying home on a Saturday night with my dad, listening to music that was recorded before I was born.

Sometimes, when I look back, I feel the flush of shame all over my body. I imagine that kind of self-absorption is normal for an adolescent, but still I occasionally feel the sting of guilt when I remember how badly I treated my dad during those years.

Already bored with Jane Austen, Sadie had wandered off to some dark corner, where she was rummaging through God only knew what. "Be careful," I shouted to her. "We don't know what's up here. You don't want to get hurt."

"It's just boxes. I'll tell you what they say. *B-E-T-H.* That spells Beth. That was my mom's name."

Beth. Midway through reading the liner notes, I carefully set down the Etta James album I held and took a breath to still the sudden racing of my pulse. I'd promised myself that I wouldn't meddle, had vowed to forget about the mystery surrounding her death. But this wasn't meddling. This was simple curiosity. I cleared my throat and said, "There are boxes up here with your mother's name on them?"

"Yup. And some pictures."

Pictures? I got up, dusted off my butt, and followed the beam of my flashlight to the corner Sadie had wormed her way into. Sure enough, four or five boxes tucked back under the eaves said BETH on the sides. Whether they held trash or treasure, they apparently were all that was left in this house of Tom's late wife. Behind them, stacked beneath the dusty sheet Sadie was holding up, were a half-dozen artist's canvases.

I squeezed in beside my stepdaughter, played the

beam of my flashlight on the top canvas, and studied it in the dim glow of light. It was a pastoral scene, cows and pastures in winter, a red barn in the distance, painted at that golden hour when afternoon blends into evening and shadows fall long and deep. In the bottom right-hand corner, in tiny white lettering, Elizabeth Larkin had signed her work.

Beth had been a painter. A very good one.

I scooched down beside Sadie, tugged the canvases out from behind the boxes, and went through them, one at a time. They were all landscapes, vividly colored, masterful in their use of light and shadow. These works of art would have held their own in any modern art gallery. They were exquisite, Beth's legacy to the world and to her daughters. They should have been proudly displayed for the enjoyment of other people. So why had somebody hidden them up here?

"Your mother painted these," I told Sadie. "Do you remember seeing them before?"

She solemnly shook her head. "They're pretty," she said. "My mom was a good artist, wasn't she?"

"Yes," I said. "She was."

"Can I have them in my room?"

There might be some good reason why Beth's artwork was up here, gathering dust and fading into obscurity. On the other hand, didn't her daughters deserve to have something of their mother to look at? Something to inspire them and give them comfort? "Pick one," I said. "We'll dust it off and hang it in your room. The rest will have to stay here for now."

After a great deal of deliberation, Sadie ended up picking the first painting we'd looked at, the one with the cows and the distant barn. We rewrapped the rest in the sheet and carried the painting downstairs to clean it. Under the kitchen sink I found a soft brush. I gently dusted off the canvas and wiped down the frame with a damp cloth. Then we carried it back upstairs and hung it on the wall in the girls' room.

Sadie and I stood for a long time, drinking it in, before we pronounced it perfect. Then, hand in hand, we headed downstairs for lunch.

We were just finishing our tuna sandwiches when the phone rang. "It's me," Claudia said. "I'm calling to extend the proverbial olive branch. I'm hoping you're not still mad at me. Or if you are, that I can bribe you with chocolate. I just made the most incredible triple fudge layer cake, and I need help eating it. I beg of you, save me from these calories that threaten to destroy me."

"Chocolate," I said. "My biggest weakness. I'd love to come over and help you manage those calories. But I have Sadie with me."

"Bring her. Dylan's been asking when she was coming over again to play. We'll pop a movie in and park them in front of it. They'll be quiet for hours."

"What about the chocolate you-know-what? Tom doesn't like her to eat—" I turned away from the kitchen and whispered into the phone, *"S-U-G-A-R."*

"Sugar!" Sadie shouted gleefully.

At the other end of the phone, Claudia laughed.

"Busted," she said. "Nice try. Give the kid a break. It won't be the first time she's eaten cake at my house. What Tom doesn't know won't hurt him."

I hung up the phone and began clearing the table. "Get your raincoat and your boots, Lady Sadie," I said. "We're going visiting."

Dylan was a robust, handsome child, with rosy cheeks, a thick head of dark, wavy hair, and lively brown eyes. He met us at the door and immediately spirited Sadie off to another area of the house. Maybe the sugar thing wouldn't be an issue after all. "What a cutie," I told Claudia. "I bet in a year or two or five, the girls will be lined up at his door."

"Yes," she said, taking a cake knife from the kitchen drawer and slicing through several layers of dark chocolate. "Unfortunately for everyone involved, my son takes after He Whose Name Shall Not Be Spoken Aloud In My House. Including the part about the girls. Too bad I didn't realize that before I married the turkey." She licked chocolate icing from her finger. "How big?"

"Oh, about half the cake will be just about right."

"Don't tell me. You're one of those alien creatures who can eat anything and not gain weight."

"Guilty as charged."

"I hate your guts."

"I've heard that more than once. But you're not exactly *zaftig* yourself. I doubt one piece of cake is going to hurt you."

"I'll take that in the spirit in which it was meant."

She set a dessert plate holding a huge slice of cake in front of me. "Forks are in the drawer to your right. Thanks for the compliment. But believe me when I say I've worked like a stevedore to maintain this body."

From my stool, I leaned, slid open the drawer, and pulled out two forks. "Nobody would ever guess."

"I run five miles a day, lift weights, and do Pilates three times a week."

I handed her a fork and dug into my cake. "You certainly do seem to have plenty of energy. You must burn the weight right off."

"It's worth what I have to go through. I used to weigh three hundred pounds."

I stopped, forkful of cake halfway to my mouth, and gaped. "You're kidding."

"I am." She grinned and popped a bite of cake into her mouth. "But the look on your face was priceless."

"You really are a bitch."

"Thank you. Seriously, though, I have to watch my weight. I was chunky as a girl. I've been fighting fat my entire life."

"You're definitely winning the battle." I took another bite of cake. "How come you didn't tell me Beth was a painter?"

Claudia slid onto the stool next to mine. "You never asked."

"Clever answer. Sadie and I were in the attic this morning, sorting through my junk, and she unearthed some of Beth's paintings. They're really good. I can't imagine why anybody would store them away in a dark corner of the attic."

"I couldn't say why. I knew she painted. Everyone did. She was really prolific, and she'd started getting some recognition for her work. Six months before she died, she had her own one-woman show at a gallery in Portland. If she'd lived, I suspect she'd have made a big splash on the art scene once she got discovered."

"It just seems a shame that the family would hide her work away, instead of displaying it." I thought about what Claudia had said. "If she was so prolific," I said pensively, "then where's the rest of her work? Sadie and I only found a half-dozen paintings."

"Damned if I know. She sold a few, but I don't know what happened to the rest. There'd probably be a couple hundred of them." Claudia saw the look in my eye, and lifted a hand as though warding off an evil spirit. "Oh, no," she said. "We talked about this, right? Repeat after me: I will not obsess about Beth Larkin. I will not obsess about—"

"I'm not obsessing," I said, taking another bite of cake to prove my point. "I'm just curious. I really like her work, that's all."

The kids wandered into the kitchen then, looking for chocolate cake. Claudia talked them into having sugar-free frozen fruit pops instead, and we dropped the subject. But I didn't forget it. I tried. I focused on everything but Beth. That night at dinner, I kept my mouth shut and listened to what Tom and his mother discussed. After dinner, I played Parcheesi

with the girls, letting Taylor claim victory. I super-
vised baths, read the girls a bedtime story, listened
to their prayers. But all the time, my mind was on
Beth Larkin's artwork.

And the contents of those cardboard boxes.

Eight

"You have to see this, Jules. It's the most amazing security system I've ever seen." Tom had spread the brochure out on the breakfast table, and he was leaning over his plate of egg beaters, devouring the fine print with a fascination I suspected I wouldn't share. It must have something to do with that Y chromosome; even a man with Tom's advanced education found gadgets endlessly captivating. I, on the other hand, lacking that crucial chromosomal distinction, had never found hardware or electronic doodads to hold my interest for longer than, oh, say, three or four seconds.

Trying to disguise my utter lack of interest behind a sleepy yawn, I said, "Oh?"

"This little gem," he said, rapping the brochure with a knuckle, "contains a complex GPS system combined with an alarm so sophisticated that if somebody so much as brushes against your car, it'll go off."

"What happens if *I* brush against my car?"

"It comes with a remote control unit that goes on your key chain. You disarm it the same way you lock and unlock your doors. If anybody comes sneaking around the yard in the middle of the night—"

"Vandals, burglars, the neighbor's cat—"

He fixed me with one of those disapproving husband stares. Because I'd been married before, I recognized it immediately. Every husband carries that stare in his arsenal of weapons. Even so, I was impressed by how well Tom carried it off. He was a virtuoso of disdain. "Don't be that way," he said. "This is important. The alarm will keep people away from your Toyota, and the GPS will prevent you from getting lost again. Plus, it includes 24-hour live access to on-call security advisors. You'll love it, I promise. I've made an appointment to have it installed next Tuesday."

"And how much will that cost?" I skimmed the fine print, saw the price, and whistled. "A little steep, don't you think?" And a little over the top, but I declined to mention that.

Disdain gave way to righteous indignation. Pointing his index finger at me, my husband said, "You can't put a price on your safety."

I dug into my bowl of blueberries, which were on the Thomas Larkin, M.D., list of approved breakfast foods. Lifting the spoon, I said, "There is that to be considered."

"You'll thank me, Jules. Believe me when I say it." Tom glanced at his watch and said, with some irritation, "Where the hell are the girls? We have to leave in ten minutes and they haven't eaten breakfast yet."

I knew they were up and dressed; I'd witnessed it with my own eyes. Normally, Jeannette would have rounded them up by now, but she had an early shampoo and clip, so she'd already left for work. I set down my spoon. "Should I go up and—"

"No." He shoved his chair away from the table. "I'm done anyway. Finish your breakfast. I'll go."

I picked up the brochure and, in the absence of more stimulating reading material, idly perused it while I ate my blueberries. Why I would need some fancy-shmancy high-tech auto security system, I couldn't imagine. Tom was becoming, to say the least, overprotective. Another word for it would be fanatical, but I really didn't want to go there. I was thrilled that he cared; I would have been even more thrilled if he'd cared just a tad less. Did my husband have control issues? I hoped not, because I have a tendency to become claustrophobic without much provocation. I don't do well with restrictions. Telling me what I should and shouldn't eat for breakfast was one thing; although he was serious about it, I took his recommendations with tongue firmly planted in cheek. But if Tom started telling me what to do in a more generic fashion—more so than the average husband might try, that is—the result wouldn't be pretty.

I was taking a bite of English muffin when I heard the commotion. It sounded like the voice of God, accompanied by the furious wailing of a little girl. "Stay there," Tom ordered.

"But, Daddy—"

"You heard me," he said grimly. "Stay put!"

I raised my reading glasses, tilted my head as his hard, angry footsteps descended the uncarpeted stairs. They continued down the hallway, growing louder and more pronounced as he approached the kitchen. He reached the doorway and stopped, his breath coming in hard little gasps, his face flushed scarlet from his hairline to the starched white collar of his dress shirt. In his hand was Beth's painting. The one I had hung in Sadie and Taylor's room.

"What the *hell* do you think you're doing?" he said.

"Eating breakfast?"

"Don't toy with me, Jules. You know what I'm talking about. How dare you go behind my back and defy me this way?"

"I didn't *defy* you. I just—"

"I expressly tell you that I don't want the girls to have any reminders of their mother. And the instant I turn my back, you hang this, this—" So furious he couldn't find words, so red of face that I feared a stroke was imminent, he brandished the painting as though it were a dead rat. Some vile, disgusting Thing. "If you don't call that defiance, then I don't know what is."

"Who the hell are you," I said, "and what have you done with my husband?"

"Stop being cute. This isn't the time or the place for frivolity."

Frivolity? My temper, which I'd so far managed to keep under wraps, lit like a roman candle. "You know what?" I said. "Those girls of yours have lost their mother. They have nothing—*nothing*—of hers to remember her by. It's possible that you mean well, Tom. I really want to give you the benefit of the doubt. But you don't have the right to take her away from them. I don't even understand why you'd want to. She's their mother, for God's sake." I ran a hand through my hair, realized that at some point I'd gotten up from the table and was now pacing. "Do you realize that after my mother left, the only comfort I had was the few reminders I had of her? The photos, the books, the—"

"This isn't about you, Jules." He'd grown cold, and somehow his silence was worse than the yelling. "And it isn't about you telling me how to raise my daughters. I thought we'd already clarified that, but it looks as though you need a reminder."

"Maybe you're the one who needs a reminder. How about a refresher course on being civil to your spouse?"

"You can't go around undermining my authority! You're setting a terrible example for the girls. How are they supposed to understand that I'm the head of this household when my own wife doesn't even acknowledge it?"

"For the love of God, Tom, what century are you living in? Women stopped being men's chattel about the same time as we got the vote. And as far as setting a good example, how do you think it looks to the girls, you rushing in here and reprimanding me like some naughty child? Is this what you want them to think marriage is all about? You could at least have the decency to scream at me in private, where the girls can't hear. Because you can be sure that they're upstairs right now, listening to every word that's coming from our mouths!"

He opened his mouth to speak, glanced toward the ceiling, and clamped his jaw shut. "The painting goes back to the attic," he said in a cold, distant voice. "And we will continue this discussion at a more appropriate time. The girls and I are already late."

And it's all your fault. That was the rest of his sentence, the part he didn't say out loud. But it was implied. It was there, written on his face, in his stance, between the lines of the words he did say, if only I were interested in reading those blame-laden white spaces.

Neither of us said another word. Tom left the painting propped against the kitchen wall, its presence a clear message that he expected me to return it to the place where I'd found it. I listened as the girls followed him downstairs, still loudly protesting his seizure of their precious *objet d'art.* They went outside, Tom uncharacteristically silent, the girls as noisy as a pair of brood hens. I heard the car doors slam, the engine start up, the faint squawk of tires as Tom left the driveway.

The breakfast dishes still sat on the table where we'd left them. Mechanically, I gathered them up, rinsed them in the sink, and loaded the dishwasher.

Both girls had left without eating breakfast. I wasn't sure Tom had even noticed, so intense was his fury toward me. With the wet dishcloth, I wiped down the kitchen table, dropped the crumbs in the sink, then turned on the faucet and rinsed them away.

Who was this man I'd married? The funny, light-hearted, caring man I'd fallen in love with had a dark side I didn't much like. It was a shock to discover he had a temper; the shock worsened when he turned that temper on me. Over something so trivial as an oil painting hung in a place where he didn't think it belonged.

Had his anger really been about the painting? Or had it, at its core, been about something more basic: his belief that, as his wife, I should obey him?

We'd joked about it more than once, this notion of men expecting their wives to kowtow to them, and every time the topic had come up, Tom had seemed to find it as ridiculous as I did. The word "obey" had deliberately been left out of our wedding vows. Even if I'd been a traditionalist, I wasn't a fool. Hell would freeze rock solid before I'd take a vow to obey any man.

But what about Tom? What if he'd been hiding his true feelings for fear of frightening me off? I'd made my opinion on the topic clear; he had to know that I'd run like a scared jackrabbit if I thought he intended to cage me. Was it possible that the man I thought I knew didn't really exist? Was my Tom, the charming man I'd fallen in love with, a figment of my imagination?

My grandmother—she of the lethal frying pan—
had been fond of apocryphal adages. One I particularly remembered: *Marry in haste, repent at leisure.*
When I was a teenager, my cousins and I used to
laugh behind her back. Now I considered that maybe
Gram was right. Had I already, after only a few
weeks of marriage, reached the repentance stage?

Impossible. No way was I that poor a judge of
character. Tom hadn't spoken the words he said to me
this morning because of some overdeveloped male
ego; there'd been something else fueling those words,
something else fueling the intensity of his emotions.
Fear? Anger? Grief? Was he still in mourning for his
first wife? Or had Beth done something so terrible
that the very thought of her sent him into a blind
fury? Was there some rational motivation behind his
seemingly irrational behavior?

Somehow, Beth was the key. I knew it instinctively, even if I didn't know how she was connected,
or what it all meant. I just knew that Beth was at the
center of all this. And as her successor, I was tangled
up in it whether or not I wanted to be.

Upstairs, they called to me, those boxes that had
been shoved way back into the shadows beneath the
eaves. I wondered what secrets they held, wondered
if I dared to try to uncover those secrets.

I considered the possibility that I was being melodramatic, that the boxes held nothing more sinister
than Beth's high school yearbook, a rusted tin box
of recipes, and a moth-eaten cheerleading sweater.

I had to go up there. Tom had made it clear that

he expected me to return the painting. If I'd wanted to be difficult, I could have told him to return the damn thing himself. But that would just prolong the argument. It wouldn't serve anybody's purposes. On the other hand, if I took it back up to the attic myself, I'd have a legitimate reason to be up there. And in order to squeeze the canvas back into the tiny space where it had been stored, wouldn't I have to first move those boxes that were in the way? The ones that had Beth's name written on the sides?

To fortify myself for the job ahead, I took the blueberries from the fridge and, leaning over the kitchen sink, ate the rest of them right from the cardboard container. Tom would be proud of my antioxidant intake. If he was still speaking to me, that is. I tossed the container in the trash, grabbed the painting, and scooted up two flights of stairs to the attic.

At least today it was sunny. I'd brought a flashlight, but the windows faced the east, so the morning sun that streamed in illuminated all but the darkest corners. With barely a twinge of guilt, I set to work dragging Beth's boxes out of their hiding place and into the square of light that fell on the floor in front of those two gable windows. With a heavy sigh, I tucked the painting back where I'd found it, beneath the dusty old sheet. I'd tried to do right. It wasn't my fault that Tom was a dunderhead who failed to understand the needs of his daughters. I'd continue to fight the good fight. Maybe, sooner or later, some of what I was telling him would sink in. Another of

Gram's old sayings came to mind: *You can always tell a doctor, but you can't tell him much.* Yeah. We had that going on in spades.

The first box I opened held treasures, but not the kind I'd hoped to find. There were no clues in here—clues to what, I wasn't sure—just random pieces of a woman's life, items that brought Beth Larkin alive for me. I took out a small, wooden music box, round and made of cherrywood. When I opened it, I found a winter scene inside, a charming cottage situated on the frozen steppes. I wound the key and the theme from *Dr. Zhivago* poured out. A little tinny; a little off-key, but its haunting melody sent goose bumps racing up and down my spine. As it played, I could clearly see the faces of Yuri and Lara, could feel the bittersweet agony of their ill-fated love. As a young girl, I'd yearned for a love like theirs, a love that transcended time and war and even death. It had taken me a while to understand that a love like Yuri and Lara shared existed only between the covers of Russian novels.

But the ghost of that romantic young girl still resided in me, and I felt a strong kinship with Beth Larkin, for at some point in her too-brief life, she'd known those same yearnings.

I set aside the jewelry box, picked up a bottle of inexpensive perfume. Uncapped it and took a whiff. The scent was delicate, faintly floral, not overpowering, but just right.

Her yearbook was next. I opened it, flipped through the pages, realized I didn't know her maiden name. There were bound to be a half-dozen Elizabeths. The best I could do was guess.

I was paging slowly through the club pages—glee club, golf club, camera club—when I heard the distinctive thud of the front door slamming downstairs. Book in hand, I went to the window, but it looked out over the side yard, so I couldn't see the driveway.

I moved to the head of the stairs and peered down into the upstairs hallway. "Hello?"

No answer. But I hadn't imagined hearing that door. Somebody was in the house. As Tom's wife—even if we were barely on speaking terms right now—I supposed it was my duty to go down there and make sure some junkie wasn't making off with the silver. There probably weren't too many junkies in Newmarket, but I wasn't so naïve that I believed there were none. Even a town like this one had its share of crime. Hadn't I already fallen victim to it myself?

On the other hand, maybe it was Tom, come home to apologize for going off on me the way he had. I descended the attic stairs and paused in the upstairs hallway. With a tremulous smile, I said, "Tom? Is that you?"

Still no answer. But I could hear sounds from the kitchen. A drawer opening and then closing. Just my luck. Somebody really was stealing the silver.

Book in hand, I crept down the last staircase to the ground floor. At this time of day, with the sun at the back of the house, the front hall had all the ambiance of a dungeon. At the end of the hall, morning light flooded the kitchen, and footsteps—footsteps that sounded furtive to me—moved about the room. I took a breath. "Hello?" I said one last time. "Who's there?"

Nobody answered, but the refrigerator door opened and closed. What kind of intruder helped himself to the leftovers in the fridge? I looked around for a weapon, decided that Beth's yearbook would have to do. Heavy as it was, I could give somebody a pretty mean whack if I had to. I crept down the hallway, raised the book over my head, took another breath for courage, and stepped boldly into the kitchen.

Just as the intruder was stepping out.

We collided. I let out a soft little squeak and raised my weapon. Riley nearly dropped his dish of ice cream, and I was halfway to knocking him senseless with the yearbook when my brain made the proper association and managed to halt my arms before the book could connect with his head.

My brother-in-law was quick. He ducked and danced, somehow managing to hold on to his bowl of ice cream while at the same time yanking the iPod earbuds from his ears. "Christ in a sidecar," he said. "What in holy hell are you doing?"

"I thought you were a burglar." Now that the time for fear had passed, my heart was speeding faster than Mario Andretti on race day. I lowered the book and struggled to hold steady the knees that had gone as weak as day-old spaghetti. "I called out, but you didn't answer."

"I couldn't hear you. Headphones."

"I can see that now. You scared the bejesus out of me."

"Likewise. My friggin' life flashed in front of my eyes. That book's a lethal weapon."

"That was the idea." I eyed his dish of ice cream with suspicion. "I thought you lived in your own apartment over the carriage house. Don't you have a refrigerator?"

"Yeah. But mine isn't stocked with Ben & Jerry's Cherry Garcia. Which is starting to melt. Do you mind?"

"Would it matter if I did?"

"Probably not. I'm headed for the front porch. You're welcome to join me as long as you promise to let me eat in peace."

I followed him out to the veranda. "Why aren't you at work?" I said. "You're always hanging around the house. I don't see any evidence that you're gainfully employed."

"I'm flattered that you've taken so much notice of my comings and goings." He plunked down on a wicker chair, raised his booted feet, and leaned back on his tailbone. "I'm between jobs. Where'd you find the yearbook?"

"In a box in the attic."

"Snooping again, were you?"

"I'm not going to dignify that with an answer. I was looking for Beth's picture in here, but I don't know her maiden name, so I couldn't find her."

"Shickler. Now can I eat my ice cream?"

"I've already forgotten you're here." I opened the book to the senior section, paged through it until I reached the *S*'s. "Sanders, Sears, Selby. Shickler," I said. "Elizabeth."

Even with the pouffy 1980s hair, Elizabeth Shickler was stunning, blond and delicate and beautiful, with a smile that could melt marble. Finally, I knew where Sadie had gotten her looks from; the family resemblance between the two was as strong as that between Tom and Taylor. So this was my predecessor. This was the woman who'd had it all and tossed it away when she jumped off the railing of the Swift River Bridge.

Or was pushed off.

Practically devouring Beth's photo, I said distractedly, "Riley? Why are Elizabeth's paintings crammed into a dark corner under the eaves in the attic?"

Riley paused, his spoon halfway to his mouth. Mildly, he said, "I didn't know they were."

"Some of them are. About a half-dozen. But Claudia tells me there should be more."

He resumed eating. "I'd think there would be," he said through a mouthful of Cherry Garcia. "Beth painted for years."

"So where are they? The rest of them?"

"Beats me. Maybe Tom sold the lot of them after she was gone. He never said a word to me."

"Hmm. Maybe." I studied Beth's senior portrait, trying to find the answer in her face. If only I knew what the question was. "That seems to be a sore spot with him. We had a massive go-round this morning because I brought one of them down from the attic and hung it in the girls' room. I did it because Sadie asked me to, and I thought it would be nice for the girls to have something of their mother's to remember her by, but Tom went into total meltdown mode over it. I saw a side of my husband I'd never witnessed before."

"And that should tell you, just in case my words the other night didn't get through your thick skull, that some things are better left alone. The topic of Beth Larkin being one of them."

"I don't understand why! What the hell is the big deal, Riley? What's the deep, dark secret that everybody knows but nobody's telling me? I'm starting to feel like a pariah."

"There is no deep, dark secret. Tom's been through a lot. We've all been through a lot. Elizabeth's death was sudden and senseless. Maybe you don't understand this, but it takes time to recover from that kind of loss. We're all just doing the best we can."

I slowly closed the yearbook. "Are you implying that I don't know about loss?"

Riley shrugged. "If the shoe fits…" And he took another bite of ice cream.

"I had a baby."

The words tumbled out of my mouth before I could stop them. He fixed me with a steady gaze that was impossible to interpret. His silence seemed to be urging me to continue, but it could just as easily have stemmed from a total lack of interest. I wasn't sure why I was telling him this, but it was too late at this point to turn back. "I carried her for nine months," I said. "I wanted that little girl—*loved* that little girl—so much. Jeffrey and I named her Angel."

Riley was silent, but his eyes weren't unkind. "Something went wrong in the delivery room," I said. "We're still not sure what happened. Angel didn't make it." The words sounded so simple, so innocuous. So detached from the crushing heaviness of the meaning behind them. "My beautiful, perfect little girl, the little girl I'd carried for nine months and already loved with all my heart, died before she could take her first breath." I stopped because my voice had become tremulous, and I didn't want to show weakness in front of him. I took a breath to steady it. "So don't tell me I don't know about loss."

He rested the bowl of ice cream in his lap and said simply, "I'm sorry."

"I'm not asking for pity. I just want you to know where I'm coming from. After Angel died—" I closed my eyes for an instant. When I opened them again, Riley's gaze was fixed on my face as though the world began and ended there. "After Angel died," I began again, "Jeffrey just couldn't deal with it. He couldn't look at my face without thinking of her. It was simply too much for him. So he left. He moved on to a new life and left me to deal with my own grief alone. It was just as well. It hadn't been much of a marriage to begin with. Still, it was one more blow after losing Angel. Then, a few months after our divorce, I lost my dad. So I've seen more loss in the last couple of years than most people have. It hasn't been easy. But I'm not the kind of person to dwell on it. I still get up every morning and greet the day, grateful to be alive. And it's getting better. Sometimes I'll go for a day or two without thinking about her. I know that's a sign that I'm healing. It can be hard to talk about Angel, but I still do, because if I stop talking about her, it'll be as though she never existed. And that would kill me. So, no, I don't understand why Tom would be so desperate to forget someone he loved. Because I could never do that."

"We all grieve in different ways."

"Maybe so, but certain emotions, certain responses, are universal."

"Has it occurred to you that maybe he feels betrayed? Rejected? Abandoned? Maybe even a little guilty? Your daughter's death, terrible as it was—and I'm not trying to minimize your pain— was one of those cruel tricks of nature. A tragedy, but apparently not preventable. You couldn't have known ahead of time that something would go wrong. It was just a miserable twist of fate. But Beth killed herself. She *chose* to die. Chose to end her marriage to Tom, to leave her family. That's a pretty strong statement to make about their marriage. If it were my wife who'd done that, you can believe I'd be spending more than a little time in brutal self-analysis, wondering whether, if I'd done something different, said something different, *been* something different, the end result would have been different."

"You think he feels responsible."

"Of course he does. It's human nature. When somebody close to us commits suicide, we can't help feeling at least somewhat responsible. Because despite what we like to believe, living in this hedonistic culture, we *are* our brother's keeper."

What he said made sense. It was possible that Tom's behavior arose from guilt because he hadn't done whichever random thing might have prevented his wife from stepping off the side of that bridge. Riley's words should have comforted me. So why didn't they?

I studied that senior portrait for a long time. Granted, the photo had been taken many years ago. But wouldn't it have shown in her eyes? Wouldn't there have been some hint of sadness, some intangible something to indicate that this young woman would someday choose to end her own life? Maybe I was being fanciful, but I saw nothing of the sort. The Elizabeth Shickler of the high school yearbook was a straightforward, open, smiling young woman who gave no hint of a dark and troubled future.

There was also nothing in her artwork to suggest that she was troubled. Yes, I'd heard all the theories about the link between creativity and depression. But there was nothing melancholy about the paintings I'd seen. They'd been full of color, flooded with dancing light. How could a woman paint something so lovely, so light and airy, so *sensitive,* and then go out and kill herself? Suicide just didn't seem to fit with the image I was gradually building in my mind of Elizabeth Shickler Larkin.

But most of all, I couldn't see her deserting her

family, choosing to leave them behind, choosing to inflict upon them the kind of pain she couldn't have failed to know they would experience with her loss. Could the woman who painted those exquisite paintings, so full of heart and emotion, have been so callous in real life that she didn't care how much her husband and daughters suffered? Suicide is seldom an impulsive deed. Most people who kill themselves think about it for a long time before acting on their feelings. Beth's daughters had to be her whole world. Although I'd known my daughter only for the nine months I carried her, my mother-love was all-consuming. Unless there was something fundamentally wrong with her—which I had yet to discover—Beth's feelings had to be the same. It was a universal emotion, the love of a mother for her child. Had Angel lived, I could never, ever have left her. It was my conviction, based on everything I'd learned about her, that Beth Larkin couldn't have left her girls, either.

Not deliberately, anyway.

Which brought me right back to my earlier conclusion: Somebody else had made the decision for her.

I broke for lunch, wolfed down a Lean Cuisine, chasing it with a bowl of the Cherry Garcia that Riley seemed so fond of. By early afternoon, I reached the last box. Whatever it held would be the final word on Beth Larkin. The last of her secrets—at least the secrets this attic held—would be revealed to me. I tried not to be relieved that it was almost over. I'd been on this wild-goose chase since breakfast, and I wasn't any closer to the truth than I'd been four hours ago. Sighing, I peeled back the packing tape and opened the flaps.

When I saw what was inside, I considered just closing the box back up without going any further. The box was crammed with books, and I'd already seen enough of my own books this week to last me a lifetime. But I'd come this far, and I'm not the kind of person to quit. Even when quitting might be the smarter course, I've been known to plow on through. At this point, it couldn't hurt me to thumb through Beth's books and find out what she liked to read.

Her collection was eclectic. A fistful of mystery novels. A few cookbooks, some art tomes, a book on digital photography. A couple of coffee-table books, meant for casual viewing instead of serious reading. And at the bottom of the box, a dog-eared paperback copy of *Dr. Zhivago*. Aha! I knew it! I knew there'd been more to it than just that tinny music. Somehow, I knew Beth had been as enchanted by Yuri and Lara as I was.

I picked up *Dr. Zhivago,* opened it to the first chapter, and began reading. Pasternak's words instantly drew me into a landscape that was both exotic and brutally beautiful, and I had to force myself to stop reading after a few pages. Otherwise, Tom might come home tonight to find me sitting here in semidarkness, flashlight beam trained on the page, tears streaming down my cheeks and ruining the pages, all because of the unjustness of the Bolshevik Revolution and Lara and Yuri's doomed love affair.

Enough already. It was time I left this dark place where day and night were interchangeable, and ventured back out into the sunlight before I turned into a mushroom. I closed the book and was about to drop it back into the box when a folded piece of paper fell from between the pages and fluttered to the floor.

Some people would have returned it to the book unread. But if you know anything about me at all by this point, you'll realize that isn't my style. Maybe if you held a gun to my head. Otherwise, there wasn't a snowball's chance in hell that I wouldn't read whatever was on that piece of paper.

I picked it up, unfolded it, flattened it out on my knee. It appeared to be a note of some kind. One that had been written but never sent.

K,

He's found out the truth. Don't ask how; it doesn't really matter now. Oh, God, what am I going to do? I can feel the hounds of hell closing in on me, their hot breath on the back of my neck. I'm not sure how much longer I can hold out. He was so furious, I thought he'd kill me. I don't know what he'll do now. I could lose my children over this. Both of them. What if he tells? If the truth comes out, what legal recourse would I have against him? Against either of them? I'm afraid the law wouldn't look too kindly on me right now.

I'm so scared. How did I end up in this god-awful mess? I have no illusions about the ease of extricating myself. I could end up losing everything. To be honest, at this point, I fear for my life. If you'd seen him, you'd understand. I've become paranoid, certain that I'm being followed. But of course, whenever I turn around, nobody's there. Just the ghosts that I can't seem to shake. Was it worth the fear and the pain I'm going through now? If I say yes, then I'm a fool. If I say no, I'm a liar. What kind of woman does that make me?

Please tell me it will be all right. Lie to me if you have to. I just need the comfort of hearing it from somebody else's mouth. Tell me I'll get through this. I have to, for the sake of my children. If I don't—no. I don't even want to go there. But I don't have a choice, do I? I have to go there. Because this is serious. If I don't make it through this, you have to swear that you'll watch over my kids. They're the only thing that really matters. They have a future ahead of them, while mine is looking less and less promising.

Beth

Whoa. Reading Beth's words was like being slapped in the face with a wet towel. The snap, the shock, the sting. I reached the end, retraced my steps, reread the letter carefully, every word she'd written, every word she'd left unsaid. Who the hell was K? Better yet, who was the "he" she referred to? And exactly what was it that he knew?

This wasn't good. A sick feeling rose in my stomach, and for an instant, I felt light-headed. What was going on here? What had happened to make Beth so afraid? Because that much was clear. She was terrified that she would lose her children. Maybe even her life.

And she had. Damn it, she had lost her life. Was this the proof I needed that something other than suicide had taken place on the bridge that night? That some unknown person had waited for the perfect moment, and found it one summer night in the swirling waters brewing beneath the Swift River Bridge?

The paper in my hand was a crucial piece of evidence. It needed to be seen by somebody. Like Dwight Pettingill. He of the Big Mac and the lite beer. Newmarket's finest. Groaning at my internal vision of this particular boy in blue, I could only hope that the Newmarket PD had somebody just a tad finer than Dwight. A tad less provincial. Dare I hope there was a police chief? Somebody who knew their ass from their elbow? Somebody who wasn't Dwight?

I shoved the letter into my pocket and dragged the boxes back under the eaves. Trembling with excitement, I trotted down the attic stairs, circled around the upstairs stairway railing, and began my descent to the ground floor.

The sun had moved around to this side of the

house, suffusing the entryway with a golden glow. I was halfway down the stairs, my mind on the note and what it might mean, when I took a step down and lost my footing. It happened so quickly, I didn't have time to react. One instant I was on my feet. The next, I was pitching forward into empty space.

I hit my tailbone against the edge of a step, bounced off it, and slammed my head into the newel post with a crack that was probably heard in five counties. I landed awkwardly, on my rump, one ankle twisted impossibly beneath me. I lay there gasping, understanding for the first time what the expression "seeing stars" meant. I think I passed out for a minute. Or maybe it was an hour. All I know is that when I finally came to, everything hurt. I felt like I'd slammed headfirst into a concrete wall without benefit of a crash helmet. My tailbone must surely be shattered—it wouldn't hurt this much if it wasn't— and my ankle, my poor, throbbing ankle, was starting to swell.

I raised my head and tried to focus on the coatrack that stood in the corner, but I kept seeing two of them. Considering how hard I'd hit my head, this wasn't any great surprise. But it still wasn't good news. I tried to sit up, but it was impossible. My balance was completely gone, and I simply fell back over, betrayed by my own body, which was as floppy as a rag doll. If not for the stairs climbing directly to the heavens right in front of me, I wouldn't have been able to tell up from down.

"Shit," I said thickly. "Shit, piss, fuck, damn."

Nobody answered. Nothing moved around me, save for the dust motes that floated in a leisurely manner above my head. I watched them, fascinated by their reflective qualities. *Tsk, tsk.* Looked like Jeannette wasn't quite the perfect housekeeper she wanted people to believe she was.

My mind wandered. What time was it? I was too whacked-out to know how long I'd been lying here, but not so far gone I couldn't wonder how much longer it would be before somebody came home and found me. It might be hours. Meanwhile, my ankle continued to swell. It was probably broken. For all I knew my ass could be broken, as well. I'd hit it hard enough on the way down.

I reached up and touched my head, wincing at the pain that went roaring through my skull at even the slightest touch. I didn't seem to be bleeding; apparently it hadn't cracked open like a melon when it slammed into solid mahogany. That was the good news, and I took some comfort from the knowledge that I probably wasn't dying. But I needed medical attention. The sooner the better, if only for the blessed analgesic relief of the drugs they'd surely give me.

Panic set in. I cleared my throat. "Help!" I croaked. "Somebody please help me!" I felt a little foolish, like a cartoon character. Sweet Polly Purebred, tied to the railroad tracks, waiting for Underdog to come and rescue her. Or was it Dudley Do-Right who rescued Sweet Polly? My fuzzy brain wasn't quite sure. "Help!" I said again, louder this time, and with more conviction. Screw it. I might not like playing the helpless female role, but sometimes you don't have a choice. Like it or not, when that role is thrust upon you, there's not a lot you can do except pray to God that somebody comes along and saves your sorry ass.

I waited. On the street outside, a car passed, the steady boom-boom of its stereo vibrating the floor I lay on. Nobody was going to come. I was going to lie here with a broken ankle, a cracked skull, and possible internal injuries, until I expired. When they finally came home, they'd find me dead on the floor. And when the pathologist was done tampering with my poor, battered body, he'd shake his head and say, "If only they'd found her in time."

"Help!" I screeched, as loud as I could manage. "For God's sake, help me!"

Nobody came. I slept again. I know they always tell you not to let a person with a concussion go to sleep, but to hell with what they say. Sleep was a welcome respite from the pain. Being awake was the hard part.

Sometime later, I was awakened by the slamming of a car door. For an instant, I was disoriented, and wondered why I was lying on the floor. My brain didn't immediately make the connection between floor, staircase, and throbbing body. But the knowledge came back to me on a wave of pain and nausea. I wet my lips, moved my tongue around inside my arid mouth to moisten it, and yelled again. "Help! Somebody please help me!"

Silence. "HELP ME!" I shouted with my last reserve of strength. "HELP ME, PLEASE!"

I thought I heard footsteps, but maybe it was my imagination. Or the unfulfilled wishes of an overfull bladder. *I'll never drink Diet Coke again,* I promised myself. *Never, never, never again.*

A door opened somewhere in the house, and a man's voice—the sweetest, most welcome voice I'd ever heard—said, "Julie?"

I wet my tongue again. "Help," I croaked. "Front hall."

The footsteps came nearer, and then Riley loomed over me, his mouth agape. "Holy mother of the sweet baby Jesus," he breathed.

"Exactly. Try to imagine this…from my perspective."

"Are you hurt?" he said, dropping to his knees beside me. "What happened?"

I was capable of responding to just one question at a time. "Pretty obvious," I said, choosing the latter, the only one that was recent enough so I could actually remember it. "I fell."

"Hold still." His hands were exceedingly gentle on my poor, broken skull as he felt for fractures. I winced, and he continued his exploration, moving southward, methodically and thoroughly checking bones as he went.

"Hey," I said at one point. "Watch it."

"I'm not molesting you. I was a medic in the Gulf War. I may not have a fancy medical degree like my brother does, but I know what I'm doing."

"Lucky for me," I said thickly, "that you're between jobs."

"I don't think anything's broken. You'll want an X-ray to be sure. And there's one hell of a lump on your head."

"Hit the newel post on the way down. Surprised you didn't hear it."

The corner of his mouth twitched. At least I thought it did. Hard to say for sure when I was seeing two of him. "Can you sit up?" he said.

"Sure. Just feels like I'm on one of those sit-and-spin toys. And my vision's greatly improved. I now see two of everything." I gave him a dorky grin. "Did you know you have four eyes?"

All four of his eyes rolled heavenward. "We need to get you to the hospital," he said firmly.

"Good plan. Just help me up. I'll walk…to car."

"Right. That should work. Damn it, Julie, how the hell did you manage this?"

"Beats me. I stepped down, and…no footing. Just…splat."

Still on his knees, he glanced past my shoulder, spied something on the floor, and crawled past me to get it. "Maybe," he said, rocking back on his heels, "these had something to do with it." He held up the two AA batteries he'd picked up off the floor. "Unless you were carrying these—" He paused, and I shook my head in denial, sending a stabbing pain from my scalp to my toenails. "Then somebody must've left them on the stairs," he said. "You hit these, on those uncarpeted stairs, and you'd just roll off into the wild blue yonder."

"Yes," I said, a vague memory prodding at my brain, a memory of the moment before I fell, that brief instant of surprise as my foot landed on something and kept going. "My foot rolled…I took a header into empty space."

"One of the girls must've left them there. I'll be having a talk with Tom tonight. They have to be made aware of how dangerous it is to leave things on the stairs."

"No." My brain was fuzzy, but this one thing I knew. I'd been up and down those stairs a dozen times since breakfast, and the batteries hadn't been there. If the girls hadn't left them, and they hadn't been there the last time I went upstairs, who had put them there? And why?

Riley pulled his cell phone from its belt clip and said, "Hang in there, Cinderella. I'm calling your coach."

I wasn't sure which was worse, the mortification of being lifted on a stretcher into an ambulance by two grim-faced EMTs who looked to be about twelve years old, or the further humiliation of being stripped in the E.R. while my brother-in-law stood guard over my poor, wretched body. It was a dead tie. At least Riley had the good grace to look away while I was being undressed like a Barbie doll and reclothed in the latest hospital fashion. He left the cubicle completely while I used a bedpan to empty my bursting bladder. Afterward, I begged the nurses to let him stay. I didn't want to be left alone with all these well-meaning strangers poking and prodding and hovering over me. Riley had called Tom, and he was on his way. In the interim, my brother-in-law was pressed into duty as Tom's stand-in.

My husband still hadn't arrived when they sent me down to X-ray, but by that time, they'd given me a shot of Demerol, and I was safely ensconced in la-la land, thanks to the magical powers of pharmaceuticals. They ran a CAT scan to make sure I hadn't fractured anything. Then, after what seemed an eternity, they wheeled me back up to the E.R., where I found my husband waiting, his handsome face taut with concern. "So glad you're here," I said as he stood beside my bed, my fingers threaded with his. "I've been so scared."

"Not half as scared as I've been." Tom's blue eyes—what I could see of them—searched mine as if he expected to find the Hope Diamond buried somewhere in their depths. "You could've broken your neck," he said. "You could have—" He stopped, shook his head in horror at what might have happened. "I don't know what I'd do if I lost you. Listen, Jules—" He glanced around, leaned closer to speak to me privately. "I'm so sorry about this morning. I was an ass. I had no business going off on you like that. You had no way of knowing."

"No problemo," I said. "I've already forgotten. Man, these drugs are great. Where'd Riley go?"

"I sent him home. There wasn't any need for him to stay."

"I'm serious," I said. "You got mad and said things you didn't mean. You're off the hook."

It wasn't the absolute truth, but there was enough truth in it to assuage any guilt I might have felt about lying. I hadn't forgotten, but I'd managed to forgive Tom for his outburst. I'd given it a great deal of thought after my conversation with Riley, who'd opened at least one or two closed doors and let in the light. At least now I believed I understood my husband's motivation. I might not agree with it, but agreement wasn't necessary to understanding.

The curtain at the foot of the bed parted, and the intern who'd examined me stepped inside the cubicle, clipboard in hand. She saw Tom, recognized him, and barely gave me a glance. What the hell, I was just the patient. Not a necessary participant in this interaction at all.

"Dr. Larkin," she said warmly. "I have the results of your wife's CAT scan."

Together, they stepped back outside, and I lay there staring at the ceiling and listening to the low murmur of their voices as they conferred, one doctor to another, too softly for me to make out what they were saying. Eventually, the curtain parted again and Tom came back alone.

"Hey," he said softly.

I opened my eyes, saw his blurry face, and smiled wearily. "Must have drifted off," I said. "What's the verdict, Doc?"

"You have a nasty ankle sprain. You'll have to stay off it for a few days. We're going to fit you with an

air cast. It'll give you the support you need until
your ankle's healed enough to support you again on
its own. You also have one whopper of a concussion.
Dr. Jankowski wanted to keep you overnight for ob-
servation, but I pointed out that as a physician, I'm
fully capable of doing any observing that needs to
be done, with the added benefit that we sleep in the
same bed."

"Mmm. Convenient. So I'm being sprung?"

"You're being sprung, just as soon as we get the
air cast fitted and the paperwork processed." He
paused. "You took a nasty hit to the head. It's a miracle your brains aren't splattered all over the entryway like scrambled eggs."

"Proves how hard my head really is. Now I know
how Humpty-Dumpty felt."

"I swear to God, Jules, those girls of mine are
going to get a piece of my mind they won't soon
forget. I've lost track of the number of times I've told
them not to leave toys on the stairs. Maybe a good
look at you, with your two black eyes, will put the
fear of God into them."

"Black eyes?"

"It's really not that noticeable. At least not yet.
It'll be worse tomorrow. But you have bigger things
to worry about than looking like a prizefighter who
just went down for the count. Come on, let's get you
dressed."

Something tickled the back of my brain, something important that I couldn't seem to remember.
Something that had to do with my clothes. What was

it? But it was gone, the thought never fully formed, escaped before I could even reach out and try to catch it.

Somehow, Tom managed to prop me upright in a wheelchair, and he dressed me the way he'd have dressed a small child. Thanks to the Demerol—not to mention the concussion—I was too out of it to put up much resistance. I just sat in my wheelchair, hunched over like an old woman, while he lifted and arranged each limb. The nurse bustled in with the air cast. Between the two of them, they figured it out, wrapping it around my calf until it fit snugly. Tom signed a sheaf of papers with his illegible physician's scrawl, pocketed the packet of pain pills we'd been issued, and wheeled me out into a small-town dusk.

It was a lovely Indian summer evening, but I was too loopy to notice. Getting me into the car was a chore, because I had absolutely no control over my body. My limbs just flipped and flopped, and Tom finally had to pick me up and drop me into the passenger seat like a sack of potatoes. He clicked my seat belt and adjusted it, planted a tender kiss on my temple, and walked around to the driver's side of the car.

We were halfway home before my befuddled brain suddenly kicked into gear and I remembered what it was that had eluded me earlier. Beth's note. The one I'd been planning to take to the police. I'd shoved it in my pocket just before I stepped on those batteries and went ass over teakettle. Just to reassure myself that it was still there, I slid my hand into the pocket of my jeans. Felt around, then dug deeper. Nothing. I knew I'd put it in there, so where was it? I flicked a glance at Tom, but he was focused on his driving and wasn't paying me the least attention. Maybe I was wrong. After all, I'd taken a hard blow to the head. My memory was bound to be a little shaky. Maybe I'd put it in the other pocket. I furtively checked, shoving my hand in deep, all the way to the bottom, and scrabbling around like a crab scavenging for food on the ocean floor. But it was pointless. An exercise in futility.

Because both my pockets were empty.

Nine

I tried not to worry about what had happened to the note, but I couldn't help myself. Had it fallen out of my pocket at some point and been picked up later by a cleaning person who read it and then discarded it? Or would the hospital maintenance crew have been trained to turn in to the nurse's station any random papers they found on the floor? I'd been gone for over an hour to X-ray. All that time, my clothing had been sitting unattended in the E.R. cubicle. Anybody could have rifled through my pockets. Riley had been there, and Tom. Dr. Jankowski, and a never-ending stream of nurses in their modern-day uniforms of pastel polyester pants and tops that featured happy little cartoon animals. The nursing profession had come a long way from the days when they wore white dresses with starched collars.

All considerations of nursing attire aside, I had a

serious problem. Somebody was in possession of Beth's note. Somebody who wasn't the police. Or me.

And I had no idea who.

To say the idea was unsettling is an understatement, but once we reached the house, I didn't have time to worry about it, because everybody in Newmarket, it seemed, was there to greet the returning invalid. Claudia was there, and even Monica, the teenage babysitter. A stone-faced Riley remained silent, but Claudia greeted me with a gasp and an, "Oh, you poor thing!" which made me suspect my appearance wasn't quite as innocuous as Tom had claimed. Sadie, big-eyed and concerned, plastered herself to my side, while Taylor, reticent as ever, stayed in the background, although her eyes never seemed to leave me. While Tom got me settled in semi-comfort on the living room couch, with a feather pillow that was heavenly and a blanket I didn't really need, Jeannette hovered anxiously, wringing her hands and casting furtive glances at Tom. "This is not my fault," I heard her say once, to nobody in particular. "Nobody is going to blame this on me."

Since nobody was accusing her of anything, I thought it strange. Was she expecting to be criticized for her housekeeping skills, allowing random objects to show up in even more random places? Or was she expecting at any minute that I would say to her, "Aha! It was you who drove home from work in the middle of the day to place those batteries on the stairs so that when I came back down from the attic, I'd fall and break my ass."

For an instant, I semi-seriously considered saying it, just to see what would happen. But I wasn't into deliberate cruelty, even towards a woman who seemed to hate me for no better reason than the fact that she could. Since the night I'd heard her arguing with Tom in the kitchen, our relationship—if you could call it that—had been civil but strained. I knew she wanted me gone from this house, from Tom's life. But I couldn't imagine her stooping so low as to booby-trap the stairs in the hopes that I'd break my neck. Jeannette might hate me, but I couldn't see her sitting in a jail cell, awaiting sentencing for her murder conviction.

But somebody had placed those batteries on the stairs. Somebody had been in the house while I was upstairs in the attic sighing over Yuri and Lara. Riley was the logical answer. He had free rein of the house, was in and out all day, and lived right there on the property. He'd already come in and scared the crap out of me earlier in the day. It would have been easy for him, on a casual walk-through, to pull two double-A's from his pocket and set them in a spot on the wooden staircase where I couldn't possibly miss stepping on them.

But to what end? What possible reason could Riley have for wanting to see me hurt? He had no reason to hate me. As far as I could tell, my brother-in-law was an amiable, mildly sarcastic slacker who was too laid-back in his dealings with the world to muster the energy to hate anyone.

The girls had been at school, which ruled them

out. That left the field open to the other six billion people on the planet. The doors were never locked. In a town the size of Newmarket, that was common practice. And knowing how the gossip vine works in small towns, probably a well-known fact. Anybody who had a strong inclination to steal the silver could have done it a long time ago.

But I was too tired to think about it anymore. My brain felt like it was clogged with molasses. The Demerol was starting to wear off, and my body was a single dull, throbbing ache. I tried to find an inch of me that didn't hurt, but there didn't seem to be one. Tom, taking note of my pale face and glassy eyes, declared that I'd had enough company for now. And like my own personal Prince Charming, he scooped me up in his arms and carried me upstairs to bed.

I was grateful for the change of venue. The bedroom was cool and dark, our bed soft and cozy. He undressed me, tucked the covers under my chin, then went into the bathroom. I heard water running, and then he was back, with a paper cup. "Here," he said, "take this."

I opened my eyes, tried to focus on the big blue pills in his hand, but I couldn't tell if there were two or four of them. He propped me up and I took them, one at a time, and washed them down with cool tap water. "What are they?" I asked afterward.

"Something to make you feel better. You should sleep like a baby."

"And wake up feeling refreshed?"

"You fell down the stairs, Jules. You're bruised from head to toe. I don't want to sound discouraging, babe, but tomorrow isn't going to be a cakewalk."

"I suppose I should thank you for telling it to me straight."

Empty cup in hand, he loomed over the bed, his shadow on the wall greatly exaggerated, and said, "Try to get some sleep."

That shouldn't be a problem. I was already halfway there. "What about you?" I asked groggily.

"I'm going back downstairs for a while. Don't worry, I'll check on you regularly."

"I know you will." I reached out, and he grasped the hand I offered. "You take such good care of me."

"Go to sleep, Jules. I'll be up to bed in a bit."

I don't remember him letting go of my hand. One minute I was awake; the next minute I wasn't. Tom was right. I did sleep like a baby. Assuming that babies experience strange and disturbing dreams, that is.

They were almost hallucinogenic in their intensity, those dreams, so vivid, so very real to me, that afterward I couldn't have sworn in a court of law that they didn't really happen. Even the impossible parts seemed feasible. At first, like E.T., I was trying to phone home to get a ride from the hospital, but I didn't have my cell phone with me, and the head nurse refused to let me make a call from the nurse's station. So I stood outside the entrance, watching strangers come and go, none of them with cell phones until three teenage boys in a souped-up old Barracuda pulled up to the entrance, hip-hop music playing so loud it shook the sidewalk. I knew these dudes would have cell phones, and when I approached the driver and asked to borrow his, he looked put-upon, but handed the phone over readily enough.

Except that I couldn't seem to dial the number. Every time I tried, my fingers slipped off the buttons, or I accidentally hit the wrong digit and had to start over. I just couldn't make the connection go through. My frustration kept building, and the kid was getting impatient, and finally he told me if I wanted a ride home, I should climb into the backseat.

I don't remember getting into the car, but suddenly there I was, sitting in the back of the Barracuda, hip-hop vibrating all around me and Beth Larkin sitting beside me. Except that it wasn't the smiling, blond Beth I'd seen in the yearbook photo. This Beth had pasty skin and dark, sunken eyes. Her hair, what was left of it, hung in black, wet strings, tangled with leaves and debris from the river. Her eyes held an emptiness that wasn't quite human. She reached out a cold, moss-covered hand and touched me, and I recoiled in revulsion. Her teeth, when she opened her mouth, were black and snaggly. "Watch your back," she said. "Don't trust anybody."

Then she was gone, and so was the Barracuda, and suddenly I was standing on the veranda of Tom's house. I tried the door, but it was locked. Inside the house, I could hear Tom and his mother arguing. "She probably put the damn batteries there herself,"

Jeannette said. "Look at all the attention she's getting out of it."

I waited for my Galahad to defend me. He didn't disappoint. "Did you look at her?" he said. "Two black eyes, a sprained ankle, a concussion. You should see her back. The bruises. She's in terrible pain, Mother. Who would do something like that just to get attention?"

Then Claudia was speaking. "What about the note?" she said. "She's read the note. If we don't do something about it, the truth will come out. And then where will we be?"

"Stay out of it," Tom barked, and then, somehow— I think I flew there—I was at the Swift River Bridge, teetering on the rail, while below me, a voice that seemed to emanate from the swirling waters themselves whispered to me, "Jump! Jump!" I released my hold on the rusted piece of iron I'd been using to balance myself, leaned forward, and was just starting to fall when a hand grabbed me and pulled me back, down off the railing and onto the relative safety of the gridwork that made up the bridge's road surface.

The body attached to the hand turned out to belong to the old man, Roger Levasseur. "Why'd you do that?" I screamed at him, hopping mad. "Why did you save me? Don't you understand that I wanted to jump?"

He stared at me with those red, rheumy eyes. I saw sorrow in them, and compassion. And an intelligence I'd missed the first time around. "But what about the children?" he said. "They need you. Taylor and Sadie and Angel and little Davy. If you jump, who'll take care of them? Not me. I'm too old."

"And you smell bad," I said.

"You have to fight for them. You have to protect them."

"How?" I asked him.

"Talk to Mel," he said. And he disappeared.

Alone on the bridge, I walked to the railing and looked over the side. Below me, water rushed and swirled. Beth Larkin, her youthful beauty restored, floated faceup on top of the water, her pale blond hair bobbing on the river's surface. She opened her eyes. They were a soft blue, the color of chicory growing by the roadside in August. But when she opened her mouth, her teeth were still snaggly and black. The blue eyes darkened with anger. "See what you started?" she said.

I awoke abruptly, my chest heaving as I gasped for breath. What the hell had been in those pills Tom gave me? I glanced over at him, sleeping still and silent beside me. Tom always slept that way, with a tidy economy of movement, like a wax doll, only the rise and fall of his chest attesting to his humanity.

Although it seemed as though I'd just gone to bed, pale morning light filtered through the gauzy window curtains. I still had a killer headache, and after a night of lying in one position, I'd added stiffness to my arsenal of complaints. Not to mention that I needed to pee like a racehorse. Trying not to disturb Tom, I lifted the covers, sat up, and carefully swung my legs over the side of the bed.

It took a minute for the room to stop spinning, but eventually it righted itself and remained steady. My head and my ankle both still throbbed, but my balance had been partially restored, and the air cast gave me some measure of support. My vision was still a little funky, but I hoped to have enough equilibrium to make it to the bathroom without falling on my ass. Moving like a four-hundred-year-old woman, I hobbled across the twelve feet of empty space between the bed and the bathroom doorway. Exhausted by the effort, I clung to the door frame and took a series of deep breaths, waiting for my strength to return. As if I actually believed I had any.

After I'd used the facilities and shuffled to the sink to wash my hands, I made the mistake of looking in the mirror. The shock nearly sent me into a relapse. It was uncanny, my resemblance to Beth. Not the live one, but the dead one in my dreams, the one with the sunken eyes and the snaggly teeth. Except that I had something she didn't: two fat, purple shiners. Jesus God. If this were Halloween, I could rent myself out as a party favor, guaranteed to terrify even the bravest of children.

I cautiously pulled my nightie off over my head and dropped it on the counter. Thanks to Tom's propensity for mirrors—or maybe it was Beth who'd had them installed in every usable inch of space in that huge bathroom—I was able to view the bruises on my back. I looked like somebody had used me for a punching bag. Not just my tailbone, but my entire backside, from my rump to my shoulders, was mottled with bruises. During the course of my fall, I'd ricocheted like a ping-pong ball off every available surface. Although I hurt everywhere, I knew it looked worse than it really was. Bruising generally does. I also knew how lucky I was. I could have broken something, and then I would've been out of commission for a long time. Nevertheless, the sight of my reflection was disheartening, as well as a stunning reminder of my own mortality, something I hadn't spent much of my young life dwelling on.

"Hey, you."

I'd been so engrossed in cataloguing my charms that I hadn't heard Tom's footsteps. I turned to him, slowly and cautiously. "Hey, yourself," I said.

"You look quite fetching wearing nothing but bruises and an air cast. Feeling better?"

"It's the latest fashion for ghouls. The vertigo's a little better this morning, and my head's not quite so fuzzy. Everything hurts, and my vision's still blurry, but I only see one of you this morning, so I guess there must be some improvement. Mostly I feel like a very old woman who just lost a fight with a Greyhound bus. And what in God's name was in those pills you gave me? I haven't dreamed like that since— come to think of it, I've never dreamed like that."

He left the doorway and came into the room. "They were just pain pills," he said. "Sometimes, they have an odd effect on people."

"I'll say." I turned back to the mirror and picked up my nightie. "Did you know we're going to have a little boy named Davy?"

"Is that so?" He stood behind me, his hands on my shoulders, his eyes on mine in the mirror.

Turning the nightie right side out, I said, "That's what Roger Levasseur told me last night in my dreams. And Beth was there, and these three teenage boys driving an old Barracuda, and you and your mother and Claudia were arguing, and—"

His fingers traced a pattern against my bare shoulder that, amazingly enough, set my motor to running. How could I possibly think about sex when I was half-dead? "What were we arguing about?" he said.

"Me, I think. Something about the batteries. Your mother thought—" As Tom's hands continued their irresistible seduction, I struggled to remember the elusive snippets of conversation that had taken place inside my drug-befuddled brain. "Now I remember. She said I probably put the batteries on the stairs myself. Engineered the fall to get attention."

His lips were soft and warm on my bare shoulder. Against my skin, he murmured, "Who in their right mind would say something like that? Believe it or not, my mother's very worried about you."

"Probably more worried," I said cynically, bunching up the nightgown and pressing it to my chest, "that I'll file a lawsuit against her homeowner's policy and her insurance premiums will go up."

Tom raised his head. In the mirror, I watched his eyes narrow. "Jules," he said in a voice he might have used to scold a naughty child.

"I'm sorry, Tom, I really am, but the woman detests me."

"You're wrong. You're not seeing her objectively."

How much more objective could it get? I'd clearly heard her tell my husband that he should send me back where I came from. "Maybe," I said, choosing my words carefully, "it's you who aren't seeing her objectively. Considering that she's your mother, and all." Studying his frozen expression, I added, "Which would be natural, of course. Seeing as how—well, you know."

"You'd better quit now, Jules, while you're ahead, because you're digging your own grave a little deeper with every word that comes out of your mouth."

A shudder ran through my body. "Please," I said. "Don't use that word."

"Which word? Grave?"

I shuddered again. "It's too close a reminder of what almost happened yesterday."

"Oh, sweetheart." He was instantly contrite. "I'm sorry." He kissed the back of my neck. My knees weakened, and I dropped the nightie and gripped the edge of the marble counter to steady myself.

Studying my poor, battered reflection, I said, "Tom?"

Distracted by his ministrations, he said, "Hmm?"

"You didn't happen to see anything fall out of my pocket yesterday, did you?"

He went still for an instant. "Like what?"

"A piece of paper. I'm sure I had it in my pocket when I fell, but by the time I left the hospital, it was gone."

"Maybe you lost it here. When you fell."

"I don't think so. Riley would have noticed. It must have fallen out at the hospital."

"Sorry, I didn't see anything." His mouth worked its way down my shoulder, and he reached a hand around to cup my breast. "Was it important? Do you want me to call the E.R. and see if they found it?"

"No," I said weakly. "It's not important at all. Tom—"

In his most seductive voice, he said, "Let's go back to bed."

"But how can we—I'm bruised all over, and I'm wearing this damnable air cast—"

"Jules, Jules, Jules. You're underestimating my powers of creativity."

"Creativity?" I said. "Oh. Well, in that case…"

Afterward, I lay beneath the covers and watched him dress. There are few sights in this world that give me more pleasure than that of a man in a white dress shirt looping and tightening his necktie. It gives a man such a crisp, clean appearance. Tom straightened his tie, adjusted his collar, and caught me watching him. With a slow, lazy grin, he said, "See something you like?"

This was the Tom I knew and loved, the playful, laid-back Tom, the one who didn't have worry lines bracketing his mouth. "I see a lot that I like," I said. "And if I hadn't already shown you how much I like it…"

"Hold that thought. There's always tonight." He

went into the bathroom, returned a moment later with a paper cup and a big cylindrical tablet. "Pain pill," he explained, and I took it without question, like an obedient child. "You should take another one in four hours. The bottle's right on the bathroom counter."

He tossed the paper cup into the trash and picked up his wristwatch from the nightstand. Slipping it on his wrist, he fixed me with a stern gaze and said, "I'm expecting you to behave yourself today."

I didn't want him to go away, the playful Tom. I saw fewer and fewer glimpses of him these days, and the serious Tom, he of the stern gazes and the worry lines, felt like a stranger. Trying to tease him into sticking around a little longer, I said, "Don't worry. The next time I decide to practice tumbling, I'll use a mat."

He went to the closet and took out a suit coat. "I had no idea that living with you would be so, ah… colorful. Are you always this much of a magnet for trouble?"

"That's not fair. The tree wasn't my fault. I was just in the wrong place at the wrong time. And the vandalism was random. Some kid saw a new car and decided to mess around with it. Also not my fault. As for yesterday, I suppose that could be explained by my own klutziness."

Tom shrugged into the suit coat. "I never took you for the klutzy type."

"I never was before."

"After you fell asleep last night, I read the girls

the riot act. They both swore they hadn't left those batteries lying around, but who else could it have been?"

My heart contracted. "Oh, Tom. Don't blame it on the girls. I really don't believe they were to blame. I really don't think—" I stopped, inexplicably reluctant to share with him my theory that some unknown person had placed those batteries in that particular location deliberately in the hopes that I'd trip over them and fall. The idea was so far-fetched that the chances were excellent it was a figment of my imagination. After all, I'd suffered fairly severe head trauma. Maybe my belief that they hadn't been there before was the result of memory loss. Maybe they'd been on the stairs all along and I simply hadn't noticed them. Until, distracted by the discovery of Beth's letter, I made that last fateful trip down the stairs.

"Claudia promised she'd be in and out to keep an eye on you. If you need anything, you're to call her. I don't want you traipsing up and down those stairs all day by yourself. Is that clear?"

"I don't need a keeper, Tom. I'm capable of taking care of myself."

"Yes. You proved that yesterday."

I felt like a nine-year-old who'd been reprimanded for something he hadn't done. Was Tom really blaming me for my accident? That seemed grossly unfair. I'd never been careless. Never been accident-prone. Why would I start now? It looked as though Good Tom had really gone into hiding, and

Evil Tom had taken his place. I was hurt, but more than that, I was irked. How could he make such tender love to me, then turn around just minutes later and, with a few well-placed words, tear me down and leave me in tatters? I held back the response I wanted to make; sticking out my tongue at him wouldn't do much to advance my case for independent adulthood.

"I'll behave," I said, because placating him was the easiest way of defusing the situation. He wasn't going to come around to my way of thinking anytime soon, so I might as well try to adhere to his. That way, everybody would be happy.

There was a knock on the door. It opened, and the girls stood there wearing identical expressions of apprehension, tempered by curiosity. "We came to see you," Taylor said somberly. "To make sure you're okay."

"You look scary," Sadie said.

I tucked the bedding tighter around me for modesty's sake and patted the bed. "Come here," I said. "It looks worse than it really is."

Sadie bounced over and wiggled her plump little bottom onto the bed. Taylor, reticent as always, followed at a more leisurely pace and stood beside the bed, examining my poor, mutilated face. "Does it hurt?" Sadie asked, studying my two black eyes with the same absorption I'd seen her give to some exotic dead insect she'd found.

"A little," I told her. "But give me a few days, and I'll be as good as new."

Taylor fiddled with the zipper to her jacket. Eyes downcast, she said, "We didn't leave those batteries on the stairs. Honest."

"I know you didn't, sweetheart. Nobody's blaming you."

She glanced up at me, her eyes steady on mine, as though gauging my sincerity. A brief smile blossomed on her face before she averted her eyes again.

"Give Julie a kiss," Tom said, "and let's get hopping. We don't want to be late."

Sadie leaned and gave me a mooshy kiss, and Taylor stepped up obediently and planted a less mooshy, more chaste kiss on my cheek. Tom's kiss was nearly as chaste. I lay there listening as they trundled down the stairs, as his car started up and drove off. When the sound of his engine had faded away, I sat up, threw off the covers, and unstrapped the air cast. There wasn't a lot I could do in my condition, but I could at least wash my body.

I stood for a long time under the hot shower, letting its soothing fingers take away the strain from my knotted muscles. Afterward, I took my time toweling off; stiff and sore as I was, every action took twice as long as it should have. After performing minimal morning ablutions—the brushing of hair and teeth—I found the loosest clothing I owned and slowly, painfully, dressed myself.

I was cautious on the stairs, moving in slow motion as my condition, and my air cast, dictated. It took a while, but I managed to get downstairs without killing myself. "Score one for me," I muttered.

Now that I was down here, my hubby expected me to stay put. I found the phone book and looked up Claudia's number. "It's Julie," I said when she answered. "I just wanted you to know that I don't need to be watched over like a two-year-old. I appreciate the offer, but it really isn't necessary."

"Honey," she said, "I almost died when I saw you last night. Mike Tyson would've been horrified. You looked like you'd been caught in a cement mixer. How are you feeling this morning?"

"Like I got caught in a cement mixer. I just want to be left alone to die. You know the drill: lie on the couch, watch *The Price is Right,* snooze."

"At least let me bring you breakfast."

"You don't have to do that."

"I want to. I just picked up the most incredible fresh-baked croissants at the bakery. They're still hot. We'll eat them with my homemade boysenberry jam."

I groaned. It sounded almost as good as sex. Almost. "You," I said, "are going to be the death of me. Don't tell me you made the jam yourself."

"Made it and grew the berries. I know it's hard to believe, but back when I was married to what's-his-name, I was a domestic goddess, until I figured out that it was just one more example of white slavery. So I'm fully capable of cooking a gourmet meal, should I so choose. Just don't tell anyone my secret. If you do, I'll have to kill you."

"I'll keep that in mind. My cooking skills are adequate, but nothing to write home about. You, therefore, are my hero."

"Sweet words to my ears. Hang in there. I'll be right over."

We sat at the kitchen table in the morning sun, eating sinfully delicious croissants with jam and drinking some kind of special dark roast coffee that Claudia was trying out. "This is decadent," I said, reaching for my third croissant. "Are you sure it's not illegal?"

"I hope you don't think that would stop me if it was." Over the rim of her coffee cup, she eyed me. "So what happened yesterday? How'd you manage to fall down those stairs?"

"Why does everybody ask me how I 'managed' to fall?" I demanded. "As though it were something exceedingly difficult to do that required a great deal of effort on my part?"

"Hey, I'm not casting stones." Claudia pointed an index finger at her own chest. "I've fallen up the stairs too many times to fault you for falling down them. I think it's just the horror of seeing how bad you were hurt that incites people to ask such a stupid question."

Slightly mollified, I said, "It wasn't my fault at all. Somebody left a couple of batteries on the stairs. Round ones. I stepped on them and my foot just rolled right out from under me."

Claudia tore off a piece of croissant. "Well, it's a miracle you weren't killed."

"I have a hard head and a soft ass. Although today, both of them are feeling the pain."

She leaned her chin on her hand. "Did they say how long you'd be wearing the air cast?"

"They didn't tell me much of anything." I rolled my eyes. "Mostly, they talked to Tom. Outside the cubicle, if you can imagine that. I felt like an afterthought."

"That's not right. You should have demanded that they tell you everything."

"If I'd been in my right mind at the time, I would have. But my brain was too fuzzy from the concussion, and on top of that, I was on Demerol."

"Ah. Happy juice."

"Exactly. So I guess they figured I needed Tom to act as a translator."

"You have to admit, it's convenient that you're married to a doctor."

Thinking of this morning, and how cleverly he'd worked his way around all my infirmities, I had to agree. It was a definite plus, being married to a man who was so familiar with the female anatomy. Warming to the topic, I said, "Can I tell you a secret?"

She leaned forward eagerly. "I love secrets. I'm all ears."

"Tom and I are trying to get pregnant."

Claudia's elegant eyebrows went sky-high. "So soon?"

"That's what I said, but he convinced me. Promise you won't tell anyone."

"I promise. Well. Congratulations. If it's what you really want."

"It is," I said. "But it's a little early for congratulations. The rabbit hasn't died yet."

The pills had made me sleepy. I'd finished my breakfast, and all I wanted now was for her to go away. I yawned, covering my mouth discreetly, hoping she'd take the hint.

She did. "Looks like it's time for your nap," she said.

"I'm sorry. The pain pills make me groggy." It was the truth. Just not all of it.

"Of course they do." Claudia stood and began clearing the table. "You should sleep. It'll help make for a quicker recovery." She put the dishes in the sink, found a dishcloth and wiped down the table. "There," she said, gathering up her jam and her coffee. "I've done my domestic duty for now. You need to park yourself on the couch and take a little snooze. I'll be back at lunchtime. Homemade turkey noodle soup with barley and egg noodles and a few other secret ingredients that nobody knows."

I wanted to protest that she was doing too much, but being spoiled was addictive. A girl could really get used to it. Besides, her turkey noodle soup sounded amazing. "Thanks," I said, genuinely gratified. "I'll see you then."

As soon as she was gone, I locked the door and hobbled from the kitchen, my ankle screaming in protest. In the front hall, I locked that door as well, and slipped quietly into the small room Tom used as a study. Yes, I was tired and groggy. Maybe even a bit loopy. But I wasn't ready to sleep. Not just yet. They say that curiosity killed the cat. In my case, the cliché is probably true. I've never been one to do what's best for me. Not when there was something more interesting to do, a mystery to solve. In the words of Jon Bon Jovi, I'll sleep when I'm dead.

In keeping with the obsessive/compulsive aspects of my husband's personality, the desktop was empty of everything except the computer and a shiny black cup that held a couple of pens. No bills, no books, not so much as a stray paper clip dared mar the perfection of its gleaming surface. I found it a little creepy, how fastidious my husband was. But that was just Tom.

I pulled out the desk chair, sat down, and fired up the computer. I was ticked off that I'd lost Beth's note, the only real evidence I had that anything in her supposedly perfect life had gone amiss. I couldn't very well go to the police with vague suspicions. But there were things I could do. In my dream last night, Roger had told me I should talk to Mel. It was good advice, and I fully intended to talk to her once I was sprung from my prison. In the meantime, there was plenty of online snooping to be done. Somewhere in the archives of the local newspaper, there had to be at least an article or two about Beth's death. The wife of a prominent doctor jumping to her death from a bridge railing would have made quite a stir in a town as small as this one. If the stories were archived, it was pretty much guaranteed that they'd still be available online.

Life before the Internet. How did people survive?

I pulled up Google and typed ELIZABETH LARKIN into the search box. It immediately pulled up 1,110,000 hits. As a research instrument, the

Internet had its drawbacks, and this was one of them. I went back to the Google search page, retyped her name and added NEWMARKET MAINE to the search criteria. This cut out about 1,109,000 entries. It still left me about a thousand hits to wade through, but a thousand was better than 1.1 million. I already knew that most of them would be totally unrelated to my search, random items that had been selected by some peculiar and inexplicable formula known only to Google.

It took me nearly a half hour to find it, in part because the pill Tom gave me had made me groggy, but mostly because I kept getting sidetracked by seductive entries that looked so interesting I just couldn't help checking them out, if only for a few seconds. Invariably, those few seconds turned into minutes and, totally immersed in something fascinating but unrelated to my search, I kept losing track of time and my original purpose. But in my own inimitable fuzzy-brained manner, despite my screaming ankle and my dull headache, I persevered.

That perseverance paid off. I almost missed the article, buried as it was between a story about the current state of the Maine housing market and a history of some woman named Elizabeth Maines who'd died in 1856. DEATH OF DOCTOR'S WIFE SHOCKS SMALL MAINE TOWN. It had been picked up by the AP, and apparently distributed around the New England news outlets. It might have even gone national, if it was a slow news day.

NEWMARKET, MAINE (AP)—The small town of Newmarket is still reeling from the death of one of the town's most beloved citizens and the wife of a prominent physician. According to local authorities, Elizabeth Larkin, wife of Dr. Thomas Larkin and mother of two young children, took her own life on Tuesday evening when she jumped from the railing of the Swift River Bridge and perished in the waters of the Swift River. Neighbors in this small southern Maine town are stunned. "She was such a nice lady," said Seth Leibowicz, a local grocer. "Always smiling, always with a kind word."

Yet other, unnamed sources say that over the past six months, Larkin had become increasingly despondent. Friends and neighbors have expressed dismay because on Tuesday night, Larkin left her two-year-old daughter in the car, unattended until a local resident found her there and called authorities. "I don't understand," said bakery owner Tess Pullman. "What kind of mother would leave that poor little girl alone like that? Not the Beth I knew. She was a good mother. She'd never do anything to traumatize her child like that. Something happened to change her, that's all I can say."

Police Chief James Andrews confirmed that after an investigation, Larkin's death has been ruled a suicide. He declined further comment. Phone calls to the Larkin home went unreturned.

Larkin leaves behind her husband, Dr. Thomas Larkin, her two daughters, Taylor and Sadie, her sister, Melanie Ambrose, also of Newmarket, and her mother, Janice Radcliffe, of Zephyrhills, Florida.

I sat there, numb, as what I'd just read gradually sank into my fuzzy brain. Sadie had been there that night. She'd sat in Beth's Land Rover, there on the bridge, and witnessed her mother's supposed suicide leap. Or perhaps she'd witnessed something else, something worse than suicide, something her two-year-old brain didn't quite comprehend but was cognizant enough to fear.

Dear God.

How long had she sat there alone after Beth went over the side? How long before this unnamed "local resident" found her, a helpless two-year-old child, alone and crying for her mother? Ten minutes? An hour? Two hours? I'd spent some time out on Swift River Road. In all the time I'd been there, I'd seen just one vehicle pass. The road was obviously not heavily traveled. At night, after dark, it must have been terrifying for Sadie. What had Beth said to her before she left the car? Had she planned not to return? Had she spoken words of comfort to a daughter she knew would never see her mother again? Or had fate, in human form, intervened in Beth's plans to return safely to her child?

There was something terribly wrong here, something so wrong I couldn't believe that supposedly intelligent people had been stupid enough to fall for it. I could see clearly what the rest of the world seemed to have missed: No mother, no matter how much she wanted to die, would kill herself in front of her two-year-old, leaving the child alone, in the dark, unprotected, on a back country road that was seldom traveled, dependent on the goodwill of strangers for her safety and an open target for child molesters and other unsavory characters. No mother would leave her child alone in a car, on a high bridge over a swiftly running river, if the possibility existed that the child might leave the car in search of her mother and fall off the side of the bridge into the swirling waters below.

Never. Not in a million years. Not even the worst mother in the world would do this. Not deliberately.

The last piece of evidence fell into place, and the tiny shred of doubt that had remained, the doubt that had allowed me to concede the possibility that Beth's death really was a suicide, was gone. I knew now, beyond any reasonable doubt, that Elizabeth Larkin, my husband's former wife, mother to Taylor and Sadie and sister to Mel, had been murdered.

The implications were staggering. Somebody had wanted Beth dead, wanted her dead bad enough that they were willing to kill her in front of her child. And either the police department was made up of incompetent idiots—which was a possibility, considering Dwight's level of competence—or a lot of people were covering up the truth.

Who knew the truth? Riley? Claudia? Jeannette?

Tom? The idea that my husband might be covering up a homicide was beyond comprehension. It simply wasn't possible. There was no way Tom was involved in any kind of cover-up. No way Tom was involved in—*oh,* God. I closed my eyes and buried my head in my hands. I wasn't even going there. Tom was a good man. A good husband, a good father, a good doctor. He'd taken the Hippocratic oath. He was not a killer.

But I couldn't shake the words Beth had said to me last night in my dream: *Watch your back. Don't trust anybody.* Did that anybody include Tom?

Fear is a peculiar emotion. It distorts your perspective, makes you see things that aren't there, prevents you from noticing what should be obvious. My thoughts raced, like a runaway locomotive, one after another. Sadie had been with Beth the night she died. I could only presume that she'd witnessed something, although only Sadie—and possibly Beth's killer—knew what that something was. Why was Tom so adamant that the girls have no reminders of their mother? Why was he so determined that Sadie not see a therapist? What memories did he fear Beth's painting might shake loose? Was he afraid Sadie might say something to her therapist that, if disclosed, could destroy his life? Was he driven by guilt, or was he trying to protect someone else? His brother. His mother. Maybe some other person as yet unknown to me.

No. I wasn't going to let myself think this way, allowing fear to overtake reason. There was absolutely no basis, aside from my own overactive imagination, for thinking that Tom might have been involved in his wife's death. How could I even consider doubting him? This was *Tom* I was talking about, for God's sake. My husband. My friend. My lover. Damn it, I would know if he were involved in anything sinister. I lived with the man. I slept with him. If that kind of evil existed inside Tom Larkin, I would have sensed it. But I hadn't sensed anything of the kind. Tom's actions weren't questionable. He was simply a concerned dad, trying to protect his little girls. And I had been reading way too many mystery novels.

But somebody was responsible. Somebody had killed Beth. I hated to even think it, but if I were to point fingers, Riley seemed the most likely candidate. After all, Beth had been his girlfriend at one time. But she'd married his brother instead of him. That had to hurt. Had it eaten away at him all these years, festering and poisoning him until, in a fit of passionate rage, he'd confronted the woman he'd lost to his brother and tossed her off the side of a bridge? Hadn't Riley always been jealous of Tom, jealous of everything Tom possessed? Jealousy was a strong motive. Was it strong enough in Riley's case to compel him to take away the thing his brother loved most in life, the woman he believed Tom had stolen from him? My brother-in-law seemed a decent, levelheaded guy. I liked him. As far as I could see, everybody liked him. Despite his occasionally acerbic tongue, he'd been kind to me. But I hardly knew Riley Larkin. All I'd really seen was the superficial outer shell. I had no idea what went on behind those blue eyes.

I didn't want to believe that Riley had killed Beth. It seemed improbable, but I'd seen less likely scenarios. And if not Riley, then who?

I considered Jeannette. Tom's mother was a very unhappy person, and that unhappiness radiated outward to everyone she came in contact with. She hated me on general principles. Had she hated Elizabeth, as well? Something Riley once said came back to me now: *Nobody's ever been quite good enough for our boy here.* The implication, which I hadn't picked up on at the time, was that Jeannette Larkin had considered no woman—including Elizabeth—to be a suitable wife for her son. Tom had admitted that his mother was overprotective. Was it outside the realm of possibility to believe that a deranged woman might consider the act of killing her son's unsuitable wife to be an act of protection? If it were Jeannette who'd done the deed, that would account for the secrecy, the knowing looks that passed between Tom and Riley, the cover-up that almost certainly was going on. Tom wouldn't want his mother, his children's grandmother, to go to prison. He would protect his mother any way he could. Motherhood was sacred; I suspected most children would do the same.

My own baser emotions made Jeannette the ideal candidate, but logic told me I was reaching. Wishful thinking, perhaps? Jeannette was a classic passive-aggressive type. To my face, my mother-in-law was

civil. Not warm, but not openly hostile. It was behind
my back that she released her aggressions. Which
meant that murdering her son's wife would be unlikely. Someone like Jeannette might be adept at
character assassination, but I couldn't honestly see
her taking the direct approach involved in actually
killing someone. I doubt she would have risked a
face-to-face confrontation. She was more likely to
kill someone with word than with deed.

I had nothing I could take to the police. I knew in
my heart that Beth had been murdered, but anything
beyond that was conjecture. I could ruminate and
analyze and explore various wild scenarios until the
cows came home, but the truth was that I had no idea
who had killed Elizabeth Larkin, or why. All the
evidence I had was little more than speculation.
Without something concrete, something that actually
pointed to one specific person, all I had was empty
hands. If I went to the cops with my suspicions,
they'd tell me their investigation was already complete, then they'd pat me on the head and send me
on my way with a strong admonition to stop playing
armchair detective.

What they wouldn't do was listen to me.

In other words, if I wanted to solve Beth's murder,
I was going to have to do it myself. Because the cops
weren't going to help me at all.

A wave of exhaustion crashed over me, a combination of pain pills and my body's own defense
system. Yawning, I closed my eyes. Immediately, a
kaleidoscope of images, vivid and surreal, danced

across my brain. Beth teetering on the railing of that bridge while Sadie watched, too young to comprehend what her mother was doing. Tom standing over me like an angry parent, scolding me for having the audacity to fall down those stairs and disrupt his otherwise smooth life. Riley, wielding that chain saw with grace and deadly accuracy. Claudia, laughing as she spread boysenberry jam on her croissant. Jeannette, casting furtive, poisonous glances across the dinner table at me. Roger Levasseur, his expression sorrowful as he studied me with those red and rheumy eyes.

I awoke with a start, realized I'd dropped off to sleep still sitting at Tom's desk. The pills Dr. Jankowski had prescribed were having a bizarre effect on me, but they kept my pain at a manageable level, so I supposed I could tolerate them a little longer. I was a wuss when it came to pain, so hallucinations and excessive daytime sleepiness were probably an acceptable trade-off.

But right now, my eyelids drooped so heavily I simply couldn't keep them open. I stumbled, woozy and weak, to the couch. Dropping my head on last night's pillow, I pulled the blanket over me and immediately fell into a deep slumber.

I dreamed. Strange, colorful and highly improbable dreams, little snippets of scene or thought or dialogue that flowed one into another in disparate entities, like a play penned by Picasso. For a time, I tried to follow them, tripping along behind like an entomologist with a butterfly net. But like the elusive butterfly, the peculiar little prisms of my dreams remained just beyond reach.

It was the telephone that woke me. I opened my eyes, squinted at the light, and fumbled for the cordless phone on the coffee table. "Hello?" I croaked.

"It's me," Tom said. "I'm calling to make sure everything's okay. Claudia said she knocked and knocked on the door, but nobody answered."

"Tom." I sat up, fighting the dizziness that hadn't been there this morning, and rubbed my forehead in a vain search for clarity. "It's these pills," I said, sounding as fuzzy as I felt. "What time is it?"

"It's nearly one o'clock. Claudia came over to bring you lunch, but the door was locked and she couldn't get in. We were worried about you."

I tried to calculate how long I'd slept. Close to three hours. Three hours, on a sunny late-September morning, seemed excessive. "Should I be sleeping so much?" I said.

"You have a concussion, Jules. Your body's been through significant trauma. Sleeping more than usual is normal. It's how your body heals."

I shoved a strand of hair back from my face. "That's what Claudia said."

"You should listen to her. And now you should get up and unlock the door. I'd just as soon you didn't lock them anyway. If you fell again, nobody could get in to help you."

"Why would I fall again?"

"Well, I don't know. Let's look at the evidence and see what we come up with. You have a concussion, you're walking in an air cast, you're stiff and bruised and lame, and you're on some pretty heavy drugs. Humor me, babe. Be a good girl and go unlock the door so Claudia can bring you your lunch."

"I'm not hungry." I realized, with some amazement, that it was the truth. The nausea that had unexpectedly rolled in had driven away all thoughts of food. For me, that was unheard of. Nothing ever chased away my appetite.

"Food will heal you, too. You need to eat, Jules."

I flushed slightly, grateful that he couldn't see me because there was just enough doubt left in me to prevent that all-encompassing, absolute trust I'd once felt for Tom. Even though I was determined not to let fear control me, I still had doubts. Questions. His wife had been murdered, and even if he hadn't been a part of that murder—and I was sure he hadn't—Tom should have pressed the police to investigate more thoroughly, should have done just about anything except what he apparently did, which was to blindly accept the ruling of suicide and continue on with his life. If it were me who died under the same circumstances, I would have expected him to leave no stone unturned until he found out the truth. The possibility that he might not do so was unsettling.

"Jules? Is everything okay?"

I reminded myself this was my husband talking, the man I loved, and that this strange otherworldliness that had come over me was a direct result of the medication I was taking, and not of any belief on my part that there'd been any wrongdoing on Tom's. "I'm fine," I said. "Just groggy. I'm getting up to unlock the door now."

"Good girl. I'll call Claudia and tell her to come back. Don't forget to take your pill. Remember, every four hours."

Good Lord. Was it time to take another of those awful things? I was barely able to function as it was. "You know," I said, "I'm not sure I should be taking them. They do really funky things to me."

In his I'm-the-doctor-and-therefore-you-should-listen-to-me voice, he said, "It's crucial that you keep the medication in your system."

"Why?"

Across miles of phone line, I heard his sigh of exasperation. "Because," he said, as though explaining something to a very small child, "as long as it's in your system, the pain won't be as bad. But if the medication wears off and the pain comes back full force, it'll take twice as long for another dose of medicine to relieve it. Do you understand what I'm saying?"

I understood, but wasn't sure I agreed with him. For all I knew, he was trying to poison me. Or keep me heavily drugged and therefore compliant. God knew, it was the only way anybody would ever see compliance from me. I wasn't sure where these dark thoughts had come from, but they hovered, improbable yet real enough to sour my disposition. "I have to go now," I said. "The door needs unlocking."

I disconnected, a little surprised to realize that I

had just hung up on my darling husband, love of my life, the man I'd allowed only hours earlier to make sweet, hot love to me. What had gotten into me? Thunderous of face and heavy of leg, I dragged myself to the kitchen door and unlocked it.

Tom was a fast worker. Claudia was already coming up the walkway, soup tureen in hand, my own little Florence Nightingale. "I thought you were dead," she said cheerfully. "Or lying on the floor at the foot of the stairs again. I must have knocked for five minutes before I gave up and called Tom. Worst-case scenario, I figured, was that if you didn't answer, he could zip home and unlock the door and we'd go in together. If we found you dead, at least we could console each other."

I glowered at her as she breezed past me into the kitchen. "Gee, thanks."

"For God's sake, Julie, I'm kidding. What happened to your sense of humor? It must be the concussion. Or the pain pills. Certain medications used to turn my grandmother into a grumpy old goat."

"Baa."

She set the tureen on the counter and removed the cover. The smell that arose from it, while heavenly, wreaked havoc with my sick stomach. "Trust me," she said, "once you've tasted Aunt Claudia's Famous Turkey Noodle Soup, your attitude will change. Satisfaction guaranteed or your money back."

"That's false advertising. How can I get my money back if I'm not paying you for it?"

"Sit down and shut up. Where do you keep the bowls?"

"How should I know? I just moved here a few weeks ago. Jeannette usually doesn't let me near the kitchen."

"That's all right, we'll find them." She opened and closed cabinet doors until she found the right one. With a pretty blue ceramic bowl in hand, she went to the silverware drawer and took out a soup spoon, then ladled a huge bowl of turkey noodle soup and placed it in front of me with a flourish. "There you go, darling. Eat hearty."

I stared at the bowl of soup. My appetite had taken a powder, and nausea still roiled in my stomach. "I'm not hungry," I said.

"Eat it anyway. You need to eat, or you'll lose your strength."

I glanced at the tureen, still steaming on the kitchen counter, then back at the bowl in front of me. "You're not having any?" I said.

"I already ate my lunch."

"Really? How convenient."

Claudia raised an eyebrow. "What does that mean?"

"How do I know you're not trying to poison me?"

Her laughter started out hearty, ended up a little shaky. "Good God almighty," she said, studying my face. "You're serious. Why would you think I'd do that?"

"I don't know." It was true. I really couldn't imagine why Claudia would want to poison me. But once the thought had formed, I couldn't seem to shake it. "You could put, I don't know, maybe window cleaner, or Vanish—it's highly toxic, you know—or even bleach, in my soup, and how would I know the difference?"

"Honey, my soup doesn't taste like Clorox. I'd be insulted if I didn't know you'd taken a hard blow to the head yesterday." Claudia leaned over the table, picked up my spoon, and proceeded to eat a big mouthful of turkey noodle soup. "There," she said, setting the utensil back down. "Are you happy now?"

"Utterly. You've set my mind at ease." I picked up the spoon she'd so recently discarded and, to my astonishment, emptied the bowl in about three minutes. "Yum," I said when I was done. "That was delicious."

"I thought you weren't hungry?"

"I thought so, too. Is there any more?"

I finished a second bowl before I was satisfied. It was the best soup I'd ever eaten. Leaning back in my chair with a sigh, I said, "Will you marry me?"

"After the way you insulted me? I have a little more self-respect than that."

"I'm sorry. I don't know what's made me so paranoid. Maybe it's the pills."

"I don't know about paranoid, but they certainly do make you sleepy. Knocking on that door was like trying to wake the dead."

"You wouldn't believe the dreams I have on that stuff. All psychedelic and Andy Warhol-ish. You should join me sometime. We could take a trip together."

"No, thanks. I'm not into that kind of trip. Have you told Tom about this?"

"I keep telling him they do funky things to me. And he keeps putting on his Serious Doctor voice and telling me why it's crucial that I keep on taking them."

Claudia rolled her eyes. "Men," she said, and glanced at her watch. "Can't live with 'em, can't kill 'em. Gotta run. Dylan has a dentist's appointment at two-thirty, so you won't be able to reach me between two and four."

"It's all right," I said. "I'll probably be sleeping anyway. Can't seem to keep my eyes open. But do you suppose—" I eyed the soup tureen lustfully before turning beseeching eyes on her. "Could you leave the soup here?"

The next few days played out with little variety. While I alternated between deep sleep and groggy wakefulness, Tom alternated between sweet concern and tough love, and my bruises ran the gamut of the color spectrum. Claudia continued to provide my meals. Jeannette remained at a distance, as though fearful I was contagious, and Riley stopped in at least once each day to check on my welfare and bring me a variety of reading materials.

Although I was grateful for the fresh entertainment, I knew better than to attempt anything as complex as a novel. In my drug-fogged state, even *Redbook* magazine ("Can This Marriage Be Saved?") was a challenge. I couldn't seem to follow a line of print to its conclusion. I'd lose comprehension—and interest—partway through. Whatever was wrong with me, whether it be the aftereffects of the concussion or side effects from the medication, it seemed to be getting worse. In my more lucid moments, I worried that Beth's note had fallen into the wrong hands. What if it had been read by somebody who knew what Beth was talking about? What if that somebody now knew I had read it? Did it mean I was in some kind of danger?

But the lucidity alternated with the cloudiness, and when the fog rolled in, I simply couldn't muster enough energy to care about anything. Jack the Ripper has read Beth's note, you say, and he's coming after me next? Cool. And would you mind moving over so I can lie down?

Riley finally said something to me about my vagueness. He'd stopped in with a box of peanut brittle and made my day. I hadn't even seen the stuff since I was a kid, when my mother used to have it around the house at Christmas. Riley sat down beside me on the couch, watching me blissfully tear into the box of candy.

"Julie?" he said. "When was the last time you saw a doctor?"

I took a bite of peanut brittle. The candy snapped with a crispness that was music to my ears. "In case you've forgotten," I said, "I live with a doctor."

"I'm not talking about Tom. I mean a real doctor."

He looked so sincere, with his shaggy hair and worn Led Zeppelin T-shirt. Over a slice of rock-hard caramel and peanuts, I gave him the evil eye. "Tom is a real doctor."

"That's not what I meant. You have a concussion. A fairly severe one. Tom specializes in the other end of a woman's anatomy. He's not an expert on head injuries. Have you considered seeing a neurologist?"

"A neurologist? Why on earth would I want to do that? Here, have a piece of peanut brittle." I held out the box. "It cures all ills."

"No, thanks. For a second opinion, if nothing else. Just to make sure there isn't something that's been missed."

"I've already had a second opinion. Dr. Jankowski examined me in the E.R. She advised me to lay low until I'm better. That's what I'm doing."

"You aren't yourself. You sleep all the time. You're confused and disoriented. That's not normal behavior."

"Tom says it is normal after a concussion. And you know I'm taking the pain pills Dr. Jankowski gave me. The side effects are bizarre."

He scowled. "That's another thing. Those pills. How long have you been taking them?"

"Ever since I fell."

"Yes, but how many days has it been since you fell? I bet you don't even know."

"Uh—well…let's see. I'm sure it's—" I tried to mentally calculate the number of days I'd spent lying on the couch in a stupor. "Three, maybe?"

"Try six."

"Six? That's not possible." He had to be wrong.

I took count again. There'd been turkey noodle soup day. Swedish meatballs day. Club sandwich day. The day we ate croissants and jam. No, wait. That was breakfast. That was the same day as...I sat there, stupefied and totally clueless. "Six days?" I said. "Are you sure?"

"At the very least, it might be a good idea for you to call up Dr. Jankowski and ask her if you can stop the medication. By now, your pain should be manageable without it."

Six days. Maybe Riley was right. I'd lost the better part of the last six days of my life, and it was impossible to retrieve them. Tom might not appreciate my interfering, but on the other hand, I was the patient. And Tom might believe he was the be-all and end-all of existence, but he wasn't my primary care physician. He wasn't even the doctor who'd written the prescription. I had every right to speak directly to Dr. Jankowski about my medical care. Those pills were anathema to me. Controlling pain was one thing. Being zonked out to the point where I couldn't recite my own social security number was going a little too far.

I called the hospital and, after working my way through a series of underlings, I finally reached Jankowski. "I was in six days ago," I told her. "You treated me for a fall down the stairs."

"Yes, of course," she said pleasantly. "I remember you. Tom Larkin's wife. What can I do for you, Mrs. Larkin?"

"Those pills you prescribed. I'm experiencing

some pretty bad side effects, and I wondered if I should stop taking them."

There was a moment of silence. "I'll have to check my records," she said, "but I don't remember writing any prescription."

"You gave them to us," I said. "For the pain. You sent them home with us from the hospital. Maybe that's why you don't remember writing the prescription. I've been taking them every four hours, and the side effects are just—"

"Mrs. Larkin? I'm certain that I sent just six pills home with you. Enough to get you through two days. If you've been taking anything else, it wasn't me who prescribed them. Are you sure Dr. Larkin didn't write you some kind of prescription?"

It was my turn to hesitate. Was it possible that Tom had written the prescription for the pills I was taking? "I suppose that's possible," I said. "These pills are blue. Huge cylindrical tablets. They taste awful."

"Well, I didn't prescribe them. The pills I gave you were round and white. Tell me about the side effects."

"Headaches, nausea, upset stomach, excessive sleepiness, lack of appetite, memory problems, brain fog, bouts of paranoia—"

"Hmm. Some of that could be due to the concussion, but the rest definitely sounds drug-induced. My recommendation would be that you stop taking them immediately. Then, if the symptoms persist, I'd recommend a full medical workup."

I thanked her and disconnected the call, slowly lowering the cordless phone to the coffee table. Riley's face was somber, his eyes troubled. "Those pills," I told him. "The ones I've been taking? They're not the ones Dr. Jankowski gave me."

Ten

"I need you to come home," I said into the phone. "Now."

"Jules?" Concern sharpened Tom's voice. "Is something wrong?"

I studied the pill bottle that sat in solitude on the end table. "There's something we need to talk about," I said, "and I'd just as soon not discuss it over the phone."

"It can't wait until tonight? Honey, I'm a little busy here."

"It can't wait another minute. Just come home. I'll explain it when you get here."

I must have frightened him, because I didn't have long to wait. I timed him; it was exactly seven minutes from the time I hung up the phone until the time he wheeled into the driveway. "Jules?" he said as he came in the front door. "Where are you?"

"In the living room."

He rushed in, worry etching frown lines at the corners of his eyes and mouth. "Sweetheart? What's wrong?"

I was determined to remain calm, determined not to panic until I had all the facts. "Sit down," I said. Tom dropped into the chair opposite me. Leaning, elbows on knees, he crossed his hands and waited. "Tell me about the pills," I said.

"Excuse me?"

"The pills, Tom. The ones you've been pushing on me every four hours for the last week. The ones that turned me into a zombie. The ones that Dr. Jankowski didn't prescribe."

He looked puzzled, an expression that did nothing to endear him to me at this particular moment. "I never said Dr. Jankowski prescribed them."

"What? You—" I halted, replaying in my brain the portions of pill-related conversation I could remember. *What are they? Something for the pain.* Had Jankowski's name ever come up, or had I only assumed? "Damn," I said.

"I had them on hand," he said. "You looked so pathetic and I felt so bad for you, Jules. I knew you had to be in terrible pain, and what Jankowski gave you was a joke. You needed something stronger. So I gave you these. I thought you knew. Didn't you read the label on the bottle?"

Of course I hadn't read the label. I'd spent half my time in a fog, and Tom had given the pills to me. I trusted him. It hadn't even occurred to me until now to question his actions. "The side effects," I said. "They're so awful. Nausea, fogginess, memory loss, paranoia—"

"Why didn't you tell me?"

"Damn it, Tom, I tried to tell you. Over and over. You just didn't want to listen. You were too busy playing the big, important doctor who knows so much more than little ignorant me."

"You're right," he said, slowly rubbing his hands over his eyes. The man looked exhausted. I don't think he'd gotten to bed before midnight in a week or more. "You're right. I've been a real ass, haven't I?"

"I hate to throw names around, but if the shoe fits, then, yes. I'd say that's a pretty accurate description of your recent actions."

"I was only trying to—"

"Don't say it. I already know. You wanted to protect me."

"You have to understand, Jules. I didn't protect Beth. I was a neglectful husband, and she's dead because of it. If I'd been paying better attention, she'd still be alive. I don't want to lose you to that same inattention."

"Trust me when I say there's no chance of that happening."

"I guess I went a little overboard in the other direction."

"I guess you did." He looked miserable, and I decided that as long as we were already there, I might as well take things a step further. "Tom," I said, "can I ask you a serious question? One you may not want to hear, but that has to be asked?"

His smile seemed a little forced. "Of course. What is it?"

"Did you kill Beth?"

His astonishment was too immediate, too visceral, to be faked. Even before he spoke, I felt myself go weak with relief. I hadn't doubted him. I really, truly hadn't. At least I hadn't thought I did. But the relief coursing through me right now said something different. Despite my protestations to the contrary, a sliver of doubt had been there all the time. "Julie," he said, sounding stunned. "Good God. You actually believed I could do something like that?"

"The thought did cross my mind."

"How could you—" He paused, sighed, ran a hand through his hair. "Never mind, I know how you could. I've really screwed things up, haven't I? To the point where you actually believed I might be a killer."

I felt just the faintest hint of shame for thinking such a thing of him. What was wrong with me? "I'm sorry," I said. "Maybe it's the paranoia. From the pills."

"You're not to take any more of them," he ordered.

"I already decided that. Without any help from you."

He stood, crossed the room, and knelt on the carpet by my feet. Took both my hands in his. His hands were warm, where mine were ice-cold. "I'm sorry," he said. "Can you ever forgive me for my lousy judgment?"

"I forgive you for your lousy judgment. And for treating me like a child."

His eyes studied mine, gauging my sincerity. Of their own volition, my fingers wandered through his hair. "I've been so confused," I said. "So afraid. Not knowing who to believe. Who to trust."

"You can trust me," he said. "You can always trust me."

"That's not what Riley seems to think."

His hand, caressing my thigh, stilled. "What does Riley have to do with it?"

"He was with me when I found out about the pills. He's the one who pushed me to call Jankowski. He's worried about me. He thinks I should see another doctor, get a second opinion."

Tom's eyes narrowed. "And when, exactly, did Riley get his medical degree?"

"It's not like that. He's just concerned."

Grimly, he said, "Stay away from Riley. He's bad news."

"Tom," I protested, "he's your brother! How can you talk about him that way?"

"You don't know him. You don't know the real Riley. You don't know what he's capable of."

"Then maybe you should fill me in."

"He's not a nice person, Jules. I know he comes off as charming, but it's just a surface charm. Underneath it, he's self-centered and irresponsible, and he absolutely refuses to grow up and accept the fact that he's not sixteen any longer."

Personally, I didn't see it. I hadn't seen any

evidence—aside from his being perpetually between jobs—that pointed to immaturity or irresponsibility on Riley's part. Even if it was true, there were traits far worse than those. But then, I wasn't cognizant of all the history between the Larkin brothers, so maybe I wasn't qualified to judge. And maybe my own judgment wasn't so hot anyway. After all, wasn't I the one who'd just accused my own husband of murder?

"What did he say about me?" Tom asked.

Brushing a strand of hair away from his ear with excessive tenderness, I said, "Nothing specific. He just made it obvious that his opinion of you isn't any higher than your opinion of him. It's a mutual admiration society."

"Don't trust my brother. I know you like him, but keep your distance. In the end, you'll be better off. We all will."

"There's something else that's been bothering me. Why didn't you tell me that Sadie was with her mother the night Beth died?"

Tom's eyes went wide. "Who told you that?"

"Nobody. I read it in the newspaper. Online." I felt a flush climb my cheekbones, but I continued to face him boldly.

"You actually went online and looked up the news reports? Why, for God's sake?"

"Because nobody will talk to me about it! If it were up to you and Riley, I wouldn't even know Beth was ever part of this family! If you'd bothered to tell me, I might have understood why you didn't want to dredge it all up again for Sadie. I'm her step-mother, for God's sake. I thought that meant I had a stake in raising her. But how can I function effectively as a parent if I don't know what's going on with the kids? Frankly, Tom, it makes me wonder how many other things you've kept from me."

"Ah, Jules, it's not like that. I've never deliberately withheld information from you. It's just so difficult to talk about. The trauma my daughter went through that night—I just can't imagine it. I also can't imagine how Beth could have done that to her own child. So there's a little anger in the mix, as well."

"You want my opinion? I think you and the girls all need therapy. You're in denial, and they're left in limbo. It's not a healthy combination."

He blinked. "Are you suggesting that I'm responsible for Sadie's nightmares? And Taylor's standoffishness?"

"In a roundabout way, yes. That's exactly what I think. Both those girls need some way of working through their feelings about what happened to their mother. But in refusing them access to a mental health professional, and then clamming up instead of talking it over with them, you've effectively closed off all avenues of resolution. You've let your own distaste for the situation stand in the way of what's best for your daughters. You have to stop doing that."

He got up, crossed the room, stared out the window, his hands buried deep in his pockets. "I have to think this over," he said. "It's possible that you're right."

"It's more than possible."

"Let me work it out on my own, Jules. I'm hard-headed and set in my ways. I need time to get past my bruised ego and find the balance I seem to have been missing."

"Fine. When you're ready to acknowledge the truth, you can find me upstairs. I'm tired, and I'm taking a nap."

Of course, I didn't sleep. I lay there listening to the soft rain outside. Every time I'd begin to drift off, I'd wake with a start and check the clock. It was a half hour before I heard Tom's measured tread on the stairs. The bedroom door opened slowly, and my husband stood there, peering into the gloom. "I'm sorry," he said.

"I'm not the one you owe an apology to."

He closed the door behind him and crossed the room. Sitting on the edge of the bed, he said, "Christ, Jules, I've made so many mistakes. How the hell can I fix this mess?"

I took his hand in mine. It was cold and clammy. "You can't change the past," I said. "All you can do is move forward. Learn from your mistakes and start doing things differently. Kids are pretty resilient. If you get them the help they need now, if you start opening up and talking to them about what they've been through, what you've all been through, it's not too late to turn things around."

"How is it possible," he said, "that I'm the one

with the medical degree, but you're the one with the common sense?"

"Dumb luck?"

"That must be it."

I ran the tip of my finger along the palm of his hand. "Do you have to go back to work?" I said.

"Actually—" He gave me a wan smile. "I wasn't sure what I'd find when I got home. You weren't exactly forthcoming on the phone. Just to be safe, I cancelled the rest of my appointments for the afternoon. Unless somebody goes into labor, I'm all yours until tomorrow."

"Really? How much time do we have before the girls get home?"

"Why? Are you thinking what I'm thinking?"

"I am definitely thinking what you're thinking."

He checked his watch. "We have approximately sixty-three minutes before they're due to burst through the front door."

"That should be enough time," I said, "for what I have in mind."

Outside the open window, a soft rain fell. Inside, we sat huddled at one corner of the kitchen table, our feet nestled comfortably together, both of us humming with postcoital afterglow. Tom reached his spoon into the carton of Ben & Jerry's and scraped at the insides. "Getting low," he said. "We might have to send out for reinforcements."

"And I was convinced you didn't believe in sugar."

"My deep, dark secret. Why do you think there's always ice cream in the house? Sugar has its time and its place. Just not in my children's daily diet."

He raised a spoonful of Chunky Monkey and fed it to me. The sheer, hedonistic pleasure was instantaneous. "You are a god," I said.

"See? Even you understand I'm really not the vile creature you thought I was."

"Not vile." I opened my mouth for another spoonful. "Just a little obsessive when it comes to protecting what's yours."

"I don't mean to be overprotective," Tom said through a mouthful of banana ice cream laced with chocolate. "It's just that responsibility was drummed into me at an early age, and I can't seem to break free of it."

I flexed my bare toes, wiggled them around and rubbed my foot, the one without the air cast, against his. "Why?" I said.

He thrust his spoon into the ice cream carton, scraped around for that last bite, fed it to me. Setting the carton aside, he said, "My dad was a doctor. A general practitioner. The kind who actually made house calls. He was universally loved by his patients, which accounted for ninety percent of the population of Newmarket. I was twelve when he died. Car accident. One day he was there, the next day he wasn't. It was tough for two young boys to comprehend. Riley was just ten. He and I both took it hard. And Mom was—" He stared out the window at the drizzle running off the eaves. "I don't know if helpless is the right word. Maybe just lost in her grief. For a long time, she walked around like a phantom. There, but not there, so insubstantial you could almost look through her. It was heartbreaking. I was the oldest, so by default, I was forced to become the adult. At twelve, I gave up my childhood to become the man of the house. I was too young to go to work, but I took care of everything else. Made sure we were warm and fed, kept the lawn mowed and the leaky pipes fixed, even scrubbed the toilets when Mom locked herself in her room, sometimes for days on end."

I tried to picture it: a preadolescent Tom, already handsome enough to break the hearts of the local girls, riding the bus home from school every day, never knowing what he'd face when he got there. While the other boys were out riding their bikes and shooting hoops in their driveways, Tom was vacuuming carpets and washing laundry, every so often sneaking a glance at the closed bedroom door behind which his mother, still in a state of shock after losing her husband so suddenly, watched the clock go around and thought about what might have been. Although I could clearly see Tom, it was hard to imagine Jeannette as a young woman. Harder still to imagine how Riley fit into this scenario. But it went a long way toward explaining my mother-in-law's bitterness toward the world. When she lost her husband, the man who lit up her life, the sun had stopped shining for her. I understood, for I'd felt the same way when Angel died. Except that I hadn't allowed my loss to make me bitter and angry. Jeannette, after twenty-five years, still cast herself in the role of victim.

"That's a lot of responsibility," I said, "for a twelve-year-old boy."

"Yes. It was." Tom got up, rinsed the spoon in the sink and put it in the dishwasher, then buried the empty ice cream container deep in the kitchen trash can. "And I took it on with zeal," he said, returning to the table, "because I'd idolized my father. Because of him, I wanted to do everything right. I thought it was what he'd have wanted. Looking back, I'm not so sure. But at the time, it felt right." He grimaced. "So I was ruthless with myself, setting impossibly high standards. Even after Mom came out of her stupor and rejoined the living, I strove to excel. By that time, it'd become routine. Simply the way things worked around here. And Mom encouraged me in my pursuit of perfection. She had great expectations of me. When I saw how much I pleased her, I doubled my efforts. I brought home perfect grades. Took care of everything around the house. I played football, not because I was interested in sports, but because my dad had been the star quarterback of his high school team, and I wanted to emulate him. As soon as I was old enough, I went to work and started contributing to the family income. I dated the 'right' girls, not because I liked them, but because my mother found them socially acceptable." Tom gave me a sardonic smile. "And," he said, "when the time came around, I applied to medical school, not because I was interested in medicine, but because my mother—and by this time the whole town—expected me to follow in my dad's footsteps and become the next beloved Doc Larkin."

"Oh, Tom. That's so sad."

My husband shrugged. "I never thought about it that way. It's just the way things were. I did it because I felt I had to. And I did it all with a smile. I held the resentment inside. But it was there. It was always there. I was so jealous of Riley that I burned with it."

"Really? Why?"

"Because nobody cared what Riley did. Nobody gave two hoots if he stayed in his room with the shades drawn, smoking weed, for a month straight. Nobody cared how many cars he totaled, nobody cared if he flunked out of school or impregnated half the cheerleading squad. Riley had it made, and I hated him for it."

Before I could respond, I heard the front door open, and the sound of running footsteps echoed down the hall. Both girls burst into the kitchen. "Daddy!" Sadie squealed, throwing herself into Tom's arms.

Taylor, as usual a little more reserved, held back. Her keen eyes took in our cozy posture and her father's relative state of dishabille with suspicion. It wasn't often she saw him in jeans and a sweatshirt at this time of day. "Why are you home so early?" she asked.

Tom swung Sadie onto his lap, and she proceeded

to wrap her arms around his neck. "Julie was lonely," he said, "so I took the afternoon off to spend it with her."

Taylor's glance in my direction was reproachful. She studied her father's face as if gauging the truthfulness of his statement. "Tell you what," Tom said. "If Julie's feeling up to it, what do you say we all go out to supper tonight? You girls can even pick the restaurant."

"Yippee!" Sadie said, clapping her hands.

"What about Grandma?" Taylor said.

"Grandma can come too, if she wants. Right, Jules?"

It would be my first outing since the accident, and although I hadn't taken a pill since this morning, I was back to feeling queasy and tired. There was nothing that sounded less appealing than going out to dinner with Tom's mother. But I couldn't disappoint the girls. It wouldn't be fair to them. I'd just come home afterward and sleep for a month. "Of course," I said.

"Can we go to Pizza Heaven?" Taylor asked, the frost gone from her voice. Children, I'd discovered, could be easily bribed. She might still not like me, but if pizza was involved, she was willing to pretend for a couple of hours.

"I don't know," Tom said. "What do you say, hon?"

The ice cream that had tasted so wonderful just a short time ago now lay like a stone in the pit of my stomach. The very idea of pizza sent waves of nausea crashing through me. But if the girls were determined to have pizza, they'd get pizza. I could nibble on a bread stick and do a little pretending of my own. With what I hoped came off as a hearty grin, I told my husband and the girls, "I say it sounds great."

The restaurant was crowded and noisy. The jukebox blasted overhead. Amid the din, waitresses scurried around us, juggling heavily laden trays of drinks and steaming pans of pizza. We were seated between a high school soccer team celebrating their recent victory and a family whose six children ran amok, without parental guidance or control, wreaking havoc with the salad bar and spilling their drinks so many times their waitress should have demanded combat pay. Ah, the ambiance of a family restaurant on a Friday night! I leaned my chin on my hand, looked deep into my husband's eyes, and said, "Promise me we won't have more than four kids. That includes the two we already have."

He leaned over the table and said to me, in a teasing whisper, "Know what the worst thing is? I delivered every one of those kids."

"Aha! So you're the guilty party. Aren't you just a bit ashamed about what you've unleashed on an unsuspecting world?"

"Julie?" Sadie tugged at my sleeve. "Can I get Jell-O from the salad bar?"

I turned my attention to her and smiled. "You can have anything you want, lamb chop."

"Come help us?"

"There's no need," Tom said, laying a hand on my arm. "I can do it. Rest your ankle."

"Is that Dr. Larkin speaking, or my husband Tom?"

"It's Dr. Larkin. Don't put undue strain on the ankle, or it'll take forever to heal. I can help the girls." He shoved back his chair, dropped his napkin on the table, and followed the girls across the three acres of dining room that lay between our table and the salad bar.

I picked up my glass of ice water and took a sip, hoping it would settle my stomach. Just the smell of pizza was making me queasy. At least I'd gotten a small reprieve this evening. Jeannette had declined to come with us. She'd had a long day, she said, and just wanted to stay in tonight, soak her aching feet in hot water and Epsom salts, and watch the evening news. The girls had been disappointed, but Tom, recognizing the tension between his mother and me, seemed relieved. I couldn't blame him. Family dinners could be difficult, given his mother's reluctance to accept me into the family and my own stubborn refusal to be ignored. The nightly battle of wills had to be trying for anybody who witnessed it.

A waitress walked by carrying a huge, loaded pizza. Bile rose in my throat, and for an instant, I feared I'd lose it, right there at the table. I looked around for the restroom sign, spied it near the entrance. Picking up my purse, I tried to catch Tom's eye and signal to him, but he was engrossed in the salad bar, and I didn't have time to dawdle. I rushed—as much as a woman in an air cast is capable of rushing—to the restroom door. It swung open and, ignoring the woman who stood primping at the mirror, I headed directly for one of the stalls.

I just made it. Dropping my purse to the floor, I fell to my knees, leaned over the toilet bowl, and lost the contents of my stomach.

I felt better almost immediately. Rocking back on my heels, I reached for the toilet paper, tore off a piece and bunched it up, and dabbed at my mouth. Behind me, a knock sounded at the door. "Julie?" said a woman's voice. "It's Melanie Ambrose. I saw you come in. Are you all right in there?"

I flushed the toilet and staggered to my feet—no mean feat considering the plastic contraption that was Velcroed to my leg. I unlocked the door, swung it open, and came face-to-face with Beth's sister. "I've been sick," I croaked. "It's these pills I've been taking. For the pain? They make me so sick. I discontinued them this morning, but they're still in my system."

Mel didn't even try to disguise the look of horror on her face brought on by my appearance. "You look awful," she said. "Let's splash some cold water on your face. Do you want me to go get Tom?"

"No. Please. We're here with the girls, and they're so excited about eating out. I can't spoil it for them."

Melanie turned on the faucet, adjusted the water temperature, and I ducked my face under the flow of water. I rinsed out my mouth, spat into the sink, and dabbed at my face with my sleeve.

"I heard about your accident," Mel said, "but I had no idea it was this bad. Here, hold on." She went into the stall, returned with a wad of toilet paper. "Wipe your face with this. It's the best I can do, now that they've replaced paper towels in public restrooms with those ridiculous electric hand dryers. You keep hearing speculation about why so many people don't wash their hands after using the restroom. Maybe it has something to do with the fact that people don't like to wait in line for one of the two dryers in a twelve-stall restroom. And they call this progress?"

I gripped the edge of the counter and didn't answer. It was okay; Mel wasn't expecting an answer. Staring into the mirror, I was shocked by my own reflection. The bruises around my eyes had started to fade, but my face was gaunt and bony, my eyes sunk deep in the sockets over lovely violet shadows. I looked like the pictures I'd seen of Auschwitz survivors after the liberation. Even my hair lay dull and flat, its gloss completely gone.

"Julie?" Mel ventured tentatively. "You really don't look so hot. Are you sure it's just your medication?"

I wasn't sure. Not any longer. The woman who stared back at me from the mirror was nearly unrecognizable. But I wasn't about to admit it to Mel, a woman whose opinion of my husband was less than stellar. She'd probably accuse him of poisoning me. "I'll be okay," I said, "once the medication is out of my system. I'm glad I ran into you. I've been wanting to talk to you. About your sister."

Some of the warmth left her. "What about my sister?"

I glanced at the door. "I can't talk here. Can we get together sometime next week? While Tom's at work?"

Her eyes narrowed in suspicion. "Why?"

"Because—" I glanced again at the door, and lowered my voice. "Because I don't believe Beth killed herself." I took a deep breath, relieved that the nausea had finally receded. "I think she was murdered."

It was raining again on Tuesday, another dark, blustery day that sent wet leaves scuttling across the yard and set the branches of nearby trees rapping against the windows. Melanie arrived at ten, an hour when I thought we'd have the most privacy. Claudia had a yoga class, and Riley a new job remodeling a kitchen for a Falmouth couple, so I knew we shouldn't have any interruptions. "You're looking a little more chipper," Melanie said, removing her coat and hanging it over a kitchen chair. "Are you feeling better?"

"A little." The bruises had almost disappeared by now, and the purple circles beneath my eyes weren't as pronounced. It had been four days since I stopped taking the pills, and I was nowhere near as groggy as I'd been. But I still wasn't myself. Bouts of nausea and spells of—to put it politely—loose bowels continued to plague me. My memory and concentration still weren't up to par. I could only read a half dozen pages before I had to put down whatever I was reading and do something else. I occasionally had trouble retrieving a word from long-term memory. Simple words, words that were part of my normal vocabulary, would simply go MIA. Sometimes, I'd forget where I was and what I was doing. My muscles occasionally twitched or jerked for no explicable reason. And I still felt achy, long after the pain from the fall should have subsided. The continued memory lapses might be due to the concussion. But the rest of it made me wonder what in hell was going on. Had I contracted some weird strain of flu in addition to all my other woes? It was a little early in the year for flu, but even Tom was starting to wonder. He'd told me that just because flu season hadn't yet hit, it didn't mean random strains of the virus weren't out there, waiting to strike the first unsuspecting person whose immune system had been compromised. And my accident, he claimed, could have been enough to weaken my immunity.

"I wasn't really comfortable coming here," Mel said. "I haven't been in this house for a long time, and I don't want to run into Tom. I probably wouldn't have come at all if you hadn't said what you did about Beth. That you don't believe she killed herself."

I'd forgotten that, as Beth's sister, she'd undoubtedly visited this house many times over the years. "I'm glad you came," I said. "I think it's important. Can I ask you a favor? Would you be willing to look around and tell me what's changed since Beth lived here?"

Mel took a second, more critical look around the kitchen. "Her clock's gone," she said. "Beth had a kitchen clock shaped like a cow. She picked it up on a trip to Boston, at one of those overpriced pushcarts near Faneuil Hall." Her voice grew wistful. "My sister had a whimsical sense of humor."

Without knowing quite why I asked, I said, "Would you mind looking around the living room, too? Just to satisfy my curiosity."

"The recliner's new," Mel said as soon as we stepped into the room. "Beth had an old wooden rocker in that corner. Tom bought it for her before Taylor was born. She nursed both her babies sitting in that chair. And rocked them to sleep."

An image of Beth Larkin was beginning to form in my head, a vision of a loving mother who breast-fed her babies and rocked them to sleep in a special rocker purchased just for them. Hardly the picture of a suicidal woman.

"And the wedding portrait's gone."

"Wedding portrait?"

"It was a huge black-and-white framed photo of her and Tom on their wedding day. It used to hang over the fireplace. There were other photos, too. One with her and the girls at Old Orchard Beach. Tom took it, I think. He's a pretty good amateur photographer."

One more thing I didn't know about my husband. Mel was proving a treasure trove of information. "Please," I said, "have a seat. Anywhere. Can I get you something?"

"Nothing. I have to admit I'm dying of curiosity. You really believe somebody killed my sister?"

"I'm absolutely convinced of it. I found a note, you see."

"A note?"

"In a box of Beth's things, tucked away under the eaves in the attic. It was stuck between the pages of *Dr. Zhivago.* I picked up the book, and the note fell out."

"That was her favorite book." Mel played with the hem to her sweater, twisting and turning it between her fingers. "She loved the movie, too. We rented it and watched it together. What did the note say?"

"I don't remember the exact wording, but it was something to the effect that *he*—whoever he is— knew. Knew what, it didn't say. She said that if the truth came out, she feared that she'd lose her children, and maybe even her life. Beth signed the note, but she apparently never sent it. It was addressed to just an initial. The letter K. Do you have any idea who that might be?"

Instead of answering my question, Mel leaned forward and said, "Can I see it? The note?"

"I'd love to show it to you. Unfortunately—" I grimaced "—I don't have it. While I was being X-rayed from stem to stern at the hospital, it fell out of my pocket and disappeared."

A frown line appeared between Melanie's eyes. "You lost it," she said.

That wasn't quite how I would have put it, but I suppose it was, on the surface at least, true. "Yes," I said. "But it wasn't my fault. I was planning to take it to the police when I fell down the stairs, and—" I stopped, because Mel had gone so pale I thought she might faint. "What?" I said. "What's wrong?"

"Don't take it to the police." Clutching the arm of her chair, she leaned forward. "Promise me you won't."

"I couldn't if I wanted to. I don't have it anymore."

"But promise you won't tell the police about it. You have to promise. You don't know him. Not really. You don't know what he's capable of doing."

I was getting a little exasperated with her theatrics. "Who?" I said. "Who is it I don't know?"

"Tom! Your husband!"

This was starting to get old. "Look," I said, "I don't know what it is you think you know about my husband, but—"

"He killed my sister! How much more do I need to know?"

"I think we're just going to have to agree to disagree about that. For God's sake, Melanie, I came right out and asked him if he killed her. I can't believe I actually said it to him. He was so hurt. But I did. And—"

"What did he say? When you asked him if he killed her, did he deny it?"

"Of course he denied it!"

"Did he actually say to you, 'I did not kill Beth Larkin'?"

"He said—" I paused, trying to remember his exact words. "I don't remember what he said, damn it! But he made it clear that he was innocent."

"You see? That's how he gets around things. It's how he always got around things, right from the time we were kids. He blinds people with his charm, with those good looks and that killer smile, so that even while he's stabbing you in the back, you're smiling right back at him and asking him to do it again."

"I think it's time for you to leave."

"Believe what you will. But you're young, Julie. A little naive. You're in love, and you're letting that love blind you. The man you married is a charming, manipulative liar who'd do or say anything to cover up the truth about what he's done. If you keep pushing this, you could be his next victim."

"That's the most preposterous thing I've ever heard."

"That's what Beth thought, too. Until she found out the truth, and it killed her. I heard about your little accident. I heard how it happened. You don't really believe it was an accident, do you?"

"If you're implying that Tom was responsible for my fall—"

"Those batteries didn't walk themselves to the stairs, now, did they?"

"Tom would never do anything to hurt me. And he was at work that day. He had neither opportunity nor motive, so there goes your theory, right down the toilet."

"How do you know he was at work?"

"Riley called him! He came straight from his office to the hospital."

"Are you sure? Are you sure Riley called him at his office? Or did he call Tom's cell phone?"

"I never asked," I snapped. "I was a little busy!" Furiously scraping my hair back from my face, I repeated, "It's time for you to leave."

Melanie stood, gathered up her purse. "Whatever. I guess there's only so much I can do if you continue to refuse my help. You know what, Julie? You're your own worst enemy. All I can say is watch your back."

After she was gone, I fretted and fumed, pacing awkwardly on my bad ankle, back and forth across the kitchen, furious with her for the things she'd said, even more furious with myself for allowing her words to plant a seed of doubt in my mind. Just when things were getting better. Just when Tom and I seemed to have regained whatever it was we'd lost. Just when I'd finally started believing in him again, the paranoia was back.

Or maybe it wasn't paranoia. Maybe it was just common sense. Maybe Melanie was right in saying that I was too much in love to see things clearly. What if the paranoia was actually my subconscious, trying to warn me that something was rotten in Denmark? *Watch your back.* It was odd that Melanie should utter the same phrase her dead sister had said to me in my dream. Did my subconscious know something my conscious mind refused to admit? Something Mel said had struck a chord in me. She'd called Tom a charming, manipulative liar. As much as I hated to admit it, there was a grain of truth in what she said. How many times had Tom lied to me, either by commission or by omission? I'd lost count. Yet every time, I'd forgiven him, looked the other way, believed the excuses he handed me. For that's what they were, excuses. Perhaps some of them were valid excuses, but they were excuses nevertheless.

For the first time since we'd met, I wasn't sure Tom and I were going to make it. How could I stay married to a man I didn't fully trust? That seed of doubt would always be there, prodding at me like an aching tooth. I might temporarily forget the nagging pain when he distracted me with pretty words or sweet lovemaking. But the minute the distraction was gone, that pain would be right back, waiting to keep me awake at night.

I loved Tom Larkin. Was I ready to face life without him? We'd been together only a short time, but already I'd adjusted to his rhythms and his lifestyle, had grown accustomed to his warmth beside me in bed at night. I thrilled to his lovemaking and laughed at his stupid jokes. Every inch of his body was familiar to me. I knew the tenderness of his touch, knew how precisely we fit together. I could gauge his moods just from his tone of voice. I knew, and finally understood, his need for order and neatness. And I respected him, as a human being, as a doctor, as a caring father who was capable of admitting his mistakes. He was my husband, my lover, my friend. Our marriage might have been brief, but it was real. Leaving him now would tear my heart in two.

And I had to consider the girls. In the few short

weeks that Tom and I had been together, I'd grown inordinately fond of them. Sadie, with her sweet face and gentle affection, was my favorite. But I also had a great deal of respect for Taylor, so fiercely independent, standing her ground no matter what the situation. They needed a mother so badly, and I'd done everything I could to fill that void. And I'd promised I'd never leave them. That promise had come from my heart. How could I justify breaking it?

But this was a crazy house, a house of mirrors, where nothing—and nobody—was what it appeared to be. Maybe it was the paranoia that had returned along with the headache, but I no longer felt safe here. I no longer trusted anybody. Not Tom, not Riley, not Claudia, and certainly not Jeannette. If I left and never returned, my mother-in-law would dance a jig. Tom would survive, the same way he'd survived after Beth died. He'd pour himself into work and neglect his family, for that was how Tom operated. Riley would pick up the slack, for that was how *he* operated. The girls would be hurt by my leaving, but I told myself that kids were resilient. They'd get over it. Eventually.

When I left L.A. six weeks earlier, I'd believed there was nothing left for me in the city. But I also knew that if I wanted my job back, it would be waiting for me. Carlos had made that clear before I headed East. "We're family," he said. "Family takes care of family. You ever need anything, you come to Carlos." What's the old saying? Home is the place where, when you have to go there, they have to take you in. That's the way it was with Carlos and me. He'd welcome me back to the fold, badger me until I caved and told him every sordid detail, and then he'd console me with Cuban rum and a day at the spa.

But right now, just the thought of Cuban rum had my stomach roiling. This couldn't go on. Something was wrong, something that scared me half to death. What if I were dying? What if I had some rare form of cancer that would leave me weak and emaciated, too sick to take care of myself, totally dependent on other people? I needed to see a doctor, one who wouldn't immediately report back to Tom. And I doubted I'd find that in Newmarket. Everybody in this town adored my husband. Everybody, that is, except Melanie Ambrose.

I guess there's only so much I can do if you continue to refuse my help. Those were the words Mel had said to me just before she walked out my door. I wondered if she could be right. I thought about it for a long time before I shambled to the kitchen like the Swamp Thing, picked up the phone, and dialed her number.

"Mel?" I said when she answered. "It's Julie Larkin. I need your help."

Eleven

Dr. Helen Kapowicz was a general practitioner affiliated with Maine Medical Center in Portland. It was Mel who found her in the phone book, Mel who arranged the appointment, Mel who drove me to Portland because I didn't trust myself to drive that far. After the words we'd had, I wasn't sure she would even speak to me again. But I should have known better. Melanie Ambrose might passionately hate my husband, but she had nothing but compassion for me. I wasn't sure how I'd ever pay her back. When I told her that, she gripped the steering wheel so hard her fingers turned white and said grimly, "I couldn't help my sister. But I'll be damned if I'm letting you go down without a fight."

Dr. Kapowicz was an older lady who listened patiently to my complaints—and to her credit, didn't even suggest I might be crazy—before she had me disrobe for the exam. She was thorough. She checked my heartbeat, my pulse and my reflexes, took my blood pressure and my temp, studied my eyes and ears with her little pocket light. She took blood and urine samples, did a pelvic exam, even examined my feet and my gums. By the time she was done, she knew me more intimately than Tom did. "Why don't you get dressed," she said, "and then we'll talk."

She didn't leave me waiting for long. "Well, Mrs. Larkin," she said when she came back, "I have good news and bad news. The bad news is, I don't know what's causing some of your symptoms. The headaches, the forgetfulness, the disorientation, could seemingly be attributed to the concussion. Except that it's been long enough since you fell that it seems as though the symptoms would be gone by now. They could just as easily be some kind of stress reaction. I'm hoping the blood tests will shed some light on that. In the meantime, the good news—at least I think it's good news—is that you're pregnant. That's probably the primary cause of the nausea you've been experiencing."

My heart began to thud. Stunned, I whispered, "Pregnant?" The thought hadn't even occurred to me. We'd only been trying for a few weeks. Frantically, I thought back, tried to remember the date of my last period. Had I even *had* a period after I came to Newmarket? Much of the last few weeks was fuzzy in my memory. And with everything that had gone on, my monthly visitor was the last thing on my mind. "How far along?" I asked.

"I'd say somewhere between five and six weeks."

"That long?" It seemed impossible. Three weeks had passed since we tossed out the Trojans and went commando. If Dr. Kapowicz was right, I'd already been pregnant when we made the decision to try for a baby. Yet up until that point, we'd used a condom every time we had sex. So much for the efficiency of that method of birth control.

"I sense a little uncertainly about this pregnancy," the doctor said.

"It's just a shock, that's all." A major one. My mind raced, like a pinball out of control, from one implication to the next. None of them were good. "My husband and I were talking about starting a family. I just didn't expect it to happen so quickly."

"Do you have children?"

"Two stepdaughters. And I gave birth to a still-born child a year and a half ago. I wasn't sure I should even try again." Tears filled my eyes, and my throat closed up. "I'm sorry," I sputtered. "This is all so overwhelming. I just got married six weeks ago. I'm not sure I'm ready for a baby. Not right now." It was what I'd wanted. What we'd both wanted. But the timing couldn't have been worse. Here I was, contemplating ending my six-week-old marriage, and now I was pregnant? The gods must be getting one hell of a laugh out of this one.

Kapowicz patted my hand. "Give yourself a little time to adjust to the idea. Finding out you're pregnant is always a shock, even when it's planned. I'll give you a prescription for prenatal vitamins and antinausea medication. And, if you want, a referral to an OB/GYN."

"Thank you. I'll take the prescriptions, but the referral won't be necessary. My husband is an OB/GYN. I'm sure he can refer me to someone he trusts."

"Well, then. I guess all we have left to do is wait for the results of the blood tests. I'll call you when they come in. It should only take a few days."

In the car, I sat in silence, still stunned by this unexpected turn of events. It changed everything. I was carrying Tom's child. How could I leave him now? Even if I tried to leave, he'd never allow me to. Not if he knew about the baby. He wanted this baby, maybe even more than I did. This little collection of cells that had burrowed into the wall of my uterus had joined us together in a way that no marriage license could ever do. No matter what happened between us, we'd created this child together, and we would be joined by that simple biological fact as long as the three of us drew breath.

"So," Mel said after several miles of trees and asphalt highway and utter silence. "How far along are you?"

I turned my head, seeming to see her as though from a great distance. "How did you know?"

"I've been there a couple of times myself. I figured it out the other night at the restaurant when I saw you on your knees in the toilet stall. With my first pregnancy, just the smell of tomato sauce was enough to send me into a violent fit of vomiting."

"Please don't tell anyone. I don't want Tom to know. Not yet." Not until I decided what to do.

Dryly, she said, "Tom and I don't exactly run in the same circles. But don't worry. I won't tell. You need a little time to sit back, take a deep breath, and get your head together."

Yes. That was exactly what I needed. I sat in a daze, pondering my options, as the fall foliage flew past my window. Was my marriage worth saving? Did I want to leave Tom? Could I possibly stay with him, knowing how conflicted my feelings were about our marriage? Was it even safe to stay? There was one conclusion I didn't need any time at all to reach. My safety, and that of my unborn child, were of paramount concern. More important than my marriage, more important than disappointing the girls, the one thing that really mattered was that I give birth to a healthy child.

Mel and I were apparently on the same wavelength. "This isn't a bad thing," she said. "Try to remember that. No matter how much of a mess your life is right now, this is a baby. A beautiful, precious new life. A joyous occasion. You and that baby will get through this together. With or without Tom."

She was right, and I was thankful for the reminder.

It was just past noon when she dropped me off at the house. I'd finally convinced Claudia that her personal Meals on Wheels program was no longer necessary. Grateful to be alone, I choked down a bologna sandwich, then I went upstairs and took a long, hot shower. I shampooed my hair, luxuriating in the thick strawberry-scented lather. I'd had a rough couple of weeks, and I deserved to be pampered.

Dressing had become a little easier. Without too much effort, I slipped into jeans and a T-shirt. I had a phone call to make. Then I intended to drive into town and fill my prescription.

I sat on the edge of the bed, debating, for a good ten minutes before I finally picked up the phone and dialed. It wasn't as though I'd made a decision to leave Tom. I was simply testing the waters, mapping out my escape routes, just in case I needed to use them. It felt wrong, going behind Tom's back like this. If he knew what I was about to do, he'd be hurt. Angry. But I had to protect myself and my baby. I was swimming in shark-infested waters, and I needed to know exactly where I stood if things got so bad I had to make the decision to get out of the water. I didn't want to believe it would come to that, but I had to explore my options, just in case.

I checked the time. It was twelve-thirty. Three hours earlier out on the Coast. Nine-thirty wasn't too early to call. Louis wasn't the kind to lallygag in bed all day. He'd probably been up for hours already, sitting on his balcony with his feet up, reading *Variety* or the racing program, and drinking coffee so black and thick you could easily mistake it for used motor oil.

Louis Coffey's age falls somewhere on a continuum between sixty and dead. In his younger days, he was a semipro prize fighter, and he has the scars to prove it. After he retired from fighting, he took work as a film extra whenever he could get it. He line danced in *Saturday Night Fever,* played golf in *Caddyshack,* and was vaporized in *Men in Black.* But that kind of work was irregular, so to supplement his paltry income, he bought up a block of crumbling apartment buildings in West Hollywood, one of which I'd called home for the past quarter of a century, and he became a slumlord. Although renting uninspired post-World-War-II-era apartments to people just this side of indigence hasn't exactly provided him with an income to rival Donald Trump's, it pays the bills.

He answered on the first ring. "Louis," I said, trying to inject a modicum of enthusiasm into my voice. "It's Julie. Julie Hanrahan. Well, Julie Larkin now."

In his gravelly Burgess Meredith voice, Louis said, "Hey, kid. How goes the battle?"

"Not so well, I'm afraid. I have a question for you."

"I hope you're not looking for a security deposit. When you and your dad moved in here, all those years ago, he was pretty much down and out. Hell, let's face it. He didn't have a pot to piss in. All he had was a few pieces of ugly furniture, and you. Most pathetic little kid I ever saw, all scrawny legs and big brown eyes and scabby knees. I couldn't say no to him. So I let him move in without a deposit. On account of you."

I assured him that I wasn't looking for a security deposit. "This is something else," I said, and took a breath. "Have you rented out my apartment yet?"

There was an instant of silence at the other end of the phone before he said, "What's the matter, kid? Trouble in paradise already?"

"It's nothing, really. I'm just looking into my options."

"The apartment's rented. I rented it a couple days after you left. Nice lady, works at an insurance company downtown. Hell, I figured you got married, maybe this time it was for keeps. Last guy you married was a loser. I was hoping that this time, you'd do a better job of picking. Listen, I got a little advice for you. Date the guys, sleep with 'em and get your kicks, but don't get married. It never seems to work out."

"It's not that big a deal," I said, "really."

He sighed. "Look, if you need to come home, I'll find a place for you, even if I have to put you up on my own couch until I can find an excuse to evict somebody. That kid in 3B's been dealing drugs. I know it. I can catch him at it, I can toss him out on his ass without the ACLU getting on my case."

Tears stung my eyelids. "Are you sure, Louis? You'd really do that for me?"

"As sure as I am that Sonja Henie won't be traveling with the Ice Capades anytime soon. Don't be spreading this around, because you'll ruin my reputation as a hard-ass, but all those years I spent losing money to your dad playing blackjack, I was also watching you grow up. I have an avuncular interest in you. And if that son-of-a-bitch you married is hitting you—"

"He's not! It's nothing like that."

"It better not be, or he'll be answering to me."

God bless Louis Coffey. "Thank you," I said. "I'm sure Tom and I will work things out and I won't need to take advantage of your hospitality. It's just that— we didn't know each other very well before we got married, and now—"

"I should think not. What was it, five days? You kids nowadays are always in a hurry. Never want to take the time a sensible person knows you gotta have before you make that kind of decision."

He was right, of course, but I didn't want to hear it. I'd already chided myself a dozen times for not waiting until Tom and I knew each other better. "Listen, Louis," I said, "I have to run, but I really appreciate—"

"You need anything," he said, "and I mean *anything,* you call me. Understand?"

"I understand."

I'd barely hung up the phone when it rang again. "I saw you with Melanie Ambrose," Claudia said. "I didn't realize you were friends."

"Just friendly acquaintances," I said. "I ran into her in the powder room at Pizza Heaven and we got to talking, and the next thing I knew, we'd made plans to go shopping together. In Portland. At the mall." I hoped to God she'd drop the subject. I was a terrible liar, and if she asked me anything specific,

I'd have to spin the lie even deeper. It wouldn't take her long to figure out I'd never been to the Maine Mall in my life.

"Wonderful!" she said. "If you're feeling well enough to go shopping, then you should be well enough for what I have in mind. Sunday, I'm taking Dylan to the county fair. We were hoping you and the girls would like to come along."

My life was in such turmoil that for an instant, I had trouble processing the fact that the normal world was still revolving out there. It was early fall, county fair season. I knew this because just last night, the girls had pestered Tom to take them this weekend. They'd seen the ads on TV and just had to go. Their father, of course, was working all weekend, and the girls had been crushed. I couldn't think of much that interested me less than going to a county agricultural fair. I'd never attended one, and it wasn't high on my list of Things To Do Before I Die. Cotton candy, terrifying carnival rides, and barnyard animals. But I knew the girls would be thrilled. And Tom wouldn't miss us. If they gave out awards for Most Absent Spouse, my husband would win the blue ribbon.

Besides, even considering the barnyard animals, going to the fair would still beat spending the day at home with my mother-in-law. "Yes," I said. "We'd love to come with you."

The next couple of days, my absent spouse was even more absent than usual. I wasn't sure what was distracting him, but I considered it a blessing. I wasn't ready to tell him about the pregnancy, not while I was still so uncertain about where our marriage was headed. And Tom wasn't a fool. Every day of his life, he dealt with pregnant ladies. Sooner or later, he was bound to figure it out. After all, Melanie had, and she barely knew me. But for now, at least, I had a reprieve. Sunday morning, he kissed me goodbye, warned the girls to behave or else, and flew out the door, still tying his necktie as he went.

We left around nine. The fair was located in Oxton, a forty-minute drive from Newmarket, one of those classic Maine "you-can't-get-there-from-here" places. In the backseat, the three kids chatted excitedly. The foliage was nearing peak, and as we drove the back roads of southwestern Maine, we saw vista after vista of stunning color. The roads were bumpy, and twisted every which way, but the antinausea pills Dr. Kapowicz had given me were helping. I still wasn't quite ready to chow down on three-alarm chili, but I felt relatively safe being away from the bathroom for more than twenty minutes.

We parked in a field a half mile from the fairgrounds. "Stay together," Claudia told the kids. "If we lose you in this crowd, you'll be thirty-five before we ever see you again."

I'd finally gotten the air cast off my ankle. My balance was a little off, but I was healing nicely, and so thrilled to be rid of the annoying thing that I didn't even care about the fact that I'd be walking for what looked to be the next two days. It didn't seem likely that we'd be able to cover the entire fair, not with three small kids. Taylor might make it, but I suspected Dylan and Sadie would tire after a couple of hours. Since I expected to tire long before that, I figured we should probably hit the don't-miss highlights early. God forbid we should leave before Sadie got her pony ride.

We started with the livestock, every kid's favorite thing. We quacked with the ducks and geese and crowed with the roosters; we petted sheep, fed grain pellets to the goats, and made tentative forays into the world of dairy cattle. Until now, the closest I'd come to a cow was medium rare, laid out on a dinner plate with salt and pepper and a smattering of A.1 Sauce, so needless to say, I kept my distance. The smells weren't pleasant, and I'd never realized just how large a cow is up close and personal. Although the farmer assured me that his prize-winning Holstein wasn't about to trample my seven-year-old stepdaughter, my heart continued to beat a little harder than usual until she was safely away from those lethal-looking hooves.

After we'd seen our fill of live creatures, Claudia and I pointed the kids in the direction of the exhibition hall, eager to see the hand-sewn quilts, the jams and jellies, the needlework and the paintings and the thousand and one other homemade crafts on display. The kids were bored and whiny until we reached the tableau of dead animals proudly displayed by some amateur taxidermist. Here, they stood enthralled with the sharp teeth and glassy eyes of one wild creature after another. "Look," Dylan said, "it's a fox! Are those real animals?"

"They used to be," his mother told him.

"Cool. These are even better than the chickens!"

Sadie slipped her hand in mine. Softly, she said, "Are those animals dead?"

Claudia and I exchanged glances. "Hey," I said, "is anyone hungry? Because I think I saw a cotton candy stand not far away."

"What's cotton candy?" Sadie asked.

"It's like eating pretty pink clouds. Sweet ones. You'll love it. Trust me."

"Daddy doesn't like us to have sugar," Taylor reminded me.

"This is a special occasion. Daddy won't mind. Honest."

She looked skeptical, but at the same time intrigued. We dragged a loudly protesting Dylan away from the wild, dead creatures, and made a pit stop in the restroom to scrub the *eau des animaux* off our hands. Then we hit the midway, along with about three thousand other people, most of them under the age of twelve. I don't think I've ever seen so many kids in one place, hopped up to a manic state on sugar and the incessant barking of the carnies: "Three tries for five bucks! A winner every time!" It was a good thing I'd brought my life savings, for everything in this place was vastly overpriced, from dollar-fifty ride tickets (and some rides took four tickets!) to four-dollar lemonade and lobster rolls so expensive you had to take out a second mortgage to afford them. We found a cotton candy vendor and bought one blue and one pink wand of the delicious confection, which the kids immediately tore into. Even Dylan, whose loud protests had been ongoing ever since we left the exhibition hall, finally forgot the poor butchered fox when presented with this sweet, gooey alternative.

By the time we were done, everybody was sticky, and I suspected the blue stains on Sadie's Dora the Explorer T-shirt were permanent, but I didn't care. The smile on her face was worth it. Dora was everywhere; I could always buy her another shirt. That is, if I was still around to buy it for her. The thought stole a little of the sunshine from my day, but I forced it aside, determined to enjoy myself with the girls. Who knew how many outings like this we'd have together? Whatever was going on between Tom and me, I could set it aside for this one day. The girls deserved my undivided attention.

The kids played a few games. Taylor proved to be deadly accurate at breaking balloons with darts. After milking me for every cent I was willing to part with, she came away with a huge stuffed Tweety Bird that I could have bought in a department store for half of what it cost her to win.

Then it was ride time. I begged off, knowing there was no way I could hold it together on one of those circular nightmares. So I juggled jackets and sunglasses, Claudia's purse and Dylan's baseball cap, and a Tweety Bird the size of Rhode Island, while they all went on the Tilt-A-Whirl. It made me dizzy just to watch, so while they were going around, aided by an ear-shattering, wobbly recording of "Boogie

Nights," I wandered over to a display of Indian jewelry, drawn, as always, by the turquoise. I set down Tweety, shifted my burdens, and picked up a necklace of hammered silver and Arizona turquoise to examine it. The quality was what you'd expect for the county fair circuit, inexpensively made using a lesser grade of turquoise than you'd find in a jewelry store. But the bauble was pretty, and the price reasonable, even taking into account the three-hundred-percent markup. I decided to buy it, and was redistributing my load to locate my credit card when I noticed the man watching me.

He was about thirty feet away, leaning lazily against a corner post of one of the game booths. Tall and lanky, he wore a John Deere cap and a wife-beater T-shirt that showed off his tattooed arms. One arm boasted a massive bald eagle, an American flag gripped tightly in its talons. On the other arm, intricately and skillfully drawn, was the head of a tiger. The man's dark hair was slicked back, his eyes hidden behind mirrored sunglasses. But I knew he was watching me, and there was something about that opaque gaze that seemed mildly malevolent. I couldn't explain why, but a shudder ran down my spine. He took a drag on his cigarette, then he tossed it onto the yellowed grass, ground it out with one booted foot, and gave me a grin.

I immediately averted my gaze. Crap on a cracker. Was he about to come up and speak to me? I'd given him no more encouragement than a brief glance. Surely he couldn't misinterpret that as a sign of interest? I was tired, my ankle was starting to hurt, and

I needed to eat something more substantial than a nibble of spun sugar with food coloring in it. The last thing I needed was to be hit on by some tattooed yokel.

But when I glanced back up, he was gone. Relief coursed through me, accompanied by acute embarrassment. Of course he hadn't been about to hit on me. The smile had been nothing more than the acknowledgment of two anonymous strangers whose glances happened to meet purely by chance. He was simply being polite. Did I really think myself so alluring that total strangers were unable to resist my magnetism?

Claudia and the kids returned to claim their possessions, I located my credit card, and I paid for the necklace. We were sitting at a picnic table, chowing down on hot dogs and potato chips, when I saw the man again. I told myself it was coincidence. The midway wasn't that big; if you kept circling around, sooner or later you were bound to run into the same person two or three times. He was leaning over a display of belt buckles, seemingly fascinated by the assortment. I ignored him, keeping my gaze focused on my hot dog. But when I glanced up, I found him staring at me. Again.

"Don't be obvious," I said to Claudia, "but look at that man over there by the belt buckles. I think he's following me."

Ignoring my warning, Claudia swiveled around to search the crowd. She might as well have sent up flares, she was so obvious. "What man?" she said.

"Don't look!" I whispered.

She arched an eyebrow. "I can't very well see him if I don't look."

"Don't be so damn obvious. He's over by the belt buckles. Skinny, dark-haired, big tattoos."

Making only a feeble attempt to be discreet, Claudia studied the mystery man. "You're imagining it," she finally declared. "I've been watching him all this time, and he hasn't even looked in our direction. The only thing he's interested in is a new buckle for his belt. Preferably one with a naked woman on it."

"He *smiled* at me, Claudia."

"Oh, well, that makes all the difference. Men who smile at women are always psycho serial-killer stalkers."

"Oh, shut up. I know what I'm talking about. The man's been watching me."

"I think you've been stuck indoors for too long. You've forgotten how human beings interact." She studied the man for a little longer. "You could be stalked by worse. He's not the kind of guy I'd want to take home to mother, but as a momentary attraction—say, for an hour or two—he'd make a very nice play toy."

I shuddered. "Not my type."

Claudia shrugged. "To each his own. Cripe, Dylan, look at the mess you've made. You look like you took a bath in mustard." She rolled her eyes and said, to me, "I must be a masochist to do this."

"It goes with the mommy territory. I—shit, Claudia,

I think he's coming over!" I felt an instant of panic before he took a sudden right and veered off course, disappearing into the crowd.

"Honey, are you all right? I've never seen you so pale."

"I'm sorry. I guess I really do have an overactive imagination." Maybe it was the paranoia, back for a return engagement.

Claudia patted my arm. "After what you've been through, I'd be worried if you didn't suffer from just a little anxiety. What you need is Valium. It did wonders for me after my divorce from You-Know-Who."

I didn't really know who, since she'd never bothered to tell me the name of He-Who-Shall-Remain-Nameless, but I got the gist of what she was saying anyway. I appreciated the suggestion, but if there was one thing I didn't need right now, it was more pills. No, I'd get through my anxiety the old-fashioned way. Time and distance did wonders for such things.

After we finished eating, we let the kids take a few of the kiddie rides, the ones that used only one or two tickets and basically did nothing more exciting than revolve in slow motion. Their choice of music was interesting for a ride designed for small children: AC/DC's "Highway to Hell." Whatever happened to "Someday My Prince Will Come"? Was I living in the Dark Ages?

By midafternoon, Claudia and I were both worn out, my ankle was letting me know that it'd had just about enough, and I'd completely forgotten Mystery Man. The kids had already lasted an hour longer than we'd predicted, and showed no signs of stopping. "One more ride," Claudia said sternly. "One more, and then we leave."

"I wanna do the House of Horror!" Dylan said, and the girls immediately added their enthusiastic agreement.

"What do you say?" Claudia asked me. "This one doesn't revolve, and there's no chance of you falling off and breaking a leg. Why don't you come with us?"

I started to decline, but Taylor stepped up to me and slid her hand in mine as smoothly as though it were an everyday occurrence. "Please," she said softly. "I really want you to come."

My heart nearly stopped beating. My throat clogged, and tears, ridiculous tears, threatened to spill. Sadie had been so easy. But Taylor, feisty Taylor, our own personal mini-Tom, had been a tough sell. Her timing was impeccable. All these weeks I'd spent trying to win her over, and now, *now,* she'd finally decided to like me.

My heart wept at the irony of it.

But I couldn't let her see how touched I was. Instead, I closed my hand over hers and said, "For you, my love, absolutely."

Before I could change my mind, Claudia hustled me into line. Somehow, I'd ended up carrying Tweety after Taylor's arms got tired. I got a few curious glances from some of the small children, undoubtedly wondering what an ancient woman like me was doing with a yellow bird the size of a house. And from their mothers, there were a few sympathetic smiles because I had to lug the obnoxiously adorable creature around all day.

"I've never been through one of these things before," I told Claudia as we inched closer to the entrance. "I don't know what to expect."

"Expect the unexpected. Just keep moving. If you stop, you'll bog down the line going through. Remember, it's supposed to be a little scary. That's what makes it fun."

"Speak for yourself," I muttered. We reached the entrance, and something—maybe just a tingling at the back of my neck—made me turn around. I caught just a glimpse of Mystery Man's face. He was hovering not five feet away, hands tucked innocently in his pockets, his eyes focused directly on me. Then before I had time to think, I was shoved through the entrance and instantly plunged into utter darkness.

"Claudia?" I said. "He's here. I just saw him outside."

"Keep moving. There's nothing you can do about it now. Dylan, stay with the girls. Don't let go of each other. Keep working your way through to the end. We'll meet you outside."

All around us, the amplified screams of the tortured and the maniacal laughter of their torturers echoed in full stereo. Ahead of us in the darkness somewhere, I heard Sadie shriek in gleeful terror. Totally blind, I fought my way through something wet and slimy that hung from overhead. I moved into an area lit with a black light. Ahead of me, I could see Sadie's T-shirt and Taylor's shoelaces glowing purple. Somebody tapped me on the shoulder. I turned, and was greeted by a skeleton in all his grinning, purple-boned splendor. He stood behind the half wall that separated the tormenters from the tormented. His bony hand lay on my shoulder and his face was inches from mine. I knew it was all in fun, but the tiny shriek I let out was totally involuntary.

I passed through a heavy curtain, into a narrow passageway where cold, clammy hands, grasping and clutching, reached out for me as I passed. I ducked and twisted and did my best to avoid them. The maniacal laughter continued. So did I. Ahead of me, something swayed. I could feel the breeze as it moved back and forth. I reached out and touched it. The instant I made contact, I realized it was a man—or rather, a replica of a man—swinging by his neck from a rope. His eyes lit up fire-red, and he looked so real that I stopped short, afraid at first to pass by. I reached out a tentative finger and poked him. His clothes were real, but the rest was electronic. Okay. I'd had about enough of this place. Which way was out?

I moved forward into another dark chamber, eager now to get the hell out of Dodge. Somebody bumped into me from behind. A hand grabbed my wrist, and I turned, expecting to see another ghoul. But I was still in darkness, and whoever had hold of me was on my side of the wall. "Let go of me," I said, but the hand held fast.

"What's the matter, Julie? Scared, are you?"

Damn right, I was scared. But I didn't intend to show it. "Who are you?" I demanded. "How do you know my name?" Ahead, I could hear Sadie's delighted shrieks, growing more and more distant. "Claudia?" I shouted.

More maniacal laughter. "Claudia's not here," he said, and clamped a hand over my mouth.

The panic was instantaneous. I struggled. He shoved me hard against the half wall that separated us from whatever electronic devices operated this house of hell. "Let go of me!" I said. Behind us, a woman screamed, loud enough to wake the dead.

"I have a message for you," he said, his voice soft enough so only I could hear it amid the din. "You need to—*oof*." I elbowed him directly in the solar plexus. Taking advantage of his momentary distress, I broke away. Fighting my way through another curtain, into yet another dark space, I became disoriented. Which way had I come? Before I could figure it out, I felt his hot breath on the back of my neck. He tackled me, and we fell to the floor, jarring the hip that hadn't quite recovered from my recent fall.

"Help!" I shouted as we rolled and tumbled on the floor. "Help me!" He cuffed me to shut me up, and the warm, salty taste of blood trickled into my mouth. I reached out blindly for a weapon. My hand came into contact with Tweety. I didn't hesitate. I picked up the giant yellow bird and began clobbering him over the head with it. "Help!" I screamed, to no avail. Everybody in this place was screaming for help of one sort or another. I bashed him one more time with the giant Tweety, took a deep breath, and yelled the one thing I figured would get anybody's attention: "Fire!"

Twelve

"So you didn't get a look at him?"

I was sitting in the first-aid tent, a damp cloth pressed to my split lip, while Claudia and the kids looked on with varying degrees of concern. I glanced at the head of security. He was seventy-five years old if he was a day, with the legacy of too many years of fried dough and sweet Italian sausage settled around his middle. "I told you," I said for the third time, "I saw him outside. It was too dark inside to see anything."

"So in other words, you didn't see him."

"Look, I know who it was. I saw him three times outside. He was following me around. I can describe him to you. Tall, skinny, greasy, slicked-back hair, tattoos. An eagle with a flag clasped in its talons. Ask my friend. She saw him, too."

"Ayuh. Do you have any idea how many fellas have that same tattoo? Especially since the Iraq War.

Everybody's patriotic these days. And you say he called you by name? Seems odd, considering you didn't know him."

"You think? Yes, he knew my name. He called me Julie. He said—"

"You don't suppose he could have heard your friend here calling you by name? You said he was standing right nearby when you were in line for the House of Horror." Barney Fife cleared his throat. "Assuming, of course, that he was the same man who assaulted you."

This was going nowhere fast. "Look," I said, "if you don't mind, I'd like to go home now. Don't worry, I'm not going to sue the Fair Committee. I just want to get out of here, go home and soak my aching body in a tub of hot water. If that's not too much to ask?"

The codger exchanged glances with the first-aid nurse and said, "I guess that would be all right. But I'll need your contact information. Just in case."

Right. Just in case the guy who attacked me walked up to him, held out his unshackled wrists, and said, "Please arrest me." Because that was the only way it was going to happen.

I removed the cloth from my lip, then hobbled the half mile to the car. The kids were oddly subdued, as if the air had been let out of them and they'd fizzled to the ground. Claudia got the two youngest into their car seats. The rest of us clicked our seat belts. My hip screamed as the car jolted over the bumpy terrain of the field, and then we were on the road and the only sound I heard was the cartoons playing on the backseat DVD player.

When the silence built to the point where one of us had to speak or we'd all go crazy, Claudia said, *sotto voce,* "Don't even say it. You were right and I was wrong. Do you have any idea how much I hate those words?"

I glanced quickly at the kids in the back, but they were all engrossed in the ongoing adventures of Scooby-Doo. Whispering so they couldn't hear me, I said, "He knew my name, Claudia. This wasn't just some random mugging. If he'd wanted my purse, he could have taken it when he ran. But he didn't. All he wanted was to give me a message."

"What was the message?"

"I don't know. He didn't get a chance to tell me. I was too busy braining him with Tweety to listen."

"Wish I could've been there to see that."

"Nobody could see that. It was pitch dark."

"Clever of you to yell *fire* instead of *help.*"

"*Help* wasn't working. Everybody in there yells for help. People just thought the ghouls were scaring me. I'd have been dead before anybody noticed." Even then, I thought, they would have just stepped over me and kept on moving, thinking it was part of the act. I turned baleful eyes on her and said, "Never again! Do you hear me? Never, ever again am I going into one of those places. You think my anxiety was bad going in? That's nothing compared to how it was when I came out, bruised and battered for the second time in two weeks."

"I'm sorry. I didn't really believe he was following you. I thought you were imagining it."

"And now? What do you think now?"

"I think you need to talk to Tom."

"And tell him what? That some strange man who somehow knew my name attacked me in the House of Horror, and I beat him with a giant Tweety Bird until he ran away?"

The corner of Claudia's mouth twitched, and she struggled to maintain some semblance of sobriety. "Something rotten is going on here," she said. "I don't think you're safe. I think—" she turned her head to me and studied me somberly. "Somebody's out to get you."

"That sounds so melodramatic. So drama-queenish. So—"

"So real?"

"Be serious. Why would anybody want to hurt me?"

She drummed manicured fingertips on the steering wheel as she considered my question. "I don't know," she said at last. "But you have to tell Tom."

Even if I'm afraid he might be behind it? I hadn't allowed the thought to take shape until now, but it had been there, lying in wait, like a lioness anticipating her dinner, ready to jump me when I least expected it. The attack hadn't been random; the man had called me by name. Somebody had been behind it. Who else but a member of the Larkin family? If not Tom, then Jeannette. Or maybe Riley, although why Riley would want to hurt me, I couldn't imagine.

"Maybe," Claudia said, thinking aloud, "he was just trying to scare you."

"Mission accomplished. I think I just got my first gray hair."

From the backseat, Sadie said, "Julie?"

I twisted in my seat until I could see her. "What, honey?"

"Did that bad man want to kill you?"

I'd thought the kids couldn't hear us. Now I wasn't so sure. Claudia and I exchanged glances and made a silent, mutual vow to change the subject. "No, sweetheart, of course not. I think he just wanted to scare me."

"Did he scare Tweety?"

"Not at all. Tweety was strong and brave. As far as I'm concerned, he's a hero."

When we got home, Tom's car was parked in the yard. As much as I wanted to postpone the inevitable, I knew it was pointless to try. Even if Claudia hadn't been gung ho on tattling, I could never have convinced the girls to keep their mouths shut. The fair had been an exciting experience, but the most exciting part, by far, had been my attack in a darkened room by a faceless assailant. So while Tom listened, on his face a look that was a mix of consternation and outright horror, I sat silent, letting Claudia and the kids tell the story. When they were done, and everyone fell silent, Tom sat there, his eyes burning a hole in me. I began to fidget. "Are you all right?" he finally said.

"My hip's a little sore, and my lip, but other than that—"

"What am I going to do with you, Jules? It's getting so I'm afraid to let you out of my sight.

You're a one-woman disaster area. Am I going to have to lock you in the house? Am I going to have to—"

"Tom." I frowned, shook my head, and gave him my best "not in front of the kids" look. He glanced at Sadie, Taylor, and Dylan—three pair of curious eyes, watching him—and, catching my train of thought, went silent.

"Listen," Claudia said, "why don't I take the girls home with me for a couple of hours? I just rented the new Disney movie, and I have a bag of fish sticks in my freezer with their names engraved on them."

Tom nodded. "Thanks, Claudia," he said. "You're a peach."

When she'd gone, I said, "That was good of her. Where's your mother?"

"She and Riley went to the movies." His words were clipped, and he still wore a grim expression I couldn't decipher.

"You can stop stewing," I said. "I didn't get hurt."

"That's not what I'm stewing about. When were you planning to tell me?"

Still preoccupied by the afternoon's events, I was a little slow at catching up. Vaguely, I said, "Tell you what?"

"It was a little embarrassing," he said, "when Sally Nixon congratulated me today, and I didn't have any idea what she was talking about."

"Who's Sally Nixon? Congratulated you about what?" And then I understood, and everything inside me went still.

"Good question, isn't it? Sally came up to me after the meeting and said she'd heard my wife was pregnant. I almost choked on my coffee. While she stood babbling on, offering her best wishes, I stood there feeling like a fool. Were you planning to tell me at some point, or just wait until I figured it out on my own?"

"I don't understand. Where did this Sally Nixon person hear that I was pregnant?"

"Her husband's cousin works at the pharmacy where you filled your prescription for prenatal vitamins. Word gets around fast."

"That's confidential information! It's illegal— not to mention unethical—to release it!"

Wearily, he said, "Welcome to small-town America." His eyelids looked heavy, his eyes sorrowful. "You haven't answered my question, Jules. Were you ever going to tell me?"

"I just found out myself a couple of days ago." I knew I sounded defensive, and I hated it, but how could I admit the truth, that I hadn't told him about the baby because I wasn't sure our marriage had a future? I didn't want to hear the death knell that admission would surely sound.

I watched my husband pace across the room, and my heart contracted. I'd seen Tom angry, and it wasn't a pretty sight. But I'd never seen him like this. Hurt. Bewildered. Scared. "I thought this was what you wanted," he said. "I thought it was what we'd planned together."

I bit my lower lip. "I thought so, too."

He stopped pacing long enough to stare at me, and the fury in his eyes made me flinch. "What the hell does that mean?" he said. "That you're having second thoughts about the baby? Or about being married?"

I raised my shoulders, took a ragged breath, and said through tears, "Maybe."

"Maybe," he repeated blankly. "Maybe which? Maybe you're not sure you want a baby? Or maybe you're not sure—" he stopped, took a breath to still the trembling in his voice "—you still want me?"

"Maybe," I said, "both."

"Shit, Jules." He gaped at me in disbelief. "Shit, shit, shit!" He returned to his pacing while I sat there feeling like some kind of monster. Wheeling on me, he said, "I don't understand. I thought we were happy together. Just you and me, forever. No lies. No bullshit. Just openness and trust. What the hell happened to that?"

"I don't know, Tom. Maybe you'd like to tell me!"

"Am I supposed to understand that?"

"In case you haven't noticed, my life hasn't exactly been a cakewalk these last few weeks. You're never here. I see more of Claudia than I do of you! I'm stuck here in this house with your mother, who hates my guts. Your daughter hasn't been far behind her. I've been insulted, injured, and now assaulted. I've been sick for weeks, and your response to that was to turn me into a zombie with your pain pills. This house is full of secrets and angry silence. You tell me your wife died in an accident, then I find out she killed herself. Or did she? Nobody but her sister has been straight with me. You tell me one thing, Riley tells me something different, until I'm so confused I don't know who to believe. How many other lies have you told me? How the hell should I even know? In this house, the truth seems to change on a regular basis, depending on whose truth we're talking about. I'm suffering from headaches and nausea and paranoia. Half the time, I can't remember my own name, and my damn hair is falling out. I'm scared, Tom. Scared! And you want me to bring a baby into this situation? How can I when I don't even feel safe here myself?"

"Why haven't you told me this before?"

I gaped at him in disbelief. Didn't he get it? He was an intelligent, educated man. How could he be so dense? "Don't you understand?" I said. "I haven't told you this because I don't trust you!"

"Jules." Bewilderment took over his face. "I love you."

"I know. I love you, too." Even as I said the words, I realized they were true. I just didn't know what to do about it. Tears swam in my eyes and I considered him through a wet blur. "Maybe," I said, "love just isn't enough."

Bewilderment gave way to anger. I could see it in his eyes, in the suddenly taut lines of his face. "You know what?" he said. "You let me know when you figure that one out. If you're lucky, I might still be waiting around. But I can't say for sure. You know how it goes. The wind might blow in a different direction. I could change my mind somewhere along the way."

"Damn it, Tom, don't be this way."

"What way would you like me to be? Because whatever it is that you're lacking, I'm sure we could figure out a way around it if only I knew what the hell it is you want. You think about it. In the meantime, I have places to go. Things to do. People to see. Don't bother to wait up for me. I'll be late."

I closed my eyes and held back hot tears as he slammed out of the house, started up his car, and shot out of the yard so fast he burned rubber. Only after he was gone did I give in to the tears, and then I cried until my eyes were red and puffy and I looked like Godzilla's second cousin. I wasn't sure what had just happened, except that my husband had just walked out the door, and I had no idea if or when he was coming back. Worst of all, it was my fault. I was the one who'd started this debacle. They say the truth will set you free. But the only person set free by my truth was Tom. Had I made a mistake? Should I have kept my mouth shut and continued to live in fear? I loved him, but marriage to Tom had not turned out the way I'd thought it would.

Marry in haste, repent at leisure.

"Shut up, Grandma," I said aloud. "Nobody wants to hear your philosophy right now."

Dinner was a somber affair. The girls were still with Claudia, and Riley had other plans, so it was just Jeannette and me around the dining room table.

"Where's Tom?" she said. "I thought his meeting was over hours ago."

"He's not here."

"I can see that. But where is he?"

I set down my fork. "If you must know, Jeannette, we had a fight. You're probably delighted to hear that, considering how fond you are of me."

"That's unfair. I never said I didn't like you—"

"Oh, can the act. There's nobody here but the two of us. You don't have to lie. I already know you hate me. See how much easier that makes it?"

Her nostrils flared. Beneath the pink pantsuit resided the heart of Satan's spawn. "Regardless of what you believe, Julie," she said stiffly, "I don't hate you."

"Then you give a damn lousy approximation of love."

"And you're a spoiled, selfish little girl. God only knows why, but for some reason, my son loves you. I don't know what you did or said to drive him away, but I knew it would come to this. You're all wrong for him, and the sooner he's rid of you, the better."

"It might not be that easy."

"Why? What are you talking about?"

"Oh, hell, I might as well tell you. Everybody else already knows anyway. I'm pregnant."

"What?" She looked so distressed, I almost felt bad for her. "It can't be true."

"Oh, it's true. Just ask Sally Nixon. She'll tell you."

"Who's Sally Nixon?"

"Damned if I know. But she managed to tell Tom before I could, thanks to some busybody at the pharmacy who spread my private business all around town."

"Is that why Tom left?"

"Why he left," I said, "is none of your business. Excuse me." I shoved back my chair, picked up my plate, and carried it to the sink. "I've lost my appetite."

A half hour later, I walked over to Claudia's and picked up the girls. They were tired and cranky, and determined to stay and watch the rest of their movie. The argument grew a little heated until Claudia turned off the television and ended it. Neither of them was particularly happy about this turn of events, but they could see it was pointless to argue. Claudia hovered, clearly curious about what had happened with Tom, but I didn't volunteer any information, and for once in her life, she had the good sense not to ask.

We got bath time over with, and I read the girls a bedtime story before I tucked them in. Taylor slept with Tweety, my hero, who took up half the bed. "Julie?" she said when I leaned over the bed to kiss her.

"What, honey?" Her hair smelled like bubble gum, sweet and fruity from the shampoo we'd used.

"Thank you for taking us to the fair."

"You're welcome, sweetheart. I hope you had a good time." Except, of course, for my assault in the House of Horror. And my subsequent interrogation by the head of security.

"I did." She hesitated, then said, "I'm glad that man didn't hurt you."

"Me, too."

"And I'm glad that my dad married you. Good night." Before I could respond, she rolled over and buried her face against Tweety's magnificent yellowness.

I slept alone that night. Tom never returned, and I woke in the wee hours and crept downstairs to find him asleep on the couch, still in his clothes. He'd shoved a throw pillow under his head and covered himself with his mother's handmade afghan. His jacket and tie were strewn carelessly on the floor, his dress shirt unbuttoned at the throat and hopelessly wrinkled. The couch wasn't quite long enough to accommodate his length, so he was curled in a fetal position, one foot bare, his missing sock tangled in the bedclothes.

Somehow, the sight of that foot, so bare and vulnerable, struck a chord deep inside me. Shaken, I bent and picked up the tie, laid it out on the coffee table. I was shaking the wrinkles from his jacket when he opened one eye and looked at me. "You didn't have to sleep here," I said, hanging his jacket over the arm of the couch.

"I'm not ready to forgive you just yet." His voice was hoarse and sleep-fogged; he didn't sound like my Tom at all. "Come here," he said. "Don't say anything. I just want to hold you."

He lifted the afghan and I slipped beneath it. Tom wrapped it around us and snugged me up tight against him, one arm around me, his palm flat against my belly. His breath was warm on my cheek, his heartbeat strong against my back. "Whatever my failings," he said, "and I know they're legion, one thing remains steady, and that's my feelings for you."

I didn't answer. But I lay my hand on top of his, there on my still-flat belly. He turned his wrist, bringing his hand palm-to-palm against mine. I threaded my fingers loosely through his and let out a hard, shuddering sigh.

We didn't sleep. We didn't talk. There was too much tumult inside us, too many conflicting emotions, too many words which, if spoken, could be hurtful or even fatal to our relationship. Instead, we just held each other in the early-morning silence. Sometimes, when the chaos of life swirls around you and there's nothing else solid to hold on to, that's the only thing you can do. Our marriage was in critical condition. Right now, I didn't know whether or not the patient would survive. I didn't even know if the man whose arms held me so tightly was a killer. All I knew was that I loved him. I couldn't guarantee that we'd stay together, but at this moment, the future lay at a great distance, and the only time that counted was now.

Our contentment didn't last. Eventually, the rest of the household began stirring. Jeannette came downstairs, took a single look at the two of us huddled together on the couch and, mouth pursed, turned without a word and headed directly for the kitchen. Upstairs, the bathroom door closed with a bang; a moment later, the toilet flushed. The scent of brewing coffee, rich and inviting, drifted in from the kitchen. With a sigh, Tom disentangled himself from me and dropped his feet to the floor. I sat up beside him and wrapped the afghan around my shoulders. Elbows braced on the knees of his wrinkled pants, Tom rubbed his face with his hands. "That couch is a travesty," he said. "It reminds me of my days as a resident, when I used to sleep anywhere and anytime I could manage. There was this hideous old orange Naugahyde *thing* that dared to call itself a couch in one of the hospital waiting rooms. I spent more than one night on that back-breaker."

I didn't say anything, just gave him a wan smile.

"Jules?" he said.

"What?"

Instead of answering, he leaned forward and kissed me tenderly. I let go of the afghan and rested my hand against the nape of his neck. It felt warm and familiar. The kiss went on for a while. We parted and drew back to look at each other. His eyes appeared as somber and uncertain as I felt. "I have to get ready for work," he said, and he got up and left me there alone.

I folded the afghan. Carrying Tom's jacket and tie, I went back upstairs to get the girls ready for school. I wasn't sure exactly when the job had become mine, but at some point along the way, Jeannette had abdicated the mommy role, and it had passed on to me. I felt honored to play mother to these two delicious little girls. My only regret was that they might sense my ambivalence toward their father. I didn't want to be the cause of any anxiety on their part. They'd been through enough already. I didn't know where any of us would be in a year. But if I ended up having to leave these two little girls, my heart would be ripped in half. Already I loved them as if they were my own. If Tom and I parted—and I couldn't believe I was even considering such a thing—I would insist on somehow remaining a part of their lives.

In spite of a tension so thick you could cut it with a knife, everybody made it out the door on time, and I was alone, the only sound that of the kitchen clock ticking. I took my antinausea medication and my prenatal vitamins and then I made myself a bowl of oatmeal. It wasn't high on my list of favorite foods, but until the pills kicked in, it was the only thing I was certain I could swallow. I hoped this nausea wouldn't go on for nine months. If it did, I'd be a skeleton by the time I was done, for even my normally healthy appetite couldn't stand up to twenty-four-hour-a-day morning sickness.

I filled the sink with hot, soapy water and proceeded to wash the breakfast dishes. We had a dishwasher, but sometimes, especially when I had serious thinking to do, washing them by hand was my preferred method. It gave me something to occupy my hands while my mind was occupied with other things. Like yesterday's mugging. It was hard to believe, with the morning sun pouring in and the songbirds hopping around outside my window, that yesterday I'd been physically attacked and could have been seriously hurt. Or even killed. Hard to believe that someone out there wished me harm.

In hindsight, I probably should have made a report to the State Police. But by the time I'd gone a few rounds with Barney Fife, all I'd thought about was escaping. We hadn't caught Mystery Man, so we had no idea who he was. I could describe him quite clearly to the cops, and so could Claudia. But unless he was a known felon, or the cops had a suspect in custody for me to identify, it would be like searching for the proverbial needle in a haystack. Besides, I had no proof that he was the one who'd attacked me. Not that I doubted it. But it had been pitch-black inside the House of Horror, and I hadn't seen his face. Even if I'd been able to identify him in a lineup, all I'd actually witnessed him doing was smiling at me. Even I wasn't stupid enough to think the cops would arrest him based on that.

Besides, unless the cops could coerce him into talking, it didn't really matter who he was. Mystery Man didn't know me, and I didn't know him. He was clearly working for somebody else, somebody who did. Somebody who wanted me roughed up and shaken. Somebody who had a message for him to deliver.

I mentally kicked myself for my quick reflexes. I should have waited to clobber him until he finished telling me what he had to say. If I'd heard the message, I might have had a clue about who had sent it.

But I was too distracted with fighting for my freedom—and for all I knew, my life—to give him time to say his piece.

If nothing else, I knew it all came back to Beth. There was no other reason anybody would want me out of the picture, and everything that had happened since I'd arrived in Newmarket seemed to be somehow tied in with Beth Larkin's death. Someone out there—almost certainly someone that I knew—was a killer. And if I wasn't careful, I might become the next victim.

If I had half a brain, I'd pack my bags and leave today. I had friends in L.A. who would help me. A place to go, a lumpy couch to sleep on. Louis and Carlos and the girls at the boutique would welcome me back with no questions asked. There was really no reason for me to stay here. No reason other than those two sweet little faces that had studied me so somberly over their breakfast cereal this morning. No reason other than their father, the man who may or may not have ended their mother's life. The man I loved. I didn't trust Tom Larkin as far as I could throw him, but that didn't do anything to weaken my wild attraction to the man.

The telephone rang, and I jumped. I was so skittish these days. I dried my hands and went to answer it.

It was Dwight Pettingill of the Newmarket PD. "Just following up on the vandalism thing," he said. "Have you folks had any more trouble out there?"

"None at all," I said. "Tom had some fancy security system installed on the car. If anybody so much as brushes against it, it'll make enough noise to wake half the county."

"That's not a bad thing," Dwight pointed out. "It would be enough to deter me from trying to break in."

The prospect of a chocolate doughnut would probably be enough to deter Dwight, but I wasn't about to verbalize the thought. I had other fish to fry. "Anyway," he was saying, "I just wanted you to know we've closed the case. We weren't able to lift any fingerprints from the belt, and without any other evidence—well, it's not as though there was any real damage done."

It seemed to me that law enforcement in this neck of the woods was pretty lax. Or maybe I'd simply met the two least competent men in the field of police work. "I appreciate everything you've done for us," I told him.

"All in a day's work, ma'am."

"And your job must be fascinating," I said, "dealing with all that crime on a daily basis."

"Well—" I could imagine him flushing red at the other end of the phone. "Sometimes we do get ourselves into some serious situations. Domestic violence, for example. Just last year there was a fellow who—"

"Do you ever investigate homicides?" I tried to inject a little breathless enthusiasm into my voice. Julie Hanrahan Larkin, police junkie and morbidly curious citizen.

"Why…yeah," he said. "Occasionally. For sure." I could tell he didn't want to admit that he'd never, in his entire career, worked a homicide case. Newmarket wasn't exactly a hotbed of crime. It wasn't often that somebody showed an interest in his day-to-day work. Probably the little woman discouraged him from talking about it in front of the kids. Wouldn't want them to have nightmares after hearing about their daddy's deadly run-in with a dangerous shoplifter.

"Like, for instance—when Beth Larkin died. Did you know it was suicide right away, or did you investigate the possibility of homicide?"

I'd put him between a rock and a hard place. If he told me they'd automatically assumed her death was a suicide, there was no place left for our conversation to go. The fish he'd hooked would break free and get away. If he said they'd investigated it as a homicide, I might be pressed to ask him for details he didn't have and couldn't make up on the spot. Dwight didn't strike me as the kind of guy who was good at thinking on his feet. I held my breath, waiting as he teetered on the fence, wondering which direction he'd fall.

He landed on the side of honesty. Probably a wise decision, given his cerebral limitations. Lies simply bred other lies, until pretty soon, they took over your life. Dwight might not be an intellectual giant, but he wasn't a fool, either. He knew his limits. "It was pretty obvious that it was a suicide," he said. "She left a note."

"Really?" I breathed, in pseudo-fascination. "Did you see it? What did it say?"

He hesitated, torn between the desire to impress me and the certainty that the information he was about to divulge was confidential. "I can't really say," he finally said, and I let out the breath I'd been holding. Damn. It was a lousy time for Dwight to discover professional ethics.

"But I can tell you it was the most pathetic sight I ever saw. That poor little girl, crying for her mother. And the mother, floating facedown in that river—" He stopped abruptly, suddenly cognizant of who he was talking to, and the fact that the victim and I shared a husband. "My apologies, ma'am," he said. "You don't want to hear this."

I had to do some quick thinking or I'd lose him. "Are you telling me that one of the girls was with her that night? Nobody ever told me that. How awful! Which one?"

"It was Sadie," he said, his voice appropriately somber. "Damnedest thing I ever saw. Beth left her sitting there in her car seat and jumped off the bridge right in front of her."

"That's terrible! How did you find her?"

"Oh, it wasn't us that found her. It was Roger Levasseur. Crazy as batshit, that guy, but he knew what to do that night. He picked up Beth's cell phone and called 911."

The neighbor I'd read about in the newspaper article. Roger Levasseur. I should have guessed. Nobody else lived out there in that godforsaken place. Now I understood the reason he'd been so concerned that day when he found me alone on the bridge, staring into the river. He knew what had happened there. He might even have witnessed Beth's plunge to the chilly waters below. Might have seen who pushed her off the side.

I had to talk to Roger.

In spite of the sunny morning, Swift River Road was as lonely and eerie as I remembered. I shuddered when I drove across the bridge, my tires singing on the gratework as the river rushed below me. I reached the other side, where the trees seemed to close in on me, turning mid-morning into twilight. I had no idea what I was looking for, could only hope I'd recognize it when I saw it. Once I crossed the bridge, the road narrowed, and then it turned to dirt. I hit a pothole and my teeth slammed together so hard it hurt. Out here, even the utility poles had shrunk, like old men lined up in a row, aged and decrepit and forgotten.

A quarter mile past the bridge, the trailer appeared, seemingly out of nowhere. One minute, I was traveling through deep, dark forest; the next, I was passing an open patch of land where an ancient silver trailer gleamed in the sun. An old blue pickup truck sat next to it, stripped of its doors and its hood, stalks of goldenrod growing up through the compartment that had once held an engine. No attempt had been made to tame the property around the trailer; straw and milkweed and wildflowers grew right up to the skirting. It looked as if the structure had been plunked down in the middle of a hayfield with no thought to esthetics or practicality.

When I pulled into the driveway, which was little more than a scattering of loose gravel, an arthritic golden retriever stood stiffly. He stretched and sniffed the air, trying to determine whether I was friend or foe, then lumbered over to greet me. I got out of the car, patted his head and moved toward the door.

The steps were wide planks propped up on cement blocks. No expense had been spared here when it came to welcoming visitors. I rapped on the rusted door. "Hello?" I shouted. "Mr. Levasseur?"

There was no answer, yet my instincts told me somebody was inside. I rapped again, harder this time. "Mr. Levasseur? It's Julie Larkin. I need to talk to you."

I heard movement inside, caught a flash of motion from the corner of my eye. Levasseur had lifted a window blind and was peering out at me. "Go away!" he shouted.

"Please," I said. "Remember me? I met you on the bridge a few weeks ago. You said bad things had happened there. I need to talk to you about that."

"I can't. I can't talk about it."

"You have to help me." I took a deep breath and followed my instincts. "I'm pregnant, Mr. Levasseur, and I'm afraid. I think I may be in danger."

He dropped the blind. A moment later, I heard him release the lock. He opened the door cautiously, and the odor hit me hard in the face. I tried to control my gag reflex, but it wasn't easy. Instead of inviting me in, he stepped outside. "Thank you," I said, coming down off the steps in the hope that he'd take a hint and leave plenty of fresh air and space between us.

He eyed my flat belly and said, "You're pregnant?"

"Yes. I just found out. I need to know what happened that night. The night Beth died. I know you were there. Dwight Pettingill told me you were the one who found Sadie there alone in the car. You called the police. I have to know what you saw."

"Didn't see anything."

"You saw Sadie, didn't you?"

"That was afterward. After she fell."

"Then you did see Beth fall?" Eagerly, I demanded, "Who was with her that night?"

"I've said too much. They'll come after me."

"Who?" I persisted. "Who'll come after you?"

"I had a wife once," he said. "And a son. He's a lawyer now, in Baltimore. That's in Maryland."

"Mr. Levasseur," I said, "I know you're an educated, intelligent man." One who'd forgotten that cleanliness was next to godliness. "You must understand how important this is. I have to know the truth. Who is it that'll come after you?"

"Go away."

"I won't. Not until you tell me what I want to know."

"No," he said. "Go away from Newmarket. It's not safe for you here."

"Why?" I grabbed his arm, no longer concerned about the foulness of his person. "Why isn't it safe for me?"

"He was there that night, you know."

"Who?"

"Your husband. Tom Larkin."

"I know he was there," I said impatiently. "The police called him and he came out to pick up Sadie. He—"

"Not then. Before."

"Before what?"

"Before she went in the water."

"What?" I knew I gasped; I felt the color drain from my face. Until now, I hadn't truly believed Tom was involved in Beth's murder. "Are you sure? Maybe you're mistaken. Maybe you only thought it was Tom. Maybe it was Riley. His brother. Do you know Riley? They look a lot alike." I knew I was babbling, but I couldn't seem to stop. I clutched his sleeve and shook it. *"Tell me, damn it!* Did Tom kill her?"

"My wife left me," he said, apropos of nothing. "Her name was Irene. She had an English degree from Vassar. And great legs. Did I ever tell you that my son's a lawyer in Baltimore?"

I gave up at that point. I wasn't getting anything more out of Roger Levasseur. I bid him goodbye and left him standing on his rickety steps with his old dog, both of them watching me drive away. I was heartsick, trembling so hard I could barely keep the car on the road. *Oh, Tom,* I thought. *Why?* What could have driven a seemingly sane man to kill the mother of his children? What terrible thing had she done to him? For I was convinced, even at this point, that it had been a crime of passion. I just couldn't imagine my husband cold-bloodedly planning a murder. That kind of cruelty wasn't in his makeup. Something must have happened, something so distressing, so shocking, that he'd flown into a rage. Maybe her death had even been accidental. They'd been fighting; he'd raised a hand to her; she'd ducked away from the blow and fallen backwards over the railing.

"You're reaching," I told myself. "You're really reaching."

Of course I was reaching. I didn't want Tom to be the villain in this piece. *Dear God*, I prayed, *let me be wrong. Let it be anybody but him.*

But the evidence was piling up, and it was all pointing to my husband. Was it really possible he'd sent that thug to assault me at the fair? Had he also been responsible for my fall down the stairs? I'd spent hours in the attic that day with no view of the driveway. A quiet person could have crept into the house and strategically placed those batteries right where I'd be sure to step on them, and I never would have known the difference.

But why? Why would Tom marry me, proclaim his undying love, then do his best to ensure that I was out of the picture? It didn't make sense. There was a missing piece to the puzzle, and without it, I had nothing but a collection of unrelated puzzle pieces.

Beth, I thought. *Cherchez la femme.* Everything had to do with Beth. And I might have no idea what was going on. But I realized, with an insight I hadn't known I possessed, that I knew who did.

I circled the supermarket parking lot twice before I found a parking spot. It was the first of the month and food stamps were out, and the place teemed with locals loading up their carts with sirloin steaks, sugary cereal and Diet Pepsi. I found Mel in the canned-food aisle, stocking cans of string beans on a shelf. "I want to know the truth," I said. "The note I found in *Dr. Zhivago.* You know what it was about, don't you? What was the big secret that Beth was keeping? The secret that's responsible for her death?"

"I don't know what you're talking about." Her voice was steady, but her eyes were downcast, and her hands, rapidly shuffling cans from a cardboard box to the shelf, were shaky.

"I was attacked yesterday," I said.

That got her attention. Her eyes widened in disbelief. "What?" she said. "Tell me."

"I was at the fair with Claudia. Some man followed me into the House of Horror and attacked me. He roughed me up a little, called me by name and said he had a message for me."

"Holy fuck."

"This is getting serious, Mel. Somebody's out to get me. And I know it's connected to Beth's death. I have to know the truth. If you don't tell me, I'm going to have to call Dwight Pettingill and tell him you know more than you're saying about your sister's so-called suicide."

"Shh!" Her gaze darted around, and then she jerked her chin in the direction of the back room. "Come with me. We can't talk here."

She led me through a swinging door, down a dingy corridor, and into an office paneled in the cheapest, ugliest fake wood paneling I'd ever encountered outside of a basement rec room. The desk was littered with coffee-stained papers and empty soda bottles. The air conditioner had developed a leak at some point in the last decade, and water stains marred the paneling below it, adding to the overall ambiance of the place. Mel shut the door and then locked it, just to be safe.

"I've thought about telling you this. I almost did the other day. But I was afraid. I didn't want it to get out. It's too late to hurt Beth, but it could hurt Sadie, and I don't want that to happen."

Through gritted teeth, I said, "Tell me."

Mel took a deep breath. Twisting the hem of her apron between nervous fingers, she said, "Beth had an affair. Tom found out about it."

"An affair?"

"That's right. By the time he found out, it was long over. But of course, he was furious. Not that I could blame him, under the circumstances. It must have been quite a shock. He was furious. Beth said he was like a wild man when he confronted her about it. She thought he'd strangle her with his bare hands."

I'd witnessed a little of that temper myself, when I hung Beth's painting in the girls' room. Grimly, I said, "How did he find out?"

"It was one of those weird coincidences. Sadie got sick. We thought she had meningitis. The hospital did blood tests. Thank God, it turned out to just be some virus. Nothing life-threatening. But you know how small-town hospitals are? Everyone knows everybody else's business—"

"Just like small-town pharmacies. Yes, I've had the pleasure. Go on."

"Some lab tech, out of the goodness of his heart or the smallness of his brain, recognized the name on the blood sample and sent the test results to Tom as well as Sadie's G.P. She was Tom's daughter, and he was a doctor, so of course this idiot put two and two together and came up with seven."

"And?"

"And one of the tests they ran, as a matter of routine, was blood typing. Sadie's blood type is A-negative. When Tom saw that, he went ballistic. You see, Beth had O-positive blood. Tom's is B-negative. Anybody else might have missed it, but he's a doctor. He knew right away that there was no way on God's green earth he was Sadie's father."

I grasped the back of an ancient desk chair for support. Suddenly, I felt as though I were seeing her through a long, narrow tunnel. "Are you telling me that some other man is Sadie's biological father?"

"That's exactly what I'm saying. Once Tom found out, Beth broke down and admitted the whole thing.

The affair, the pregnancy—she'd never been sure, you see. She'd known it was a possibility, but because the affair was over and she'd stayed with Tom, she put it out of her mind. As far as she was concerned, Tom was Sadie's father, and that was that. But Tom couldn't accept it when he found out. He was crushed. He worships that little girl. And he was so furious with Beth for what she'd done that he made her life a living hell. She cried, and apologized, and begged him to forgive her. But the damage was already done. He threatened divorce. Threatened to take her girls away from her. So she did the only thing she could. She decided to take the girls and leave him instead."

"Beth was going to leave him?"

"She planned to, as soon as she could find a job and a place to live. She told me about it a few days before she died. She'd been hoarding away money, and she almost had enough to start a new life without Tom. But it never happened. He won the battle, and the war." Mel's words took on a bitter flavor. "I never saw her alive again. Now do you understand why I'm so certain he killed her?"

This was more than I could take in at one time. My head was spinning, and if I didn't sit down soon, I was afraid I'd pass out. "Julie?" Mel said. "Are you all right? You don't look so hot."

"I just need—" I looked around for a place to sit, eyed the grimy desk chair, and sat in it anyway.

"Julie?" Mel's voice carried a distant echo, as though she were speaking from miles away, even though she was so close I could reach out and touch her.

"I just feel a little faint," I said. "I need to rest."

"Oh, hell. You're not going to keel over, are you? We're not even supposed to be in here. If you pass out in here, Mr. Bronson will have my head."

"No. It's just—" The room was swimming, and I clutched frantically at the worn chair arms in an attempt to stabilize myself. "Tell me," I said.

"Tell you what? Should I call you a doctor? You're white as fresh snow."

"Tell me who. I have to know who Sadie's father is."

I already knew the answer. I knew it even before she said it. But I needed to hear it anyway. Needed to confirm what my instincts were screaming at me. Mel's face was growing long, stretched out and twisted like the reflection in a fun house mirror. "Nobody else knows," she said. "Just Tom and I. But it's Riley. Riley is Sadie's father."

Riley, I thought, just before I passed out. *Of course.*

When I came to, I thought at first I was dead. All those kindly, concerned faces encircling me, gazing down from above, reminded me of every near-death experience I'd ever read about. Except that they were all strangers, and not previously deceased relatives come to ease my way into the afterworld. All of them, except for a stout woman in a blue warm-up jacket with a white athletic logo, were dressed in teal smocks. That was a little disconcerting. I presumed their presence meant I was still breathing, although I couldn't imagine what had happened to cause these identically-dressed strangers to be staring at me so oddly.

The woman in the athletic jacket held a Dixie cup of cold water to my lips. "She's coming around," she said to the room at large. To me, she said, "Here you go, sweetheart. Have a drink of this."

I lifted my head obediently and sipped. The water felt soothing as it trickled down my dry, scratchy throat. "What happened?" I said.

"You fainted, hon. No big deal. That happens sometimes in early pregnancy."

I glanced around, desperately seeking a familiar face, to no avail. The woman patted my hand. "It's okay," she said. "I'm a nurse."

"All right, people," said a male voice, "party's over. Get back to work and give the lady a little breathing room."

The sea of Shop City smocks parted, and I finally saw Mel's face. I'd never been so happy to see anybody in my life. Her fellow associates filed out of the tiny office, and Mel knelt beside me. "I am so glad Gloria was here doing her weekly shopping," she said. "I didn't have a clue what to do. I've never seen anybody faint before. You went down like a pile of bricks. It's a wonder you didn't give yourself a new concussion on top of the old one."

"It's all right," I said. "Acquiring new bruises seems to have become a daily thing with me. Can I sit up now?"

The two women helped me to a sitting position. "As long as you're sure you're all right," Gloria said, "I really need to go. My ice cream is sitting out there in my shopping cart, melting."

There was no disaster worse than melted ice cream. I thanked her, and she left me alone with Mel. "I think I should drive you home," she said.

I started to protest, then realized I wasn't sure I had the energy to drive, let alone the ability to remain conscious long enough to reach our driveway in one piece. "Fine," I said. "I can pick up my car later."

The ride home only took five minutes. One of the advantages of living in a small town. We pulled into the driveway and parked behind Riley's pickup truck. Riley Larkin, Building and Remodeling, it said on both doors in a bold, modern font. "Riley doesn't know about Sadie," Mel said.

I gave her a long, hard look. "Your point?" I said.

"Sadie doesn't know, either," she said softly. "She's been through so much—"

"Don't worry. She won't hear it from me. I'll be too busy trying to stay alive." I opened the door and climbed out of the car.

"Listen, Julie, if you need anything—"

"Right. I know who to call." I slammed the door and walked away.

The house was empty. I walked through the rooms, one after another, wondering how I could ever have thought this house was beautiful when in truth, it emanated a malevolence so thick I could taste it. Everything inside was tainted with it. Poisoned by the knowledge of what had happened to its mistress.

Upstairs, I lay on the bed in a daze. What a mess I'd fallen into. My own personal House of Horror. I'd been in denial for so long, but I couldn't deny the truth any longer. The puzzle had finally come together, and the resulting picture was heartbreaking. My husband, the man I adored, had killed his first wife. And Riley wasn't blameless in this thing, either. The philandering son-of-a-bitch had cuckolded his own brother. What kind of man would sleep with his brother's wife? Not to mention conceive a child with her? Not that his actions—or Beth's—excused what Tom had done. There was no excuse for murder. But none of this would have ever come about if Riley'd been able to keep it in his pants.

I was so tired. I hadn't experienced it with my first pregnancy, this kind of soul-sucking, overwhelming exhaustion. I closed my eyes for a moment and was instantly asleep. I found myself back in the rear seat of that Barracuda, hip-hop music thumping and thrashing about my head. The three bellicose teenagers were there, and Snaggle-Tooth Beth. "I'm missing something," I told her. "What is it that I'm missing?"

Beth opened her mouth to respond, and a worm crawled out of that dark hole. I watched in horrified fascination as it crawled across her mossy face. "Nothing is what it seems," she said cryptically.

"What the hell is that supposed to mean?" I

shouted at her, so angry I wanted to jump up and down and stamp my feet, like a three-year-old in the middle of a temper tantrum. "Stop talking in riddles! Tom killed you! There's nothing left to know. Why are you making this so difficult for me?"

"I tried to warn you, but you didn't listen."

Somewhere in the background of my dream, a phone rang. Ignoring it, I said, "Warn me about what?"

"I tried to warn you to watch your back." The phone kept ringing. "The puzzle's not complete yet."

"Goddamn it, Beth, you're still talking in riddles!"

"Figure it out for yourself."

I awoke with a jolt. It felt as though I'd slept for only about ten minutes, but when I checked my watch, I discovered that I'd been out for four hours. *Four hours?* It was nearly dusk, and I'd slept the afternoon away. That was so unlike me, it was scary.

The puzzle's not complete yet. That's what Beth had said to me this time around. What was that supposed to mean? What was she trying to tell me? Not Beth, I corrected myself. I'd read somewhere that the people in our dreams are actually symbolic of various characteristics of the dreamer's own personality. I wasn't sure I believed that, but I wasn't crazy enough to think I'd actually spoken with Beth Larkin. It was my own subconscious that had given voice to Beth's words. What had I missed? Overlooked? What threads had I left untied?

The note. I hadn't followed up on Beth's note.

I'd been too busy recuperating from my fall and, in my foggy state, I'd simply forgotten it. I got up from the bed, still groggy from my nap, and went downstairs. I got the phone book from the kitchen drawer and looked up the number to the hospital emergency room.

A pleasant, well-modulated female voice answered. "Newmarket General Hospital, Acute Care Center, Debbie speaking. How may I help you?"

"Hi, Debbie," I said. "This is Julie Larkin. I was in there a couple of weeks ago, after I fell down the stairs."

"I remember you. What can I do for you, Mrs. Larkin?"

"While I was there that day—possibly while I was upstairs having my CAT scan—I seem to have lost a piece of paper. I think it fell out of my pocket when I undressed in the cubicle."

"Uh-huh."

"I was just wondering if you'd found it after I left."

"As a matter of fact, we did."

"You did?" My heart raced with either excitement or terror. I wasn't entirely sure which it was. "What did you do with it?"

"We gave it to Dr. Larkin when he came in asking about it a few days later. I guess he forgot to tell you."

"I guess he did."

I hung up the phone, my heart continuing to thud a steady rhythm against my ribs. So Tom had the note. He'd read it, and he knew damn well that I'd read it, as well. He had to know I suspected something. I might not know the entire story yet, but what I did know—coupled with my suspicions about the rest—was enough to render me a threat. A liability instead of an asset. If I uncovered the rest of it, I could destroy his life. Tom would never let me do that. He'd never let me send him to prison and leave the girls fatherless.

Which meant he had no choice but to kill me.

The only proof I had of anything was in that note. I had to find it.

In my pocket, my cell phone chirped. I pulled it out, read the words on the screen: ONE VOICE MAIL MESSAGE. That must have been the phone I heard ringing in my dream. I flipped the phone open, checked the calls received list. The last call had come from a number within the 207 area code, but it wasn't familiar to me. I didn't have time right now to deal with it. I had a killer to catch. Steeling myself against the hard truth of those words, I flipped the phone closed, shoved it back into my pocket, and headed down the hall to Tom's study. If the note still existed, it would be in here.

The desktop was, as always, immaculate. I slid open the top drawer and began rummaging through its contents. Nothing of any significance. I closed that drawer, knelt, and opened the heavy file drawer on the side instead. It was filled, as I had suspected, with green hanging files that Tom had clearly marked and neatly filed in alphabetical order. I began working my way through the tabs. AUTO LOANS, HOME REPAIRS, HOME-OWNER'S INSURANCE, MEDICAL/DENTAL, MISCELLANEOUS, and UTILITY BILLS. I wasn't sure what I was looking for. A file folder marked HOMICIDE, perhaps? As anal-retentive as Tom was, nothing would surprise me. I continued on through what could only be described as personal files, one for every member of the household: JULIE, MOM, SADIE, TAYLOR, TOM.

Good Lord, the man kept file folders on us? What on earth would he put in them? Reports of our daily activities? Scowling, I pulled one out at random. It was Taylor's. I opened it up. Inside, I found her kindergarten school photo and her first-grade report cards. Her immunization records—all her immunizations were up-to-date—and a copy of her birth certificate. And in a little plastic sandwich baggie, a perfectly formed baby tooth.

It was the tooth that got to me, that carefully preserved memento, that shining example of doting fatherhood. How could a man so sentimental he'd save his daughter's baby tooth in a sandwich bag be capable of murder? What if I was wrong? What if I were looking at the wrong brother? Riley'd been in that hospital cubicle with me. He could have seen the note when it fell out of my pocket. It could have even been Riley who removed it from my pocket. I had no proof it had fallen out; I just knew it had turned up among the missing. And Riley'd had ample opportunity to place those batteries on the stairs. After all, he was the one who was at home that day, the one who'd "found" me as I lay there, helpless and screaming for assistance.

"Looking for something?"

As if my thoughts had conjured him up, there stood Riley, in the flesh. Looking better than any man had a right to look, he leaned casually against the door frame, a cold chicken leg in one hand. Eating again. The man was always eating.

"No," I said, my pulse accelerating slightly. He'd startled me, and right now, for more reasons than I could count, he was the last person I wanted to see. "I'm just—" I waved my hand vaguely while I tried to find a reasonable explanation.

"Snooping," he said, and took a bite of cold chicken.

"I am *not* snooping! And why aren't you working? I thought you had a kitchen to rebuild?"

"Chill, Julie, I'm just teasing you. Whatever Tom has in those files couldn't possibly be worth snooping to see. I mean, how many dental X-rays and electric bills would it take to put you to sleep?"

In my heightened state of paranoia, his words seemed to have more than one meaning. What did he mean about putting me to sleep? Was it some kind of veiled threat? Had he killed Beth and, now that I'd learned the truth, was he coming after me?

"Julie?" he said. "Are you all right?"

"I'm fine!" I snapped, my anxiety giving way to annoyance. This man was undoubtedly the cause of all the ills in my life. Because of him and his inability to control his sexual urges, my husband would probably go to prison. And I might just end up dead. "I just want to be left alone!"

"Okay," he said, looking a little surprised. "Jeez. I can tell when I'm not wanted. You don't have to say it twice." He hesitated a moment, opened his mouth as if he were about to say something more. Then he thought better of it, and with a slight nod, turned and left me alone.

What in hell was wrong with me? My personality had changed so much in the past few weeks, I barely recognized myself. When I wasn't in a fog, my emotions careened back and forth between anger and fear like a crazed pinball. Could this possibly be due to the hormone changes of pregnancy? I'd heard horror stories about women who had worse side effects from pregnancy than other women did from PMS.

Maybe I was just losing my mind.

I gathered up the contents of Taylor's folder and returned it to the drawer. I paused, my hand hovering over the JULIE folder, before I swooped down and grabbed it. I couldn't imagine there'd be anything in it of any value to me. I'd only been here a few weeks, too short a time for Tom to have accumulated anything of significance.

The folder contained only one item, a folded sheaf of papers covered in fine print. I unfolded it, read the lettering at the top. *Life Insurance Policy.* I squinted to focus on the tiny print. Ignoring all the legalese that insurance companies were required to toss into their policies to confound policy holders, I read between the lines and got the gist of it.

Dropping it as though I'd been burned, I gaped at it in horror. But like a bystander passing a horrific car crash, I couldn't seem to take my eyes off the damn thing. I picked it up gingerly and reread it, over and over, until I convinced myself that my eyes weren't deceiving me and I really was holding an insurance policy on my life. For two million dollars, payable to Thomas Larkin, beneficiary.

Dated three days before I fell down the stairs.

Thirteen

I sat on the floor of Tom's study for a long time, holding on to what amounted to my death warrant. My breath came in little short gasps. My mouth had gone dry, and my heart was thudding. If I died, Tom would reap two million dollars. That was a pretty big payday for a marriage that had lasted less than two months.

Hurt doesn't begin to describe how I felt. Betrayed comes closer, but it's still too weak a word. Devastated? Crushed? Destroyed? All of them were accurate, none of them sufficient to describe the pain I felt at the demise of my marriage to a man I'd loved with every fiber of my being. Instead of responding in kind, he'd crushed that love like an insect under his shoe. Ground me into the dirt and spat on me for good measure. I'd been right all along. The man couldn't be trusted. Usually, it felt good to be right. So why didn't I feel any satisfaction?

In my pocket, my cell phone rang again. I pulled it out and stared numbly at the digital readout. It was the same unfamiliar number as before. I thought about ignoring it, but it was easier, in my deadened state, to just deal with it now. I flipped open the phone and said dully, "Hello?"

"Mrs. Larkin?"

"Yes."

"This is Dr. Kapowicz. Did you get my voice mail message?"

Voice mail message? Um, no. It seems I'd been a little distracted by the fact that my husband wanted me dead to the tune of two million dollars. "Sorry," I said. "I haven't checked my messages. Why did you call?"

"I have the results of your blood tests. Mrs. Larkin, have you ever heard of diazinon?"

"Diazinon? No. Why?"

"I never would have thought of it, but something you said just clicked. I think it was the hair loss that got me to wondering. I looked it up after you left, and every one of your symptoms could be explained by it. The nausea. The confusion. The anxiety. So I decided, just to be sure, to have your blood checked for insecticides. And there it was. Diazinon. It's an insecticide, one that's highly toxic to humans. There's an inordinately high level of it in your blood-stream."

"I don't understand," I said. "How can that be? How could I have been exposed to something like that?"

"I don't suppose you live on a farm? Or near one? Have you spent any significant amount of time in a public building that's regularly sprayed for insects?"

"None of the above."

"Has anybody else in your family exhibited the same symptoms as you?"

"No. Just me."

"That's what I thought. I hate to say this." She hesitated. "But considering the high levels, even if you'd answered any of my questions in the affirmative—I just can't justify calling this accidental."

It took a minute for her words to sink in. Even then, I didn't want to believe them. Prayed I was wrong. "You're saying that somebody has been deliberately poisoning me?"

"It's not an easy conclusion to reach. I've never before been in the position of pointing the finger of blame. But in the absence of any other rational explanation, yes, I do believe that somebody has been deliberately poisoning you."

The room, and everything in it, grew smaller and more distant. My husband was a doctor. He'd know about poisons. And if I died, he'd be two million dollars richer. *Tom,* I thought. *Oh, Tom, how could you?* I wet my tongue, which seemed to have grown three sizes in my mouth. "How?" I said. "How would this exposure happen?"

"Possibly through ingestion into the digestive tract. Somebody putting it into your food. You could have breathed it in, although that seems unlikely, since nobody else in your family has exhibited symptoms, and the levels, coupled with the nature of your symptoms, suggest to me that the poisoning is probably chronic, rather than acute. It could have even been through dermal contact. Sprinkled onto your clothing, or mixed with something you use regularly—bath powder, shampoo, liquid soap."

In my dazed state, the implications were just beginning to sink in. This wasn't just a matter of my being poisoned. I was pregnant. Anything that went into my bloodstream also affected my baby. Woodenly, I said, "What about the baby?"

"That's my second biggest concern, right after you. This could cause innumerable problems. Birth defects. Possibly fetal death. We just don't know. There isn't enough empirical evidence to make that kind of conclusion. All we know is that it can't possibly be good. Not for the baby, and certainly not for you."

"I don't know what to say."

"Don't say anything. Just get out of that house. Go to a motel, or a friend you can trust, preferably one who lives at a distance. Don't take anything with you. No food, no cosmetics, no shampoos or bath oils. Just a few clothes, and I'd replace those as soon as possible. You do realize—" She paused again, sighed. "You do realize that I'm obligated, by law, to report this to the authorities? They'll be stopping by with a search warrant. If they find the diazinon, and if they find out who's done this to you, that person could be charged with attempted murder. Two counts, since you're carrying a child. If anything happens to either you or the baby as a result of this, then that charge could be upgraded to first-degree homicide."

I heard the back door open, heard footsteps in the kitchen, and excited voices as Jeannette and the girls trooped in. "Mrs. Larkin?" the voice at the other end of the phone said. "Are you still there?"

I took a couple of deep breaths. "I'm still here," I said.

"You'll leave the house?"

In the kitchen, Sadie and Taylor were chatting merrily about their respective days. Innocent. Unaware of the firestorm that was about to descend on top of them. "I'll leave," I said wearily. "Thank you for calling."

It didn't take me long to pack. After what the doctor had told me, I was scared to touch anything. I crammed a change of underwear, fresh jeans and a T-shirt into an overnight bag. I didn't dare to take my hairbrush, or even my toothbrush. All that could be replaced in a quick trip to Rite Aid. I slung the strap to my overnight bag over my shoulder, and that was when I realized I didn't have a car. I'd left it at Shop City when I'd landed in an unceremonious heap on the floor of the manager's office. Now what? It was dark outside, and raining. I couldn't just take off on foot.

I pulled out my cell phone and dialed Melanie Ambrose. She'd promised to help if I needed anything. I could only hope she really meant it.

But the phone just rang and rang. Nobody was

home at the Ambrose residence, and they didn't appear to have an answering machine. Gaining strength from the adrenaline that raced through my veins—the old fight or flight reaction—I disconnected and dialed Claudia instead.

"Are you alone?" I said when she answered.

"Utterly," she said. "Dylan's with Mr. Unmentionable tonight. Why?"

"I need a favor."

"Say the word, sugar plum."

"I left my car at the grocery store earlier today, and I need to pick it up. Then I need the name of a reputable motel. And a reputable divorce lawyer." I paused to take a breath. "I'm leaving Tom. Don't ask. I'll explain everything when I see you. Right now, I just need to get out of here. Can you help me, or do I have to call a cab?"

"Of course I'll help you. I'll be there in five minutes."

I closed the phone and returned it to my pocket. When I turned, he was standing in the doorway, his shadow, heightened by the hallway light behind him, falling in exaggerated proportions on the wall. My Tom. The man. The monster.

"You're leaving me?" he said incredulously.

I struggled for breath. He was blocking the doorway, and there was no other exit to the room, except the window and a two-story drop to the ground. I could try to make a run for it, but he was bigger than me, and far stronger. Especially in my weakened condition. The only way I was going to escape was to talk my way out of the situation. "I don't think you want to have this conversation right now," I said. "Not with the girls downstairs."

"I don't understand. This morning—"

"This morning I didn't know the truth. Please, just let me go."

"Not until you explain why you're doing this. For Christ's sake, Jules, it's only been six weeks. You're carrying my child. You're not even willing to try to work things out?"

He didn't intend to make this easy. Why hadn't I called the police to escort me from the house? "If anything happens to me now," I said, breathless, "you won't get the money. They'll be watching you, especially after Dr. Kapowicz calls them—"

That now-familiar vertical frown line appeared between his eyes. "What money?" he said.

"The two million dollars! The life insurance money. I know, Tom. I know everything. I know about Beth, and the diazinon. And the note. You took it so it wouldn't fall into the wrong hands. Because it was the only piece of real evidence I had. You—"

"What the hell are you talking about? Diazinon?"

"I'm not sure if you were trying to kill me, or make me just sick enough so you could keep me in line, like you did with the pain pills. If it wasn't for Dr. Kapowicz, I never would have known. My God, Tom." I fought back tears I couldn't afford to show, for they were a sign of weakness, and I didn't dare to appear vulnerable before him. "How could you do this to our baby?"

He took a step toward me and I shrank back. "Jules," he said, "I don't have any idea what you're talking about."

"Don't come any closer. Come a single step closer and I'll scream. I'll scream so loud they'll hear me downtown."

He raised his hands, those lovely, manicured hands with the long, elegant fingers I'd always loved. "I won't come any closer," he said. "Just let me say this. Whatever it is you think I've done, you're wrong. I would never do anything to hurt you. Or our baby. Damn it, Jules, what the hell is going on?"

"Oh, Tom. I'm so disappointed in you. Are you going to stand in front of me and keep denying that you killed Beth? I know the truth. I know about the blood tests. I know who Sadie's father really is. You thought when you killed Beth that you were in the clear because everybody believed it was suicide. But when I started snooping around, you realized I was a liability you couldn't afford. So you decided to kill me, too. The fall down the stairs didn't do it, so you turned to the diazinon instead. And at some point along the way, you decided that since you were going to all the trouble of having to kill me, you might as well make something on the deal. Two million dollars. Is that what a wife is worth these days?"

"You have it all wrong," he said. "I didn't kill Beth. I've told you that before. And the rest of this— you're not making any sense at all."

"I know you were there that night," I said, "on the bridge. Roger Levasseur saw you."

"Yes, I was there! I followed her there. We argued. Beth stalked off and disappeared. I waited ten or fifteen minutes, but she didn't come back. She'd said all she had to say to me. So I gave up and went home. The last time I saw her, she was still alive."

"You don't really expect anyone to believe that lame story?"

"It's the truth!"

"Let me out of this room, Tom. If you kill me now, you won't get away with it. Too many people know pieces of the truth. If I don't walk out of this house alive tonight, by tomorrow morning, you'll be behind bars. Give it up. Let me go. If you do, I won't press charges. All I want is a divorce." It was a little white lie. A divorce wasn't the only thing I wanted. There were two other things I highly coveted, two other things I intended to fight for. They were both downstairs in the kitchen right now, making dinner with their grandmother. I'd vowed that I wouldn't leave them, and I intended to keep that promise. I might be walking out tonight—assuming Tom didn't kill me first—but I intended to be back, if only to collect the daughters of my heart.

"Jules," he said, sounding so wretched I had to steel myself against the pain in his voice. "Don't do this."

"Let me go! Claudia's waiting for me!"

He closed his eyes, squared his shoulders. When he opened them again, I saw the glassy sheen of tears. "I love you," he said, and stepped away from the doorway.

"I can see that," I said, and rushed past him, my heart hammering at triple speed. I clattered down the stairs as though the devil himself were at my heels. Claudia was waiting in the kitchen, looking like an old sea captain in her oversize yellow slicker. The girls looked somber. Taylor eyed my overnight bag and her eyes grew accusatory.

"What's going on?" Jeannette said. "We could hear the two of you arguing upstairs, but we couldn't make out what you were saying."

"You'll have to ask your son about that." I knelt and beckoned the girls. They came forward, and I drew them into my arms. "I love you," I said fiercely. "I love you both so much. You know that, right?"

Somberly, Taylor said, "I knew you wouldn't stay."

"Listen to me. I know you don't understand this. I don't expect you to. You're just kids. Your dad and I—it simply didn't work out. Sometimes that happens. But you know what? I'm coming back for you. Nothing, not even your dad, will keep us apart. I swear." I hugged them again, and then I stood. "Goodbye, Jeannette."

"I can't believe you're doing this to him," she said. The woman looked so distressed that, if I hadn't known better, I would've thought she actually wanted me to stay.

"This is nothing," I said, "compared to what he's done to me." I took my raincoat off the hook by the back door and shrugged into it. "Come on, Claudia. Let's go."

We stepped outside into the driving rain and ran toward the car that sat there with lights on and wipers slapping. I was almost there when I felt Tom's hand on my shoulder. Adrenaline shot through my body. I wasn't going to get away after all. He was going to kill me, right here in the driveway. How many domestic violence cases had I read about where the woman was shot in the back as she left? How many women were killed each year, trying to escape their tormentors? Was I about to become one more statistic? Why the hell hadn't I called the cops?

I turned to face my nemesis. Tom loomed over me. Drenched, his hair plastered to his head and rivulets of water pouring down his face, he looked like the villain in some terrifying teen slasher movie. "Jules," he pleaded, "don't do this! Talk to me! We'll figure this out!"

"Are you going to let go of me?" I said. "Or is Claudia going to pick up her cell phone and call Dwight Pettingill?"

He just looked at me, and then his hand fell from my shoulder, limply, like the hand of a dead man. For an instant, I felt guilty. As though I'd been the one to shoot him in the back, instead of the other way around. How could I possibly feel sympathy for the man, after everything he'd done? Steeling myself against my own roiling emotions, I gave him a single parting glance and then I ran for the car. Slamming the passenger door behind me, I told Claudia, "Drive. Now. Go!"

She put the Subaru into Reverse and raced backward out of the driveway, tires squawking on wet pavement when she crammed it into Drive. "Oh, my God," I said. "Oh, my God." I dropped the hood to my raincoat and leaned back against the passenger seat. "I didn't think I'd get away. I thought—" My voice broke, and a sob escaped. "I thought he'd kill me. He killed Beth. He shoved her off the side of that bridge and then went home and pretended to be the grieving husband. And he's been trying to kill me. He's been poisoning me with some insecticide called diazinon."

Quietly, Claudia said, "I know what diazinon is."

"I still can't believe it. I thought I knew him better than this. He seemed like such a decent guy. A good husband. Good father. He loves his little girls so much. And I really believed he loved me." I was trembling all over, whether from the cold rain or the aftermath of terror, I couldn't be sure. "I'm so worried about the girls," I said. "You don't think he'd do anything to them, do you? I'm going to call Dwight Pettingill as soon as I get settled. Tom can't think I'll let this lie. He has to be stopped. He has to—" I realized I was babbling. I glanced over at Claudia, who was uncommonly quiet. "I'm sorry," I said. "I realize this must be as much of a shock for you as it is for me. You've known Tom all your life."

"Yes," she said. "I have."

In the dark, with the oversize hood of the yellow slicker hiding her face, she bore an uncanny resemblance to the grim reaper. The executioner. A shiver skittered down my spine, and I shook it off. I was safe now. I glanced in the side-view mirror. Nobody was following us. Tom had really, truly let me go. I could relax now. It was over.

In the darkness of the grocery store parking lot, reflections from the red-and-white Shop City sign fell in bloody pools on the wet pavement. Claudia pulled into the empty parking space next to my Toyota Highlander. I fished my keys out of my purse and blipped my doors open. Turning to Claudia, I said, "I don't know how to thank you. You've been a good friend. I'll miss you."

"I'll miss you, too, lovey. Take care."

I scurried to the Toyota and climbed in before I could get any wetter. As if that was possible. I cranked the engine and turned on the heater, and was sitting there shivering, waiting for the windshield to defog, when the passenger door opened and Claudia climbed in beside me. "I forgot to give you directions to the motel," she said.

"Oh. Right."

"You go two blocks down on Main and take a right. Turn left at the first intersection. It's just down the street. The Maineway. You can't miss it."

I hunched my shoulders and rubbed my cold hands together. "What would I do without you?"

"It's a good question. One we'll never know the answer to. It's a damn shame it had to go this way, but sometimes you just don't have a choice."

Something odd in her voice, some peculiar inflection, caught my attention. She dropped the hood of her slicker, and that was when I saw the gun in her hand. "Sorry, snookums," she said, "but there'll be no motel for you tonight. Or any other night, for that matter."

"I don't understand."

"Of course you do. Give yourself a minute to think about it. I'll wait." She smiled, looking smug and more satisfied than I'd ever seen her. "I'm in no hurry."

I have to give myself credit; I never do anything halfway. When I'm wrong, I'm spectacularly wrong. There's nothing like a fatal miscalculation to ruin a girl's day. Maybe if I hadn't spent the last few weeks in a diazinon-induced fog, I might have figured it out. Or maybe not. As I reached back frantically in my memory—what there was of it, between the gaping holes that would remain forever empty— every shred of evidence, every subtle nuance, had pointed directly at Tom.

Which was, of course, exactly the way Claudia had planned it.

Staring down the barrel of that Saturday-night special, I wasn't sure whether to laugh or cry. I know this sounds crazy, but through the terror—and believe me, you haven't known fear until you've found yourself facing the business end of a gun—another emotion kept fighting its way to the forefront: elation. Sheer, undiluted joy. Because if Claudia was the villain in this piece, that meant Tom wasn't. He was innocent. It was probably too late for that knowledge to do me any good, but at least my instincts had been correct. I'd known, right up to our final confrontation in the driveway, that something didn't feel right about this. The Tom I knew, the Tom I loved, couldn't possibly be the monster he appeared to be. *I'm sorry,* I told him silently, regretting that I'd probably never be able to tell him just how remorseful I really was. *I'm* so *sorry I stopped believing in you.* I focused on the single bright note in all of this: the girls wouldn't lose their dad. They'd grieve my death, but they hadn't known me for long, and eventually, they'd forget about me and move on with their lives. I could live with that. Or, more accurately, I could die with that. Especially knowing that they wouldn't lose both of us, that Tom would still be there for them.

"Drive," Claudia said. "Any funny stuff and I'll shoot you."

All-righty then. I might be a little slow at times, but I wasn't stupid enough to argue with a woman pointing a loaded gun at my head. I backed out of the parking space, shifted into Drive, and headed for the exit. "Turn left," she said.

After I'd made the turn, I said, "Where are we going?"

"Never mind. You'll find out when we get there. Just drive."

Trying to keep the conversation going while ignoring the thumping of my heart, I said, "So it was you all along. Not Tom."

She smirked. "Had you fooled pretty good, didn't I?"

"I don't understand. Tom said he followed her there that night. But she was alive when he left her."

"Darling Tom. Beth called me, in a tizzy because they'd had a terrible row. I told her to meet me at the bridge. We used to hang out there when we were teenagers. Drink some beer, smoke a little pot, make out with the boys. So it didn't seem strange to her that I should suggest the bridge as a meeting place. I let her go ahead of me, which was a good thing, because Tom went after her. He flew past me out on the state highway, so I pulled into Lasselle's convenience store and waited until he came back without her. I didn't want him to see me and put two and two together."

"Of course not. What about the suicide note? Mel said it was in Beth's handwriting."

Claudia smiled. "I can make anybody do anything when they're on the wrong end of my gun." She punctuated the statement by kissing the gun barrel lovingly.

"Why did you kill her?"

Claudia's smiled disappeared. "The bitch deserved to die after what she did to Tom."

"You mean cheating on him with Riley?"

"Cheating on him and getting pregnant. For God's sake, had the woman never heard of birth control? It almost killed Tom, you know. He was so much in love with her. And then there was Sadie—he loves that kid so much. He was devastated when he found out she wasn't his. Beth came sniveling to me for sympathy. I pretended to give it, even though I could clearly see the truth. Tom wasn't going to be happy until he was rid of her forever. So—" Beneath the slicker, she squared her shoulders. "I took care of it for him."

"I don't understand. I thought you and Beth were friends."

"We could never be friends," Claudia said bitterly. "She had Tom, and I didn't."

So it was as simple as that. Call it jealousy, call it unrequited love or even obsession, but what it boiled down to was that Claudia wanted what Beth had, and was willing to kill for it. And now, as Tom's wife, I was in possession of that same coveted treasure. The moment I married Tom, my fate was sealed.

I cleared my throat. "Why didn't you ever tell Tom how you felt about him?"

"I tried once. During his blackest period after Beth died, he came over to my house one night for a drink and a sympathetic shoulder. We ended up having several drinks, then tearing each other's clothes off and having screaming sex. Afterward, I was in bliss. I really believed this was it. The man I'd secretly loved for half my life was finally mine. And I made the mistake of telling him I loved him. But instead of saying it back to me, the way I'd imagined, he got up, put on his clothes, and went home. The next day, he called to apologize. He said the whole episode was a mistake, that it had arisen out of loneliness and grief and an overabundance of alcohol. He was too much of a gentleman to mention the confession I'd made. And I pretended right along with him that those words had never been spoken. I told him not to sweat it, that the night had meant nothing more to me than some good, healthy sex, and that we could go back to being just friends, with no hard feelings between us." Her laugh was brittle. "I'm one hell of a liar. He bought it hook, line, and sinker. For me, it was one of the most painful, embarrassing moments of my life."

"I'm sure it was."

We were headed into the wilderness, and a suspicion began to nag at me. Unless we changed course soon, which didn't seem likely, we were headed directly for Swift River Road. Returning to the scene of the crime, perhaps? The woman didn't have much of an imagination if she always killed her victims in the same location. On the other hand, if not exactly imaginative, reusing the bridge was at least economical. She didn't have to waste gas, at three dollars a gallon, driving around looking for potential homicide sites.

I was right. Funny how being right was no longer satisfying. We took the turn onto Swift River Road, leaving civilization—such as it was—behind us. Here, there were no streetlights to illuminate our way. Heavy rain clouds had blotted out the moon. With only the Highlander's headlights to guide us, Swift River Road was dark, and wet, and more than a little creepy.

"So let me get this straight," I said. "You put those batteries on the stairs?"

She laughed, a deep, whiskey-throated laugh. "I was hoping you'd break your neck. But as it turns out, you're tougher than I thought. And wasn't it just like Riley to be your knight in shining armor? Sometimes I really hate that guy."

Maybe she hated him, but I didn't. I still wasn't impressed that he'd slept with Tom's wife, but now that I knew he wasn't a killer—I couldn't believe I'd actually suspected both of them at varying times— I was willing to forgive him for his indiscretion. And I was damn glad he'd been there to scrape me up off the floor and dial 911. "And the diazinon?" I said.

"It's a pesticide, snookums. I own a greenhouse. Without pesticides, all my precious babies would be eaten alive by multilegged little monsters. The diazinon keeps them healthy and beautiful."

While it kept me nauseated, headachy and paranoid. Grimly, I said, "How'd you do it?"

She grinned, inordinately pleased with her own cleverness. "I mixed it with your shampoo, sweetie. That nauseating stuff that makes you smell like strawberry shortcake. I did it the day you fell. While you were on the couch that evening, being fussed over by the entire neighborhood, I slipped away and went upstairs. It only took a minute to mix it in and shake it up."

What if I hadn't been the only one who used that shampoo? What if the girls had used it, or Tom? What about my unborn baby, who'd done nothing to deserve this? But of course, Claudia didn't know I was pregnant. If she had, would it have made a difference? Probably not, since she hadn't cared enough about Tom or the girls to even conceive of the notion that one of them could have been sickened right along with me.

You bitch! I wanted to shout. *You miserable, unfeeling bitch!* But I couldn't. Not while the woman had a gun pointed to my head. I was almost certainly going to die, but there was no sense in antagonizing her and hastening the process.

"What about Mystery Man?" I said instead. It should have occurred to me at the time that Claudia was the most likely person to have sent him on his evil mission. But I'd been distracted. I'd just found out I was pregnant, and I was still wrapped in a diazinon cloud.

"Oh, him." She dismissed him with a wave of her free hand. "While you were in the bathroom with the kids, I paid him fifty bucks to follow you around and scare you. I was just toying with you. Trying to keep you off balance."

"And the belt? You're the one who cut the belt on my Toyota?"

"I was particularly proud of that one. My uncle Ernie was a backyard mechanic. I spent half my childhood scooched down beside him, passing him wrenches. It was a piece of cake, so easy a baby could have done it. I came over in the middle of the night with my sharpest kitchen knife, slid under the car, cut the belt, and was back home in less than five minutes. I knew I was safe. You would never have suspected me."

Ahead of us, the bridge loomed, its skeletal, hulking form barely visible in the glossy headlight reflections. "Drive up onto the bridge and park," she instructed. "Leave the headlights on. I don't suppose you have a flashlight in this thing?"

I did. Flashlight, flares, jumper cables, the telephone numbers of everyone from AAA to Newmarket General Hospital. Just in case. After my breakdown, Tom had equipped the vehicle with everything I might need if I should ever undergo another automotive emergency. How could I have ever imagined him to be a killer, this man who cared so deeply about my welfare? But the human brain has an amazing capacity to distinguish patterns. We look at a work of art that consists of nothing more than a few lines which, up close, appear to be nothing. But when we stand back, our brains fill in the empty spaces, connecting those lines until we see whatever it is the artist intended us to see. A house, a tree, a hippopotamus. So it was with me. Claudia had drawn a series of seemingly unconnected lines. But when I stepped back and looked at them as a whole, my mind filled in the empty spaces and I saw exactly what Claudia had intended me to see—my husband's guilt.

If she hadn't been about to kill me, I might have admired her cleverness.

We got out of the car. The rain was coming down so hard now it was almost blowing sideways. We both lifted our raincoat hoods—like it was going to matter if my hair got wet, since I was about to die— and with the gun still trained on me, Claudia opened the trunk, found the flashlight, and took it out. "Over there," she ordered, flicking the switch. "Move it."

With the gun at my back and the flashlight beam dancing ahead of me, I let her guide me over the metal grating to the bridge railing. Below, I could hear the rushing water. The current was swift, the river engorged because of the recent rains. "Climb up on the railing like a good girl," she said, while I just stood there, looking at her stupidly. I'd thought she was going to shoot me. At least shooting would be quick and, as far as I knew, most likely painless. Death by drowning seemed so much less appealing.

"I'm not going over the side," I said, the first time I'd argued since she first pointed that lethal-looking little gun at me.

"You heard me," she said. "Do it!"

I glanced down at the rushing water and thought about all the afternoons I'd spent at the Y, learning to swim. If I survived the fall, there was a slight possibility I might survive the river. I'd never survive the gun. Either way, the odds weren't in my favor. I vacillated, torn between a quick, painless death and the possibility of survival in those cold, turbulent waters.

Headlights appeared in the distance. We both saw them at the same time. "Shit," Claudia said. "Say a word, and you're dead. Not one word!"

"And how do we explain to some passing motorist that we're just out taking a stroll in the pouring rain on a rickety old bridge in some remote area of the wilderness?"

"Shut up! I'll deal with it. If I have to shoot him, I will."

"What's wrong, Claudia? Aren't Tom Larkin's

wives enough? Now you're killing complete strangers?"

She shoved the gun against my kidneys so hard I'd be peeing blood tomorrow, if I survived tonight. Through her teeth, she ground out, "Not. One. More. Word."

We watched the car approach. Instead of driving up onto the bridge, it stopped behind my Toyota. The driver's door opened, and a dark figure got out, indistinguishable in the rain and the glare of the headlights. The anonymous figure moved toward us, into the headlight beam, and morphed into my husband.

I had no idea how he'd found us here, but I was inordinately happy to see him. Claudia, needless to say, wasn't as enthused as I. She muttered a curse and pressed the gun harder against my back.

"I lost one wife because of my stubborn pride," Tom said, peering into the driving rain. "I don't intend to lose another one because of the same weakness. You're wrong about me, Jules, and you're going to hear me out." He looked around, seemed for the first time to realize where we were. Hoarsely, he said, "What in God's name are you doing out here?"

"Surprise," Claudia said brightly. "Your wife was just about to jump off the bridge. Weren't you, precious?"

"Death by bullet would be a lot easier," I said. "Tom, I'm so sorry. All this time, I thought it was you who killed Beth, but it was really—"

"Shut up!" Claudia raised the gun and cuffed me with it. For an instant, I saw stars. Blood trickled from my ear. What else was new? By now, my body was used to being a human punching bag.

"You hurt her," Tom said, "and I swear to God, I'll kill you."

"That would be hard, wouldn't it, since I'm the one with the gun?"

"Claudia—"

"I'm sorry, Tom. Truly, I am. But this has gone too far to stop now. And I'm having far too much fun." She gestured with the gun. "Julie, get up on the bridge railing."

"No!"

"Fine. Then I'll just shoot your husband." And she leveled the gun at Tom.

I didn't think she was kidding. "No," I shouted. "Wait! I'll do it." I grasped the cold, wet metal, found a fingerhold, and began climbing.

"Jules! No!"

"Isn't this touching," Claudia said. "Just like Romeo and Juliet."

I climbed higher. Grabbing an upright beam, I hoisted myself onto the narrow railing. I teetered, only too aware of what seemed like miles of dark, empty space between me and eternity. I didn't dare to glance down. I have a horrific fear of heights. I'm not that impressed by raging rivers, either, just in case anybody was wondering. Was I really going to have to take my chances with that boiling, bubbling, frigid mess below?

"Jump," Claudia ordered.

"No!" Tom said. "Don't listen to her, Jules!"

I swayed, trying desperately to keep my hold on the beam as the wind whipped around me. I could see that Claudia was getting edgy. She had the flashlight trained on me, but the gun pointed at Tom. Handling both of us was getting to be too much for her. With the gun wavering back and forth between Tom and me, she shouted, "Jump, damn it!"

Tom took advantage of her split second of distraction. In a move that would have made Knute Rockne proud, he rushed Claudia, catching her off guard and knocking her off her feet. They fell to the ground together, and on the rain-slicked bridge grating, while I looked on in horror, they rolled and kicked and punched, grappling for control of the gun.

Suddenly, the gun went off, with a boom that seemed to echo off both riverbanks and ricochet on down the valley. A splotch of red appeared on the front of Tom's dress shirt. "No!" I screamed as his lifeblood began to trickle out of him. He turned his gaze on me, and I expected to see reproach on his face. After all, I'd done this to him. If only I'd listened. If only I'd trusted him the way he trusted me. But all I saw on Tom's face was tenderness. No anger, no blame, even though this was all my fault. Just love.

Then he closed his eyes, and I felt myself go dead inside.

Claudia scrambled to her feet and pointed the gun at me. "Goddamn it," she said, "I told you to jump! Why didn't you listen to me?" Her hands were shaking violently, and I saw the glimmer of tears in her eyes. But despite her grief over what she'd just done, I had no doubts about what would happen next. I'd just seen her shoot the man we both loved; she wouldn't hesitate to shoot me.

Behind her, Tom moaned. He wasn't dead yet. If I took my chances with the river, there might be a sliver of hope that I could save him. If not, at least I'd die trying.

So I did the only thing I could do.

I let go of the beam and stepped off the railing.

The fall seemed to take forever. It's true what they say; your life really does flash in front of your eyes. But not the way I always imagined it would, thirty years of life playing out in fast-forward, beginning to end. It was only the highlights I viewed as I moved through the air in slow motion. I saw my mother, the long-haired hippie girl, younger then than I was now, reading a Dr. Seuss story to me as I lay in bed. And I saw Dave, not as the frightened, dissipated man he became before he died, but as the young rock god he'd started out to be. There was Lucky, the puppy I'd had when I was eight, and Troy, the first boy who'd kissed me when I was twelve. I saw Jeffrey on our wedding day, and Angel as I held her in my arms on the day she was born, every inch of her perfect despite the fact that she'd never drawn breath. I saw Tom, the love of my life, standing on a moonlit beach, dressed entirely in white, looking at me through eyes of love, vowing to make that love last a lifetime. I saw the girls, little moments we'd spent together: Sadie, her hair tangled with twigs and leaves as she helped her daddy pick apples. Taylor, slipping her hand in mine at the fairgrounds, touching my heart with this first tentative foray into love. I saw their smiles and their tears, saw the disappointment on their faces when I walked out the door.

I saw it all. And then I hit the water.

I knew if I did a belly flop, it would be all over, so I deliberately hit feet first, toes poised like a ballerina, hoping to slice through the surface like a knife. Even so, I still landed with the force of a Greyhound bus slamming into a concrete wall. It was like diving into a vat of ice. The cold was needle-sharp, stunning. The water slowed my fall, but still I kept plunging, deeper and deeper into the swirling, muddy mess, until I felt the soft, squishy river bottom on my feet. I had only one chance at survival, and that was to get back to the surface and out of the water before hypothermia set in. Once my limbs stopped working, I could kiss this mortal coil goodbye.

I kicked off my shoes, braced my feet against the muddy river bottom, and pushed off with every ounce of my rapidly waning strength. Upward, upward I swam, my arms and legs barely functioning, they were so numb from the cold. The water swirled around me as I struggled with the current. Because the night was so black, I had no idea how far I was from the surface. It could be two feet, or twenty. My lungs started to burn. I was running out of air. If I didn't reach the surface soon, it would be too late.

One lungful of that muddy river water and I was as good as dead.

I was starting to weaken. My lungs were screaming for oxygen. I wasn't going to make it. I would die here, at the age of thirty, in this frigid water, in the same place Beth had died, while on the bridge above me my husband slowly bled to death.

No. I'd come this far. I couldn't quit now. Not while there was a chance of survival. Not while there was even a glimmer of hope that I might save Tom. With a burst of strength I hadn't known I possessed, I kicked through the icy water. I broke the surface and, treading water, took a huge gulp of air. I drew it, moist and life-affirming, into my tortured lungs. And then I took a look around.

The current had carried me a short distance downstream. I could see the hulking frame of the bridge, could see the car headlights shining in the mist. What I couldn't see was Tom. Or Claudia. The water around me was turbulent, the current powerful. I'd always been a strong swimmer, but my recent illness, combined with the time I'd spent fighting for my life in the river's frigid depths, had weakened me. The battle wasn't over yet. I struck out for the shore, not thirty feet away. But the rushing current kept sweeping me downstream.

And then I heard her. Sounding as though she were a million miles away, her voice floated over the water. "Julie," she called in an eerie, singsongy voice. "Julie, Julie, Julie…where are you?" She played her flashlight beam—or, more accurately, *my* flashlight beam—over the river's riotous surface, over the jagged rocks at the water's edge. Hoping to find a body washed up there. My body.

She turned the beam in my direction, but it wasn't powerful enough to reach me. I'd floated too far downstream. Unless she wandered down the riverbank, she wouldn't find me. Let her think I was dead. That way, I might have a chance of making it.

I tried to figure out where I was, but it was impossible to get my bearings in the dark, especially being tossed and turned in the billowing current. Downriver, I saw lights, faint and twinkling. A house, perhaps? Or a dam? Was there another road somewhere nearby? Or was I about to be washed over some massive waterfall and crushed to death on the rocks below?

In the distance, Claudia was still calling my name. Nearby, from the riverbank, came a soft whistle. Somebody was out there. Still treading water, I narrowed my eyes. "Who's there?" I said, in a voice I hoped was loud enough to be heard, but too soft to carry upstream. "Help me!"

"I'm throwing you a rope. Try to catch it."

I knew that voice. "Roger?" I said, dumbfounded. "Roger Levasseur?"

"Here it comes. Grab it!"

The coiled loop of rope landed five feet away from me. I tried to swim toward it, but the current moved me away too quickly.

"I missed it," I said. "Try again."

The rope disappeared. My hands were starting to

go numb. It felt as though I'd been in the water for months, but in actuality, it probably hadn't been more than five minutes. It's odd how, when life and death hang in the balance, time ceases to have meaning. Minutes become hours, hours become days, days become years. I'd come here six weeks ago as a young bride, overeager, naïve, and brimming with optimism and hope for the future. I wasn't the same person now; in those six weeks, I'd aged twenty years. Most of them in the past twenty-four hours.

"Here it comes again," Roger said. "Ready?"

"Ready!" This time, I was prepared. When the noose landed, I looped it around my wrist. "I have it!" I said.

"Hold on. I'll haul you in."

My fingers had gone so numb the knuckles didn't want to bend. So I wrapped the noose of dirty yellow rope around my waist instead, cinched it tight, and let the batshit crazy former MIT professor haul me in to shore like a fish on a line.

I landed facedown on the rocky shore, too tired to care that I was lying on a pile of rocks, and too grateful I was alive to care about the stench that hung over my rescuer, so thick he might have sprayed it on with an atomizer. I was alive, and for a moment, that was the only thought that filled my mind. And then I remembered. I moved my mouth to speak, but nothing came out. I tried again. My lips were stiff. Rigid with the cold. I probably looked like Leo DiCaprio in *Titanic*. Blue all over, except where I was bone-white. "My husband," I said. "He's been shot. Is he alive?"

"I don't know." As lucid as the day he was born, Roger added, "Wrap this around you," taking off his jacket and handing it to me.

I shrugged into it and tried to absorb the heat from his body. "How'd you know?" I said. "How'd you happen to be out here?"

"I saw the headlights from my trailer, and I figured that anybody who sat on the bridge in this kind of storm was either in trouble or up to no good. So I came out to see what was going on. I was hiding in my fishing shack under the bridge when I heard the shot. I saw you go into the water, and I grabbed my rope and went after you."

Thank God for curiosity. It might have landed me in a heap of trouble, but it had also saved my life.

In the distance, Claudia continued her search. "I'll take care of her," Roger said.

I clutched his sleeve. "She has a gun. She shot Tom. She's—" Not quite right in the head, I almost added, until I remembered who I was talking to. Instead, I said, "I'm going with you."

"You're half-dead. Your shoes are gone. It's thirty-seven degrees outside, and you're wet to the bone."

"And I'm going with you."

"Fine. Slow me down, and I'll leave you behind."

Like a good little soldier, I fell in behind. My bare feet were so numb that I couldn't feel the roots and rocks ripping my skin. It was probably just as well. I held the jacket tight around me and stuck to Roger in the darkness. Through bushes and over logs, slogging through the mud and the crud, the grass and the brambles, like a couple of navy SEALS on a secret mission, we circled around behind Claudia, who was still fanning her flashlight beam over the riverbank in search of my dead, bloated body.

Thirty feet behind her, Roger paused. In silent pantomime, he told me to stay put. My body heat nearly depleted and my limbs growing limp, I nodded, too weak to argue. From somewhere under his raggedy sweater, Roger produced a gun. I didn't know much about guns, but this baby was no little Saturday-night special like the one Claudia carried. This was a serious gun, the kind that could blow off the top of your head if it had a mind to. I didn't know where he'd gotten it, and I was pretty sure I didn't want to know.

"Joooo-leeeeeee," Claudia called in that singsong voice that sounded just this side of madness. Or maybe she'd already crossed the line. She didn't have far to go. "Oh, Joooo-leeeeeee, darling, where are you?"

I cast an anxious look at the bridge. I was close enough now to see Tom's body lying there, silent and unmoving. My heart hurt. I could actually feel it hurting, there in my chest. Surely he was dead. I'd seen the blood seeping through the hole Claudia had blasted in his side. How could he possibly survive something like that? Especially out here in this cold?

Thirty feet away from me, moving so silently even I couldn't hear him, Roger stepped up behind

Claudia and pressed his gun to the back of her head. "You don't know how long I've been waiting to do this," he said.

Oh, no. Was he going to kill her? Hadn't there been enough bloodshed?

But he didn't kill her. Instead, he said, "Drop the gun. Now, please."

"What if I say no?"

I stood and said, "It's over, Claudia. Put the gun down and let's end this now."

"So you're alive," she said. "Bravo. You win."

"This isn't a game," I said fiercely. "My husband's up there on that bridge, bleeding to death. You told me once that you loved him. But you know what, Claudia? What you feel isn't love, it's obsession. Love doesn't destroy what it holds dear."

In the distance, a siren wailed. "Drop the gun," Roger said gently. "The police are on the way. I called them. They know everything. Give it up now. It's time."

For an instant, she hesitated. I could almost read her mind as she weighed her options. Escape versus surrender. Freedom versus incarceration. Life versus death.

I knew it, the instant she made her choice. Still, as closely attuned as I was to her, I was a half second late in recognizing her intent. I opened my mouth to protest, but she was quicker. In a lightning-swift move that would haunt my nightmares for a long time, Claudia raised the Saturday-night special to her own temple and pulled the trigger.

The gunshot echoed across the water and back, ricocheting the way the earlier one had, until finally it died away. Then all I could hear was Roger's labored breathing and the water lapping at Claudia's crumpled body. And the eerie whine of the approaching sirens.

I could see the lights now through the trees, screaming down Swift River Road. The electric blues of the police cruisers, the flashing red of Newmarket Rescue. I reached out and rested my hand on Roger's shoulder. He turned those sad, rheumy eyes on me, and for a long time we just looked at each other.

Then I wrapped his coat tighter around me and went to meet them on the bridge.

Epilogue

I was lucky. I only spent a few days in the hospital. When they took me in, I was weak and dehydrated—ironic, I know, after spending all that time in the water—and suffering from hypothermia. But I was alive, and that was what mattered.

Tom wasn't as lucky as I. He lost a great deal of blood, and almost died on the way to the hospital. He was hospitalized for nearly a month, in excruciating pain for a good portion of it. I spent most of that month at his bedside. He doesn't remember much of those first couple of weeks, when they kept him doped up on morphine. But I remember. It's not the kind of thing you forget, seeing someone you love in that kind of pain.

The day after they brought us into the hospital, I was dozing by his bedside, attached to my own portable IV, when Jeannette stuck her head through the door. "Can I come in?" she said.

"He's your son," I told her. "Of course you can come in."

She walked silently into the room and stood by his bedside, her hands gripping the bed rails and a single tear tracking down her cheek. Tom's face looked pale and waxen, corpselike. The morphine had him so heavily sedated that the only evidence of life was the whoosh of the respirator. It must have frightened his mother half to death.

I got up and stood beside her. "He's a strong man," I told her. "And a hero. He saved my life last night."

"Dwight Pettingill told me all about it. Do the doctors really believe he'll survive?"

"He has everything to live for. Two little girls who adore him. A wife who'd be dead if not for him." I paused, unable to speak past the lump in my throat.

"And a mother who's been a fool."

"No." I took her hand in mine, seeing for the first time the hardened calluses, the reddened skin. "You're not a fool. You just wanted to protect your child. That's admirable."

"Oh, Julie. I've treated you so abominably. It wasn't personal. Really. It's just that—oh, God, how can I admit this? I thought Tom killed Elizabeth. What kind of mother does that make me?"

"A human one." I couldn't very well cast aspersions on her when I'd believed the same thing myself.

"They'd been fighting that night," she said. "The

night Beth died. She told him she was leaving him. Tom went upstairs, and she put Sadie in the car and drove away. When he came back downstairs, he ran out after her. Just like he did with you last night. And then she turned up dead. What was I supposed to think?"

The same thing I'd thought. I shook my head in sorrow. How could two rational women have believed such a thing of a man like Tom Larkin?

"I can see it now," she said, studying me.

"What? What can you see?"

"How much you love him. Your eyes haven't left his face since I came in the room. You know, I've been deathly afraid of you."

"Afraid of me? Why on earth—"

"I believed he'd killed Beth. No mother wants to believe that of her child, but it's the truth. When you came along, the two of you seemed so close, and I was terrified that you'd unearth his secret. It would be just like Tom to tell you something like that. If you found out, the truth would destroy us all." She hesitated, gripping the bed rails so hard her knuckles turned white. "Except that I was wrong, and both of you almost died anyway."

"But we're both alive," I said. "And we have to believe Tom will recover. I won't accept anything less."

"Can you forgive me? You probably hate me, but for Tom's sake, I wish you could find it in your heart to forgive."

Still holding my mother-in-law's hand in mine, I said, "There's nothing to forgive."

It was an epic moment, a moment of true healing. That afternoon, standing by Tom's hospital bed, marked a new beginning for Jeannette and me. At first we took baby steps. Learned to crawl before we could walk. But eventually, we came to understand and respect each other. More than that, we became friends. Not just for Tom's sake, but for our own.

Two days after Jeannette and I called our truce, I lost the baby. Dr. Kapowicz said the fetus simply couldn't take the strain that was put on it, and the miscarriage was nature's way of protecting both of us. I was crushed, but Tom was philosophical. He said there would be other babies. That we had plenty of time, and an abundance of love to give.

One sunny October afternoon, Tom and I walked slowly, laboriously, down the hospital corridor to sit in the solarium. There, amid the thriving greenery and the last of the fall foliage, we sat holding hands while Tom filled in the rest of the blanks for me. If I'd gone a little further the day I went through his desk, in the TOM folder I'd have found an identical life insurance policy, with me as beneficiary. He'd opened them both shortly after we were married, knowing if anything ever happened to either of us, the other—and the girls—would be taken care of. After Beth had died so young, he didn't want to take chances. Life is unpredictable, and so precious. Although we didn't talk that afternoon about how close we'd come to using both those policies, I saw it in his eyes. And I'm sure he recognized that same knowledge in mine. We'd come very close to losing each other on the bridge that rainy autumn night.

Tom told me about the silent fear he'd lived with these last two years, the fear of losing Sadie to his brother. It had been with him, dogging his steps and weighing down on his shoulders, since before Beth died. Then, when he read her note—the one I'd lost from my pocket at the hospital—he'd realized he had nothing to fear, because Riley already knew the truth, and hadn't acted on it. Riley, it seemed, was the furious man Beth had written about. It wasn't her husband she feared, but her lover. When he'd found out he was Sadie's father, he'd threatened to take her away. But clearheadedness had prevailed. Riley realized he was in no position at that point to be anyone's father. And his brother had been Sadie's dad for two and a half years. As much as he loved her, he couldn't tear her away from the only father she'd ever known. So Riley had made the decision that he would remain her doting uncle, and never claim what he had every right to lay claim to. When Tom brought him Beth's note after my fall, Riley had torn it up. There were still hard feelings between the two of them— after all, Riley had slept with Tom's wife. They might never enjoy the warm camaraderie that most brothers enjoyed. But at least they'd called a truce. It was a start.

Tom also cleared up the mystery of who the note was addressed to. The mysterious "K" was actually Melanie. Her childhood nickname had been Kitty, and that's what Beth had called her even as an adult.

Why Mel hadn't admitted this to me when I asked, I'll probably never know. Maybe it was fear. But I decided to let it be. It didn't matter anymore.

The last hole Tom plugged that October afternoon was the mystery of Beth's paintings. The rest of them, he told me, were in a gallery in Boston. A few had already sold, and the gallery director had great expectations for the rest. The profit from the sales was going directly into a college fund for the girls. No matter what the future brought, Beth's daughters would be taken care of. That's something Tom and I both knew Beth would appreciate.

My recovery from the results of chronic poisoning has been gradual. Dr. Kapowicz says I'm very lucky. I could have died, or spent the rest of my life in a vegetative state. She's closely monitoring the situation, but so far the only symptoms I've experienced are headaches and the occasional memory lapse. I forget people's names, sometimes search diligently for a word but find only blank space. But that's slowly improving, as well. Dr. K. says we may not know for years whether my body suffered any permanent damage. Because I've personally experienced the overwhelming fragility of life, I choose not to look that far ahead. I'm simply grateful to be alive, with Tom by my side.

It's been eighteen months since that terrible night. We have so much to be grateful for, Tom and I. We have each other, and neither of us seems to have suffered permanent damage from what we went through. We have the girls, and a newfound appreciation for all the gifts that life has given us. Six months ago, we gave the girls a baby brother. We named him David, after my dad, but we call him Davy. He's a happy, healthy child, full of love and bubbly laughter. He resembles both of his sisters, and he looks a little like Tom, but most of all, Davy looks like himself. And that's fine with us.

I'm in the process of adopting Tom's girls. As far as I'm concerned, they're already my daughters. Sadie started kindergarten last fall, and Taylor has grown up so much, she's become my best girlfriend. Once a month, the girls and I do a mother-daughter movie night together. But most of the time, we just stay home with Tom, who took on a partner and cut his patient load in half. It's made a big difference in him. He's more relaxed, less stressed. He's even been known to hang his clothes—believe it or not—two inches apart, instead of a half inch. I'm not sure if I should worry, or rejoice.

There've been other changes in the last eighteen months. A nice young couple bought Claudia's house, and we've become friendly with them. Dylan went to live with his dad. They moved to upstate New York, and last I heard, he was doing well. The police found the diazinon exactly where Claudia had said they would—in my strawberry-scented shampoo.

A few months ago, we took the kids to Los Angeles for a visit. We went to Disneyland, bought a map of where the stars live, shopped on Rodeo Drive, and had lunch with my crusty old friend Louis. The girls gave the city their seal of approval. Louis gave his to Tom. "You got a winner this time, kid," he said when he hugged me goodbye. "And those kids—" If I didn't know better, I'd have sworn I saw tears in his eyes. "Hang on to this one," he said, and shook Tom's hand vigorously. With Louis, you can't get a higher recommendation than that.

Jeannette has a new beau. His name is Arthur, and he's a building contractor who Riley introduced her to. They're taking it slowly, but she's started spending nights at his house, and I swear I can hear the sound of wedding bells just down the road.

A month after Roger Levasseur saved my life, I tracked down his son, the Baltimore attorney, who hadn't heard from his father in years and had no idea if he was even alive. He came to Newmarket to visit his dad, and between the two of us, we convinced Roger to give up the filthy old trailer and move into a senior's housing complex in town. To my surprise, it turned out that he's loaded. Back when he was an MIT professor Roger invested wisely, and he's been living on those investments for years. Tom gave him a complete physical exam and referred him to a psychiatrist who put him on a new psychotropic medication that's done wonders for him. Roger now has a home health aide who comes in a couple times a week. Tom and I help him with groceries and take him out for dinner once in a while. He's made friends at the complex. There's an ongoing chess tournament in his building, and so far, nobody's been able to beat him.

But the biggest surprise of all came from Riley

and Melanie Ambrose. They started dating after they ran into each other at the hospital. Last June, they got married. I'm happy for my brother-in-law, and pleased to have Mel as a sister, especially now that she's apologized to Tom for all the dreadful things she believed about him.

As for Tom and me, we're doing okay. It took almost losing each other for us to realize just how much we meant to each other. We were in family counseling for a while, all four of us, but after Davy was born, we graduated. Having a stable family has been good for the girls. Taylor's now more open and accepting of people, and Sadie finally stopped having nightmares. For both of the girls, life is good.

We don't talk much about that night. We decided it was more healthy to put it behind us and move forward with our lives. But I did ask Tom, one evening when we were curled up together on the couch, how it was he found me that night.

"It was the GPS system," he said. "The one you couldn't see the reason for. The one that, when I waxed rhapsodic over it, you just rolled your eyes and left the room."

"Enough," I said. "Leave me a little dignity."

So that's my story. My new beginning didn't go quite the way I thought it would when I married Tom. Like most things in life, the ending to my story—or maybe I should call it the beginning—has a bittersweet component, a sharp edge to remind me that my current state of contentment was bought at great cost. I lost my baby, nearly lost my husband,

and came very close to losing my life. That's a heavy weight to carry around. But Tom and I both hope it's made us better, stronger persons. The one lesson I know we both learned from all this is that you should never take for granted the people you love. Tell them you love them. Show them, every day, in a hundred different ways, how much you care. Because you never know when the unthinkable might happen. Life is precious. Treat it that way.

That's what Tom and I are doing.

REQUEST YOUR FREE BOOKS!

2 FREE NOVELS
FROM THE ROMANCE/SUSPENSE
COLLECTION PLUS 2 FREE GIFTS!

YES! Please send me 2 FREE novels from the Romance/Suspense Collection and my 2 FREE gifts (gifts are worth about $10). After receiving them, if I don't wish to receive any more books, I can return the shipping statement marked "cancel." If I don't cancel, I will receive 4 brand-new novels every month and be billed just $5.49 per book in the U.S. or $5.99 per book in Canada, plus 25¢ shipping and handling per book plus applicable taxes, if any*. That's a savings of at least 20% off the cover price! I understand that accepting the 2 free books and gifts places me under no obligation to buy anything. I can always return a shipment and cancel at any time. Even if I never buy another book from the Reader Service, the two free books and gifts are mine to keep forever.

185 MDN EF5Y 385 MDN EF6C

Name _____ (PLEASE PRINT)

Address _____ Apt. #

City _____ State/Prov. _____ Zip/Postal Code

Signature (if under 18, a parent or guardian must sign)

Mail to The Reader Service:
IN U.S.A.: P.O. Box 1867, Buffalo, NY 14240-1867
IN CANADA: P.O. Box 609, Fort Erie, Ontario L2A 5X3

Not valid to current subscribers to the Romance Collection,
the Suspense Collection or the Romance/Suspense Collection.

Want to try two free books from another line?
Call 1-800-873-8635 or visit www.morefreebooks.com.

* Terms and prices subject to change without notice. N.Y. residents add applicable sales tax. Canadian residents will be charged applicable provincial taxes and GST. Offer not valid in Quebec. This offer is limited to one order per household. All orders subject to approval. Credit or debit balances in a customer's account(s) may be offset by any other outstanding balance owed by or to the customer. Please allow 4 to 6 weeks for delivery. Offer available while quantities last.

Your Privacy: Harlequin is committed to protecting your privacy. Our Privacy Policy is available online at www.eHarlequin.com or upon request from the Reader Service. From time to time we make our lists of customers available to reputable third parties who may have a product or service of interest to you. If you would prefer we not share your name and address, please check here. ☐

BOB08R

LAURIE BRETON

32427 POINT OF DEPARTURE   ___ $6.99 U.S. ___ $8.50 CAN.

(limited quantities available)

TOTAL AMOUNT	$ _____
POSTAGE & HANDLING	$ _____
($1.00 FOR 1 BOOK, 50¢ for each additional)	
APPLICABLE TAXES*	$ _____
TOTAL PAYABLE	$ _____

(check or money order—please do not send cash)

To order, complete this form and send it, along with a check or money order for the total above, payable to MIRA Books, to: **In the U.S.:** 3010 Walden Avenue, P.O. Box 9077, Buffalo, NY 14269-9077; **In Canada:** P.O. Box 636, Fort Erie, Ontario, L2A 5X3.

Name: _____
Address: _____ City: _____
State/Prov.: _____ Zip/Postal Code: _____
Account Number (if applicable): _____

075 CSAS

*New York residents remit applicable sales taxes.
*Canadian residents remit applicable GST and provincial taxes.

MIRA®

www.MIRABooks.com   MLBI1208BL